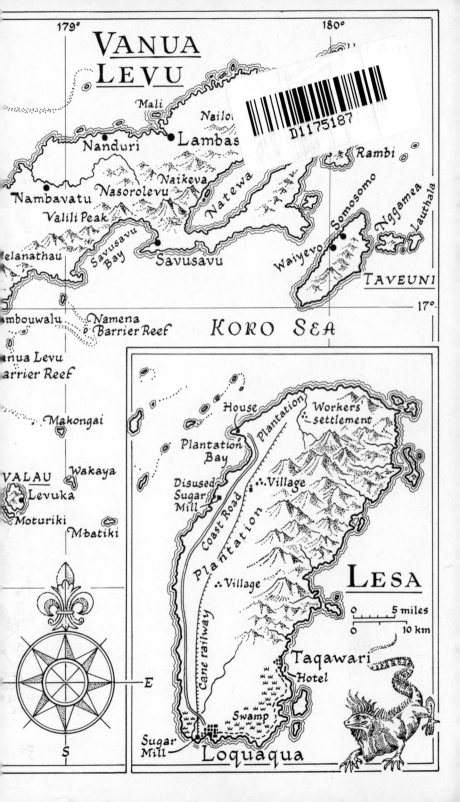

VANUA LEVU

Mali

Nailou

Lambas

Rambi

Nanduri

Naikeva

Nasorolevu

Natewa

Somosomo

Nggamea

Lauthala

Nambavatu

Valili Peak

Savusavu Bay

Savusavu

Waiyevo

TAVEUNI

elanathau

17°

mbouwalu

Namena Barrier Reef

KORO SEA

nua Levu arrier Reef

Makongai

House

Plantation

Workers' settlement

Plantation Bay

VALAU

Wakaya

Levuka

Disused Sugar Mill

Village

Moturiki

Mbatiki

Coast Road

Plantation

Village

LESA

0   5 miles

10 km

Cane railway

Taqawari

Hotel

E

Swamp

Sugar Mill

Loquaqua

S

AN ABUNDANCE OF RAIN

Also by Carol Drinkwater
THE HAUNTED SCHOOL *(for children)*

CAROL DRINKWATER

AN ABUNDANCE OF RAIN

Michael Joseph
London

MICHAEL JOSEPH LTD

Published by the Penguin Group
27 Wrights Lane, London W8 5TZ, England
Viking Penguin Inc., 40 West 23rd Street, New York, New York 10010, USA
Penguin Books Australia Ltd, Ringwood, Victoria, Australia
Penguin Books Canada Ltd, 2801 John Street, Markham, Ontario, Canada L3R 1B4
Penguin Books (NZ) Ltd, 182–190 Wairau Road, Auckland 10, New Zealand

Penguin Books Ltd, Registered Offices: Harmondsworth, Middlesex, England

First published 1989

Typeset in Linotron 11/13 pt Electra by
Goodfellow & Egan Ltd, Cambridge
Printed and bound in Great Britain by
Butler & Tanner Ltd, Frome, Somerset

A CIP catalogue record for this book is available from the British Library

ISBN 0 7181 3253 X

In loving memory of Neil Cunningham,
A cherished adventurer.

And for my father, Peter Regan, with love.

Author's Note

This story is set in Fiji and its islands during the last months of 1986 and the early part of 1987. All characters, locations and situations are entirely fictitious.

I hope that those who know and love these islands, as I do, will not judge too harshly the many liberties I have taken.

My very special thanks to Michel Noll, my husband, Christopher Brown, my dear friend, Susan Watt, my editor, for much appreciated support and input.

Carol Drinkwater, February 1987

PART
1

Chapter 1

'Are you all right, Mrs De Marly? You're looking a bit frail, dear,' whispered an elderly widow from Toorak, Melbourne.

She was sitting to Kate De Marly's right at the Captain's table. It was a kindly, tactful tone.

'I'm fine, thank you,' Kate replied courteously.

'You've hardly touched your food.'

'I'm fine.'

Although unwelcome, the observation had been quite accurate. Kate had hardly touched her plate. Indeed she had hardly eaten a morsel since the cruise ship had left Sydney. She was still in a state of shock, still unable to face anything, still suffering from the blow that she had received five days earlier.

Kate had set off from her gracious home in London almost a week earlier; she was travelling with her French husband, Philippe. On arrival at their hotel in Sydney, she had put through a call to her father at his sugar plantation in Fiji. She had not seen him since she was a small girl and had been longing for the reunion. She wanted to be sure that he had received her letter, to be certain that he was still expecting her.

A woman had answered the phone. She had been confused by Kate's request.

'Sam? You want to speak to Sam? Just a minute.'

The unknown woman had passed Kate on to a Mr Robert

Stone, the Plantation overseer, who had told Kate that her father, Sam MacGuire, had been dead for ten days.

'Dead for ten days!' She could hardly believe what she was hearing! To have come so far! To have been so close to meeting him after all these years and now to have lost him forever!

'Sssh, don't upset yourself,' Philippe had consoled in their hotel room. 'We'll take the next plane straight back. Go to Europe instead. You musn't upset yourself, my *chérie*.' Her husband had soothed her, holding her, stroking at her tender, tear-stained face.

'I can't go back! Not now. I want to go on, visit the Plantation, see his home.' She had wept in his arms.

The memory of this caused Kate to want to sob again; tears came, catching in her throat.

Her neighbour was saying something to her. 'You're disembarking tomorrow, is that right?'

She had to return to her cabin before she made a fool of herself, weeping in front of other passengers. She threw a helpless glance across the silver-laden table towards her husband, Philippe, who was locked in conversation with a flawless middle-aged woman from Berlin whose name Kate had never quite caught. He looked irredeemably bored.

'Help me,' she begged him, but he had not observed her silent plea.

'Would you all please forgive me,' she announced manfully into the jabber of *soignés* first-class passengers seated around the Captain's supper table, 'I'm feeling a little tired,' and she rose deliberately, maintaining poise, and placed her starched white napkin on to her almost untouched plate. 'Good night,' she murmured to the nine silenced diners including the Captain and Philippe. They nodded at her politely, all assenting to her exit.

'Good night Mrs De Marly.' 'Get some sleep,' one or two muttered kindly. She turned away, emitting a silent sigh of relief. She was preparing to forge herself a path across the crowded dance floor, simpler than attempting to negotiate her way around the clusters of tables, when her husband grabbed her by the wrist.

4

'Want me to come too, Petal?' he whispered affectionately.

She shook her head and set off alone across the polished, sprung dance floor, zigzagging her neat way around couples of all ages, locked in one another's arms smooching happily, or simply shuffling aimlessly to and fro. No one paid her any attention. She pressed on, detouring towards the bandstand where the resident sextet, Les Hawks and his Gay Knights, were making an unremarkable down-tempo stab at 'Somewhere over the Rainbow'.

A strawberry-blonde songstress, in a shimmering evening dress, with blood-red lipstick set in a permanent sultry scowl, was just completing her rendering of the much-sung lyrics.

The singer sat down at the edge of the bandstand and stared disinterestedly into the late-night crowd. Then, with seemingly little relish, she lowered podgy, long-nailed fingers towards the ground searching for her advocaat and lemonade. It was placed discreetly under her chair. At that same moment a passing dancer knocked Kate off balance. She stumbled against the stage, grabbing at the rostrum, and accidentally upset the moving glass, capsizing it, sending it spinning, tumbling to the dance floor, crashing and sprawling like a broken yolk.

'Oh, Jesus Christ, you've stained my dress, you silly cow!' the blonde cursed foully under her sodden breath.

Kate bit her lip, shocked by such a response. She smiled an apology, 'I'm so sorry!' then she hurried away as Les Hawks himself stepped across the stage, trumpet in hand, smiling extravagantly to ease his singer's fury. Dancers stepped aside, amused by the incident, and then swung on as Philippe, anxiously watching Kate's face, half rose from his seat, before deciding not to follow.

We should have just returned to London, he reflected silently, watching his retreating wife. Pointless to continue.

Kate had reached the exit at the end of the ballroom, and paused to draw breath before slipping lightly through the swing doors which closed automatically behind her. And, as if securing a hermetically sealed lid, the drab music, the smoke, the dissatisfied singer, the clatter of dessert plates being removed and coffee cups being served, the overly ebullient chatter of bronzed tourist passengers and the clinking of melting ice against stamped glassware were all, mercifully, cut off from her. Only the tonal snore of the engine chugging below in the engine room could be heard now and that she found rhythmic and soothing.

She hurried the length of the deserted, mahogany-walled corridors, as if blindly through a maze, up one flight of a narrow stairway and on, into the silent, womb-like sanctum of their comfortable suite.

The coverlet on their double bed had already been removed by an anonymous nightmaid, the fan switched on and the sheets folded back, ready for sleep. Kate, not troubling even to undress, flung herself, stomach down, on to the bed and buried her face in the comforting, sweetly scented linen pillowcases. She fumbled for her stilettos and flung them, one muffled thud after another, on to the thickly piled carpeted floor and closed her weary eyes before falling asleep.

Minutes later, when the door reopened and Philippe stole into the cabin, she heard nothing. His worried gaze found her lying carelessly, like an elegant, discarded doll, across their bed. Her sleek, calf-length evening dress, spotted with advocaat stains, had ridden up above her knees exposing her bare, stockinged ankles and lower legs.

It was an inviting tableau. Her fragility was a powerful component of her sexuality.

She's sleeping. That's something, he thought, closing the door noiselessly behind him so as not to wake her. He leant his muscular weight back against the cabin wall and watched her silently as he began removing his black bow tie. How he hated dressing for dinner! Her delicate body lifted with the regularity of its sleeping breath while her right arm hung over the side of the mattress towards the floor with fingertips barely brushing against the beige-based carpet.

He flung his unknotted bow tie on to the dressing-table stool, on the left side of the room, and then followed it with his black dinner jacket which touched the seat momentarily before sliding silently, unnoticed, to the ground. Kate stirred,

6

disturbed by the movements in the room, and then drifted back into sleep. He watched her for a few moments longer. He was feeling tired himself, ready to sleep, but decided after all to leave her alone for a while. In need of a stroll and a breath of late-night air he headed briskly back towards the upper deck, along deserted corridors where voices droned sleepily behind closed doors.

Moments later he was leaning, portside, out over a metal and varnished wood railing, watching the ocean, or more precisely, watching the liner churn leaping waves into the water beneath him. He glanced upwards towards the heavens. It was a beautiful night and the discharge of ozone refreshed and relaxed him, lifting his previously downcast spirits.

Outbursts of drunken though not raucous laughter to the right of him, further towards the bow of the ship, disturbed his contemplative mood. He turned and peered into the night searching for a glimpse of the unknown gigglers. A young couple, probably in their mid-twenties, still in full evening dress, were leaning against one of the lifeboats, fooling together, bent double with carefree laughter. He leaned, idly watching them, envying them their high spirits. Such frivolity seemed a stranger to him now.

'Feeling all right, is she, your wife?'

The voice came from Philippe's left. Its owner had approached unobserved, while Philippe had been watching the young couple. He recognised the northern accent at once. It was one of the passengers, one of the guests at this evening's dinner table. An Englishman, older than himself by twenty or so years, also travelling with his wife. Philippe couldn't place the accent. His English was perfect but even now, after almost twenty years in the country, regional accents were still confusing to him.

They had sat opposite one another at the Captain's table this evening but had already crossed paths several times during the past four days. Philippe thought him an interfering bore. 'A pain in the arse,' he had said to Kate a night or so earlier.

The older man stood lighting his pipe, settling to the pleasure of it and the idea of whiling away a short time in Philippe's company.

Blast! Philippe thought irritably. He had been enjoying his solitude, indulging in a moment's wistfulness, mourning his lost youth.

'She's fine,' he replied eventually, curtly though not overly impolitely. He was accustomed to disguising his feelings, feigning an engaging manner when business or social demands called for it.

'We were sorry to hear about her father's death.'

Philippe did not reply, merely nodded abruptly.

'I believe she told my wife that you were leaving us tomorrow?' the stranger continued. 'Disembarking in Fiji? She says you've not been there before?' He puffed away contentedly, enjoying the conversation. Had it not been for the liner's movement creating a strong breeze and dragging the tobacco smoke behind them Philippe would have become overtly irritated by both the questions, which he read as small-minded prying rather than casual small talk, and the pipe. He decided against answering the questions, supposing them to be rhetorical, part of the tiresome fellow's meandering, undiscerning mind. The stranger seemed to know more about their private affairs than he, Philippe thought scathingly. He felt a moment's irritation towards Kate for telling so much, for allowing her anxieties and shock to leave her so unguarded.

What business was it of anyone that this was their first trip to the South Pacific and that she had been on her way to visit a father she had never really known? No doubt she had fallen prey to their bored, inquisitive lives and had told them everything.

'We spent our first holiday in Fiji,' Philippe's companion continued, 'after we emigrated from England. Late fifties, it was. Can't remember the exact year. You'd have to ask Betty, she never forgets a date.'

'Betty?'

'My wife. Anyhow, it was when the British were still in Fiji.

8

Lovely spot, I thought. Was then anyhow. Not the same now, of course. Got a bit of a problem there, now. Too many Indians. Always happens though. Soon as the British leave. Places go to pot and they all end up killin' one another. It'll be the same when your lot leave New Caledonia.'

Philippe rubbed at his face, distorting classic features with the flesh of his fingers and then scratched at his collar bone exposed beneath his open-necked dress shirt, shadow gestures expressing his building irritation. 'I think, if you don't mind, I'll wander off and get some sleep. Good night.' He turned swiftly but the man stepped after him.

'Yes, I might as well walk down with you. It's getting pretty late. My Betty'll think I've jumped overboard!'

The young couple were silent now.

Ignoring his companion, Philippe moved away from the railing, glancing in their direction, to where they had been standing. He glimpsed them, shadows of them, wrapped in one another's arms, kissing and clutching passionately. How he wished his unwelcome companion would disappear! Had he been alone he would have dallied a while longer to enjoy the brilliance of this newly discovered stirring southern sky while listening to the liner churning through the water. Instead, he strode purposefully on ahead and, while the older chap paused to bang his pipe against the varnished wooden railing, he took the chance to call out another brusque 'Good night', hastening away, down the steps towards his suite.

When he unlocked the door he found that Kate had climbed into bed and was now curled up beneath the sheets, fast asleep. Her dress lay like a dead skin on the floor beside his jacket. He crept, tiptoeing, towards them, dropping them untidily on to the stool before wandering across the room to kiss and stroke his wife's sleeping head.

No longer tired, he decided to read for a while. He was still having difficulty adjusting to the time differences, and the late-night stillness would be useful. He already had plenty of work to catch up on and a new batch of telexes from his London offices had been delivered to their cabin just before supper.

An hour or so later, exhausted by concern rather than concentration, Philippe walked through from the bathroom where he had been working. He found his wife, no longer sleeping, lying loosely, naked, limbs thrown in various directions, a white sheet coiled around her feet.

'You must be tired, little petal,' he whispered affectionately, sliding himself next to her, on to the slightly damp sheet. 'You mustn't keep upsetting yourself.'

'Mmmmm,' she droned listlessly.

He held the weight of his vigorous body on one elbow and leant close to her, stroking her stomach solicitously, as the liner rolled beneath them carrying them towards their destiny.

Kate had been dressed for hours. She was restless, and had been ready for disembarkation since dawn. She and Philippe breakfasted together in their cabin and afterwards she left him alone to work, saying that she preferred to read on deck.

It was a glorious morning, but for her no ordinary day. She was anxious about their arrival but no one, except perhaps Philippe, would have detected her agitation. She settled to her book, on a lounger alongside the swimming pool, but very soon abandoned it, deciding instead to take a stroll along the crowded, sundrenched deck.

Here and there someone called to her, passengers idling in the sunshine. A cluster of small islands was appearing on the horizon. Kate paused to observe them. She inhaled a deep salty calming breath, and then exhaled deliberately, wrapping her delicate, well-manicured hands around the white metal railing. Excited passengers were gathering all around her but she resolutely refused to be jostled by them. She stood elegantly erect, gazing out on to the endless, beryl-blue tropical water, watching mainland Fiji draw closer into vision.

A tall, gangly, sandy-haired fellow in unflatteringly brilliant Bermuda shorts bumped unsteadily against her left arm, causing her to lose momentarily her well-poised balance.

'Oh damn!' she cried, thrusting her right arm on to her

10

windswept head to save her newly acquired hat before it disappeared overboard.

'Ooh, sorry sheila,' he belched. ''S 'bit rough for me,' and, to Kate's horror, the rough-spoken, bleary-eyed redhead bent close to her face. His eyes squinted at her as he tugged her hair in a kindly, vain attempt to straighten the straw bonnet and undo his carelessness.

'Thank you. It's all right,' she muttered, smiling politely, swiftly averting her eyes back towards the water. The stench of alcohol on his breath made her quite giddy. She was also feeling vaguely seasick she now realised, or perhaps it was simply her nerves.

'If you would excuse me please!' she heard from somewhere behind her. It was her husband's voice. Too brusque to be described as plummy. His accent was strongest when he was short-tempered.

Philippe pushed his way forcefully through the bunched tourists reeking of duty-free.

'C'est pénible!' he whispered curtly. 'I shall be glad to get off this damned boat. Have they announced what time we dock?'

'Within the hour. That's the last I heard. What's the matter?' Kate replied, still focusing on the approaching land and choosing to ignore any accusation intended by him about the cruise.

'Nothing. I wanted to get a telex through to London. It's not urgent. It can wait. How are you? Better?'

She nodded silently.

'We don't have to go through with this, you know. It seems rather pointless. Why don't we just send a message saying that we've had to return urgently to England?'

'Because I want to go. I'd like to see the place.' She sighed. 'Did you organise the luggage?' she continued indifferently.

'One of the chappies'll take it. We'll collect it before Customs.' He paused before adding, 'I hope there's no hiccup this end.'

Kate vaguely wondered why there might be but said nothing. She noticed that her recent companion had found a friend and was now pushing his unsteady way along the

11

crowded deck, leaving the space vacant for Philippe to close in beside her. She watched dispassionately as the sunburnt fellow hugged, kissed and then fondled a short, plump woman bedecked with streamers. The woman was also wearing shorts.

'A mistake,' Kate observed disparagingly. She took great care over her slender, graceful frame.

'Did your father mention in the letter what the distance is between Lesa and mainland Fiji?'

'He didn't mention it, Philippe. You know he didn't,' she replied, observing his short temper, thinking that he was as anxious as she. No doubt for different reasons.

In spite of sixteen years of marriage she and Philippe had never travelled such a distance together. He hated to be out of contact with the office. He had always been a regular 'short hop' traveller, particularly in the early days when he had been working for Crédit Suisse as a trader on their London foreign exchange desk. Weekdays had frequently been spent in Switzerland. Never any hiccups there. Philippe was a perfectionist. He hated what he referred to as 'hiccups'. They disturbed his meticulously planned days and such confusion made him peevish.

Of course he and Kate had always taken holidays together. Two a year, generally speaking. Usually in France. Philippe had school chums who had a house in the South and his French parents still had their apartment in Paris although they had retired now to a villa on the Cap at Antibes. Or there was the small house in the Alps, in Courcheval, which they rented almost every Christmas. Philippe loved to ski. Kate had never learnt as a child, there had never been the money for such 'indulgences' particularly once her father had left home. She had a private instructor now in Courcheval and she was very competent but, of course, if you haven't learnt as a child, it's never quite the same. But they both enjoyed the mountains.

Philippe had recently been toying with the idea of investing in a place of their own on the Continent. 'I can't think why we never have,' he had been saying to her at regular intervals as he poured enthusiastically over glossy Swiss brochures or property columns every Wednesday in *The Times*. We could pop over most weekends.'

Yes, they could. But would they? she would ask herself silently. He worked so hard that persuading him to go anywhere was a struggle and once out of contact with the *Financial Times*, the *Wall Street Journal* and telex, telephone or fax machines he became quite intolerable, though, no doubt, both could be installed.

She had persuaded him to take her to the Far East a few years earlier. A Kuoni Tour. Three countries, seventeen days. Singapore, Thailand and Bali. Bali had been particularly difficult because Philippe had spent almost the entire time inside the hotel room on the telephone.

But there had been temples, a couple of days' relaxation on the beach and then plenty of shopping in Singapore before flying home. She had enjoyed wandering around the Buddhist temples, particularly in Bangkok. And would have preferred to stay longer there. Fascinating too, to observe all the petite, young Asian girls dining at the hotel with obese German businessmen. And English and Frenchmen too, she had to admit that.

It had caused her to wonder about Philippe. What if he had been there alone? It was something she never allowed herself to consider. All those trips he took to Europe, alone. Loyalty was a virtue she depended upon.

Perhaps because of her father.

Her thoughts drifted again towards her father. She thought of his letter and the reason for her journey. It seemed so bitterly unfair, so cruel that after all these years of silence, years of missing him, longing to hear from him, loathing and resenting him, growing up without him, never knowing what had happened to him, that she had finally heard from him. He had finally summoned her. And now he was dead. And for some inexplicable reason she was terrified.

'There's the port!'

'That's the main city of Suva!'

Kate's attention was nudged abruptly back into the present. The passengers all about her had started pushing, some were cheering while others were shouting raucously. She felt momentarily panicked. It was like being surrounded on New Year's Eve in Trafalgar Square, she thought mockingly as she reached her hand a few inches along the metal railing in search of Philippe's firm grip.

She smiled at him. 'Stay with me,' she seemed to say, and then she peered hard at the tropical island quayside looming into view. Her heart was pounding as matchstick silhouettes evolved into urgent people scurrying about, busying themselves around the wharf. She saw half-naked Indians heaping precariously balanced wooden crates on to small metal trolleys, while elsewhere, powerfully built uniformed natives, as rich a brown as iroko wood, lounged elegantly in white scalloped knee-length skirts. Other less elegant fellows were crouching like primates and glaring mistrustfully at the arriving liner.

Escorted by bustling terrier-like tugboats the majestic cruise liner negotiated its sleek, foaming path towards the quayside, announcing its arrival with several dark blasts on its imperious horn.

Hordes of impatient tourists, either side of Kate and Philippe, began preparing to disembark. Down the wooden ramp on to the Customs Wharf in search of trinkets, postcards and foreign adventure.

Chapter 2

It was already noon in Suva's bustling streets. Young Ami Chand hurried out of a duty-free store, ran towards his tired Suzuki jeep and tossed a brown paper package, containing black-market video cassettes, on to the passenger seat. He glanced at his watch. Past noon. He was cutting it pretty fine!

He scooted around the bonnet of the truck while grappling impatiently in his jeans pocket for his keys. Generous drops of warm rain began to smack against his harassed young features. Ami glanced skywards. It was overcast, threatening a tropical downpour.

'Jesus!' he blasphemed, kicking frustratedly against the open red door of the jeep. He was having a rotten day!

Why did nothing ever work out for him?

The brakes on his truck were badly worn. They were dangerous in the rain but in spite of that he was going to have to dash. He had left his son, Jal, with his parents, promising to collect the boy after his meeting, but he had been kept waiting, his meeting with Ashok Bhanjee had run late and now he was going to have to look sharp, leave his son for another hour, and get directly to the port. He couldn't afford to lose his job at the Plantation, precarious enough since old Sam's death!

Nimbly he jumped into the open truck, started up the sluggish engine and flicked the button to start up the worn rubber wipers. They began to swish heavily to and fro. He threw the gearstick into first and stared miserably at them, cursing them as they laboured their way back and forth across the dusty, now muddied, windscreen. The thick drops of tropical rain were beating fast against the glass, thudding on to the uncleaned windscreen like birdshit fired from a machine gun, while the inept wipers juddered back and forth, creating a coagulated mass of red mud that smeared the entire screen and annihilated all chance of visibility.

'Why now?' Ami begged. He crouched on the worn seat, pulled out a piece of ragged cloth from his back pocket, normally used as a headband, and lunged his hand out of the window, hastily wiping the cloth across the screen. This done he threw the soiled, sodden rag on to the passenger seat, sat comfortably, checked his digital watch and, once more, set the brooding engine in motion. He might not be too late!

He weaved his way swiftly, darting recklessly in and out of undisciplined, unthinking traffic, negotiating a dangerous path around scurrying pedestrians all fleeing from the unexpected downpour. Until suddenly, spontaneously changing his mind, quite characteristic of him, he executed a dare-devil U-turn which he accomplished in one bold gesture, turning the beaten old motor full lock and swinging the jeep back along the opposite side of the main road, then sharp left into a narrow, almost boggy lane cluttered with untidy sprawling piles of coconuts. All for sale.

He had decided to collect his son after all.

Here was the main entrance to the market, next to Suva bus station. It was recognisable by the clusters of brightly coloured Fijian natives and ethnic Indians. With a bias towards the Indians, famed traders of the world! Ami parked, or rather dumped, the truck and ran into the market, smartly pushing his way through the throngs of shoppers and traders. Many of those not directly engaged in business turned their heads as they were brusquely shoved aside. Several recognised him, he had been brought up here on the mainland. They shouted to him, warmly greeting him in Fijian Hindi.

'Ami! *Kaise hai?*' they called to him.

'*Accha,*' he repeated several times, boasting confidently with gestures and facial expressions about his good health and his accumulating, although truth to tell non-existent, prosperity.

'So your brother's made his fortune and left for Canada, eh Ami?' shouted one young fellow across colourful displays of fruit. 'Your turn next, my friend?' another teased.

'Yes. Very soon. You wait and see,' Ami retaliated.

Behind him as he pushed his hasty way ahead he could hear his fellow Indians laughing, harmlessly lampooning him. They might laugh, he thought, but he'd get to Canada one day! He was going to be very rich one day!

At the far end of the narrow market lanes he spied his father standing in front of their neatly arranged yet cluttered family stall. He was engaged in a sale. His mother, the holder of the purse strings and collector of debts, was seated discreetly at the rear of the stall. Her arms jingled with gold bangles glinting in the darkened light of the covered market. At her side stood Jal, her five-year-old grandson, who watched admiringly, mesmerised by his grandfather.

The old man, Jal's grandfather, was persuading an elderly tourist, eager to return home laden with souvenirs, that here was an opportunity to purchase a work of art. The price, the only barrier to owning the 'piece', was being tossed back at the potential customer with the agility of a trampoline artist who delicately, slowly now, brings himself to rest, feat accomplished. Grandson Jal was enthralled by the dexterity, the deftness of the negotiation, practised, though he could not yet know it, during decades of hardship, poverty and indentured labour, honed to a skill which had helped to earn them, these exiled Indians, their price of freedom.

Ami crept in apace, watching while his father reverently handed his satisfied customer the hand-carved wooden Ganesh wrapped in a local supermarket bag. The tourist was smiling. He smugly believed he had driven a demanding bargain and had 'put one over' the Indian. Mr Chand graciously accepted the dollars, watching as each note

17

was counted into his fair-skinned palm, then he bowed his head in thanks to his customer, who disappeared into the milling crowds as Chand turned to pass the dollar bills to his ever-vigilant wife. As she counted and folded each warm note the bangles on her arms clinked and collided with one another like dancing Spanish castanets.

Ami held back until the transaction had been completed. In spite of his haste he knew better than to break the spell. Now, seeing that the goal had been scored, he pushed his way forward, through the shuffling crowds shopping for food and *kava*, alongside sauntering tourists greedy for a bargain.

His mother was the first to see him approach. She nudged her adored grandson forward knowing through experience that her son would be in a hurry. Ami scooped Jal into his arms, bare beneath the rolled-up sleeves of his prized flying jacket, whilst digging deeply into the rear pocket of his jeans. Swiftly, and not entirely discreetly, he passed a rain-dampened wad of local dollars to his mother who proudly added them to her cherished growing bundle. She bowed her head in thanks to her second son, who bragged about 'plenty more to come where that was made!'

They did not need his support but, as the only son remaining, his successful elder brother Roshan having left with his family for Canada several days earlier, Ami was encouraged to continue the ritual of family support.

With both parents nodding approvingly Ami slipped back along the narrow garbage-ridden passages of the thriving market with his boy still wrapped around his waist and clinging to his neck. Out into the wet, navy noon they stepped. Swiftly he deposited the child on to the passenger seat, sweeping the muddied rag and the package of cassettes to the ground, and started up the tired engine which shimmied like an overweight belly dancer.

'Shit!' he swore at the damp engine before it finally fired and roared into life.

The rain was bucketing down now as he hurtled back along the main road towards the port, dangerously avoiding a

18

sauntering chicken, on his way to collect the English arrivals who were, no doubt, becoming anxious.

But this was the South Pacific. Fijian island time!

'Kate! We'd better make a move,' Philippe called above the hubbub of anticipation.

The liner had landed. An air of impatience pervaded as people stood bunched together, anxious to break loose. Kate cast an elegant eye down on to the quayside.

Quite suddenly, it had begun to pour. Noise and rain bombarded her. People were bustling to and fro carrying large packages, cheaply made suitcases or heavy cartons. Everywhere brown-skinned bodies hurried for shelter as the storm sheeted on to the concrete dockside.

She breathed deeply and exhaled. Her heart was pounding. Everything smelt alien. The air was reeking of dampened soil, diesel and heavy fruit perfumes. The tropics, one of those tropical downpours!

It had been the same that July in Bangkok, she remembered. Their holiday had coincided with the rainy season in Thailand but she hadn't minded. Quite the reverse; she had loved it, the force of the weather. Everywhere she had breathed lush, sodden vegetation. She had found it purging, liberating, wet clothes against her fair skin.

'Hey, wake up, *chérie*! Let's get moving!' Philippe put an arm around her slender waist She was wearing an elegant, light blue, floral silk dress that she had bought at Harvey Nichols two months earlier. The day after she had received her father's letter. A celebratory treat, she had told herself. Philippe's strong, sure arm, clammy against the yielding silk, guided her close to him, negotiating excited crowds pushing their way down the ship's stairway, determined to live to the hilt every moment of their cruise stopover. 'Stay with me!' he shouted above the noise of high-pitched chatter, pounding feet and ever-increasing rain.

She held her wide-brimmed straw sunhat firmly on her head. It was beginning to sag under the weight of the deluge and probably looked awful, she thought sadly, turning to glance briefly at her husband. He seemed to be thoroughly disgruntled, and drenched. His shirt, open to his chest, was clinging to his skin and she could clearly discern his nipples, overly pink through the white sodden cotton.

They ran the last few steps, dashing to find cover under the corrugated iron roofing of what, she supposed, was the Customs Hall. Outside, barely audible car horns were baying like dogs while within, the rain thudded against the roof like children beating tin drums. Indian porters clanked trolleys of luggage to and fro, friends cried out to others glimpsed waiting through Passport Control, lost tourists shouted names anxiously in search of loved ones, disorganisation and chaos reverberated throughout the open, barn-like building.

Philippe wiped the drips of rain from his sodden hair with a spotted silk handkerchief and glanced about him.

'There's our luggage! That was quick,' he announced triumphantly, disappearing amongst bustling and bemused groups. He headed resolutely towards a short, stocky Indian patiently standing guard over their cases. Kate followed. Between them they gathered the several designer-embossed pieces on to a trolley and hurried to join the queue, or rather gaggle of visitors and homecomers waiting to be cleared through Immigration and Customs. It all seemed a formality. When their turn came, surprisingly swiftly, they were smilingly waved through.

'Now.' Philippe spoke purposefully. 'I wonder where this Stone fellow will be waiting.' It was more a thought to himself than to Kate who, in any case, was not listening. Her attention had been drawn by a commotion that had broken out behind them. She had turned to see what was happening.

Two Indian customs officials were shouting at a third arriving Indian, insisting that he open up his luggage. As far as Kate could tell he was reluctant, clinging passionately to his brown plastic cases held together with worn cord. Kate watched with fascination as he explained in painstaking detail the problems involved in retying the suitcases. Unfortunately, the customs men were obdurate and waited in grim, unrelenting silence. The poor fellow's hangdog expression wrung Kate's heart.

Finally, seeing no way out, he conceded, fumbling nervously to loosen the offending ropes. One of the customs men, the more officious of the pair, with his thin black moustache and bored angry face, began to rummage impatiently, like a dog in search of a misplaced bone, through the first case, while the owner stood looking on helplessly, watching miserably as his underwear and striped pyjamas were pulled from the plastic case and strewn across a long wooden trestle table.

Curious to know what he was thinking Kate turned to observe the owner of the cases. He was looking tense. Beads of sweat bejewelled his dark, oily hairline as he dragged desperately on a cigarette like an asthmatic sucking into a void for oxygen. She concluded that he must, after all, be guilty. And apparently she was right.

At the bottom of the case several video cassettes were found. The grim-faced officials were triumphant. They leapt into animated life like water diviners whose search was at an end. Kate assumed that the cassettes must be 'blue' because the now terrified-looking little man was arrested noisily. Silence fell momentarily across the hall as all forgot their own story and looked on in curious disbelief.

Two newly arrived officials, tall burly Fijians, not Indians, grabbed him forcefully by his upper arms and led him smartly through a bottle-green door at the back of the echoing hallway. The arrested man continued protesting his innocence until he was out of sight. His cases disappeared through the same door moments after him but the flannelette pyjamas, still strewn across the counter, were brushed to the ground, forgotten.

Kate recalled visiting an uncle of hers in hospital when she was a child. He had worn the same pyjamas.

The next in line, an elderly European couple, walked gingerly forward, stepping on the unnoticed stripes as they approached the now smiling officials.

'There seem to be a lot of Indians here,' Kate remarked. 'They've just arrested one for smuggling.' She turned back to Philippe. He wasn't listening.

'I suppose he would carry a sign letting us know who he is.'

21

'Who?'

'Stone. He isn't damned well here!'

Jarred back into the present, Kate looked about her, hoping she might be able to spot their man. 'Is that him there?' she enquired hopefully, pointing at the only white man immediately in view apart from the arriving tourists.

'Don't be silly. Of course it's not him. At least, I hope it isn't.'

The man she and Philippe were referring to was a portly, florid-faced fellow, in his late fifties, looking as though he might be suffering from the climate and the gin. They were looking for someone fit enough to run a large plantation.

'I hope to God they radioed through my telex. You can never tell with these remote places. They just don't understand the importance of communication.'

'Look!' Kate had spotted, across the hallway, a small hand-painted sign nailed above a booking desk. It read: 'FERRIES TO THE ISLANDS.'

'I'll go and ask.' And before Philippe could stop her she hurried off, heading in the direction of the booth where she found another Indian. He was settled at a desk in an inner office.

'We want to go to Lesa, to the Lesa Sugar Plantation. Is there a ferry that goes there?' she asked politely. There seemed to be no sign that he had heard her.

'Excuse me. Do you speak English?' she enquired again. This time more forcefully.

'Yes.' The Indian replied without lifting his head but implying, quite plainly, that he had understood the first time.

'We were expecting to be met here but . . .' Her voice trailed away feebly at his show of apparent uninterest in her dilemma. And then, 'What time is the next ferry to Lesa?' she continued with renewed enthusiasm.

'One stops there every three hours. Last one left twenty minutes ago. Or you can take a seaplane, but not from here.'

'Where?'

'Outside town, twenty-five minutes, eighty-five dollars.' The Indian returned to his seat and his Hindi film magazine,

22

leaving Kate staring at him helplessly. She was feeling wet and quite miserable, more so now at the prospect of returning to Philippe with the news that they had a three-hour wait ahead of them or they would have to go in search of a seaplane, when a breathless voice behind her spoke her name.

'Excuse me missus, are you the English lady, Mrs De Marly?'

Relieved to have finally been recognised Kate swung swiftly to meet Mr Stone. 'Yes, I am,' she answered.

'Sorry to be late, missus.' Ami Chand grinned warmly at her. His raven hair was glossed wet against his handsome young Asian face.

'Are you Mr Stone?' she asked, astounded, eager to disguise the surprise she felt at the sight of an Indian. She had no reason to suppose that Stone was not Indian.

'He couldn't come today.'

'I see. But you are from my father's plantation?'

The young man nodded.

'I'd better get my husband.'

Philippe had already seen Kate in conversation with the young Indian and was hurrying towards them, followed by the ever-patient porter still struggling with the trolley and their hand luggage.

'Are you here to meet us?' Philippe was approaching as he spoke.

'Yessir. Mr Stone couldn't come today. Busy with repairs.'

'You're late.'

Ami said nothing as he deftly gathered up their luggage and led them outside, hurrying towards the waiting truck, parked a hundred yards or so along on the opposite side of the narrow, littered street.

It had stopped raining but the heavy clouds hung like clusters of charcoal in the low sky above them. Beneath, the dusty unswept streets were covered in rivulets of mud which gurgled and seeped into Kate's open, slingback sandals.

The noise of the hooters, the roaring motorbikes and the vibrant life in the overcrowded Suva Port suburb overwhelmed them as they followed awkwardly behind their agile young

23

guide who sprinted on ahead, leaving them to weave their way in and out of passing cars, vegetable carts and folk sauntering by on numerous bicycles.

Ami threw their luggage carelessly into the open back of the truck and opened the passenger door. 'Down you get,' he said to his son in Hindi. 'My son,' he explained proudly to the arriving foreigners.

Jal clambered out obediently, shuffled shyly past the foreign couple, his head firmly bent to avoid any possibility of eye contact. With the aid of his young father he vaulted over the rusted side of the truck, burying himself and a treasured transistor radio amongst the strangers' luggage.

'I'll get in first,' Philippe murmured to Kate, leaving her free to indulge in the pleasure of discovering her new surroundings.

'We cross by speedboat. From here to the landing stage,' Ami assured, 'will take us about fifteen minutes, once we're out of the city traffic.'

He shoved the gearstick into first and the truck lurched forward. With his right hand on the wheel and his elbow resting against the open window (English driving regulations remained as witness to the islands' British colonial past) he used his left hand to search for a desired radio station. Perhaps it was the city traffic, the recent bad storm, or simply the age of the radio but nothing more than an unpleasant high-pitched crackle was transmitted. Philippe, feeling short on patience and infuriated by the time they had been kept waiting, longed to tell him to turn the damn thing off but thought better of it, not wanting to upset his wife whose head was now leaning contentedly out of the window, oblivious to his irritability.

They began making their way out of the city along the coastal road towards a small landing stage where the Lesa Plantation dinghy awaited them. Ami pointed out to them, with much charm and confidence, that it would give them an opportunity to glimpse a little of the mainland before setting off for the island.

Ahead of them, to their left, were mountains, pale and smoky in the overcast distance like drawings in childhood

Western comics. Kate glimpsed fleeting images of native homes as the truck hurtled by. She smelt the damp leaves and the faint perfume of banana trees.

'Fijian houses!' Ami shouted across Philippe. 'Fijian name is *bure*.'

They were built from dried palm leaves or corrugated iron. From their lush green gardens, made all the more brilliant by the recent rain still dripping from the giant leaves, friendly smiling Fijian women called out to her.

'*Bula!*' they shouted, in deep resonant tones. It was a greeting. An expansive welcoming 'hello'.

She smiled shyly, intrigued by what she saw. She wondered what might have induced her father to settle in such a place. A world so alien to her. Goats tethered to gateposts, trees or abandoned wheelless rusted automobiles paid her no attention while cows roamed obliviously along the roadside, sauntering lazily across Ami's path, causing him to swerve dangerously towards the open ditch on the opposite side of the cambered road. He was happy that his passengers knew nothing of the unreliability of the brakes!

'Excuse me, stop here, two minutes,' Ami announced outside a small isolated general store. Without switching off the engine he reached swiftly under the passenger seat, took from behind their ankles his brown paper package and leapt from the truck before Philippe had time to say a word. Philippe glanced at his watch. It was already quarter to one.

'This is intolerable,' he muttered.

They watched silently as a middle-aged Indian waited at the door of the impoverished store. He shouted to Ami as the young man sprinted along the pathway towards him.

'Who is this boy? Did he say?'

Kate shook her head. 'I suppose he works at the Plantation.'

Philippe sighed in disgust.

The man seemed impatient. Ami tore into his package and handed something to the shopkeeper who began waving his arms impatiently, angrily regarding whatever it was that Ami had brought him.

'I think he's arguing with the other man,' Kate observed.

25

Ami gestured towards the truck, towards the waiting passengers, grabbed what looked like a paper bag from the shopkeeper and hurtled back along the pathway towards the waiting jeep.

'Sorry about the delay,' he announced smilingly, thrusting the brown package and paper bag under his own seat.

Neither Kate nor Philippe responded.

They drove onwards again, along this coastal highway, for longer than his promised quarter of an hour, probably twenty-five minutes. It was an uncomfortable journey due to poor suspension. Their damp clinging clothes and the humidity, not lessened by the recent downpour, added to their aggravation.

Along the shoreline Kate saw transparent plastic bottles lying discarded on the perfect white sand. Old shoes, the soles of old shoes, broken beer bottles and bruised shapeless tinnies. The dregs of life rolling lazily to and fro as the quiet waves lapped against them. And across the fertile green land surrounding them they saw rusted cars piled high, one on top of another, manmade mountains of discarded automobiles scarring the deluged landscape. Trash jettisoned or heaped everywhere, surrounded by towering, majestical tropical beauty.

Eventually they approached the deserted landing base, no more than a raft floating idly in the turquoise water. Close by Kate spied three tall Fijians, thick, sinewy young men, naked from the waist upwards, standing proudly, prattling together, barefoot against the damp terracotta earth. They turned to gaze into the passing truck and spotted her. Their faces lit up and each smiled expansively, exposing large mouthfuls of gleaming ivory teeth beneath flat, spatulated features. One blew an enthusiastic kiss, the second shouted a hearty, full-throated, 'I love you' and the third yelled happily, 'Whisky!' All three erupted into gales of laughter, overjoyed by their own boldness. Their enthusiastic grinning and playfulness made Kate laugh too. She wanted to wave and smile but feared the gesture might be wrongly interpreted and instead turned coyly towards her silent husband who sat, overtired, staring straight ahead of him.

The truck slowed down on the perilously potholed road and swung to the right, rolling on to soft, damp sand.

'There's the Plantation speedboat,' Ami explained as they

pulled up on the sand. 'We'll leave the truck here and take that across to the island.'

He parked the vehicle within the dappled shade of towering palm trees, still dripping from the recent storm.

Kate stepped from the rusty truck, sank her weight into the damp sand and stared out across the crystal water.

A multitude of islands speckled the horizon.

'Which one is Lesa?' she called to the Indian who, with help from his small child, was lugging their bags towards the elegant white motor launch.

'That way.' He was pointing northwest. 'You can't see it from here.'

Kate peered through the sharp light, following the direction of his finger. Two months she had been waiting for this day. Perhaps, in truth, much longer. She sighed, feeling saddened at the thought that her father would no longer be there to greet her. A stab of anxiety pierced her. Perhaps she should have listened to Philippe. Perhaps they should have just turned back and gone home. But then she would never have known anything about him, this stranger that had been her father.

Chapter 3

'Lesa is famous for its rare, crested iguana,' Ami shouted to them, once at sea, to be heard above the sound of the spray and the chuntering diesel engine.

Kate nodded politely, clutching desperately on to her sunhat with one hand and gripping tightly on to the side of the speedboat with the other. Strands of her light brown hair had blown across her face and had lodged uncomfortably between her lips.

A school of fish leapt from the water. They swam between the numerous coral reefs which jutted above the transparent water's surface.

Kate was longing now to ask their Indian guide about the Plantation, knowing that with every wave that crashed lightly against the side of their boat her arrival became more imminent, but he could not hear her.

Her heart was beating fast now. She turned to Philippe for reassurance but he was looking decidedly uncomfortable, even wetter than before. Poor thing, she thought. He's hating all this. I know he is.

So she contented herself with her enforced silence and watched the island of Lesa loom into view. It appeared greener, lusher, larger than she had been imagining.

'Over there's the port of Loquaqua.' Ami pointed to his right, as they chugged around the foot of the island. 'That's the only town on Lesa.' Ahead of them to the west, a tanker coasted distantly beyond the reef. 'He's on his way to the mainland.'

Kate glanced at the sky. All the clouds had disappeared. It was a clear, liquid blue. The sun beat down on them, drying their briny skins as swiftly as the salt spray showered them.

'You'll be able to see the Plantation soon. The house is on a headland.'

Finally, they were arriving!

Six days of travelling would soon be over. It had seemed endless, and then the brutal, unexpected news of Sam's death. The cruise had been her idea. She had needed a few days to recover from the shock but it had not been a success. Both she and Philippe had hated every moment of it. But now her journey was almost over. They were finally approaching his home.

She wondered how long he had lived there.

'Look now!' Ami pointed towards a building, revealed like a solitary hill station on a cliff-top, way above them. 'That's it.'

The house faced west, out across the reefed water towards the ocean. It overlooked the various smaller islands and atolls, to the left of them now as they approached.

'Lesa Plantation House,' the Indian shouted proudly. 'Nice house, missus.'

Kate squinted to avoid the direct glare of the late midday sun as she stared up at the building growing in the diminishing distance. She could hardly believe her eyes. Not in her wildest imaginings had she expected such a place. 'What a spot to build a house!' she sighed, more to herself than to anyone around her. 'That crafty old devil,' she murmured with unexpected admiration for this stranger, her father. It was not that the house seemed large or overly luxurious, but its location! She could understand its attraction now.

Suddenly she was feeling elated. Her spirits had lifted more than she could explain or even understand. All the anxiety and sadness that she had been feeling during these last few days disappeared. Fears were abating, simply seeping away at the sight of the imposing yet inviting edifice. So this was where he had disappeared to.

And as the small boat leapt and bounced on the spray, so too did her heart, eager to discover now, hurrying her onwards towards their destination. At that moment she noticed the small Indian boy, staring at her again. He had hardly looked anywhere else since they had left the beach on the mainland. It had made her feel awkward, highlighting her own nervousness, but now she smiled at him encouragingly. He simply closed his round, black eyes and buried his face in his hands.

'Do you live at Lesa too?' she shouted, pointing with her eyes. The boy had not heard her or had chosen not to hear. His shyness appealed to her, made her grin.

She turned her attention, for the first time, towards his father who was singing happily to himself as he steered. Kate noticed how handsome he was, and fit. He had taken his shirt off when they had climbed into the speedboat and had buried it with his satin flying jacket, wedging both between the luggage. It left him naked to the waist.

Silently she watched him. His naturally dark skin gleamed in the heat while the salt spray clung to him like fine white talcum powder. She watched the back of his black-haired head moving from side to side in time to the music inside his head.

For his part, Ami had forgotten his passengers and was quite alone with his song, lifting his own downcast spirits, musing over his meeting, temporarily assuaging his earlier disappointment.

His ill-fitting, sodden jeans clung to him and a gold chain hung around his neck glinting like paste in the heat. Kate studied him for a moment longer until, as if feeling her eyes on his naked back, he turned his head and grinned broadly at her, remembering his passengers and his duty once more.

'Soon be there,' he reassured warmly. She smiled.

For a fleeting moment his regard reminded her of someone else, a Thai tourist guide that she had met one solitary, hot, empty afternoon in Bangkok. A slender, breathtakingly handsome young man who had shown her around the Golden Temple while Philippe remained at the hotel, working. She had been feeling lonely, as she so often did, lacking her overly busy husband's attentions, and had innocently flirted with the youth.

30

'You want number one man in your room, missus?' he had asked her guilelessly, as she tipped him probably rather too generously.

'Good God, no! I'm a married woman!' she had explained, remembering now how shocked and uncomfortable his bluntness had caused her to feel. The young Thai boy had simply shrugged and wandered off, amused by her, leaving her feeling foolish that she had so adamantly expressed her discomfort.

She smiled now at Ami and his young son.

Later that same afternoon in Bangkok, as she had strolled back alone towards the Orient Hotel, she had wondered what it would have been like . . . number one man in her room . . . She had tried to dismiss the thought but it had persisted, disturbing her. That evening, at supper with Philippe, she had secretly compared them, ruminating on her unsolicited invitation. And for a short while she had regretted her reaction. Her reticence, as she had perceived it later.

She turned to her husband. He looked ready to land. He caught her eye and smiled.

How many times during their marriage had Philippe railed at her for what he called her 'reticence with life'? She supposed he was right.

'I'm looking forward to some lunch, Petal. How about you?' he yelled over the putting of the engine and the spray.

Kate nodded, returning his smile. He had not wanted to make this trip. It had been she who had insisted. Even in Sydney after the news of her father's death it had been she who had wanted to continue.

'Why don't we return to London and when the estate is settled we can just sell the place?' he had said to her after she had told him the news. 'I can't think why you want to go there. It can't mean anything to you.'

She hadn't been able to explain why. 'Because he was my father,' she had reiterated insistently.

'But you didn't know him.'

'That's why.'

Finally he had conceded. 'All right, if it's what you really want, then we'll go. And then sell the place. I suppose the old boy's lived there for donkey's years. God alone knows what sort of place it will be.'

She had never understood why Philippe insisted on referring to him as the 'old boy'. He had never met him. Sam was a shadow from Kate's distant past, almost never mentioned, particularly by her mother.

'I don't want to talk about him, Katy.'

In the beginning Kate had persisted, questioning regularly: What was he like? Where had he disappeared to? Kate's questions tormented her poor mother who had never been able to forgive him. They tore at an already festering sore.

'God alone knows where he is. Dead I suppose!'

There had been a violent row one Christmas Eve. Kate, still only seven, had witnessed it. She had been sitting with her parents eating supper. They were bickering. It had been no more than usual until, suddenly, tempers began flying, and they had started shouting at one another. In the heat of their argument they must have forgotten that Kate was still there. She had said nothing, would not have dared, silently watching as they screamed at one another, accusing one another, of what she had long since forgotten, growing more aggressive and insane with every curse.

'Jesus, woman, I'd like to kill you!' her father had yelled, violently hurling himself at Kate's mother who, terrified, had thrown herself backwards from her chair, knocking her skull against the living-room wall, against the burgundy wallpaper. Kate could still picture it now.

She and Sam were paralysed with fear, watching the crumpled creature on the ground. Blood began trickling through her mother's dark hair. It ran down the side of her cheek. She began to whimper and then her tears became more forceful until she was wailing uncontrollably. Sam had stared at his young weeping wife, all the while scratching nervously at his face.

'Dear God Almighty,' he breathed, and turning to Kate, he said softly, 'I have to get out of here, Kathy . . . Will you come with me or stay here with your mother?'

Kate had started to cry. 'What about Mummy?'

32

She wanted to be with him, she loved him so much, she couldn't bear to lose him but she wanted to be with her mother too.

'I'll stay here with Mummy,' she had choked, hoping that if she stayed he might not go, or if he did, he'd come back.

But he never came back.

He clung hard against her, giving her a long, rough hug and then, without saying another word, he had turned and walked out of the door.

'Daddy, please don't go,' Kate had begged hopelessly.

She only ever saw him once again. She never knew what had happened to him or where he disappeared to. Not until a couple of months earlier when she had received a typewritten letter from him, telling her that he was living in Fiji and that he wanted her to visit him on his sugar plantation.

'I have put the Plantation in your name. If anything should happen to me I want you to have the place. If you can forgive your old man, why don't you come and see it?' he had written to her.

It had seemed incredible, to receive such a letter after all those years. She had supposed him already dead. Almost never a word from him since he had deserted them, leaving her mother unforgiving, bitter and angry. Kate rarely recalled this memory. It was too painful for her, even after all these years. She had never forgotten the sound of that dull thud as her mother's head hit the wall . . . and the fear of what might have happened. She had run down the street, to the neighbours for help, and they had driven her mother to hospital.

She breathed deeply now and let her left hand, the one clutching tightly on to the side of the speedboat, fall easily into the spray. The water was cool against her burning skin. She was feeling anxious again and tilted her head towards the jutting headland, directly in front of them now, staring uncertainly at the Plantation House. It towered majestically, standing alone, looking out over the calm, turquoise ocean. Her breath caught in her throat and her head began to spin.

'Too much sun,' she told herself.

33

She had wanted so much to understand Sam, and to forgive him. To know what had happened to him during all those silent, absent years.

'I'll land the boat on the beach in that bay and we'll take a jeep up to the house.' Ami skidded the elegant white speedboat skilfully through the shallow reef water and landed easily on the blindingly white sand.

From where they disembarked it was an uncomfortable couple of miles along a dusty, coastal hillside road towards the house on the headland.

'Excuse the tin biscuit!' Ami joked self-consciously as he banged his hand flatly against a burnt-orange-coloured, battered and rusted Volkswagen jeep which they found waiting for them within the shade of a sandied coconut grove.

'What?' Kate asked as she threw her leather shoulder bag on to the dusty back seat and clambered in after it.

'This. She's so old. At the house they joke that she's made like a Japanese tin biscuit,' he joked.

'I think he means biscuit tin,' Philippe whispered to Kate as he climbed in after her.

Kate sat impassively. She was feeling exhausted now and overly sensitive. Her skin was covered in a light film, a mixture of reddish dust from the road and drying salt from the spray. It stung and creased against her light flesh. She noticed the little boy's ragged clothes and his unwashed, mud-caked feet and, for no apparent reason, the sight of him so dishevelled suddenly aggravated her. He had, at last, ceased staring and was now amusing himself with his rediscovered, oversized transistor radio.

As Ami started up the engine the whirring wheels sprayed them with sand. She sighed irritably. Philippe took her hand, squeezed it and smiled reassuringly, before turning his attention to the surrounding stretch of deserted beach.

An endless expanse of sugar-cane fields unfolded to the right of them as they set off along the coastal road; a sea of ripe green stalks, glinting silver-tipped in the still heat. Beyond, the mountains; rising dramatically in the central distance, blue-black and amethyst, like bruised, gigantic volcanic larvae. Everywhere heat, beating, still and silent.

To the left, as the jeep struggled to climb higher, Kate beheld a pure turquoise lagoon hemmed by laced rock fringes of reef. Beyond it, stretching endlessly towards the horizon, was cobalt-blue ocean. The water was so clear she felt able to count each grain of golden sand shifting imperceptibly beneath it.

She realised with relief that the throbbing heat was easing. Cooled, as they climbed higher, by a light breeze.

They reached the pinnacle of the towering cliff-top. The headland jutted west from the northern point of the island.

Kate stepped from the jeep and stretched her limbs. It was markedly cooler here. She found herself, not in the tropical jungle that she had been expecting, but in a manicured, secluded garden dappled and umbrellaed by a mass of flame and acacia trees as tall as coconut palms. The air was still. Silence, save for a generator humming contentedly somewhere behind the main house and the swish of breezes high above in the tall trees.

It was ravishingly beautiful, so tranquil and so entirely unexpected. In spite of her exhaustion Kate paused to imbibe the living silence surrounding her. Everywhere, flowers and fruit: papaya trees, taller than men, bore clusters of fruit hanging like unripened green breasts; an array of small bushlike plants blossomed brilliant vermilion-red flowers; dead sawn-down coconut trunks still rooted in the earth were overgrown with living foliage, giving new life and colour to them, while all about the garden hacked or damaged coconut husks had been gathered into neat piles and placed at the feet of the flame trees, like sacrificial offerings, waiting to be used later for burning.

Kate tilted her head and gazed upwards, towards a swimming-pool-blue sky peering back at her through a forest of swaying susurrant leaves. An unseen bird screeched a raucous welcome as she sauntered, loosening her tired muscles, towards a gravelled pathway that led to the house.

The verandah, with its inner door open to the day, was

35

about fifty feet long. It stood bordering the length of the house, like a frill on the hem of a faded skirt, and was cluttered with ageing, weatherbeaten, rattan furniture placed anyhow. Burmese, or perhaps they were Tibetan, bronze bells, hanging from a wooden rafter, tingled in the light breeze.

Unlike the garden, the house seemed empty, neglected, deserted even. Behind her, as Kate faced the house, less cared for than she had deduced from the speedboat, could be heard the constant sound of the waves rolling, beating sensuously against the reef.

Two tall, honey, thin mongrels came bounding towards her, startling her, all the while panting and barking. Kate laughed loudly at their sudden, unexpected welcome as the bitch leapt against her, knocking her off balance. She began making her way along the path towards the unknown house. The dogs followed, pestering playfully. She turned to Philippe who was with Ami organising the luggage.

'I'm going inside. To have a look around. Are you coming?' she shouted, stepping gingerly on to the porch and taking off her sadly misshapen sunhat. A rangy, tired-looking fellow in his mid forties stepped through an open doorway and stood in the hallway, watching as Kate approached.

'Calm down,' he commanded. The mongrels obeyed instantly, settling themselves amongst the rattan terrace furniture, panting contentedly. 'Hello there.' The stranger smiled, moving towards Kate as she arrived. 'I'm Rob Stone, Plantation Manager. You must be Sam's daughter? We spoke on the telephone. Welcome to Lesa.' He spoke with an Australian accent. She had been so distressed by his news on the telephone that she had not noticed it.

'Yes, of course. Kate De Marly. How do you do?' Kate offered her hand. 'And this is my husband, Philippe.'

Philippe joined his wife and the stranger inside the cool, darkened hallway. Kate glanced furtively about her. The fan above them was whirring rhythmically, easing them into the new environment. She noticed a damp smell, a mustiness permeating, and hated it, finding it an uncomfortable, unwelcoming odour, like mothballs in a strange bedroom. It reminded her of visits to her widowed grandmother, when she was a child. The house felt neglected, dusty as the memories of her father. Like creeping into a long-forgotten attic where time had somehow stood still.

'We were expecting you to meet us at the port. I suppose you received my telex,' Philippe accused tartly.

Kate noticed the faint hint of reprimand in her husband's voice. She knew it well. She had heard him using the same manner with his staff, when displeased. It had an unnerving effect on them but not, she observed, on Stone. This blond, burnt man, with his strong, swarthy, unshaven face, was not going to be alarmed by any city businessman.

'Had a lotta trouble with a cyclone back in the early part o' the year. Still got some damage. It's gotta be seen to if we don't want the crops to suffer next year.'

Stone was lying. There had been a certain amount of damage several months earlier but it had long since been settled.

Philippe stiffened perceptibly and glared into Stone's grey-blue eyes. For a microsecond Kate watched the two men regard one another warily, as if sniffing one another out, jealously marking out their territorial paramountcy. She would have broken the moment, capably insisting that a wash would be in order after such a journey, had not Stone, with laconic ease and antipodean charm, stretched out his right arm and said, 'Bedroom's on the right up the stairway. Get yourselves washed up. When you're ready I'll introduce you to Timi, my foreman, and show ya 'round a bit.' With that he turned and disappeared into an office, closing the door firmly behind him. His statement of privacy.

Kate and Philippe exchanged a glance and returned outside to find Ami and their luggage.

Within the cool stark untidiness of the Plantation Office, Timi, the native foreman, sat with his head bowed into his large brown hand, cradling his forehead. The wooden fan whirring above him was disturbing the papers on the desk. In his other hand he held a plastic Bic Biro which he was tapping against a china mug filled with the dregs of pale, cold tea. It was the only external expression of his agitation.

37

There was an uncertainty about their future. Times were going to be tougher for them without Sam.

Timi and Stone were close friends. They had been working alongside one another on the Plantation for more years than either bothered to remember, brought together by the guiding hand of Sam MacGuire. All three of them had weathered troubles and good times together.

Timi, still tapping his Biro, watched Stone pace into the room. The Australian rubbed impatiently at his chin, lit himself a cigarette, walked over to the window and peered out.

'She looks a bit like him. Strange to see her.'

'How are they?' Timi asked.

'He's a bit bloody formal. Real city slicker. Won't be easy,' Stone replied, after some moments.

The jeep, partially in view, had been parked at the far end of the gravel pathway, between the house and the edge of the headland.

He watched, dragging hard on his cigarette, as Kate, sophisticated, elegant, in her thirties, and Philippe, perhaps forty, certainly a little younger than himself, in a creased pale blue suit but correct-looking, wandered about the garden. The dogs were worrying playfully at the unknown couple, barking for attention.

Stone frowned his concern. 'He's an arrogant-looking bastard, her husband . . .' he mumbled reflectively.

Kate, watched by Stone, wandered towards the cliff's edge and looked out across the water. Her skirt ballooned erotically in the breeze. He saw her calling animatedly to her husband, beckoning him to join her, which he did.

'I'd forgotten they were arriving today!' He turned back to Timi who was still sitting at his desk, working now. 'Did you organise the lift?'

Timi, taciturn now, replied without looking up. 'Yeah. I sent Chand to meet them. Thought it might do him good to get off the island for a bit, get away from the Plantation. Anyway he said he had something to do on the mainland.'

'I suppose he had business there,' Stone replied scathingly as he turned back to the open window. 'More blue movies for

Loquaqua,' he muttered as he eyed Kate trudging her way in a light frock along the gravelled path followed by Ami struggling with their luggage.

De Marly walked more slowly behind them, stopping occasionally to take stock of the exterior of the house. He was making a comment which Stone could not hear; nor, apparently, could his wife who continued on her way towards the porch without looking back.

'She's a good-looker. Trust ol' Sam,' he breathed, and turned back again to Timi, looking less perplexed than previously. 'Well, I better put on the charm, eh? Listen,' he continued, making his way towards the desk, his mind on business once more, 'just keep that damned Indian kid busy and out of my hair, will ya? Leastways till we get this place sorted out.'

Timi, never a loquacious man, simply smiled sagely. 'Keep calm, Rob.' He spoke without pitching his voice, conscious of the new arrivals moving about outside in the hallway. 'They fight between themselves all the time, the Indians, you know that. All right, sometimes they fight with us too, but it's usually just one of their family feuds. And that's all this was.'

Stone shook his head adamantly. 'I think you're wrong. I think this time it was different. Chand's been edgy since Sam died. He's been drinking hard, too. I've watched him. No one 'cept Sam could keep him in line. He's a bloody little troublemaker but if I fire him now we'll have a goddam strike on our hands. And that won't keep us the Plantation. Just keep him outa husband's way.'

Ami, already upstairs, leant over the wooden bannisters and grinned at the white couple in the hallway beneath him. 'Bags are in your room and the fan is on,' he announced.

Kate hurried on, leading the way, leaving her husband contemplating the closed office door, before stepping briskly up the stairs after her. She hurried on into the bedroom, threw herself across the substantial, overly soft mattress and pulled impatiently at her slingbacked sandals, releasing, with a sigh, her swollen, dust-caked feet. Moments later Philippe appeared and made his way towards the closed window.

Kate closed her eyes, thankful to rest her aching body and careful to avoid Philippe's temper. She heard him push irritably at the window latch which had jammed.

'*Merde!*' He swore at it under his breath, pushing more forcefully until, finally, it opened, flooding the musty room with birdsongs, chattering coloraturas into the heat.

The quiet drone of voices in the office below drifted through the floorboards and sandwiched her comfortably under the irregular circling of the throbbing ancient wooden fan.

'I think I'll go down and have another word with Stone. Meet the foreman,' Philippe said restlessly. 'Perhaps he can drive us to a restaurant for some lunch.'

No air conditioning, Kate thought as her limbs drifted into sleep, easing her away from the anxieties of the tiringly long journey and an approaching migraine.

Chapter 4

A light tapping on the wooden door roused Kate to consciousness. She opened her heavy eyelids, fighting for comprehension, but was unable to identify the sound that she was hearing nor the pale, apple-green walls surrounding her. Above, a fan throbbed relentlessly into the thick, warm air. She groped for a trigger, something to remind her. Outside a bird screeched and she turned her head to the right, towards the window. It was broad daylight, blinding sunlight was beating through the glass.

'Mrs De Marly.' A voice reminded her, someone outside the door was calling.

She pulled herself from the bed, smoothed her creased silk dress and walked to the door with limbs as heavy as a drugged beast's struggling for balance. She had taken a Mogadon earlier, she recollected hazily. She turned the quaint porcelain door-handle – it felt cool against her fingers – and discovered, standing in front of her, the young Indian who had collected them from the port.

'Yes?' she demanded awkwardly, feeling discomfited by his intrusion.

'I brought you some tea, Mrs De Marly.'

She needed air.

Without a word she pulled back the door, walked to the window, pushed hard at the sticking frame, liberating the glass a little further, and gazed out on to the fresh afternoon.

41

No sign of anyone below. The garden was ablaze with brilliantly coloured flowers. From this angle it was a cultivated patch of reds and purples. The heavy, heady scents wafted up into the room, seducing her sleepy mind. Beyond the headland, in front of her, it was low tide. The sound of the waves had receded. She spied three native fishermen wading inside the reef. 'Have you seen my husband?' she enquired of the boy, without turning.

'Mr Stone took him to see the Plantation, missus.'

'Have they been gone long?' She faced the handsome boy, gazing at him as he placed the teacup carefully on a dark, wooden, carved chest at the foot of the bed that she guessed to be Indonesian. The lemon cup sat on a cream saucer, rather fifties in style. There was no teapot or milk jug in evidence. The cup contained the brew. A solitary teabag floating in uninvitingly tepid water. The poured tinned milk seemed to sit independently on the buoyant muslined weed. She turned her gaze from it fearing she might vomit. Tropical tea! Her delicate stomach was not yet accustomed to these foreign savours! When the cup was safely settled the young man stood, almost to attention, with the round tray firmly grasped in both hands and pressed against his chest.

'Just after you arrived. About three hours ago,' he proffered.

'What?'

'Your husband left here.'

'Oh yes, thank you.'

Watched by Kate, Ami made his way to the partially opened door. He was wearing a clean white shirt with a pastel-coloured sarong. His thonged, rubber shoes slapped against the polished wooden floor. Her mind returned to the image of him steering the dinghy, singing, wet and salted, naked to the waist.

'What's your name?' she asked spontaneously.

'Ami Chand, missus.'

She nodded, silently appraising him. 'You seemed to be in difficulties this morning, Ami?'

He did not understand her remark. She supposed him shy.

'The man this morning. He seemed to be angry with you.'

42

Ami laughed comprehendingly and glanced towards his feet. 'No trouble, missus. I have business to do. Sometimes people get angry with prices. It's not my making.' He shrugged easily. 'I have a son to keep. It's hard.'

'Yes, it must be . . . Do you live here, Ami, or just work here?'

'Yes, missus. Live here now. On the Plantation.'

'Did you know my father?'

'Yes, missus.'

'Did you like him?'

'Very kind man.'

'He died fifteen days ago. Is that right?'

'Very sad, missus.' The young man shuffled awkwardly. Ill at ease in her company, she supposed.

'Do you know where he's buried?'

'Down in the valley . . . Fijian village.'

'Perhaps tomorrow, when I'm rested, you'll show me.'

Ami stepped awkwardly, clutching on to the tray. 'Have to go now, missus.'

'Thank you for the tea, Ami.'

He nodded as this trim English lady smiled at him, a beautiful lady considering him. It was a gracious smile but one that allowed no further conversation. Hesitating a brief moment, he watched as she walked purposefully to the still unopened, polished leather luggage standing on their well-crafted bases, but she did not look back. Unnoticed, he slid from the room.

Before she began to unpack the cases Kate glanced around the attic bedroom, the only room on the upper floor of the house. There were no photographs, no revealing signs of a personal life. Someone, perhaps the Australian, had cleared everything away. She did not feel ill at ease here. It must have been her father's room.

In a vain attempt to hold himself steady while his body was pitched from side to side, Philippe gripped on to the scranching, loosely locked rusty door. He had been sitting in the battered jeep for two arduous hours.

43

Conversation had been quite pointless. He hardly possessed the breath. The truck bounced to and fro on the dusty, stony track and the rough, worn engine roared defiantly, conspiring to impede all hope of discussion. Their two-hour journey had taken them, him and Stone, the length of the newly acquired estate but not around the entire boundary.

'For that you'd need the entire day, mate,' Stone had informed him earlier, before they set off from the main house.

The young green sugar cane, Philippe had been assured, looked the same from every fertile acre.

'And there's no point starin' at the other few acres. That's just barren volcanic rock. Nothin' grows there. That's way over the other side towards the mountains. Roads're pretty crude over that way. No one hardly goes there. No point.'

Philippe had settled for being shown the coast road. He had already seen part of it when he and Kate had arrived earlier, but he felt it would be an opportunity, or so he had supposed, to direct a few questions at Stone about the economics of the place, discover some facts, and, more crucially, ascertain a thing or two about the old boy's representative, Stone himself, who, Philippe had already concluded, was a 'rude bastard'. But now they were on their way back, rattling up the steep winding roadside that led from the bay to the cliff-top house. And no more than a few trivial words had passed between them.

Apart from his physical discomfort Philippe was experiencing a growing sense of irritation towards Stone who, he felt, might just be doing this deliberately. Stone had not warned him about the conditions on the road and surely the man could not have believed that his European companion might want simply to stare at mile after mile of sugar cane and eat dust?!

Stone pulled up unexpectedly and turned off the engine. He opened the door and got out, stretching his legs and pressing the palm of his hand into the small of his back as he did so. If Philippe was feeling tired, sweaty and uncomfortable in the heat, how much worse to be driving?

'Why have you stopped?' the Frenchman enquired as his

44

Australian companion strolled to the cliff's edge overlooking the vast expanse of ocean.

'I'm taking a leak,' the other shouted disdainfully, without bothering to look back.

Philippe decided to use the moment to stretch his own aching muscles. He pushed hard at the troublesome door and stepped down on to the parched, shaly soil. His head was reeling from too much sun. It was, after all, only a few hours ago that he and Kate had disembarked.

He wandered aimlessly towards the cliff's edge and looked out across the South Pacific water. Low tide. The wind must be picking up somewhere further out, he thought. The water, beyond the reef, was beginning to look choppy.

He took a moment to enjoy the view and the refreshing breeze that lightly caressed his dusty skin. He looked down to gauge how high they were. Certainly nothing dramatic, perhaps one hundred feet. Engrossed as he was by his new surroundings, he did not notice his Aussie companion finish his business, zip himself up and saunter back to the waiting jeep.

'Are you coming or not?' Stone called to him.

'What's that building down there?' he asked, staring back along the route they had travelled and ignoring Stone's question. He had spotted what looked like a disused factory built close to the water's edge. He wondered how he could have missed seeing it when they must have driven almost alongside it, judging by the outline of the road.

'Used to be the Plantation sugar mill. In the old days the Plantation crushed its own cane, loaded it straight on to the boat and sent it direct from here to the mainland. That was way back before the big mill at Loquaqua was built. It's not used for anything now.'

'How far is Loquaqua from here?'

''Bout thirty-five miles 'long the coast as the crow flies.'

'Is it all our land between here and there?'

Stone turned his head south, looking along the coast towards Loquaqua, looking away from Philippe. It made his gut churn to hear this stranger talk about the land as his. 'Pretty much, give or take a bit.'

45

He swung himself back into the jeep, slammed his door shut and started up the engine. 'It'll be getting dark soon. I got work to do up at the house. You coming or not?'

Philippe strode purposefully towards the jeep and stood beside Stone's door, directly confronting the other man.

'I was hoping we might have had a chance to talk. There are one or two points I'd like to know about the place . . . about the economics of it all. I made a few enquiries in London and . . .'

'Sure we can talk but not now. I got work to do.'

Once more there was a moment's edginess between them. Philippe hesitated. 'Well then, after supper tonight?' he suggested. 'Let's have a drink on the porch about nine.'

'Suits me. Get Timi along too. He knows more about the place than I've forgotten. Almost started it, he did, with Sam.'

Appeased if not satisfied, Philippe crossed behind the jalopy and settled himself on to the spartan dust-smeared seat as Rob Stone shoved the gearstick into first and they pulled away, up the rambling hillside road that led them both back to the Lesa Plantation House.

'He's a difficult bastard. Doesn't want us here as far as I can see. Probably expected that we'd never show up. Resents us, I'm sure.'

Kate was sitting on the bed in her underwear, white lace cotton briefs, no bra. It was too hot, she preferred wearing none. She was only vaguely listening to Philippe who was shouting from under his running shower. He had only just arrived back, dusty and exhausted.

'It's a big place. There's a hell of a lot of land. Sugar's the problem.'

'Why's that?' Her eyes were swiftly scanning the room. They had bought some whisky. Where was it? She spied it, sitting close by the window, in a plastic bag on the dressing table. She tossed her worn emery board on to the bedside table, wandered across the room and pulled the bottle from the well-travelled bag. Sauntering aimlessly about in search of glasses, she recollected seeing two tumblers somewhere.

They were in the bathroom above the basin. Gliding easily across the room, she pushed at the unlocked door on the steamy cubicle with her toes and leant in cautiously, so as not to allow her meticulously curled hair to droop in the damp and steam.

Philippe turned off the shower, climbed out looking scrubbed and pink, and stepped dripping wet on to the primitively tiled floor.

'The market's unstable. Unsteady world prices for sugar. You know, I think Stone was hoping the ol' boy would leave the place to him,' he mumbled, toothpaste in his mouth.

'Have you seen how many Indians there are here?' Kate asked suddenly. 'I noticed it today at the port, and then driving out of the city. There seem to be more Indians than Fijians.'

She pulled a towel from the rusting chrome towel rail, threw it across to him and then, creeping a little further into the room, she put her toothbrush into one tumbler, threw Philippe's brush to him, rinsed the other tumbler under the warm tap, half filled it with cold water and took the glass and the bottle back into the bedroom.

'Thanks,' he said rubbing vigorously at his wet skin. 'Yes, that's the root of the troubles here.'

'What troubles?' She paused before unscrewing the gold cap and pouring herself a small measure.

'It'll take too long to explain. I'll tell you another time. There's no ice up here. I've already looked,' he shouted after her.

'I don't care,' she called lazily, wondering why he wouldn't explain now.

He followed her through into the bedroom with the towel now wrapped around his waist. His dark hair stood in every direction, dripping on to his carelessly dried shoulders.

'What troubles? Why won't you explain now?'

'I told you, because it will take too long, my little petal.' He brushed his fingers through her combed hair.

'You caught the sun,' she grinned at him, beating her fist lightly against his flesh. 'On your face and a V-shape on your

47

chest. You look bright fuchsia.' She started to giggle. 'It suits you,' she taunted, irritated that he wouldn't explain now. 'Very chic.'

'It was damned hot out there,' he retorted.

'I can't think why you went. It was bad enough coming over in the boat. I'm still whacked.' She strolled back to the bed with her loaded tumbler and picked up a small bottle of nail varnish for her toes. 'You're the same colour,' she teased again, waving the bottle between her fingers.

'I went because we can't afford to waste time. I want to find out what our options are. Freehold land is like gold dust here but there are problems. The price of sugar is being bolstered by the government and certain overseas agreements. It has no relation to the open market. This could be a bad time to sell. Anyway,' he continued, stepping into his newly pressed white pants, usually reserved for sailing weekends, 'I've had an idea.'

'What sort of an idea?' she asked, cautiously lifting the brush to her left foot, held steady by her left hand.

'Oh, just an idea. We can discuss it later. Have you seen my blue shirt?'

'It's here on the bed. Why can't we discuss it now?' Kate asked, looking up from her nails and addressing her husband directly. He was standing, combing his hair, in front of the circular dressing-table mirror. That, like the teacup earlier, had a fifties feel to it. Quite out of place, Kate felt, with so much of the rest of the oriental house furniture.

'Because,' he said, crossing to her and stroking her with a small, perfunctory kiss, 'there seems no point in discussing it until I know what the possibilities are. And until I've spoken to the solicitors and the transfer of ownership has been confirmed. I'm starving. Are you ready?'

'Oh, Philippe, of course I'm not ready! I'm in my under-wear and you've just smudged my nails!'

Feeling disturbed with him Kate swung herself from the bed and walked over to the polished mahogany wardrobe, her wet toes curled into the air. It was an awkward, graceless move-ment, balanced on her heels. She grabbed a flower-printed sundress from a wooden hanger which clattered against the wardrobe and then fell forgotten to the floor.

'Will you zip me up, please?'

Swallowing the last slug of her whisky he put down the now empty glass and crossed to where she was standing in front of the mirror.

'How do you know all that about sugar prices and the problems here?' she asked, holding her dress, waiting for him.

'Ugh! I don't know how you can stomach that warm whisky. It's disgusting,' he said as he reached her, drawing up the zipclip, hanging at the small of her back, with his finger and thumb. 'I asked one of the young juniors at the office in London to find out for me.'

The zip began to ease its way up her back towards her neck. Philippe paused for a moment, slipping his hand inside the garment, still hanging sensuously from her shoulder, and slid it round to touch her left firm breast. He bent to kiss the slender pale skin on the nape of her neck. Delicate and soft as an apricot, he thought.

'Je t'aime, Petal,' he murmured inaudibly as his lips touched her flesh. Kate leant forward and scooped a pair of gold earrings into her manicured fingers, clipping them into her pierced ears.

'Why did you ask one of the juniors to find out?' she asked.

'Just to know the facts when we got here,' he said.

It surprised her, that he had done such a thing. 'We'll be late,' she said.

Philippe's hand slid out from beneath the soft material. He pinched her buttock jovially and sauntered to the side of the bed to slip on his shoes. Kate finished her zip by herself.

He had not taken this moment as an affront. He had almost not noticed it. After sixteen years of marriage many moments had passed between them, unnoticed.

The sun had set, augmented its colours, streamed strips of light across the distant islands sleeping in the sun, like giant, immobile *bêche-de-mer*. In its place a newish, melon slice of a moon was rising. Several brilliant stars were shining on to the water. It was a little after nine.

Above them, hanging from the peeling, grey-blue rafters,

was a naked bulb spilling shafts of light on to wilting flowers in cracked pots.

'Curious, that they should be so neglected in a garden where every plant receives such meticulous attention,' Kate observed idly.

Philippe sipped at a Scotch, fancying he could see the Southern Cross. They sat together, lost in their silent reflections, listening to the night crickets, and to the tingling of the Tibetan bells, waiting for Stone. Kate watched the bells dangling from one of the wooden beams, rippling in an occasional whisper of sea air. She wondered who had hung them there. Her father? Had he bought them in the East? Likewise the various pieces of oriental furniture scattered about the house. Had he travelled greatly before settling here? Certainly he had dreamt of it. When she was tiny he used to say to her, 'One day, my little Katy, we'll buy a big sailing ship and set off to see the world. Just you and me, eh?' In those idle dreams he had promised to conquer the world for her.

Suddenly a hymn began wafting from the valley below, out across the vast expanse of ocean. That too reminded her of her childhood. These days as an infrequent visitor to church she only heard hymns sung at Christmas, when, creeping into Midnight Mass, listening to familiar carols, she indulged her last gesture to her childhood Catholicism. As a child it had always been her mother who had taken her to Mass. Her father, though a Catholic, was judged by the rest of the family, and her school, to be a heathen. The sisters at the convent had chided her, forewarning her that he would 'rot in hell for his heathenism'.

And alone at night, how that had made her weep for him. Fearing for his soul and his eternal salvation. She had bottled up her longing to warn him of his danger for fear that he would become impatient with her mother and shout at her for 'putting nonsense into the child's head'. And once he had left . . . Who but she had prayed for him?

Raw young fears. Broken buried images. She had forgotten them, until now.

'I wonder why they're singing Christian hymns,' she mused,

rocking herself backwards and forwards on a much-lived-in raffia chair.

'Because they're Christians,' Philippe replied glibly.

They were both tired. An early night would have been a better idea than a business meeting.

She laughed. 'I thought they were all cannibals and ate the missionaries.'

'They did. Perhaps they still do, here, on these islands away from the mainland,' he teased.

Rob Stone was the only white man living in the Fijian village. Sam MacGuire, his closest friend, had always stayed up at the Plantation House; but Stone, preferring the native lifestyle, had built himself a more modest dwelling in the village down towards the valley, inland of the coastal road to Loquaqua. Though a loner most of his adult life he enjoyed the company of families and women. The generous, extrovert Fijian way of life suited his more earthbound nature. So he ate with the locals, joked with them, spoke their languages and knew and understood their customs. Most of his adult life since leaving Australia, where he had worked on a sheep station as a greenhorn jackaroo, he had spent travelling the Pacific Islands, but here, he believed, he had found his 'roots'. And the Fijians, recognising this, loved him and welcomed him as warmly as one of their own.

While the newly arrived European couple sat silently in the fading evening light, Stone stood alone on his more modest terrace, drinking a beer, smoking a cigarette and contemplating the arrival of the De Marlys. He was feeling uneasy. Earlier, having eaten supper with Timi and his sons outside their palm-thatched bure, he had returned to 'collect some cigarettes', and to the privacy of his own thoughts. He had been feeling uneasy all afternoon. He wiped the residue of beer away from his mouth and saw Timi, his foreman, six foot three, burly and proud, waving to him in the distance. The sight of this warm-hearted, mellow companion made him smile. They had been working together since Stone had first met MacGuire and signed on at the Plantation.

51

'I'm right with ya, mate,' Stone called to him, picking up his hat from the table beside him. Timi had been his most loyal asset and now, without Sam, who else was there? He himself had never understood the Indians. Before he had arrived on the islands, during the 1969 canecutters' strike, Timi had succeeded in keeping the Indians working, thereby meeting their deliveries at the mill. They had been the only plantation not hit by the strike. Stone shook his head with pride. If anybody could handle De Marly, he thought, Timi would. He ground the stub of his cigarette into the rough wooden floor beneath him, slid his glass on to the table and stepped off the porch.

Timi, smiling, strode past the small, whitewashed Seventh-Day Adventist chapel. Hymns, enriched by the fervency of faith, were ringing out. He smiled contentedly to himself, humming a note or two. He loved the glorious tunes and their religious sentiments and, when work at the Plantation had not prohibited him, had sung in the choir himself. He was a locally born, baptised Seventh-Day Adventist. Church mornings, dressed in his *sulu*, a white shirt and an English tie, his only tie, he had stood proudly at the side of his abundant wife, Miriam, who had been sporting her Sunday best too, a cherished chapel bonnet.

As he strode easily along the dust path towards Stone he inhaled proudly, considering how much he loved his family. They were a much-admired couple, he and Miriam, highly regarded amongst their own village, he being grandson to the *Ratu*, the Village Chief, and they, the parents of three strapping young sons.

Whatever should happen at the Plantation this life of his was complete. Fiji was his home, and this village, his life.

A figure creeping from within the chapel caught his eye. It was one of his grandfathers stealing from the choir practice to enjoy a solitary cigarette, in the lengthening evening shadows. The thin, wizened old man crouched on his haunches, alone on the threshold, and lit his home-rolled weed. He was one of several respected village elders, over ninety years old.

'No praying tonight, grandaddy?' Timi joked.

The old fellow, lost in memories, merely nodded his tightly curled, old grey head and closed his stoned sunken eyes, red as beetroots from years of imbibing kava, the local root crushed and soaked in water to make their potent, soporific grog.

'*Bula*, grandaddy!' Timi laughed loudly as he strolled on.

Stone and he turned from the village path and began to climb the hill, in silence.

Stone led the way, pacing steadily. He was in no hurry. He agitated his hands in his khaki trouser pockets, cleaned and sharply pressed thanks to Miriam. He had barely noticed the melodious notes of worship. So much a daily part of the village life were they, that he never gave them a thought. Besides, his ruminations were elsewhere, chewing over his afternoon drive with De Marly and, more importantly, the meeting that lay ahead of them. He was feeling more at ease at the prospect of it, knowing that Timi would be with him. Steady, that was Timi, he reassured himself once more. He, Stone, had not taken kindly to the Frenchman, he found him arrogant, but that, alas, was of little importance now. De Marly and his wife, Sam's daughter, were the legal owners of Lesa now, although it was still his 'home', his world. The only one he'd known these past eleven years.

He had carried a certain hope, perhaps even expected, that ol' Sam might've left the place to him. They had worked together as brothers and friends. He had known that there was a daughter, somewhere. Sam had mentioned her once or twice, in passing, but he had known nothing about her or her whereabouts. Neither had Sam. Or that was what he had always assumed. But they had both been secretive, independent men, he and Sam. He had rarely talked about his own past either. That had been part of their comradeship. They had understood and respected that privilege in one another. Just two travellers who had landed up in the same place at the same time. And there wasn't too much to say about it.

He felt no resentment about not possessing Lesa but he did care for the Plantation. He feared for its future. Now more than ever. He knew that, politically speaking, the situation on

53

the islands was pretty precarious. 'This is goin' to take some clever handlin', boyos,' ol' Sam used to say when things were getting hot. Between them, he and Sam, and Timi of course, they had kept the place going. He didn't want all that to change now. He didn't want some foreign bastard to just step in and thoughtlessly destroy all that they had worked so hard to build. And he didn't trust De Marly not to do that. He was too brusque to see how things should be.

And he didn't trust himself not to lose his cool with the guy.

'That sounds like him now,' Kate said, breaking their silence, rocking herself to and fro.

She fancied, against a backdrop of choral prayer, that she had heard the distant humming of voices on the hill and then bootsteps on the skerried path below them.

Stone paused for breath at the summit of the hill, and to wait for Timi, striding just a few steps behind him. Side by side they strolled, their feet crunching on the stones beneath them.

The Australian cast his eyes towards the house he knew so well and caught sight of the two figures silhouetted beneath the bare bulb, seated in semi-darkness. He lifted his hand and pulled off his misshapen, dust-caked old hat as he strode towards them and reached the step.

'Evenin',' he said drily.

'Pull up a chair, Stone, and sit down.' Philippe spoke tersely without raising his eyes. The half-lit cigar clenched between his teeth was illuminated by a match flickering in his right hand. He drew hard, waved the match vigorously until the flame died and then threw it on to the ground. It landed on the gravel close by the newly arrived pairs of feet.

Kate sat, still rocking incessantly to and fro, watching as Stone stepped on to the rundown porch and pulled over another wicker chair, dragging its hind legs, scuffing it along the well-trodden floorboards. Timi stood lounging against a pillar in the shadowed light, choosing to wait for an invitation. Kate smiled to encourage him but he hadn't noticed.

'Come on up, Timi, and sit yourself down, mate,' Stone

said, realising that De Marly was not extending the invitation to his companion.

'Kate, *chérie*, fetch another couple of glasses.'

Obediently she placed her bare, nail-polished feet on to the rough wooden flooring, idly pushed herself from the rocker and walked through into the unfamiliar house. She had no idea where to find the kitchen but supposed it to be at the back of the house. Their supper had been served by Miriam, Timi's easy-going wife. It had been she who had cleared away the plates from the round, weather-beaten porch table after their meal had been eaten, or, in this instance, not eaten, and had then bidden them good night, hurrying off down the hill to the company of her own family. No staff, as far as Kate had noticed, lived in the house.

She wandered along the semi-darkened hallway that only hours earlier had been her first glimpse of her inherited home. It felt suddenly sinister, creaking in the darkness. She was not entirely sure that she liked the place, fancying she sensed her father watching her. The musty, mothball smell had been overridden by pungent cooking fumes, now dispersing. She followed the rancid and spicy smells towards a door on the left at the far end of the long hallway. It must be there, she thought. She was feeling unaccountably nervous, as if expecting a hand to leap at her through the shadowed walls. She had always hated strange houses and always, since her childhood, had felt anxious in the dark.

As she approached she thought she heard a cupboard door close inside the room, yet there seemed to be no light within. It was a hot, humid night, too still for any wind to have blown something shut. She dismissed as foolish the notion that her father's ghost was waiting for her inside the scullery. Fanciful nonsense, she told herself sensibly, but her heart was pounding nevertheless. She nudged at the door tentatively, nervous of disturbing anyone, though whom she could not tell, knowing that they were alone in the house.

Standing in the half-open doorway she groped for the light. The melon-slice moon was shining a shaft of lemon

55

light through the window. It created spooky, angular spectres of the furniture looming in the darkness.

Something moved! Kate clenched a fist.

Her fingers scuffed against a switch and fortuitously flicked it alive. A dusty bare bulb swinging from a fraying plaited electric cord lit up a sparsely furnished, old-fashioned scullery, grimly painted in the same apple green as their bedroom upstairs, except that this had been dirtied and discoloured by grease and dust. It was in direct contrast to her own elegant London kitchen, with its gleaming strips of Poggenpohl and Gaggenau aluminium. She scanned the room uncertainly in search of a cupboard that might house the requested glasses and was astonished to see a child hiding in the shadow of a tall, cream-painted fifties dresser.

The boy from the boat, Ami's son. He looked guilty and terrified.

'What are you doing here?' she asked softly, conscious that the male voices droning outside in the warm night air might hear her, and fearing that she might terrify him further.

Close to where he was hiding, to the left of the room from where she was standing, a back door was open. She reasoned that he must have crept in that way earlier, thereby avoiding the adults on the verandah. The boy's almond, oval eyes were locked on to her. She supposed from his guilt that he was forbidden in the kitchen either by his parents or house rules.

'I'm looking for glasses,' she announced conspiratorially. 'Do you know where they might be?' Including him in her quest, she felt, would be the surest way to make friends with him.

Reticently, he pointed a finger to the two dresser cupboards towering beside him. In his hand was a half-chewed, soggy biscuit. Realising that his gesture had exposed his minor theft he quickly withdrew the guilty fingers and hid them safely behind his back. Too late though for Kate not to have discovered his petty misdemeanour.

'Is that what you were doing? Searching for sweets?' she asked casually and kindly, as she unclipped the glass-panelled doors and peered inside. 'Where's your father this evening?'

56

The boy shrugged uninterestedly and stepped away from his hiding place, the better to observe her. She threw him a snatched and, she hoped, unobserved glance and noticed that his second hand, the one he had been careful not to expose, was crammed with stolen biscuits!

'Did Sam give you biscuits?' she laughed.

The boy nodded uncertainly. It could have been a lie.

'Kate! What are you doing? We're waiting for the glasses!' The distant call of her husband!

'I'd better get a move on,' she said, grabbing two upright tumblers and shutting the cupboard doors, taking care not to rock the precariously stacked assortment of china, which, she promised herself, in a few days' time she would reorganise.

'You'd better get off home too. Your mother will be worried. Come and see me tomorrow.' She turned and hurried to the door. As she reached the light switch she glanced back at the boy who was still standing motionless, watching her, fascinated.

'Go on! Off you go! And close the door after you.'

The boy turned on his heels and scurried guiltily from the scullery as Kate switched off the light and stepped swiftly back along the dark hallway towards the parched, waiting men.

'And the racial problem here? Does that trouble you?'

Philippe glanced up at his wife as she crept unobtrusively back to her rocking chair and put the two plain tumblers on to the round, wooden table, placed between her and the two newly arrived strangers. 'Where have you been, darling? These fellows nearly died of thirst!'

Stone unceremoniously helped himself to a slug of Scotch and poured another for Timi. He placed the bottle back on the low table and pushed it across in the direction of De Marly who ignored it, preferring instead the pleasure of his very occasional cigar.

Kate, surprised by Philippe's question, unaware that any racial problem existed here, looked at Stone for a reassuring answer, or explanation. Instead she caught a conspiratorial glance shared between himself and Timi as the whisky glass passed between them and she wondered if Philippe had noticed it. She sensed Stone play for time, moments only, but she was sure of it. He took a hit of Scotch and lowered his glass to his lap.

He was sitting well back in his chair with his long legs loosely astride, comfortably at ease with himself in these surroundings, in this climate, and with his strong, rangy appearance. He smiled broadly at her husband. It was the first time that she had scanned his face, his features and she decided that he was handsome, in a beaten, lived-in kind of way. Rugged good looks. Not a look that might appeal to her.

'You mean the Indians?' he asked, finally.

'I mean the Indians and the natives working together. Side by side. What's the predominance now?' Philippe demanded, directing his question to Stone.

'More Indians,' Stone conceded.

'And the percentage?' Philippe persisted.

Stone scratched at his chin. 'Aaaw, I guess . . . what is it Timi . . . 'bout fifty-one per cent of them? Forty-six per cent Fijian natives, and the rest are Europeans, Chinese.'

'Does it affect productivity? Do they fight? Resent one another? I believe, according to the constitution, the Indians are not allowed to own the land here. That must make them resentful, right?'

Kate noticed an edge in Philippe's voice, an impatience in his questionings. He was less at ease than Stone. Were these the 'troubles' he had referred to earlier?

'I think Timi here, as one of the "natives", is better equipped to answer that one,' Stone drawled. As he spoke, with his long lean legs weighted firmly on the ground, he pushed his creaking chair backwards, swaying as it carried the bulk of his entire body on its two back legs. He addressed the remark more to his companion than to Philippe, skilfully handing the ball into the other's capable lap. Timi, he knew, had had years of experience, of tactical negotiation, under his belt. That had never been his strong card and both he and Timi knew how much depended on the answer. De Marly, not his wife it seemed, would be the one to make the decision about what the future of the place was likely to be. He might take the Plantation for himself, or worse, give it to another team, thereby depriving them both of their work and livelihood, and the land that had taken so much of their sweat.

In Stone's mind Sam had given the place to his daughter, a woman. That way, he figured, it stayed where it was. He, Stone, could run it for her, as he always had done for Sam. Until De Marly's telex from Sydney there had never been any mention of a husband. He, and he supposed Sam, had not reckoned on this.

During their meal earlier in the evening he and Timi had been talking things through. They had sat together, as they did most evenings, outside Timi's bure, his native house, in his village, smoking *tavako*, locally grown tobacco, sharing a meal. They had talked through everything they thought De Marly might want to discuss.

The economics of the place? They were both honest. Neither had made any real money from the place, occasionally not even a living!

Their experience, their dependability? No question!

The pitfalls of running the Plantation as a profitable enterprise? Risky, like anything else on these islands.

And the undercurrent of resentment between the Indians and the Fijians? That, they had both agreed, was their weakest point. The brewing racial disharmony on the islands could deaden the enthusiasm of any overseas investor.

Had they not, only a day or so earlier, discovered Ami brawling with another employee? The fellow's leg had been seriously gashed with a knife. In this instance, it had been another Indian, a canecutter, but it could, as reasonably, have been a Fijian. Fighting was not uncommon here. Though never on their plantation. Leastways, not in Sam's days. But, truth to tell, the two races detested one another. It would take very little to upset the precarious balance of peace that existed between them. Not least, a stranger, an outsider. They could not know what this Frenchman knew about the islands, or its problems. But they felt certain that no one, and this was their trump card, could run the place as efficiently and as smoothly

59

as they. They had always kept the Plantation operative. The Indians understood them, trusted them, and a foreigner, these days, would not be welcomed.

And Sam's death? What if Sam's daughter asked about his death? Whatever Stone feared or felt, it had been written 'death by natural causes'. And that is what he would tell them. Nothing more.

Stone did not welcome these questions. If De Marly dug too deeply he would draw back the curtain painted with the tourists' idyll of banana trees, beaches and smiling faces. He would soon dislodge the racial tensions that were breeding like maggots beneath the sweltering, tropical surface.

'It's like this, sir,' Timi began in his mellifluous and ever-patient bass voice. 'We keep this place lucrative, more or less, depending on crops, world prices etc. Sure, it's not always easy, living side by side with the Indians and working together. Though if I may say, it is not entirely true that the Indians cannot own land here. Seventeen per cent of all land on the islands is freehold and available on the open market. Like this place, this is freehold land. This is the biggest piece of freehold land on any of the islands. The rest, as you say, belongs to us, the Fijians. It can't be sold. That's the law. There's a Native Land Trust Board, run by Fijians, that regulates things. The Indians want access to the land and a right to rule here. We don't want that. We believe the islands belong to us Fijians. That causes tensions. But here, on Lesa Plantation, things are different. Thanks to Sam. He saw to that. This place has always been owned by a white man. Normally the Indians don't work for them but Sam was different. He understood and respected them. And looked after them. There's never been a strike here. It's a tradition. And Mr Stone and me, we're part of that tradition.'

Philippe sat for a few moments in silence, his head bent forward, contemplating his hands resting, clenched, in his lap.

No one spoke.

'What are you two trying to tell me?' he asked, lifting his head and looking keenly at the two men facing him. 'That you're the right guys to run this place?'

Stone relaxed his feet and the chair thudded back on to all fours.

'That's about it, De Marly,' he said and leant forward, stretching for the whisky bottle.

Kate laid her aching, brown head against the musty, vaguely yellowing pillowcase and stared at the ceiling, watching the fan, listening to a mosquito buzzing annoyingly around her head and to the muffled sounds of her husband gargling in the bathroom.

She thought of her father, ol' Sam, and wondered if he had died here in this room. And what he might have died from. This man who had cared for the natives and the Indians and whom her mother had so strongly railed against. She closed her heavy eyes, trying to conjure him up while listening to the fan creaking irregularly overhead.

Nights in the tropics. The heat was intense. Crickets and fruit bats were screeching around the garden. She was feeling very tired, vaguely despondent and abandoned.

Philippe turned the tap off in the bathroom. She heard him cross through into the bedroom. He lowered himself beside her on to the bed, and began to caress her tired body. His fingertips were searching, finding and then meandering through her tiny forest of dark blonde, curly pubic hair. Kate rolled over on to her side, away from him, curling her feet towards her knees, keeping her eyes shut tight.

Undaunted he inched towards her and held her dainty frame within his robust arm. His leather-strapped wristwatch glinted in the porthole moonlight, creating unobserved, dancing shadows on the walls. His other arm, the one he had been resting against the sheet, slid towards her white buttocks and negotiated them towards him, carefully resting their delicate crack against his desiring, consenting organ already sticky with anticipation. He slid himself towards her pudenda, damp only from the heat, and found his way into her soft, warm hovel.

Slowly he wrapped himself more forcefully around her, taking her tiny breasts in both his hands, massaging her still unwilling spine with his moist, muscular stomach. He found the back of her neck buried beneath her hair, and with his lips

61

he bit gently, pecking at her downy, white skin over and over again, chorusing the motion of his lower body.

She heard his breath on her shoulder and felt her body juice being drawn from her. Like water from a well it was pumped from her. In spite of herself she could not resist it. His hand slid from her bosom and found her labia. It searched on, clumsily reaching for her clitoris, pushing at it, forcing it towards upheaval.

She felt his own pace begin to quicken. She heard his breath grow vocal as his finger danced and prodded. She straightened her bent legs and began to release herself, to induce her own pleasure. His head relaxed behind her, brushing his face from side to side with her long hair, as she felt him moving faster towards his own destination. She moved her hips desperately, pressed her own, until now, limp hand against his busy fingers, forcing him to excite her, to take her with him, moving herself towards a temporary oblivion.

She felt his weight thrusting forcefully against her, moaning as he quickly toppled.

Too soon!

Was Sam's presence here, somewhere, witnessing this?

She forced his now less willing finger onwards, to complete its promise, until she, too, legs writhing in minor spasm, puled with delight.

Kate loosed Philippe's strong, sated grip and edged herself towards the other side of the bed, turning her body on to her damp back, easing herself towards sleep, as she lay under an ever-whirring fan. Together they drowsed, side by side, heavy and silent, wet and emptied.

Chapter 5

As Philippe approached the town, dust in his mouth, on his clothes and clinging to the sweat on his open-pored skin, he saw funnels of black smoke belching from the sugar refinery into the oven-hot air.

Loquaqua looked like a dump.

Along the downtrodden outskirts debris and poverty were everywhere. Solitary Fijians squatted expectantly outside patchwork pockets of erratically constructed shanty shacks, with half a dozen root vegetables at their sides, hoping that some passer-by might stop and buy their paltry wares. And, to the right of him, as he drove, the muddied and infested mangrove swamps seeped towards the ocean.

He proceeded on to a bridge, unsteadily. It swung precariously, hardly wide enough even for a single lane of traffic. At the far end a bus stood waiting; grunting, snorting diesel and bulging with passengers like some cartoon drawing. The Indian driver waved as Philippe pulled off the bridge on to the road and headed forward into the town. It was almost three o'clock. He had timed his journey accurately, was feeling hot but satisfied with himself and looking forward to a Scotch and ice.

Loquaqua was the main town on the island of Lesa. Hardly a town in the accepted sense, it boasted a port and one main street, dilated with Indian commerce and traders. These were surrounded by numerous shanty lanes bursting with prefabricated houses

and peopled almost exclusively with Indians working in Loquaqua or its surrounding sugar areas.

Its sugar mill, the only one now on the island, gave off an
aroma of acrid-sweet burnt molasses which pervaded the entire
area. Daily cargoes of crushed sugar were freighted from the mill
to the mainland, en route for Australia, England and other, less
profitable, markets. An ailing industry bolstered by unrealistic
government prices, waiting, like a pack of precariously stacked
cards, to be blown to the cracked, sunbaked earth.

Philippe saw a small sign cut from wood and shaped into a
thick arrow. It pointed to the Planters' Club. He turned the jeep
off the main road and headed towards where the sign had
pointed, hoping that this God-forsaken, infested hole kept a
decent brand of Scotch.

In the days before Sam had arrived on the islands, even before
the Second World War when the Fijians had fought for the
British and been honoured in Malaysia and the Indians had
refused to fight thereby creating yet another rift between the two
races, Lesa Plantation had been owned by several smaller
planters. It was only in May 1948 that a European, a German,
had bought all the available sugar-growing plots, combined
them and created the wealthiest independent sugar plantation on
any of the Fijian islands, the Lesa Plantation.

In those earlier days the only transport across to the mainland
had been by steamer, daily from Loquaqua port. The journeys
from the various small plantations would have been long and
tedious, across rocky tracks by cart or on horseback. Sweltering
journeys across routes that possessed no roads. These several
planters had grouped together and financed a building which
they named the Planters' Club, where, upon arrival in Loquaqua
en route for the mainland, they could refresh themselves and,
when necessary, find a bed for the night. It had been a club in the
sense that only the contributing planters were entitled to mem-
bership. It became known as the Loquaqua Planters' Club; still in
existence, it was where Philippe was now heading. Nowadays
with no planters left on the island, save Sam, or his inheritor, and
only a handful of Indians leasing Fijian state land, the club had
fallen into disuse. It was now no longer a club, merely a bar,

without rooms or facilities. The only remaining concession to the days of its more glorious, vigorous past were the international sugar prices still pasted daily on to the club noticeboard, but now hanging skewwhiff, against a peeling wall.

Philippe, as he stepped from the plantation jeep outside in the overgrown entrance gardens, let out a sigh of despair. This unexpected rendezvous had better be worth the journey, he thought, because he seriously doubted if he would get a decent drink.

Within, the shabbiness outclassed that without. A darkly lit lobby, depleted of all furnishings, housing a cloakroom locked with rusting padlock and a seedy urinal, led to the main bar-room.

Philippe made his way, through an open door, into the bar-cum-ballroom. Several curtainless windows brought light into the shabby place which faced, beyond once elegant grounds, on to the silted backside of the port. A scuffed grand piano, a relic from more unbuttoned times when this empty cavernous meeting place would have been alive with partying colonial planters and their European companions, stood on a small rostrum in the corner of the room close to the bar. Its silent keyboard sang out with more poignancy than had its evergreen tunes, now accompanied only by ghosts of drunken voices. Like a whore whose age has passed, whose purpose has been laid to waste, this place reeked of solitary gins.

Philippe scanned the desolate room. A white man was waving a finger in recognition, an obese fellow sitting smoking at the far end of the room. His appointment. Philippe ambled towards him.

As he approached the occupied table an elderly gibbous Indian appeared, silently awaiting his order.

'Large Scotch, please. Plenty of ice,' he demanded, conscious of his dark voice echoing around the room.

The barman bowed compliantly and withdrew behind a grimy, plastic, corrugated arrangement several decades past its prime, the bar, leaving Philippe and his clammy companion alone. Alone, that was, save for a spattering of early afternoon Europeans dotted about the place, drinking, slouched across glass-topped tables, talking in huddled twosomes. Hushed conspiratorial notes, as if ashamed that conversation might be overheard. And at the bar, one grey-haired wrinkled Fijian sat drinking beer.

'Robert Danil?' he addressed the fat man when he reached the table. 'I'm Philippe De Marly.'

The man gestured half-heartedly to the seat opposite him but did not rise himself. Philippe settled himself into a creaking, turquoise-painted Lloyd-loom lounge chair.

'Kind of you to come, Mr De Marly. It's a long drive in this filthy heat.' Philippe nodded and smiled perfunctorily, negligent of small talk, assessing his companion.

'May I get you something to drink?' the other continued.

'I've ordered a Scotch, thank you very much.' Philippe glanced about him, staring at the drunken native chuckling at the bar, unscrewing the cap of yet another beer bottle. He was assessing the general feel of the place and more importantly his present companion.

'No work today,' the old Fijian rasped gleefully. His soft, tobacco-ridden voice resounded through the shabbily furnished, barnlike room of the Loquaqua Planters' Club.

Philippe wondered how his companion had recognised him. Probably from the cut of his clothes, his general appearance, a London-tailored lightweight suit, English shoes and socks.

In this dusty, dreary port town teeming with Indian canecutters and leasehold farmers the Planters' Club still sported a reputation for being a civilised refuge, far removed from the bustling world of mill employees and trade folk. In reality, Philippe now witnessed, it was a seedy, dismal joint patronised by a few remaining heat-infested, drunken Europeans unable to face the realities of a lost empire and a harsher, northern clime.

He would, of course, be instantly recognisable in this environment.

Only the sound of ice being dropped into a tumbler followed by bottled liquid slithering between the frozen diamond rocks served to break the cavernous silence and the gloom of the wooden overhead fan creaking monotonously.

He turned back to face his opponent, ready now to speak.

66

'So, you want me to accept your bid for the Plantation?' he asked finally.

Danil nodded appreciatively, expending a minimum of energy. 'It's a generous offer, Mr De Marly.'

'Who are you acting for?'

His obese companion, Danil, a self-satisfied New Zealand lawyer, took a slow, considered drag on his cigarette and then held the burning weed within inches of his face, screwing up his eyes to avoid the smoke. The cigarette ash hung precariously without Danil paying heed to it. 'I must disappoint you, I'm afraid, Mr De Marly. I am not at liberty to divulge that information,' he replied finally, with a dry, condescending smile.

Philippe felt irritated by the sheer indolence of his corpulent companion who seemed, rather theatrically, to be playing his sentences.

'I can assure you, though, that our offer is genuine and, once accepted, would be handled without delay. My client is a man of his word.'

'I don't doubt it,' Philippe replied tersely, turning to accept his Scotch from the waiting Indian at his side. 'Thank you. I wonder though, Mr Danil, how you knew my plantation was for sale . . . given that it has not yet been formally put on the market and assuming, that is, that it will be for sale.' Philippe swirled the ice cubes in his glass, watching his companion before taking a slug of the whisky.

'Who is left to run it, Mr De Marly? Surely you do not intend to give up your own successful existence to settle here? And I doubt that a man of your obvious business acumen and style will leave the place in the hands of that Australian cowboy. No, due to Sam MacGuire's unfortunate demise the Plantation, necessarily, must change hands.'

Philippe, silent, maintained a steady gaze. His dark, penetrating eyes remained unconvinced.

'Mr De Marly, allow me to explain. I think, perhaps, you do not realise the situation here. Freehold land is a rare commodity. It sells for the highest premiums. You are in possession of the largest privately owned estate on any of the islands. This land that you have inherited will be in great demand. That I won't deny,

67

nor would I pretend otherwise. But the offer I am making to you is, shall we say, seductively high. You won't find a better price than ours. On that you have my word.'

'Does your "client" intend to keep the place running as a sugar plantation?' Philippe persisted.

'But of course.'

'Really you surprise me, Mr Danil.'

'I have no reason to suppose otherwise.'

'But your offer is in excess of any realistic profit return.' Philippe studied Danil sedulously, waiting for his reply. He didn't like the look of the man. But there was something else. His instinct told him so. Beneath the measured, calculated exterior lurked something blacker, reptilian.

'Freehold land, Mr De Marly, creates its own price here.' Danil lifted his left hand. Throughout their exchange it had been hugging his large gin close to his abundant, heaving chest. He had never leant forward to place it on the small, glass-topped table between them. He sipped now at his drink with the daintiness of a delicate woman, and then lowered the glass to its original position. Ash had fallen on to the generous thigh of his beige, Singapore-styled suit. He hadn't noticed. Philippe observed the damp circles under the arms of his striped shirt. The sweat of one who has too much flesh, he thought to himself scathingly.

'I am sorry, Danil,' he said, suddenly rising from his seat. 'Tell your client that my plantation is not for sale.'

Kate strutted energetically, vigorously crunching her way along the gravel pathway towards the verandah as Sally and Poncho, the two overattentive honey mongrels, came bounding towards her, barking and greeting her amorously. She was not in the mood for them but in search of Philippe, whom she found crouched uncomfortably on the wooden-slatted porch floor-boards. 'Philippe?' she said as she approached.

Engrossed in his project his reply was inaudible.

'Philippe, Ami said to tell you that a friend of yours has telephoned from the mainland,' she announced. Her tone was crisp.

'Yes, thank you, he told me. Where have you been, *chérie?*'

'I went to see where Sam is buried. I looked for you but couldn't find you. Stone said you'd gone to Loquaqua.'

'Yes, I had a meeting there.'

'Who with?'

Philippe was poring over a map of the island spread out on the ground in front of him. He had jettisoned the wicker furniture to the various corners of the verandah to give himself extra space.

Kate pulled off her straw hat, pitifully misshapen now, fanned herself with it and finally stepped impatiently on to the porch. In spite of the hour, almost six, it was still depletingly hot. She was feeling flushed, having just climbed the hill in a hurry because she was mad with Philippe. 'I don't understand why you didn't tell me that you have a friend here, on the mainland. I didn't know you knew anyone here. And I resent hearing it from Ami. It makes me look foolish,' she announced crustily.

'Why are you so upset about it, Petal? I was going to tell you about him when I found you. Where've you been?'

'I've just told you, I went to see Sam's grave. Who is this friend?'

Kate stood hovering beside her squatting husband, immersed in his map, hoping that an explanation might be forthcoming, but it was not. She moved away to a shaded corner of the verandah, pushed several stacked chairs noisily out of her way and sat on the raffia chaise longue, furiously fanning herself with her straw bonnet.

'Philippe.'

'His name is Shyam Khumar. I haven't seen him for years. He stayed with my family in Paris in '68. Bit of a revolutionary in those days. I've invited him for supper tomorrow night. Thought I might pick his brains. Find out a few facts.'

'What about?'

'Mmm, nothing special. Mechanics of the place, that sort of thing.'

Kate sighed. 'Who were you meeting in Loquaqua?'

'A lawyer.'

69

Kate let her right arm, the one holding her sunhat, flop idly at her side. She watched silently as Philippe slipped his pen into the top pocket of his short-sleeved shirt.

'What are you marking on that map?' she asked, unable to disguise the growing agitation in her voice. She was feeling raw and upset about Sam; seeing his grave in the tiny churchyard, here on this distant island, had reminded her how little she had known him and what a stranger he had been, and now Philippe's reticence to share anything with her was beginning to enrage her.

'Nothing, I was just looking at it. I've finished now,' he said rising, smiling disarmingly. Philippe had a pronounced dimple on his chin and dark blue eyes. His were handsome, classical features. When he smiled he was irresistible.

'Fancy a drink?' he called back to her as he walked into the open house, carefully folding the map. A cooling breeze wafted out on to the terrace from the fan whirring above him in the hallway.

'Philippe, why are you being so bloody secretive? Everything I ask, you say, "It's nothing, I'll tell you later".'

'You're being oversensitive, Petal. No French wine, I'm afraid. Château Lesa gin and tonic suit?' He grinned playfully.

She nodded, exasperated.

'Besides, *chérie*,' he said, disappearing into the corner of the room, out of sight, 'I do have a secret.'

'What secret?'

'Later,' he tantalised her.

Kate settled back into the chaise longue, lifting her legs on to the cushions, listening to her husband clink ice into glasses somewhere behind her. She watched a lizard scurry across the wooden beams above her, pause for a moment, and then hurry along on his way. She wondered despondently why Philippe never bothered to share anything with her. She had wanted him to accompany her to Sam's grave but he had disappeared without saying a word to her.

And then she had felt foolish when Ami had been so obviously impressed about this friend.

'Your husband has very important friend, missus,' he had

70

said when she had met him earlier on the roadway. 'He will change the world for us.'

'Who, my husband?' she had asked mockingly, half in jest.

'Shyam Khumar,' Ami had continued enthusiastically, entirely missing any sarcasm she had intended. 'He will give the land to us Indians and give us power. Help make me a rich businessman.'

'Have you seen my husband, Ami?' she had asked, crisply cutting short his eulogising, feeling certain that he had seen her confusion and bad temper.

'Kneeling on the verandah, missus,' he had replied and driven off with silent Jal at his side, in the burnt-orange jeep, in the direction of Loquaqua.

'A large one, please,' she called now into the house, to her husband mixing the drinks, thinking about Sam's solitary grave.

The two dogs – were they Stone's dogs or Sam's dogs? – had finally stopped their yapping and were snoozing in the shade out of the heat. Everything was silent, save for the fan whirring and the distant, constant sound of waves breaking on the reef beyond the headland.

Philippe walked back on to the porch, handed a drink to Kate and grabbed himself a chair which he placed at her side. 'One large gin,' he said, '*santé*,' touching her tumbler with his own.

'Cheers. Your nose is peeling.' She took a sip and enjoyed how foolish he looked with a reddened face and peeling nose.

'Was it horrid, seeing his grave?'

Kate nodded. Philippe lightly stroked her face. 'You should have waited. I would have come with you.'

'You weren't here. Ami drove me down the hill. Pointed out the way. He's in a teeny little graveyard with a little whitewashed chapel. Really quiet. Lots of big flowers growing nearby.' Kate sipped her gin and breathed deeply. 'So who's this man then? The one you knew in Paris?'

'He's a rather esteemed lawyer.'

'The same one you met today?'

Philippe shook his head. 'No, no, not him. This fellow's an Indian. In politics here. His family were rather influential here earlier this century, during the fight for Indian freedom. He was

71

studying in England at the time, and had been given an introduction to my parents; wrote to us, and they invited him over for a visit. He came several times during '67 and then again early '68 but he got involved in the student demonstrations . . . and . . . it rather upset my father. Unusual chap, though. I quite liked him. But we were never really that close.'

They both took another leisurely sip before Philippe spoke again. 'I have a surprise for you. It seems that the news is about that you are the new owner here.'

'Why do you say that?'

'We've had an offer for the Plantation.'

'Did we?' Kate sat up excitedly. 'Is it a good one?'

'Too good. I told them it's not for sale. Not yet, anyway.'

The next evening, as tawny-haired, wiry curs barked incessantly against the throbbing, irritating heat; as full-bosomed, black-skinned matrons chattered, joking lewdly together whilst preparing suppers of various root vegetables and locally caught *ika*, sea fish; as tired, work-weary Indians hawked their wares outside gaudily decorated, proudly owned boutiques in nearby Loquaqua; and as Kate sat drinking gin aperitifs in the shade of the wooden verandah, awaiting the unknown guest whose arrival from the mainland was imminent, Philippe faced Stone, alone together in his office.

'Why don't you sit down, Stone.'

'This is just fine, thanks, mate,' Stone retorted, leaning, apparently nonchalantly, against the window frame.

'All right.' Philippe glanced at the untidy desk in front of him, and sighed. 'I might as well come straight to the point, Stone.' He paused. 'Frankly, I've been thinking of changing the face of things here, so I won't waste my breath or your time with recriminations. I've been right through these figures and, quite honestly, in spite of what you tell me, I have my doubts about the profitability of the place. And, frankly, there's not much of a business attitude here. That would have to change whatever the produce.'

Stone, with piercing grey-blue eyes, stared coldly at the

72

man, this city businessman. He said nothing, just waited quiescently to hear what was to come.

'As I see it, world prices for sugar are falling. Beet sugar is proving to be a decent enough competitor. Given that we keep the place, though we have had a very good offer, we could go one of two ways . . .' Philippe strummed the tips of his fingers ruminatively against the desk while Stone leant, arms folded across his chest, watching him. 'We could either look out for another crop for the Plantation, something with a higher yield, less farmed here, such as vanilla, maybe maize or ginger, or we could change tack altogether. Frankly that's where my instinct lies. It seems only right to give you fair warning. Give you a chance to look out for something else.'

Philippe paused, regarding his adversary. Stone waited.

'Six months for the changeover seems fairly reasonable to me. I shall be needing another man here, anyway, one with the experience I require should I decide to turn the place into a holiday resort.'

A holiday resort! Jesus! Stone thought. Sam would turn in his fucking grave! But he said nothing.

'It's nothing personal, Stone. Obviously Mrs De Marly's father was no businessman. I'm afraid that won't do for me. I shall be looking out for a new team, whatever the new proposals.'

'Well, you've obviously made up yer mind,' Stone said sharply, and picking up his hat from the debris of papers and notes on the desk in front of De Marly, strode from the office. He paused on the terrace, facing the horizon, wiping his weary eyes with the palm of his hand, his stomach tightly pounding, unaware of Kate sitting alone in the shade with her gin and an untouched book.

'Mr Stone?'

'Yeah?'

'Are you all right?'

'Jus' terrific,' he mouthed sarcastically. Breathing deeply to alleviate the blow, he set off down the heat-dried, winding cliff path, still contemplating what had just been dealt him by his newly inherited boss, son-in-law to Sam (would that he had known it!).

'Bastard!' he cursed soundlessly. Stone paused to contemplate the view across to the other islands, several of which had been turned into exclusive island resorts. He plunged his hands into his working jeans pockets and kicked a small stone over the cliff's edge, watching as it plummeted to the water. He'll have a bloody riot on his hands, he thought bitterly.

Sure, there would be plenty of jobs created for the Fijians, serving drinks, smiling obsequiously, welcoming the tourists; but what about the Indian population? They were never employed in the resorts, except as cashiers. It didn't look good for guests to arrive at a tropical paradise and find that they were surrounded, not by native Fijians, but by Indian labour. No local atmosphere and colour! So, what would all the canecutters do now? Hundreds of Indians had been working at the Plantation since Sam had built the business into a profitable enterprise. Where would they go now? How would they take the news?

Never mind the bloody Indians, he thought. They can take care of themselves. What was *he* going to do?

Overhead he heard the trolling engines of a small seaplane crossing from southeast of where he was standing pondering his future. In from the mainland, he mused. He gazed up at the small buzzing creature, screwing up his face and squinting his eyes against the still sharp early-evening light, watching it curve north preparing to make its landing in the bay along the coast. Lesa Plantation Bay, it sat a couple of miles further south.

He turned and stepped on down the hill having lost interest in the plane. He had decided to get drunk, roaring drunk. The local kava would do the trick, after a few beers. He hoped that at this very moment Timi and Timi's gloriously voluptuous wife, Miriam, would be awaiting him, pounding up the root and mixing it. He thought of Timi and Miriam. What would be their reaction to the news? For the time being he would say nothing, unless De Marly said anything. Time enough for that later.

He hurried on down the path, his spirits temporarily revived by the prospect of a drunken evening away from the Plantation, away from De Marly and away from his wife. Gone, he thought despondently, were the days when he and Sam had taken the speedboat around the island and landed it at Taqawari. They had spent many drunken evenings together, carousing in the tiny Fijian port, in its fleapit of a hotel, inaptly named The Great Southern, with its own friendly bar, friendly prices and an excellent, although not always entirely clean, whorehouse.

'Shit,' he muttered, remembering his favourite woman, Felise, a formidable mulatto whose ambrosial laughter used to take the roof off the small corrugated hut in which she served him. He stepped up his speed, hurrying on his way towards Timi's place in search of home-made, alcoholic solace.

Close by, the small water-winged plane had skidded through the previously calm water and landed like a dragonfly, amber in the evening light, on the sand. Shyam Khumar, the sole passenger, emerged and Philippe stepped forward to meet him.

Ami Chand, hardly able to contain his excitement, waited breathlessly at the end of the dust track that led to the beach, watching; standing erect beside the battered orange jeep which he had spent the better part of the afternoon cleaning, although, with its history of numerous collisions, it resisted any attempt at ceremony.

He watched as the formidable Indian politician, a charismatic, looming presence in a lightweight wheat-coloured suit, hurried forward to shake hands with Philippe De Marly before being led towards him and his waiting truck.

'The man who will give us our future,' Ami repeated silently to himself.

Chapter 6

'You see, Philippe, after Oxford I was restless. I couldn't settle in England.'

Kate leant forward, listening attentively to the prepossessing stranger. Her figure caused an elongated, flickering shadow on the peeling sunstripped wall behind her as she helped herself to another small handful of pecan nuts from the table in front of her. She was feeling vaguely tipsy and wishing that she had not drunk two gin martinis, both of which she had concocted to be deliberately potent.

Shyam Khumar turned to address her. 'It was the late sixties, Mrs De Marly, there was an atmosphere of great hope in your country. Student revolutions taking place all over Europe. In 1968 I took a coach from Oxford to Paris to protest, along with others of my generation. It woke me up, dragged me from my formal education, allowed me to understand, and believe, that change was possible . . .'

She leant back again, watching his ebony-black eyes shining into the falling darkness. He smiled, thoughts elsewhere, and then addressed himself to Philippe once more. His voice was soft, yet commanding, while his features expressed a tenderness.

'But change was happening here too. Drawing me back. It was the build-up to our Independence. The British were leaving and we, too, had expectations. We Indians, for

76

example, craved the break with Britain. We saw it as our opportunity, our chance to begin to build our own future, to slip the rope of colonialism and imperialism and, for most of us, build a bridge between ourselves and the Fijian natives . . .' He fell silent for a moment, questioning the honesty of his own statement. Hadn't he, in reality, in his younger, more credulous days, encouraged another form of prejudice? Breaking the shackles of British dominance to create the same for his fellow Indians?

Against the backdrop of a darkening silver horizon, palm trees jutted and bent like strange, twisting figures in a shadow dance. Beyond the headland, beneath the vast expanse of glittering sky, waves turned and rolled. They, all three, sat listening to the power of the hot, tropical night.

'But these years, Shyam, since 1970, since Independence, must have shown you that your dreams were just an illusion, that it can't work. There's more racial hatred here than ever before,' Philippe said, breaking into the evening's spell, warmed by the light from the storm lamp placed in the middle of their table of drinks. His tone hinted a certain weariness, an agitation. Kate watched him as he flicked at a moth circling his glass.

'On the contrary, I still believe it is possible. Otherwise what is my work about?' Shyam lightly teased. 'But it will take a common desire, amongst Indians and Fijians both, to make the islands work for us. If we squabble amongst ourselves, ultimately we will be playing into the hands of a third, external party.' He pressed the paler tips of his nutmeg fingers together, reminding Kate of the priests she had known in her Catholic schooldays. She watched him stretch thoughtfully, and lean elegantly towards the table. He picked up his whisky glass and then leant back into the wicker chair, slowly turning the grasped glass in his hands. The ice clinked and swirled and the chair creaked beneath him.

'Yes,' he continued, 'I loved England in those days. It was an invigorating country. A perfect time to be a student and young lecturer, particularly for me.' He turned to Kate, smiling, his eyes glinting with relish, the pleasure of his long-held, harmless addiction.

77

'But my passion is jazz, Mrs De Marly. It kept me bankrupt! I used to spend my rather meagre salary travelling from Oxford to London, and on to Paris, when Philippe's family would tolerate me! I loved Paris! Yes, I succumbed to the music of the Left Bank! And still, occasionally, dream of it.' He laughed boyishly, took a sip of his whisky and rested his loosely cut, long black hair against the high back of the chair, still smiling unselfconsciously to himself.

Both she and Philippe, sitting beside one another, listened to him silently. No one spoke. She tried to picture him almost twenty years younger, perhaps a little slimmer, less tired-looking, enchanted by Paris, its underground jazz clubs, passionate about his music and his politics. She wondered who, apart from her husband, might have shared those obviously carefree days with him.

'But I couldn't settle in Europe. I felt my difference. I was always a stranger. A solitary guest in another man's home. England, although I loved her culture, and still do, was always the benevolent mother of our imperialism. It is a country that has given so much to these islands and, with the other hand, created so much strife and unhappiness here. In my own homeland. I would have felt a traitor. So I had to return. I knew that it was time. And I wanted to be a part of our new world here. I still do.'

'Youth's idealistic dreams, eh, Shyam?' Philippe challenged, pouring them both another Scotch.

Kate sat spellbound. She wondered how much was the effects of the alcohol. Her cheeks were flushed, her palms clammy and pulsating. She found it difficult to imagine that this stranger, this alluringly remote man, had been friends with her husband during those student days. Their worlds appeared to be entirely contrasting. Philippe seemed almost brutish beside Khumar's serenity. She had never considered her husband in such a light before, it quite shocked her, but the thought presented itself each time she looked from one to the other, sitting together discussing those student days, a world before she had met Philippe, obviously so long ago.

'And what of you, Philippe? You wanted to go into finance.'

'Yes, I've been fortunate. Initially, I joined up with a Swiss company and was posted to London. Worked as one of their traders on the foreign exchange desk. The opportunity proved to be fortuitous . . . I met Kate,' he smiled, 'and professionally, I had great fortune. I was approached by a London house to manage deposits, bonds and gold . . . it seemed to be pretty successful. These days I play international capital . . .'

Kate closed her eyes briefly and tried to picture Philippe again as he had been when she had first met him. He had only recently left France; dark, clean-cut. She had found him arrogantly handsome, dashing, with a roguish but sophisticated charm, a possessor of great self-assurance and superiority. That had intrigued her. She who had been so shy, so unsure of herself. He had never lost that certainty, that social confidence. Was he so very different now or had the same qualities simply lost their enchantment for her? She had never really stopped to consider it. Certainly he was maturer, and physically thicker. Too much whisky and not enough exercise. She was always telling him. But otherwise? Little about him had changed. It had been bred in him. That polished, unshakeable certainty about his role in life. The two male voices droned mellifluously beside her into the hot night air, liberating her. She was feeling intoxicated by the balmy night, the gin martinis and the unexpected sorcery of their guest.

She had met Philippe at a party. She had hardly known a soul there and had spent a good deal of the evening wandering from room to room, occasionally creeping unnoticed into corners of others' conversations, and disappearing again, equally unnoticed. She had lost track of her flatmate, the girl she had arrived with, and it was getting late. She was feeling awkward and self-consciously unattached.

And then Philippe had appeared; smiling, gracious. He had approached her to dance, charming her, just when she had decided to leave.

'Not disappearing are you? Just when I wanted to say hello. I've been watching you. I thought you might like to dance.'

'Hey Jude'. The Beatles record. And then 'Strawberry Fields Forever'. He had insisted on driving her home, in spite of her protests, to her rather shabby flat in Notting Hill Gate which she had shared with one other girl, both private secretaries from the same college. It had been a warm August night. He had driven his car, a white, convertible Peugeot 404, too fast and the wind had whipped her long hair against her face.

It had been thrilling.

She had been twenty, impressionable and impressed.

He had invited himself in 'for coffee'. He had been her first lover. Her only lover. A shy Catholic girl from a broken home, she had been attracted to his strength – he still possessed that – and the consummate ease with which he had approached life. He had seemed to her then not to be afraid of anything, quite unlike herself who had been lost and tentative, grappling for guidance, for someone to take care of her.

She used to imagine that he had swept her off her feet.

Silly, she thought now, such a childish, romantic idea.

Miriam trundled heavily on to the wooden-boarded verandah to announce that supper 'was waiting and would soon be cold'.

Kate rose quickly and made her way on ahead of the two men who were still both discussing Philippe's success in business and his present expectations about future international mergers within his firm.

Tonight would be the first time that Kate and Philippe had eaten inside the house. The dining room was opposite the scullery kitchen. Kate had crept in a couple of hours earlier to inspect the table. There was little communication between her and Miriam, who went about her work in a methodical yet uninterested fashion, never pausing to enquire whether there was something that the De Marlys might particularly require. She had been cleaning and cooking at the house for many years and the arrival of two strangers made little difference to her patterns. It was her role, as she saw it, to run the house, adequately but without an excessive expenditure of energy, and once her chores were performed and the dusk was descending she would lope her bulky weight back down the hill, singing loudly to herself, happy to be on her way back home to Timi and the boys and their neighbours, with whom she would pass the starry evenings, drinking *yangona*, talking, tattling and joking merrily together.

It would not have occurred to Kate to impose another way on this woman who, clearly, did not regard her as 'the boss'. To Miriam, the De Marlys were merely transient guests in an otherwise settled rhythm whose appearance had disrupted her carefree family evenings.

However, on this particular morning Kate had informed Miriam that as there was going to be an extra guest for dinner she would prefer it if they ate more formally, in the dining room.

'It'll be pretty hot in there, Mrs De Marly,' Miriam had rejoined but had conceded when Kate had insisted. Busy with her own chores, Kate had found no time to peek again into the old-fashioned room with its mahogany dining table and its almost suffocating atmosphere.

The fan above them dragged now through the stiflingly thick heat as tortuously slowly as a donkey turning a water wheel and Kate was wishing that she had not interfered and had allowed Miriam to serve supper on the terrace as usual.

This was a dark room with six, high-backed wicker chairs placed formally around an oval table, two each side and one at either end. It reminded Kate of rather morbid visits to her Irish grandmother, Sam's mother. A lady whom after the disappearance of her father she and her mother had rarely visited. The table had been laid avoiding both ends, in an attempt to create a little informality in an otherwise imposing atmosphere.

She placed Khumar at her husband's side and she sat alone, opposite them both. The door creaked open and, within seconds, a tray laden with steaming plates appeared followed by Ami.

'Where is Miriam?' Kate asked incredulously.

'I help tonight, missus,' he announced proudly. With delicate attention and not a small amount of reverence Ami placed Khumar's plate in front of him and then paused, balanced, waiting for acknowledgement.

Khumar, noticing this, interrupted his discussion with

Philippe to thank the young Indian whom he addressed by name. Plates on the table, Ami slid self-consciously from the room with the clumsily exaggerated grace of a clown. Kate giggled silently.

She bent her head and began her soup. It was turtle. Too heavy for the climate but, she supposed, a local speciality. 'Ami seems to be rather in awe of you.' She was regaining her equilibrium and with it a certain confidence that served her so well in London at her own, highly esteemed dinner parties, mainly given for clients of Philippe.

'We have met before, many times. He used to work for a friend of mine who lives outside Suva. A doctor, also an Englishman. You should meet him. He was an old friend of your father's. They had been together in Malaysia, I think, for several years before settling here. In fact, I believe it was Sam who encouraged Patterson to make his home here. Ami was Patterson's houseboy. I hadn't realised that he had moved over here.'

'I understand from Rob Stone, my father's overseer here, that Ami can be a little troublesome. Apparently there was a rather serious fight here just before we arrived.'

Philippe placed his spoon back into his soup bowl, not attempting to hide his surprise that Kate should be party to this information about which he knew nothing.

'I'm sorry to hear that. Although I have always known him to be restless.'

Philippe interrupted. 'I didn't know that! Did Stone tell you who he had been fighting with?'

Kate shook her head, anxious suddenly to change the subject.

'Philippe tells me that you are in politics, Mr Khumar? Are you in the government here?' she enquired diffidently, listening to her voice topple from her lips with the uncertainty of a beginner on the nursery slopes. She was heartily wishing that she had not been so tactless about Ami. She liked him, enjoyed his mettlesome nature and had said as much to Stone earlier before Ami had taken her to see Sam's grave. Her question had been merely an expression of her desire to understand the youth better.

82

Khumar laughed openly at her, yet there was no malice, no mockery in his amusement. 'No, no. Certainly not! And please call me Shyam. No, my politics are not comfortable enough for the government. They are hardly comfortable enough for my own party! I lead the opposition here. It is an Indian party, seeking equality for both races.'

She watched as his expression changed. For the briefest of moments the warmth was gone and in its place was something which seemed to her akin to despair. His dark penetrating eyes, chestnut in the light, bored into her although he seemed not to focus on her at all.

'It's a difficult task we have set ourselves. As you said earlier, Philippe, we have not yet succeeded. There is still much anger here, much frustration and mistrust. And there is corruption . . .' His thoughts drifted as she watched him delicately place his spoon into the barely touched soup.

'Yes,' Philippe replied, seizing his moment. 'I want to ask you about the tensions here. For an overseas investor, would you consider these islands promise a secure future?'

'You know, Philippe, these islands have been ruled by the same party since Independence in 1970. It is a Fijian party, predominantly. A few Indians in office but predominantly Fijian. Many would say that its interests are biased, that its *raison d'être* is to uphold Fijian interest. The status quo as laid down by the British for the Fijian people. Many would like to see a change. We Indians are the majority race here now. We are the economic strength of the islands. There are members of my party as well as numerous others outside any party who want Indian Rule here. They are bitter that their voice has been suppressed for so long. They would do much to see that their voices are heard. I, too, would like to see a change of government here. But my belief is that only by working with the Fijians, allying ourselves with them, can we create any fundamental change. It is up to us to make the future secure for overseas investors, such as yourself, and for those of us who are living and growing up here.'

Replete and drowsy, the newly acquainted threesome sat

together on the porch, quietly enjoying their coffee, gazing out on to a world of lapping water and distant island lights where sleeping tourists drank the worry-free draughts of natural beauty.

'It's a very particular spot your father found here. I confess I always envied him this place.' Khumar spoke softly, careful not to disturb the workings of the tropical night.

'I hadn't realised that you knew him?' Kate asked with innocent surprise as she leant close to refill his coffee cup.

'No more for me, thank you. I must leave early in the morning, I have plenty of work to do tomorrow. Yes, we were acquaintances really, rather than friends. In fact, it was Patterson who introduced us. You remember the English doctor I mentioned to you earlier? Sam was over on the mainland for a day or two on business. A task he preferred to avoid! Quite understandably he hated leaving here, even for a few days. Patterson had been threatening to introduce us for quite some time. He invited us both for dinner. I liked him immediately. He possessed a spontaneous, irreverent love of life. He was an unconventional and honest man and he looked after his labourers with kindness. He was loved and respected by both races. No mean feat here where there is so much racial misunderstanding. Perhaps he actually achieved here on this plantation, in his microcosm, what I dream of achieving throughout the Pacific Islands.'

Kate paused from her pouring of the coffee and sat under the starry night, transfixed. She found it difficult to imagine that they were remembering the same man.

'I was very shocked to hear about his death. It seemed so . . . unlikely.'

She waited, listening, but he said no more. Rising, he turned and held out his hand to her. 'Well, if you'll excuse me, I must get some sleep. Thank you so much for your hospitality.'

Philippe, who had been ruminative for quite some time, rose hastily. 'I'll show you to your room, Shyam. Give me a moment to find the keys.' And he hurried off inside the house, in search of the keys to the guest annexe that Stone had left for him, earlier.

Left alone with Khumar Kate suddenly felt gauche and awkward. 'How did he die, my father? I haven't heard.'

'Oh, I see,' he began cautiously. 'Well, I don't know the exact details. I believe there was some uncertainty about it. He was found lying near a derelict building, somewhere here on the estate. I understand from Patterson that, at one point, they feared foul play or that he may even have taken his own life.'

'Taken his own life!'

'That was quickly ruled out. The final verdict, I believe, was death by natural causes.'

'I had no idea that it was so late, Shyam! You should have said something sooner,' Philippe apologised, as he hurried out on to the porch. 'I've found the key. God knows why they keep the place locked. There's certainly nothing to steal there!'

Once more Shyam bid her good night and the two men disappeared into the house. She listened to the faint murmur of their voices retreat into the distance, as she leant her weight against one of the porch timbers, inexplicably shocked by what she had just heard. Her arm outstretched above her, she strummed her fingers lightly against the bells. They vibrated cleanly in the darkness.

This man, her father, was a stranger to her. He was not the man that, for so many years, her mother had so vehemently raged against. She did not know this 'island' man. She pondered for a moment the idea that his death had been cloaked in an uncertainty and wondered what guilt or despair might have driven him to take his own life. Less than two months earlier he had contacted her, asking her to visit him. And she had replied, warmly accepting his invitation, telling him how elated she had felt to hear from him. He was expecting her, his little girl. Why would he kill himself? And why should anyone want to kill him? Somehow she could not picture it.

The next morning it had begun to shower. Khumar peered out of the curtainless window at the rear of the house and spotted one of the two mongrels howling close by the generator sheds, expressing his irritation at the light drizzle. The damp animal was baying fruitlessly into the uncaring dawn in an attempt to stop the weather or, at best, to conjure sympathy. Both proving to be futile, he sank back miserably on to his haunches accepting his predicament. It was a little after dawn. The sun was rising, a marmalade orange, creating a misty glow across the mossy, forested, volcanic mountains.

Khumar looked at his watch and supposed it was still too early for his hosts. He would set off silently then, without any tea. He turned away from the window still smiling at the antics of the foolish dog.

As he crept from the unadorned, cell-like room in search of the lavatory he listened but heard no sounds of people stirring. Only the occasional creakings of a well-worn building. He threw an unthinking glance along the hallway towards the porch and saw someone seated, bare back to him, looking out towards the misty morning ocean.

It was Ami, waiting for him no doubt. The dark-skinned youth sat dressed only in a sulu, drinking tea from a mug which he occasionally rested on the porch step. Khumar called good morning and headed across the hallway, through the scullery towards the extension bathroom that Philippe had unlocked for him only a few hours earlier.

'Apologies for the facilities. It's a bit like student days! Not my doing, you understand,' he had said. Shyam had smiled without replying, too tired to care, and more than ready to sleep.

He reflected now on the conversations of the previous evening as he tugged at the stiff chrome taps on the antiquated bath system. The released water began to leapfrog from the central faucet.

De Marly had changed almost beyond recognition, he felt. He would hardly have known him, although truthfully, he was not physically so much altered. Certainly he was carrying a little extra weight, but the same could be said of himself, he reflected! No, it was Philippe's manner that had surprised him. He had not remembered him being quite so abrasive. But, he thought sadly, they had both been young, optimistic and more idealistic.

He had found Philippe's wife, Kate, quite beautiful in a shy, uncertain English way. He smiled melancholically to himself, remembering another in earlier days, released the towel wrapped around his waist and stepped into the weak, tea-coloured water. It must have been a while, he mused, since someone had used this annexe.

Upstairs, disturbed only by the steady sounds of her husband sleeping soundly at her side, Kate lay listening to the disgruntled belchings of the ancient plumbing. She had not been awakened by the noise. On the contrary, she had been relieved to hear movement. It had been a long, slow march towards the dawn and the sounds of the early morning life beneath her had brought her some comfort.

She had remembered a passage in her father's letter which had disturbed her and in the light of what Shyam had said to her had unsettled her. 'I have put the Plantation in your name. If anything should happen to me I want you to have the place,' he had written to her. 'If you can forgive me . . .'

She toyed with the idea of going downstairs, making coffee for Shyam and sitting with him for a short while before he set off in the jeep with Ami but she decided against it, knowing that she would be unable to resist the desire to question him further about her father, his death and other questions about Shyam himself.

Perhaps she would try to sleep a little and then later, when Ami had returned and she was more rested, she would find time to question him instead. It seemed curious to her now that she had not considered talking to Ami about her father but it had simply not occurred to her that the boy would have had any real contact with him. The idea pleased her. It seemed easier than approaching Stone who was behaving as though he resented their arrival here.

And then, spontaneously, she pulled back the sheet, careful not to disturb Philippe, walked through to the bathroom, washed, wrapped herself in a sarong and hurried down the stairs to make breakfast, or at least coffee, for their departing guest.

She found him sitting alone on the terrace, where she had last seen him.

'Oh, good morning. I hope I haven't woken you?'

She shook her tousled head and sat beside him at the terrace table. 'I was already awake,' she muttered faintly, her voice still scruffy with sleep.

'I was just about to set off when Ami insisted I sit down for a mug of tea.' He held the inelegant mug before him, smiling mischievously.

'Shall I make you a fresh pot?' she grinned also.

He shook his head. 'No, really I should've been on my way already but I was tempted by the light on the ocean . . . even in the drizzle it's a magnificent spot. You're very fortunate.'

'I came here to meet Sam. But he'd died a few days before I left England. No one notified us.'

'I'm sorry.'

'I lay awake last night thinking about what you'd said. . . . I grew up hating Sam, believing that he had betrayed us . . . he left home when I was quite small and . . . I never really knew him. . . . And then, when I hear . . . Has he really created something special here? Timi, our foreman, and Stone, who looks after the place: they both said that Lesa has achieved more in some ways than any other plantation, due to Sam.'

'I believe that's true. How long will you be staying here?'

Kate shrugged, wondering why she felt such a need to talk to Khumar. She wanted to tell him that she had visited Sam's grave, how ashamed it had made her feel for judging him so harshly, how isolated she was feeling now . . . Why had she never tried to find• him? Why had she just accepted her mother's word that he was dead, gone from her life? 'I'm not sure. Philippe is anxious to get back to work. I suppose it depends on what happens here. Another week at the most, I would think.' Had Sam contacted her knowing that he was dying? Was that what he meant by 'if anything should happen to me I want you to have the place'?

'Why don't you, and Philippe, when you are on the mainland, come and have supper with me? Perhaps we can persuade Doctor Patterson to join us, though he's a bit of a recluse these days. He was a great friend of Sam's.'

'Yes, I'd like that, thank you.'

He rose, and stood a moment beside her. 'I must be on my way.'

Kate, awkward, rose too. 'Yes, of course.' She considered walking with him to the jeep but changed her mind.

He held out his hand and formally shook hers. 'See you soon. Thank you for your hospitality.' With that he stepped from the verandah and crossed the grass to where Ami sat waiting in the parked jeep, leaving Kate feeling strangely saddened by his departure.

An hour or so later, a telex from London was delivered from Loquaqua for Philippe. He was restless. He had to make contact with his office, the house radio was inadequate. He headed off for the mainland, on the next ferry. 'While I'm gone,' he said, 'I'm going to dig out some information about Danil, see if I can find out who his clients are, something about his background, and I'll make an appointment to see the "Chief" at the Sugar Company.' Kate spent almost the entire day alone.

Feeling too unsettled for anything more active she decided to pass the time reading on the porch. Later Ami's son, Jal, appeared. He played close by in the garden. Idly she watched him. On several occasions she called out to him but he refused to respond to her beckonings, taking shy refuge behind the Indian gardeners working around him, silent beings whose baggy trousers hung from their insubstantial waists like the loose flesh on a lizard's legs.

'Have you seen your father?' she called, finally, to the lone boy but he only giggled and ran off mischievously, scampering out of sight down the hillside pathway. So she left him to play in peace, wondering why she had never seen the boy's mother. She settled to her book. It was a blisteringly hot day, tough to concentrate, and her mind drifted constantly to thoughts of her father, his death and to Shyam Khumar, lost to her now on the mainland.

Chapter 7

'Send him up, please.' Shyam Khumar replaced the internal telephone, pursed his lips in thought and waited for the heavy footsteps to ascend the stairs. Impassively he slipped his hand into one of the drawers of his desk beneath him and drew out a packet of aspirin. He helped himself to two tablets and downed them with water from a nearby glass. Five hours' sleep and too much whisky had done nothing to enhance his wellbeing. His head, which had already been pounding, had worsened during the hour since Ashok Bhanjee had telephoned. Because of his insistence Khumar had been obliged deftly to rearrange a tightly organised schedule, so that he and Bhanjee could have an hour together for discussion in the privacy of his office.

A light tapping, and Khumar's secretary opened the door. A heavy man in his late forties, wearing a light-weight Pierre Cardin suit, sharp against his Indian complexion, strode into the office. His black hair was sleeked with oil; his broad moon face split by a nylon smile. This was Ashok Bhanjee.

'Come and sit down, Ashok. Excuse the papers every-where. No time to hide them from you.' Khumar, with tired features, managed the weary joke as he rose, and leant across his desk to shake hands.

Their palms met. One plump, bejewelled hand against

90

another's lean fingers. Any stranger could read, no clearer perhaps than they, that these men had little in common.

Ashok Bhanjee was a businessman. More, he was a dollar multi-millionaire businessman. Some might say he possessed the temperament and ethics of a Sicilian but he was in fact a Gujarati Indian from north of Bombay, southern India. King of the Duty-free Markets, a growing industry on these intercontinental islands, and the Godfather of the Burgeoning Bhanjee Empire, these were his uncrowned titles.

He had given his life's work to the expansion of the family business, and had achieved a thirty-million-dollar-a-year enterprise. This success had left him at liberty to indulge his 'hobby', politics, and in that he was carving as formidable a reputation as he had in commerce. A long-time working associate of Khumar, he had lately been elected deputy party leader and had become the loudest, most vocal critic of Khumar's moderate policies, publicly accusing him of communist allegiances. He was now rapidly emerging as a self-appointed rival.

Khumar mistrusted him. He was uncertain of his integrity, distressed by what he read as Ashok's commercial motives and was tiringly aware of the growing threat to his leadership. Their only common bond was politics, and in that they rarely saw eye to eye.

Ashok Bhanjee had pressed for this rendezvous, insisting that he had news that needed to be heard. Now he sank his heavy sprawling weight into a chair opposite Khumar's desk. Khumar threw him a packet of cigarettes.

'What is it, Ashok, that couldn't wait until our next meeting?' Khumar asked directly.

Ashok slipped a cigarette from the carton and threw the packet on to the desk. From his pocket he withdrew a Dunhill lighter.

'These are promising days for us, our party, the Indian people. The end of the year is in sight, Shyam, and a new year is on its way. A year with spring elections looming. I have great faith in the future.'

Khumar laughed boldly. 'Is that your news, my friend?'

91

Ashok lit his cigarette and inhaled, slipping the lighter back into the chest pocket of his tailored shirt.

'Shyam, I have come,' he said, 'to warn you that the majority of our party are anxious about their future. They cannot wait any longer. "We want Indian control now," they are saying.'

Bhanjee continued, 'They are whispering amongst themselves. Some have evil tongues. They are saying that they are no longer willing to support you. That's not good, my friend. It does not bode well. They are saying that you promised us power, leadership; that we Indians would in time take our rightful places as the rulers of these islands. And that now you care more for the Fijian natives.'

Bhanjee's news did not surprise Shyam. He had sensed, even known, that there had been discontent growing within his party, agitated, he believed, by Ashok himself. He himself frequently felt discontented, frustrated by the powerlessness of their situation, but he had faith.

Until recently he had read their dissatisfaction as a desire for change. A desire committed to the islands as well as their fellow Indians. But the choice of Ashok Bhanjee as deputy leader had troubled him. Ideas were altering, he feared, loyalties vacillating. And he worried that he could no longer support what he believed was now the quest within his party: Indian Rule for the Indian people.

That was not his vision. His vision was not a national one. These islands were Fijian and part of a greater whole, a South Pacific Basin, a melting pot of nationalities who must, he believed, learn to work and live together. But in his solitary darkness he wept for his Indian companions. Perhaps, really, I have betrayed them. My party and the Indian people, he questioned as he had many times before. And that questioning had made him restless, despairing.

But what had been growing between him and Bhanjee, stark as their southern light, was also the cause of his present despondency. 'Shyam, we cannot afford to wait any longer. If we don't take control now by whatever means necessary, all possibility of power will have evaded us. Times are changing here, Shyam. Faster than we can perceive. Television is coming to the islands. This is our opportunity. People will never again be satisfied with what they have. We must move with these changes and use them to help us. We are sitting in a major port here. The busiest in the South Pacific. We could, with a little help from more resourceful neighbours, build our own Singapore. Think of it, Shyam, a duty-free stopover between Australia and America. That's my dream, Shyam. There will be work for everyone . . . New hotels, shopping malls, nightclubs, a livelier tourist industry and massive business potential. Poverty will disappear but we must move fast.'

Bhanjee paused, breathless with anticipation. His over-fleshed face had broken into a smile revealing white teeth bolstered by gold. A resistant silence sat between them, disturbed only by the high-pitched whirring of the inefficient office air conditioning.

'Wake up, Shyam,' he barked at the sight of his companion's reticence. 'Power will be with those who have the potential for economic growth. Indians! We are willing to work! To make money! You are dreaming with your talk of Pacific Identity. We must protect ourselves. Television can be our opportunity. It will be a playground for advertisers. Investment will pour in from all over the Western World. And they will support Fiji. But our fight, the Indian fight, will be lost if we are not in control of those investments, if we do not ally ourselves with overseas support. Shyam, we Indians, we are the workforce here. We are the power. Not the native Fijians. They are idle and unambitious. Investment, overseas investment, is the key to our success.'

Khumar picked up his cigarettes from the desk in front of him and held the packet hovering in his right hand. 'Ashok, your vision is a myopic one. You talk only of material power. What have we been working towards, dreaming of, planning for, if money is to be the deciding factor?' He slammed the packet restlessly back on to the desk. 'Christ, my friend! Are you suggesting that we stand with open arms and welcome the debris of the Western World? Why do we always look to

93

Europe and to America to set our standards? Our codes of thinking must be our own! I am not interested in the power you talk of! I know our people are impatient. I, too, am impatient, but I will not leap to choices that will finally strangle us. We have to find a way to work together and live here together. Fijians and Indians! We must not create a society that is built on racial prejudices, on power for one race. That is what you are suggesting. It's a short-term dream, Ashok!' he implored. 'What I am suggesting takes time, my friend. These islands have been gripped by the strong arm of the British for a hundred years! What have we been dreaming of if not to give back a pride and identity to us all? All of us, Ashok! Every single human being living here! Fijian and Indian creating together! And, my friend, you blindly fool yourself if you believe that we will be the controllers, simply backed by overseas investors. That is more of the same, Ashok!'

He paused, in his anger, to light a cigarette, throwing the burnt match on to the desk in front of him. 'And I will not take control by "whatever means necessary", Ashok. What the hell does that mean!'

Bhanjee waited, rubbing his lowered lids with plump fingers.

'Shyam,' he began then, coolly directing his phlegmatic gaze towards his long-time associate, 'I have suggested a referendum. Let the party members speak for themselves. It will, after all, give them a chance to reaffirm their loyalty towards you.' He spoke with the artifice of one affecting sensibility to another's torment.

'And what if they do not reaffirm that loyalty? Who will lead them – you, Ashok?'

'That is not my decision.'

That same day, later in the afternoon, spreadeagled in a black leather swivel chair installed untidily behind him, Ashok Bhanjee lovingly placed an opened newspaper on to the desk in front of him. It was not his desk, not his office, but his cousin Raj's desk, an employee of his; and it was piled high with overseas invoices.

Bhanjee settled himself against the soft leather, feeling gratified. He felt it had been a positive morning.

Resting his elbows against the chair's side wings he brought his plump gold-ringed fingers together as in a gesture of prayer, revealing a chunky gold identity bracelet hanging ostentatiously from his right wrist. He held the tips of his fingers lightly touching as, silently, supremely satisfied, he perused himself in print.

Four entire pages, with photographs and interviews, had been devoted to the opening of the new, 'ultra-modern' Indira Gandhi Memorial School. His own photograph, not a bad likeness, he felt, led the article and consumed almost the entire left column on the first page. But that was as it should be, he reflected, given his position as treasurer of the Gujarati Society. It was he who had been the driving force behind the new Indian school. It had been his vision, his voice of persuasion and, to a not inconsiderable degree, his money, donated from his substantial personal fortune, that had helped to finance the building. And so, all acknowledgement that was given to him was his due. He felt satisfied.

An audio cassette of American rock music, Bruce Springsteen Live in America, penetrated the paper-thin walls, causing them to shudder. This small cramped space, unlike his own luxurious offices, was tucked away to the rear of one of his electrical goods stores situated in Suva's flourishing, blinking, gaudily dressed Duty-Free quarter. The room, always alive with popular music on sale in the store, was maintained for accountancy purposes, private 'business' trans- actions and for his Gujarati manager and cousin, Raj, to eat his lunchtime sandwiches without disturbance and without needing to leave the premises.

Suddenly the door opened, blasting him with the thumping bass rhythm of this latest, pirated, Bruce Springsteen album. Ashok Bhanjee looked up hastily. He had been disturbed without warning. In his minutely structured empire, where order and respect reigned, this was sacrilege. He was King of the Duty-Free Markets on the islands, Godfather to the blossoming family Empire. Nobody crossed him. His features broke into a scowl which remained when he saw the cause of the intrusion. His languid, semi-hooded eyes stared with contempt as he spoke. His voice was deliberate, with only the merest hint of ill-humour which was entirely missed by his irascible young intruder.

'Has no one ever taught you, Ami, that it is impolite to walk into a room without knocking? Is Raj in the store?'

'Yes, he's serving. Sorry, Ashok. I'm late, I have to get back to the Plantation.' The words rushed nervously from the Indian boy's lips. 'But I needed to see you first. Collect my money and . . .'

'Raj would have seen to that. You know I am a busy man and don't like to be disturbed.'

'Listen, Ashok. I need more work! Something better. You promised me more responsibility. I have a son to feed. I want to give him a home, a big car, like you with your sons. You promised me that when . . .'

Bhanjee sat regarding the mettlesome young Indian restlessly pacing the length of the tiny jam-packed office.

'You'll wear yourself out with your impatience, Ami. You'll never make a successful businessman until you learn to curb that.' He spoke calmly with almost a note of jocularity but a more discerning listener than Ami Chand would have sensed the incisive note of intolerance.

'I'm fed up with plantation life. You gave my brother a chance. I want the same. I want to manage one of your shops.' The dark-haired young man with his earnest features and burning, oval eyes stopped his pacing and leant over the stacked desk, directly challenging his bull-like opponent. 'You owe me a chance, Ashok,' he added firmly.

Ashok settled his gaze on to the youth's impetuous face and smiled, eyes glinting dangerously like a well-sharpened razor, pausing for a moment before he spoke.

'Ami, my friend, this is not a question of owing. Take the cassettes and your well-earned percentage and be easy. I haven't forgotten you. I enjoy, even respect, your . . . hunger, but you are not ready yet. I promise you, your time will come, just like Roshan. I have something very special in mind for you. Trust me. Have I ever let you down? Did I ever let your brother down? But you are not your brother, Ami, and you are still learning.'

The boy withdrew from the desk and sighed. Ashok Bhanjee was not a man to do battle with. Anyway, he was already late. He glanced at his watch. He leant forward and picked up a large, meticulously wrapped paper package and a sealed envelope from his side of the desk, opened the envelope, counted a plump wad of local dollars, put them into his back jeans pocket and slid the parcel inside his brightly coloured satin flying jacket. He glanced at Bhanjee, who sat patiently watching him, and nodded half-heartedly, almost regretting his outburst. Feeling defeated for the moment but knowing that he would be back, he turned and swaggered proudly into the vibrating world of the duty-free emporium.

As Ami strode, to all unknowing observers like a victor, towards the open street door, he flicked a glance at one wall of the store stacked floor to ceiling with video cassette tapes for rent or sale, sporting titles such as *Burning Passion*, *Coolie*, *Caged Love*, *Rambo*, even *Two Faces of Lust*. Furtively his eyes crossed the store to regard Raj, the highly successful manager and salesman, who was locked in negotiation with ageing Australian tourists haggling over the price of a National Cassette Radio bigger than a car. Beside them, a free-standing Japanese electric fan whirred silently, cooing at them as they bargained.

Raj lifted his eyes in Ami's direction, giving the boy a nod yet careful not to disturb the interest shown by his willing customer whose plump wife was now peering covetously into glass cases laden with alarm clocks, with Seiko watches, digitals, pocket computers of every size, price and skill, cameras from Canon, Yashica, Minolta, and numerous others. In every available corner of the store Japanese-marked cardboard boxes stood stacked four or five high, all stuffed to bursting with hardware for sale at knockdown, duty-free prices.

Ami, envious of this fellow Gujarati Indian, yet impassioned by his own fantasies of salesmanship and percentages

97

still to be scored, swung out of the store gyrating to the pounding music oblivious to the watchful, critical eyes boring into his back.

Bhanjee let his freshly lit cigarette fall to the mock-marble tiled floor, and crushed the burning stub with the sole of his Italian leather moccasin. He directed a surreptitious nod towards Raj, signalling him to join him in the back office, and returned to the desk, leaving the door a crack ajar in expectation of Raj's immediate arrival. Once at the desk he poured himself a Scotch from the half-empty bottle always within reach and stared thoughtfully into the distance. Seconds later Raj joined him, sale accomplished, and helped himself to a cigarette from a packet lying, torn open, on the desk.

'We'll have to keep an eye on that boy or he's going to be causing us trouble.' Bhanjee spoke without facing his cousin and paced, glass in hand, back around the desk. Downing the Scotch in one agitated gulp he folded up his newspaper, discreetly shutting away the pleasure of his recorded triumph.

Later, that night, in the solitary sanctum of his elegant study, overrun with files, books and law reports, Shyam Khumar stood alone. He was tired yet unable to rest, unable to stop his thoughts dragging him back to earlier that afternoon, to his meeting with Ashok Bhanjee, whose printed photograph lay open on his desk. Spoken in syllables cloaked in affection, yet it seemed, in retrospect, Bhanjee's betrayal of him was drawn from a long-buried anger, a burning resentment. And could it be even a loathing of him?

They were two Indians who, though of different religions, Bhanjee a Gujarati Hindu and he, a Muslim, had grown up alongside one another, and had been schooled in infancy at the same Indian school. In adolescence, as second- and third-generation brothers in exile they had been drawn together, despite their differences, by their passion to see their peoples honestly represented. Their paths had rarely crossed but Khumar had always counted on the support of this man, and had never questioned that loyalty. Until Bhanjee, a magnate in his Duty-Free Kingdom, shifted his ambitions towards politics. And Khumar began to see things differently.

He turned now towards his laden desk, towards the photos of the Indira Gandhi Memorial School, a modern, highly equipped new school for Indian children. Khumar bowed his head. These photos saddened him. He, who had been fighting so tirelessly for multi-racial schools. Was that not the first place to teach tolerance and understanding? One of the first changes his party planned to implement would be non-segregated schooling throughout the islands. He had promised that.

Seeking solace in work, longing to rid his mind of what was troubling him, he closed the newspaper, threw it into the basket and stepped towards his desk. His fingers ran easily along the spines of meticulously dusted rows of leather-bound law books, imported from England after university days. He could, of course, relinquish control of the party before the referendum, graciously handing over to Ashok Bhanjee the means to change direction. And he simply continue his career as a lawyer. Christ, no! He banged his fist angrily against his desk. Files fell to the ground.

What had he been working towards these sixteen years? To see his fellow Indians, through sheer weight of numbers, snatch control in a violent longing for power, simply to rule and suppress the Fijians in the same way that they had been oppressed? No, he would die first!

He dreamt of peace between the races. More! He dreamt of Indians living and working alongside the Fijians towards a common goal. A goal that would give them a degree of pride and economic independence. Was this so naïve? Had he really fed his people nothing more than false hopes and unrealistic dreams? Would they now, at the forthcoming referendum, give their support to Ashok Bhanjee?

He eased his exhausted body into the well-worn leather chair, resting his head against its high back, closed his eyes ringed with dark, sleepless circles, and sighed.

Had there been anyone in his life who noticed these moments they would have caressed his arm and told him softly: 'You're tired, Shyam, get some rest.'

But she had long since died, leaving him in the capable hands of caring staff who, though utterly loyal, never presumed to question his relentless drive. He opened his eyes and glanced briefly at the minute quartz clock positioned discreetly on the small circular wooden table close to the window, dwarfed by the pot containing a thriving bonsai tree. Khumar's relaxation was partially sought through his fascination for plants, Japanese plants particularly: their delicacy appealed to him. It was difficult in the darkened light to make out the face, which read ten minutes to two. It had been a very long day. Breakfast at Lesa, watching the early drizzle disperse with the heat from the dawning sun, listening to Mrs De Marly, watching her, sharing her thoughts; it seemed a long while ago now.

He leant forward and picked up his sleek, black pen. Thinking once more of Kate, he slowly unscrewed the cap. One set of papers to sign, he promised himself, and then sleep.

It was after four when he stood again, exhausted from concentration. In the silent stillness of the sleeping house he walked to the door of his study, opened it carefully, fearful of waking his three Indian staff, and climbed the stairs that led to his solitary bedroom.

Un vent de fronde souffle, he thought wearily.

Chapter 8

Philippe had returned from Suva, harassed and ill-tempered. 'There seems to be a bit of a crisis building in London,' he said. 'Something about a takeover bid. I think we might have to leave.' He had spent the entire day on the mainland, on the telephone to Europe. 'I'm going back to Suva in the morning. If nothing's blown over we'll book a flight home.'

'What about Lesa?' Kate asked in dismay.

'I'll put it in the hands of an international agent. There's no sense making a decision until I know what's what.'

'What about Danil and the Sugar Company?' she asked him when he returned. 'Did you have any luck?'

'I haven't found out anything about Danil. He's well known here. I asked about if he was reputable. No one seemed too certain. I've made an appointment to see the boss at the Fijian Sugar Company tomorrow afternoon. Sort out what kind of contract they have with this place,' he explained, but his mind was elsewhere. He had temporarily lost interest in the Plantation, in the light of his concerns about England.

'Shall I come with you tomorrow?'

'Stay here and swim, enjoy your holiday. There'll be nothing for you to do over there. I shall be sitting with telex machines, and telephones.'

Philippe worked late that night, leaving Kate to disappear upstairs alone. The house creaked its late-night emptiness.

Alone in Sam's bedroom she was feeling turbulent, blaming it on the hot, muggy nights, telling herself that they were sapping her energy, gnawing into her strength; but in truth she knew it was not so.

She was in need of company, someone to talk to. To confide her fears. Ironically, it was Sam she craved. She had been feeling uneasy, since the evening that Shyam Khumar had come to stay. His conversation about her father and the news about his death had unsettled her, had dogged her with a haunting fear. Why had no one else mentioned the question of a suspected suicide, or foul play? Philippe had dismissed any question of suicide as melodramatic nonsense. 'Don't be foolish, Petal, why should the old boy do such a thing?' But then he had been preoccupied, too busy with his work.

The following morning, when Kate awoke, Philippe was already on his way. She lay in the empty bed, arms stretched above her head, listening to the activity in the house beneath her, thinking about Lesa. The idea of leaving and returning to London depressed her. In spite of her strange sense of misgiving she knew that she did not feel ready to leave. Below, in the hallway, Philippe called out to her.

'See you later, *chérie.*' And he was gone.

'Yes,' she whispered.

She peeled off the muslin-thin white sheet and wandered towards the open window, lace curtains fluttering in the morning breeze, and peered out. Philippe was already setting off in the jeep with Stone. She envied him, wishing that she had insisted on going with him . . . she thought of Shyam Khumar and realised how very much she wanted to see him again. Sighing at her own indolence, she let go of the loosely hanging curtain, and decided to take a shower.

Dressed and downstairs she was still feeling despondent and strangely ill at ease. The thought of another empty day here filled her with dismay. Something about Lesa was nagging at her.

Ami had returned to the Plantation House.

'Ami!' Kate called as she glimpsed him passing the

verandah, flopping through the garden in rubber-thonged sandals, jeans rolled to his knees, pushing a wheelbarrow heavy with shiny new gardening tools and kitchen provisions fresh from the mainland.

He rested the barrow gratefully on the ground in front of him and turned to answer her call. His skin, damp from exertion, glistened in the heat. As she stepped on to the soft grass and headed towards him he watched her, grinning broadly.

'I wanted to thank you for helping with the supper the other evening, Ami,' she said as she approached, squinting to avoid the glare from the late-morning light.

'No, missus. It was special for me. He's the leader of our party, the Indian Party.' He took hold of the two string-covered handles on the battered wheelbarrow and began pushing it again across the well-cared-for lawn, around the side of the house towards the sheds, past a stacked pile of sawn-off palm-tree logs.

'And will he be Prime Minister, Ami?' Kate asked, sharing his enthusiasm.

'There's no Indian Prime Minister, missus. Always the same man wins. The Fijians don't let us rule.'

'Why's that?'

'They're afraid, missus.'

'Of you?' she smiled, doubting him.

He nodded.

'Am I disturbing you?' she asked casually.

He shrugged.

'Can you spare me a few minutes more? I'd like to talk to you. I won't detain you for long.'

Ami lowered his eyes, uncharacteristically sheepish or reticent, but he said nothing. He continued wheeling his provisions. Kate walked at his side. They reached the shed where he had to unload and pack away various hoes, rakes and shears. He began stacking them up against one of the outer walls. The putting of the generator and his continual goings and comings made it impossible for her to strike up any conversation so she strolled a few steps away from the throbbing noise and waited for him to finish.

'Would you like a glass of lemonade?' she invited warmly.

103

Ami laughed loudly, his eyes burning with life. 'Thanks, missus.'

They walked together to the scullery door, towards Jal sitting huddled expectantly on an outer step, Ami pushing his wheelbarrow of coffee and fresh vegetables. Inside Miriam was singing with the brio, if not the skill, of an Italian opera star. Her hand appeared through the scarcely open door. She passed biscuits to the waiting child who grabbed them readily. Then, seeing his father approach with Kate, he scuttled out of sight. The door opened wide and Miriam tossed breadcrumbs and tit-bits into the yard where greedy mynah birds, alert like soccer players, competed and fought for yet another meal.

'You're late with these, Ami,' she chided kindly.

'Miriam, could we have two glasses of lemonade, please?'

Miriam trundled inside.

'Did you go to visit your family yesterday?' Kate asked, chattering while they waited, unsure whether 'family' referred to his wife, or his parents.

'Yes, missus.' He was beginning to feel disconcerted by so many questions.

'And Jal stayed here?' Kate was curious to know why Jal had spent the day playing in her garden while his father was away on the mainland.

The cold lemonade appeared in two tall tumblers.

'Let's walk over towards the promontory,' she suggested, leading the way, carrying the glasses.

They settled themselves further up the hill, on the grass at the side of a six-foot-high, red poinsettia plant, out of sight of the main house. Kate handed Ami his drink. Their view out across the endless ocean was clear, a crisp lucid light.

'I want to ask you about my father,' Kate began.

Ami sipped his glass of lemonade and wiped the sweat from his brow with the tail of his stained T-shirt. . . .

'Yes, missus?' His eyes searched her uncertainly.

'Have you worked here long, Ami?'

'About a year.'

'You told me that you thought Sam was a kind man. Did you and he often talk to one another?'

104

'Sometimes.'

'What did you talk about?'

'I used to tell him about my plans. Business ideas. He liked to hear.'

'Did he tell you about his plans?'

'Not really, missus. He was a pretty quiet man.' Every answer Ami gave his voice questioned her, fearing her reasoning, yet drawn by her without knowing why or where she was leading him. She watched his gestures, searching for a clue.

'Did you ever think that perhaps he was quiet because he was depressed or worried about something?'

The boy looked surprised by the question. He screwed up his features, thinking for a moment before shaking his head.

'Do you know anything about his death? The circumstances of it, Ami?'

He stared dumbly, eyes wide as apples. She waited, compelling an answer. 'Do you, Ami?'

'Accident,' he replied brusquely.

'What, when he died?'

'Yes, missus.' He looked tense, lowering his eyes towards his glass. Cupping the tumbler in both hands, he rubbed at it with his fingers. It let out an unpleasant squeal like a trapped animal. The noise cut into the surrounding sounds of the day and then escaped across the promontory towards the horizon.

'What sort of accident, Ami?' she pressed.

'Hurt himself, missus, fell over. Too much alcohol.'

'Fell over drunk? Is that what you mean, Ami?'

'Yes, missus.'

'The day you drove me down the hill to see his grave. Why didn't you come with me?'

'Fijian land, missus. I'm not easy there.'

'All right, Ami, thank you. I'd better not keep you any longer.'

The young Indian got to his feet, ditching his half-emptied glass on the grass beside Kate, still seated. She saw his relief at being dismissed as she watched his back disappear out of sight, flopping off in his thonged sandals, back down the hill to his

105

wheelbarrow waiting by the back door. Idly she tipped the glass on to its side and watched the sticky, warm drink bleed out and seep into the crusty, grassed earth beneath her.

There is something else, she thought inexorably, something unspoken about Sam's death.

An accident? Suicide? She had supposed that he had died peacefully in his sleep. In truth, she had not paused to consider the cause of his death at all! During the two and more weeks since receiving the news of his death, her thoughts and questions about him had centred on his life, not his death, particularly those years after she had lost contact with him.

Ami had seemed ill at ease, almost unwilling to discuss it.

Why should Sam have been drinking so heavily? Why would anyone suspect foul play, or suicide? Or were Khumar and Ami simply confused?

Later, sitting alone at a hand-carved Burmese writing bureau in the living room, she settled to scribbling some letters. A letter to a gay friend in London, expressing her fears here. She had met him several years earlier in his antique shop in Notting Hill Gate, close to her home in Holland Park. Their friendship had blossomed instantly. On many a lonely afternoon she had wandered through the park to sit and talk with him. But the letter was a half-hearted attempt. In the midst of such isolation she felt the emptiness of her existence.

In the distance the old jeep could be heard revving its way back up the hill towards the rear of the house. She paid it no attention.

Minutes later Stone crossed into the living room on his way through to the office. 'Message from your husband,' he announced laconically.

'Oh?'

'Says he's got a coupla meetings that could take him all day. Says he'll be on the five o'clock ferry and back here after six.'

Sally, the smaller and less wiry of the two mongrels, padded in from the porch. She paced out a circle around Stone's feet and finally settled herself at his side, resting her gently panting torso against his bejeaned leg.

'Thank you,' Kate said, tentatively smiling before turning

106

back to her papers. Stone hesitated momentarily before moving towards his office.

'Listen,' he said, 'if it's driving you crazy stuck up here all day just yell, I'll get someone to drive you to Loquaqua this afternoon. You could mebbe take a look around, do some shopping. Meet your husband off the ferry. It's a bit of a hell hole though.'

'Thank you,' she said again, smiling at his thoughtfulness. 'Actually, I thought I might have a stroll later, walk down to one of the beaches and swim. It's quite safe here, isn't it?'

'No sharks, if that's what you're thinking. Leastways not inside the reef. Coupla danger spots though. Underwater caverns, strong currents. Stay close to shore, that's all.'

She noticed the beads of sweat drying around the rim of his well-worn, dust-caked panama. His face, unshaven – as always in the mornings, she had noticed – seemed more than usually jaded today. Looks like he's been drinking, she thought. She watched him gently nudge the mongrel whose snoozing body had collapsed over his left foot.

'Come on, gal,' he drawled softly. The animal sat up immediately, grateful for the attention, and lifted herself eagerly, tail wagging, ready to follow Stone into his office. Kate continued to watch him as his check-shirted back disappeared from view. She assessed that he must be at least fifteen years the junior of her deceased father and she wondered whether the changes, the loss of his boss, were the cause of his weariness, his recent surliness. It must be hard for him, she reflected, to accept Philippe and me.

'Mr Stone,' she called, surprising herself. He turned back to face her, leaning against the door frame, his face half shadowed by the brim of his hat.

'Yeah?' he muttered. The dog padded back and waited patiently, panting, at his side.

'Is the dog . . . was she my father's dog?'

'Yeah. Both were his. He liked dogs, Sam did. Specially mongrels. Waifs and strays.' He turned and disappeared. Kate got up and wandered out on to the porch.

Yes, Sam had always loved dogs. Their household had

107

always included at least two. Usually somebody's reject that Sam'd found in the street, or been given by a friend. The appearance of these strays had usually caused an argument.

'Don't bring him in, Sam. You don't know where he's bin. And it'll be me has to look after him,' her mother would argue. But the dogs always stayed. The mongrels and strays.

Kate lolled against the timbers and toyed with the paper-thin petals of the bougainvillaea, delicate as *papier poudre*, curling and twisting around her, the glorious blazing mixtures of purples, peaches and reds. A small ugly bird, brown, black and white in colouring with a custard-coloured beak and splayed custard feet, came to rest on the table close behind her. The mynah bird tore greedily at the congealing mess of Kate's untouched breakfast, screeched raucously at her and flew off, out of sight.

She sat on one of the rattan chairs but could not settle. The stillness, or perhaps the heat, was nagging at her. She stepped down from the verandah and wandered out into the late-morning sun shadowed by tall, overhanging branches. Every-where was still, quiet, save for the constant smothered sounds of distant cicadas, stirring waves and a putting generator.

Perhaps, in the end, Sam had needed me, she thought. Perhaps that's why he wrote.

Inside his office Stone watched her from behind his open window. He saw her bend and pick up a discarded coconut husk. Her light, short-sleeved frock billowed gracefully, like silent bubble gum, and fell to lean against her bent hips. He saw the line of her slender thighs through the delicate, lightweight material. She stood and walked to the edge of the headland which swept dramatically away from the house, and she paused for a moment before hurling the hirsute shell, sending it miraculously spinning into the shimmering hot light, before it plummeted to its rest, thudding against the damp, low-tide sand almost three hundred feet below her.

With her back to the house, she gazed out on to the water, hands clasped behind her like a schoolgirl and skirt flapping invitingly around her calves. She watched a scattered group of Fijian women idly fishing, wading up to their skirted thighs in the cobalt-green, transparent sea. The minute waves nudged against them like tongues caressing.

Stone turned away from the window, dug into his jeans pocket, pulled out a crushable packet of cigarettes and wandered slowly towards his desk. He picked up his zip lighter, buried beneath a mass of papers, and ignited it. The breeze from the window and the creaking overhead fan excited the lambent flame. Impatiently, he cupped his left hand, dragged on his cigarette and strode out on to the verandah, throwing the lighter back on to his desk as he left the office. The weight of it thudding on to the papers quietened their easy fluttering.

The bitch, Sally, who had been dozing beside an overly cluttered plastic waste-paper basket, opened her eyes and watched him leave, one ear cocked in anticipation, before deciding to pad along after him, out into the noonday stillness.

'I'm driving out to some o' the canefields. You wanna ride? Take a swim from one of the bays nearby, I'll drop you there,' he called, cigarette still in the corner of his mouth.

'Thanks.' She smiled, spinning to face him. 'I'll get my stuff.'

They rode together for a while in silence.

It was the first real opportunity that Stone had taken to observe her at such close proximity. She resembled his friend in a way, perhaps it was the aquiline nose. A strong feature in a man, but in a woman? Particularly a woman as fragile as she? It was too harsh for his taste. Even so, he found her attractive, and could not deny it.

Further down the hill the land flattened out. Green patchwork pockets of cane were growing in the sun. Other fields were black, burnt to the ground. Wide-open plains of plantation land unfurled before her. They passed a flame tree. It stood eloquent and alone. Its dark bean pods swung pendulously reminding Kate of gypsies' earrings.

'What's that burning?' she asked as they travelled downhill, inland towards the flat, still land.

'Canefields . . . those they've cut. It's good for the soil to burn them off. Kills off the rats and hornets too.'

109

Dark, distant smoke columns swirled into the compelling, cloudless sky like strands of wispy curled hair blowing in the wind.

They turned right, off the road, on to a pinkish, lateritic dust track that ran through the centre of two green, towering canefields, ripe for cutting. The jeep crossed over a two-track iron railway line embedded in the cracked earth.

'Know what that's for?' he asked her warmly.

Kate shook her head. She had not even noticed it.

'Sugar train. Collects the cut cane and takes it back along the track, all the way to the mill at Loquaqua.'

She had not noticed the track because she had been watching a dozen or so Indians working silently in a field to the left of them. They were cutting the cane with machete knives. The movement of the knives swinging through the still air created sounds of a whiplash cutting into the heat.

'Are they working for us?' she asked.

'Sure are,' he said. 'You're a rich little lady. You and your husband,' he added sardonically as he stopped the jeep and stepped out. 'Excuse me. I gotta talk to the guys.'

Stone crossed to where the men were working, calling to them as he strode. One Indian stilled his knife, dropped it to the ground and moved towards Stone. He wiped the sweat from his naked torso with the light palm of his hand. Kate watched as Stone gestured, pointing emphatically. He lifted a handful of ripe cane from the ground and the two men stood examining it, talking animatedly.

It was hotter here, away from the headland; no sea breeze. A little after midday and more than ninety-five degrees Fahrenheit. The Indian canecutters wore wide straw hats, broken and stringy round the brims. Behind them, where their work was finished, the field had been flattened. Dried broken cane lay discarded on the razed ground like carelessly laid rush matting. Two cows, white and beige, so thin their ribs created bow shapes down the side of their emaciated carcasses, grazed amongst the trammelled residue while birds and flies found their food on their backs and faces, clustering like currants in a cake around their doleful eyes.

110

Stone clapped the fellow lightly on the shoulder, took off his panama, wiped his brow with his shirt sleeve and sauntered back towards the jeep, looking ruminatively towards the sky as if searching for something. He climbed back into the jeep, started up the engine and they began to creep forward. Tall fields of green cane either side of them.

'We've been cuttin' almost 3000 tons o' sugar cane here each season. Never hadda a strike and never hadda a problem with being on time at the mill. It's a good track record. Sam was pretty proud.' Stone turned his concentration from the track and faced Kate directly. 'You don't have any feelings for him?'

Kate stared in disbelief. 'For my . . . for Sam? Yes, of course I have! What makes you ask that?' She averted her eyes and stared into an endless stretch of tender young cane, its tips shimmering in the sunlight.

'You've never asked anything about him. Nothing at all. No photos or anything. He said he hadn't seen ya for years.'

'Whose fault was that?' she cried angrily before rounding on him, adding defiantly, 'And what about you, Mr Stone? Do you have any family?'

'Sure, I got a family, somewhere. But that's different.'

'Why? Why is that different?' Kate was not sure why she was becoming so upset. Was he blaming her? She felt tears inexplicably surfacing. Her voice quivered and her throat felt heavy.

'Because, Mrs De Marly, I am not living in their place and planning to knock it all down, change it, without knowing what it meant to them.'

'Change it . . . what do you mean?' she stammered. A tear ran treacherously down her cheek toward her burning ear. She felt relieved that it was her left ear, so he could not see it.

'Your old man died for this place. He didn't want no one to take it away from him.'

'Died for the place . . .' She felt her stomach heave with fear. 'What are you talking about?' She saw him pause before speaking, as if considering what to tell her.

111

'He said no matter what they offered he wouldn't sell. And now you're turning it into a bloody holiday resort!'

'Holiday resort! . . . But what . . . Did Philippe tell you that?'

'He sure as hell did.'

One of the cows mooed into the heat. She could hear someone shouting across the field behind her. '*Khana!*' another called. Incomprehensible words.

'What's happening?' she asked him.

'They're calling to one another in Hindi. Time to eat,' he explained.

'I need a glass of water,' she sighed. She needed time to collect her thoughts. In spite of her sunhat she was feeling queasy. She supposed it must be the jostling of the jeep combined with the overpowering smell of leaking diesel, and she wanted more than anything in the world to get out of the truck and away from Stone.

She rummaged nervously in her cotton beach bag in search of a handkerchief. The gesture was reminiscent of her mother who had always kept one close by her, for use during the long silences at mealtimes. Kate pictured her mother now: a lonely, brooding creature who had never forgiven Fate for the loss of her husband. Who had never understood Sam's desertion. She had always carried a handkerchief, repeatedly blowing her nose, twisting and aggravating the thing between her brittle fingers to break the monotony or ease her despairing, forlorn incomprehension. A Catholic girl who lived and died trapped in her own loneliness. Kate had been with her. 'You care more for those bloody dogs than you do your own, Sam,' she used to say to him. 'What about Katie and me?'

'You all right?' Stone asked uncertainly.

She nodded, clutching the white linen to her lips, struggling to breathe deeply. Her heart was beating in her mouth. She kept inhaling, slowly and deeply, trying to calm herself. She was feeling stunned. Stone put his left arm uncertainly across the back of her seat, gently brushing her shoulder, in a gauche effort to understand and console her. She stiffened.

'I want to know what you mean about my father . . . dying

112

for the Plantation.' She spoke slowly, like a dumb creature struggling to form sounds. Stone sighed and eased his arm from her shoulder but leaving it seconds longer resting on the back of the seat. He was searching uncertainly for words, for a place to begin, tapping the outside of his jeans in his agitated hunt for cigarettes. He discovered them in his left pocket.

'Listen,' he said finally. He stuck a cigarette in his mouth and continued the search for his lighter. It was on the desk in his office, holding the papers in place. 'Shit! Gotta light?'

She shook her head so he took the unlit cigarette from his mouth and held it in the same hand as the crushed packet which rustled each time he made a gesture.

'I'm not great with explanations and I don't know the score. Sam didn't discuss it with me, except he said something about getting an offer for the place. I think it was some guy he knew, he didn't say, but he did say that it was a bloody good offer and he'd be a fool to refuse . . .' Stone began automatically to lift the cigarette to his lips before realising that it was still unlit. 'I gotta get a light for this damn thing.' He was restless and agitated. Kate could see that. He stepped on the idling accelerator and, after several shots at a three-point turn in the narrow lane, he swung the jeep around and was heading back along the track to where the Indians had been working and were now lunching from their packs.

'But you said . . .' She had to raise her voice to be heard above the roar of the engine. He was driving fast. 'You said he didn't want to sell? That he died for the place?'

A small group of Indians sat squatting close to one another, eating with their fingers. Kate could not clearly discern what, but supposed it must be some sort of bread and vegetables. Stone stepped out of the jeep and walked back towards the men. She watched him as he bent low and took a light from one of the crouching labourers, pocketed some matches that they gave him in his wash-worn denims and returned to the truck. His boots pounded into the dry earth causing dust to leap about around his legs.

113

'Let's get outa here. Find some shade,' he said.

Once again they were driving in silence, for what seemed to her several miles, twisting and turning along dust-track lanes, bumping along past waving sugar plants or fields with scorched, cindered stubble. The native village homes were corrugated shacks in various shades of rust. One or two were painted a Calor-gas blue to match the endless sky, creating the illusion of patchwork villages. Everyone smiled and waved as they hurtled by but, unusually, neither of them responded to the warm-hearted greetings.

In the distance behind them as they drove away from the canefields could be heard the low, slow moan of the sugar train. Whoooo! Oooo! it brayed, echoing against the distant mountains, warning of its empty passage back along the track from Loquaqua towards the cane-workers hacking in the heat.

Kate sensed an anger burning in Stone, firing him with silence. He flung his smoked cigarette butt on to the passing roadside and drove with his eyes concentrating on the road.

'What happened to the offer for the Plantation? Why didn't Sam sell it?' she asked eventually, nervous of disturbing the wall of silence that had grown between them. He made no response.

Once more they turned off the asphalted main road, this time to the left, and wound their way along a path that was encrusted with thick, dried tyre tracks. Then the ground beneath them began to change consistency. It was becoming sandy. Stone drove onwards, towards a dilapidated building directly ahead of them. It seemed to be a small factory with sections fabricated from corrugated iron sheeting overgrown with vegetation. He halted the jeep some twenty yards in front of the building and pulled on the brake which screeched like a dying rodent.

Growing alongside the building were walls of banana trees laden with unripened fruit. Two hundred yards or so in the distance, beyond the building, Kate could make out the dulcet sounds of the sea with its tranquil, early-afternoon tide. Waves, such as they were, licked the shore. The entire building, as far as she could tell, was surrounded by a casing of curled and rusting barbed wire. To the left of her, in front of the primitive wiring, stood a tall wooden sign, splintered and discoloured by the sun and the briny air. Printed in bold white lettering, it read:

'LESA SUGAR MILL. KEEP OUT.'

And underneath, in Hindi:

'LESA KI CHINI KI KHETI.
ANDAR ANNA MANNA HAI.'

'In the old days, before my time here or Sam's, Lesa crushed its own cane. That was done here. The main entrance is around the other side, facing the water, where the freighters stood waiting for the sugar cargo. But the place hasn't been opened for donkey's years. All our sugar is crushed at the Loquaqua mill now.'

Stone sat for a moment contemplating the ugly building. Then he pushed open the truck door, climbed out and strode towards the wire wall. Kate remained a few moments, confused as to why he had brought her there, deciding whether to follow him. Finally, she shoved at the broken door with her left shoulder and moved towards him. Her flat, open sandals gathered sand beneath her feet. She considered taking the shoes off before noticing the refuse dumped in amongst the hardy weeds growing like brush in the arid soil: broken bottles, a perished Wellington boot, beer cans, even a recently dead cat, circled by flies, its face frozen into a snarl with its stiff tongue hanging out, as though strangled.

Swiftly she averted her gaze, fearing she might gag; hurried towards Stone and stood beside him, to his left. He was staring, apparently at nothing, transfixed by the ground in front of them, between them and the building. 'Twenty-six years Sam owned this place. Came over from Hong Kong. Made some good money there, he said, and wanted to settle a bit, make something of himself. Lesa had gone to seed. He got it cheap, worked at it, built it up. Made a reputation for himself. Anyone would've worked for him . . .' Stone stood quiet and then, 'He

115

used to come down here regularly, just to sit on the beach. God knows why. He called it his "spot". And this is where they found the old bugger,' he mumbled, almost inaudibly.

They stood together in silence; several small butterflies fluttered noiselessly amongst the sand weeds. Overhead Kate could hear gulls screeching greedily, cracking into the solemnity like nutcrackers into a walnut. Eventually Stone kicked at a misshapen beer can and wandered off alongside the building, in the direction of the beach, where he crouched in the sand like a native, and lit himself another cigarette with the matches given to him by the canecutters.

'He said,' he began as Kate approached and sat silently at his side, 'mebbe we'll sell the old place. Make a killing for ourselves, move on, and go buy the biggest goddam farm in Western Australia.'

'What happened?'

'I don't know. He changed, became sullen and angry, disillusioned. Said he wouldn't sell the land to nobody, no matter what they offered, said he'd rather die first.' Stone took a long drag on his cigarette and then hurled the half-smoked butt towards the water. He watched it smoking in the scorching sand before its light died.

'I asked him what was going on but he refused to talk about it. Just started working longer hours, spending time over with the cutters, drinking. I knew something was eating him but he wouldn't discuss it with me. All I knew was we weren't selling and all he'd talk about was responsibilities . . .' He turned to Kate and smiled at her, a soft, bruised contact. 'I watched him. I knew your old man pretty well. He was a hot-tempered Irishman, a tough-drinking wanderer, but a fair boss and an honest man. We drank together and whored together. Had done for years.'

Kate felt herself wince at this remark but hoped he hadn't noticed. 'When was all this?' she asked.

'Four months ago, mebbe three. I'm not exactly sure. It was going on for some time. I thought the old bugger was cracking up. Went off plenty of nights on his own and got pretty loaded. Then one dawn, about four weeks ago, he was found down here. Been dead a coupla hours.' He paused to wipe the palm of his hand across his salivaed mouth and then, cupping his stubbled chin in his stained fingers, he kneaded it like dough. A newly lit smoking cigarette caused his uncommonly bloodshot, pouched eyes to water.

'Perhaps that's why he wrote to me.'

'Fell in the dark and hit his head. They said it was an accident.' He stood up and walked towards the sea, leaving Kate alone to watch him, chewing on what she had just heard.

'You wanna ride back up to the house?' he called as he trudged, minutes later, along the warm sand towards where she was still sitting.

'No thanks, I'll swim and then walk back. It's not too far, is it?'

He shook his tousled head and stared back towards the headland. Kate shaded her eyes to follow his gaze and could just make out the house. She accompanied him back towards the parked jeep – neither spoke – and collected her bag from the back seat. It was covered in a light film of dust.

'You take care now,' he said softly. 'The sun is pretty strong.' He opened the door and swung himself into the driver's seat. Kate made no move.

'Mr Stone?'

Stone lifted his hand away from the key and looked up at her.

'What's that?' he asked.

'Sam's accident . . .' she stumbled, 'A friend of my husband's came to supper last week . . . he mentioned something about suicide, or . . .?'

'Who, ol' Sam? Bullshit!' He started the engine and the jeep jolted backwards and then swung around beside her, ready to make its way along the rutted lane towards the road. 'Listen,' he yelled above the chuntering, spitting engine, 'walk on about half a mile towards the house. Don't swim here. Strong currents. Head towards Plantation Bay.'

Without waiting for a reply he took off, leaving a trail of sand clouds swirling in the lane behind him.

Chapter 9

Kate stood watching the diminishing jeep until it was out of sight then turned and faced the sugar mill, scene of her father's death, to gaze up at its inert form. She felt a relief knowing it hadn't been suicide – after all, he had been a Catholic – but she wondered what he might have been doing there that fatal night. She drew closer, two or three tentative steps only, longing to know something about the man, as if willing the impassive, inaccessible edifice to shed its lurking secret.

But the impudent mill remained motionless, veiling itself in a cloak of corrosion and creeping vegetation.

All at once the air about her smelt acrid yet sweet. She shuddered and hurried towards the beach, clambering over several yards of untidy, rusted measures of barbed wire sinking into the soft sand. They had somehow disentangled themselves from the prohibiting wall, or perhaps been dragged at some earlier time by trespassers, and lay partially covered in the sand. This fallen wire had left an opening in the fencing. Hardly big enough for a human, she observed, but she made her way towards the jagged, forbidden entrance just the same. Her unexpected discovery made her careless in navigating the displaced wire and as she stepped over it, too quickly, she tore the flesh on her right calf and let out a piercing yelp which cut into the chasm of still, awesome heat. The cry disturbed something. A small, lizardy, green-banded creature with markings as brilliant as its camouflaging vegetation scurried out from under a nearby bush and swaggered off, terrified, in search of less distressing surroundings. Kate held her ground until the primeval-looking reptile had disappeared and then slowly she inched her way towards the rusty gap and peered beyond it into an overgrown yard. It was impossible to see anything beyond burgeoning foliage so, still clinging to her scored leg and too shaken to squeeze herself through the ripped wiring, she paused to catch her breath.

All was quiet once more, save for her knocking heart, the buzzing of the crickets and something else. She closed her eyes and listened hard. It felt too still. The suffocating heat gave off a stench. It felt foetid and evil. She imagined silent eyes watching her. And then something stirred, rustled, close by the banana trees. It began moving, hurrying towards her. Terrified, she let go of her damp flesh and fled from the infested place across the white sand towards the sea in search of somewhere cool to bathe her still bleeding leg.

Sitting in the salt water she heard a cry like a banshee wailing into the heat for her dead father, and glanced back fearfully towards the building. It was a scrawny ginger cat, wild-eyed and hungry, stalking in the undergrowth.

Having unstrapped her sandals and sluiced the congealing blood from her lower calf Kate began to make her way along the endless stretch of deserted beach, feeling glad, in the relentless heat, to have a hat. Her cotton beach bag swung loosely over her shoulder as she splashed her bare feet, still swollen and aggravated by the sand in her shoes, against the barely lapping waves, causing the salt water to sting her grazed flesh.

She felt entirely isolated and relieved to be so. She craved space; a timeless term of solitude. Once or twice she passed black-breasted fisherwomen wading silently in the warm reef waters. One caught sight of her and waved lazily but Kate simply moved relentlessly onwards. Although hot and tired, she was restless, unable to stop, fearful of pausing, even to swim. A Fijian native with shining skin smothered in coconut oil watched her from the root of an upturned coconut tree. He sat ruminatively smoking, surrounded by green-meshed fishing nets drying in the sun, following her with his languid eyes as she marched self-consciously on; hurrying on her journey to nowhere.

She shielded her eyes and glanced upwards, along the uninhabited coastline towards the headland and, catching sight of her Plantation House, she longed never to have set eyes on it. She was feeling tremulous and uncomfortable. From high above the jagged cliff face she felt she was being beckoned by an alien hand. A familiar yet disturbing voice was calling to her, asking something of her, and she feared she had no courage to answer it.

She came across a turtle lying dead in its upturned shell; its stiff flippers rose helplessly into the brittle heat. She thought of her father lying drunk and helpless, dead in the early dawning light, and it made her weep, mourning that she had not helped him, that she had never known him.

Minutes passed; unknown time passed. And still the heat from the overhead sun beat down on her, weakening and tiring her. She kept walking until, it seemed finally, she reached Plantation Bay where she threw her bag on to the white sand and herself after it, still clinging to her sandals, one in either hand,

She lay listening to the water splashing softly against the shore; a soothing, whispering rhythm. Her skirt billowed in the late-afternoon breeze and floated down against her face, leaving her thighs naked to the burning heat. She glanced up at the cloudless sky. A gull was loitering above her, hovering on a current of warm air. She closed her eyes but was still disturbed by thoughts of her dead father. The stranger who, after years of silence, had reached out to her from another life. Her hand searched blindly for the top button on her light dress which she released allowing her slim, pallid form and white breasts an introduction to the sun. Recklessly she spreadeagled herself, mingling her delicate flesh with the welcoming bed of sand.

An unidentified figure, a silhouette imperceptible as a dot on the horizon, has observed her from the cliff-top and has moved slowly down the track towards where she is lying, sandlogged.

He, this white man, creeps towards her and finds her on the ground, unable to move.

He stares down at her. His swarthy face is a mass of hirsute skin with grey-blue eyes shining, brilliantly dangerous. He takes her by the hand, whispering her full name, 'Katherine', and tries forcibly to pull her up but she is afraid and won't move from her place on the sand, lying amongst the waves that have swept up around her and cradled her sodden body. Her long hair streams about her in the water like soaked samphire.

'Hey lady,' he says, softly shaking her. 'I think you oughta get in outa the sun.'

Katherine does not respond. He stands watching her naked body, motionless except for her breasts bobbing in the waves. They are burnt and pink. He kneels down, touches them, caresses them and then presses both his arms into the sand beneath her. Lifting her up against his rough, sunbleached check shirt he carries her to a cave; dark, dank, sepulchral, where two other figures are standing in the shadows patiently waiting.

Are you waiting for me?

Inexplicably, the cave is familiar to her. The older of the two men, dressed in a chasuble, stands with his back to her, leaning forward, lighting two tall white candles. A scraggy ginger cat sits at his side wearing a Tibetan bell around his neck.

The second man is an Indian. He steps towards her and leads her towards the older, leaning figure. At the same time he hands matches to the one who has carried her into the cave and orders him to stand guard at the rocky entrance lest any intruder should dare to enter.

Katherine confesses to feeling afraid. Her voice echoes and sounds unfamiliar to her. She fears her husband. What if he should find me here, in the company of strangers . . .?

She begins to panic but the unknown, unrevealed figure turns to pacify her. He is holding his fingertips together as in prayer. She sees now that his long robe is the dress of a priest in service. His voice is rough, yet soothing, a familiar brogue, but his face is invisible.

She is led by the Indian to a darkened corner and told, softly,

121

to lie down. The ground is rough and without protection yet it feels moist and welcoming against her skin. The rock floor changes to a cushion of earth smelling of undergrowth, oozing and briny. Small sand weeds begin to grow around her, encircling her limbs with rusting bracelets of barbed wire while the Indian stands above her, shadowing the candlelight from her face and creating a giant black, flickering adumbration on the cave wall.

Slowly, he kneels at her feet and, desirous of her, lays himself upon her with the carnal ease of an incubus. His slender weight melts into her like thick, warm oil. She turns her head away from his libidinous gaze and watches his other figure, the overgrown shadow puppet, moving rhythmically on the cave wall, as she feels him draw her apart and love her.

'This is the land of lotus eating,' he whispers. 'We will not betray you.' The whites of his eyes glow like eggshells in the dusky light.

The faceless, cloaked man looks on encouragingly, moving his arms in a motion of blessing. And then he stops, turns towards the cave entrance, growing angry. His non-existent face has transformed itself into a devilled creature's with pouched, bloodshot eyes. He growls in fury as Katherine turns to discover her husband, standing over her, watching her . . . bellowing like an enraged beast, holding a shining knife above her which he plunges into the back of her lover . . . his roar echoes through the cave . . .

Kate sat bolt upright, trembling and frightened. Where was she? She looked anxiously about her and realised that she was still lying in the sand on the beach at Plantation Bay. It was evening with a sting still in the setting sun. She rubbed at her throbbing head. She had been dreaming. An ugly dream. It had unnerved her, confused her.

Dusk was beginning to fall. Her skin was prickling, and she was shaken and afraid. She looked about her and, seeing in the distance the early-evening kerosene lamps lighting up, one after another, shining out across the water from the house, she realised that she still had a long walk ahead of her, negotiating the unfamiliar hill in the falling darkness. She lifted herself to her feet, gathered up her bag and began to trudge unsteadily along the beach in search of a path that led to the hillside road.

Philippe would be back from the mainland already, around six he had said, and would be wondering what had happened to her. Hadn't he asked her to do something, or was she just confused? Her dream horrified her as she walked.

Chapter 10

Philippe was standing alone, amidst the darkening reflections of twilight. Receiver to his ear, he was staring absent-mindedly out of the window down on to the water, on to the sinking remnants of what had been a flaming sunset. Beside him, well-thumbed documents fluttered lightly on the desk, beneath an idly whirring fan. The tips of his hair had been bleached blond by the tropical sun but he was looking exhausted. He was speaking on the telephone to Danil.

'Mr De Marly,' the odious New Zealander breathed casually into the phone. 'My client feels that you are driving a very hard bargain. He regrets that it would be difficult for us to exceed our present, rather exceptional offer, but he has reminded me that I had rather foolishly omitted to mention the . . . er . . . let us say . . . arrangements of the settlement.'

Philippe listened with a certain curiosity and more than a little disgust. Danil, he felt, was no ambassador in the game of business in which he considered himself an accomplished master.

'I thought that I had already made it clear to you, Danil,' he baited, 'that my plantation is not for sale, at any price.'

The obese, unseen breath drawled and began again.

'We understand that you have been making tentative enquiries about releasing the Lesa Plantation from its contract with the Fijian Sugar Company two years before its contractual completion date. We also understand that you have plans for using the land as a holiday resort?'

Philippe felt a nerve bruise momentarily. It had been no more than a few hours since he had left his meeting with the general manager of the Fijian Sugar Company. And indeed, having learnt the terms signed by the Lesa Plantation, he had made an offer to buy out his contract. Danil, the old fox, was wilier than he had supposed.

'What is it that "your client" wants to add to his offer?' he demanded brusquely. In the yard outside the dogs began barking vigorously. Philippe took no notice, except to feel aggravated by the distraction. The crackling on the line had already caused him to miss Danil's vital words. 'I can't hear you. It's a poor reception this time of day here. You'll have to speak up!'

'I said, all monies owing to you would be paid into whatever country would best suit your needs. We were thinking that perhaps Geneva, Switzerland, might seem attractive to you. Obviously, you would stipulate your choice of currency.'

Philippe waited, allowing the line to fall silent, save for interference. He heard Danil's asthmatic breath heaving and wheezing into his ear. And still he remained quiet.

'What is your answer, Mr De Marly?' the insidious spokesman hissed.

'Perhaps, Mr Danil, I should talk directly with your client –'

'Mr De Marly, as you will appreciate,' Danil cut in abrasively, 'time is of the essence, to us both. Bureaucracy is our burden here and change creates suspicion. Let me remind you that you are an outsider here, Mr De Marly. There will most certainly be opposition to your development. That I can promise you . . .' He hesitated. 'But this way, if you wisely accept our offer, your rewards will be immediately realised. These islands are in a time of change and neither sugar nor tourism are secure industries . . .'

'So what's in it for you, Danil? What's your client so certain about?' Philippe caught the sound of the lawyer's breath as it wavered and gasped perceptibly.

125

'Don't be foolish, Mr De Marly. We, quite simply, are locals, and freehold land, as you well know, is a rare enough commodity here. But we are fortunate enough to have the resources to offer you a more than fair price,' Danil purred, at the helm once more.

'I'll let you know,' Philippe concluded, flipping the worn Bakelite switch on the antiquated radio telephone to OFF, thereby shutting out the constant intrusive crackle on the island reception wave. Pensively, he recradled the receiver. The sun had set, leaving the office in blackness and Philippe a solitary shadowed silhouette contemplating Danil's latest move. Outside in the yard one of the mongrels continued to yap.

Unexpectedly the office door opened. It was Stone followed by Sally trailing at his work-soiled boots. Before Sam's death and the arrival of De Marly, Stone had always worked into the dusk, sometimes later. He and Sam had frequently polished off the best part of a bottle of Scotch while going through papers, talking tactics, ordering supplies or simply sitting in the evening light getting as drunk as fish. Tonight it was exceptional that he was not already settled for the evening in his village. He had worked until after five and then, before De Marly's return, had set off down the hill but Kate had not returned and it had concerned him. 'I'll swim and then walk back,' she had said. That was early afternoon. He had put it to the back of his mind until he had stepped from his shower and realised that his lighter must still be on his desk. Then he had been glad to have an excuse to return.

He paused now in the doorway surprised to find anyone in the shadowed office, a room that he considered to be his private territory. He switched on the light. It momentarily blinded the pensive De Marly who had not heard the latch turn.

'Stone, have you seen my wife?'

'Nah, I don't think so. Leastways not for a few hours,' the Australian replied, lifting his head to regard the man who was still standing at his desk.

'That's strange, I mentioned that I was going to the

126

mainland this morning and told her that I might need her when I got back. I thought she'd be here. You gave her my message, I hope?'

Stone nodded. 'Yep.'

'When she turns up,' Philippe continued, 'be so kind as to tell her that I'm in the living room and that I've got something for her to sign, will you please?' The two men crossed one another as Philippe headed towards the doorway and Stone to his desk. Stone sat shuffling through the papers in search of his misplaced lighter.

Philippe swung round as he departed, casually leaning back into the office. 'I don't suppose you have a Qantas timetable, do you? I've had no time to get one this afternoon.'

'Sorry, mate. We don't have much call for that sort o' thing out here,' Stone replied sarcastically, not bothering to look up.

'Mmmm.' Philippe moved across the high-ceilinged hall-way and into the expansive, open-plan living area where he had thrown his briefcase and tortoiseshell spectacles before hurrying into the deserted office to answer Danil's unexpected call. He made his way thoughtfully back to the sofa, a primitive two-seater adorned with two neatly pressed, white lace antimacassars, sat down, opened up the sleek leather case, and pulled out several foolscap brown envelopes, each containing similar-sized typed sheets of papers, forms or contracts.

He unclipped his black and gold Mont Blanc from a leather pen holder in the top of the briefcase and settled back into the seat in preparation for a little study, before realising that he was thirsty, or more accurately, in need of a drink. Danil's challenge, for that was how he perceived it, was orbiting inside his mind. Carelessly, he threw the papers on to the empty couch cushion beside him and looked around. The room had recently been dusted and all signs of life had been lovingly tidied away, replaced by painstakingly arranged frangipani flowers resting on beds of their own tropical leaves, left there to brighten this sparsely inhabited room.

There appeared to be no cupboard or sideboard that could contain bottles. The room was furnished with a multitude of

127

cane chairs; the one sofa; a bookcase crammed with shabby paperbacks, post-war orange Penguins, and other yellowing-paged stories telling of love, lust and cannibalism in the South Pacific; several carved wooden lamps; twin brass lights and the dark hand-carved Burmese writing desk that Kate had sat at earlier in the day. It was still covered with her blue airmail envelopes and sheets of blank paper curled by the day's heat.

Philippe lifted himself impatiently from the seat, still grasping his pen, and walked to the door. 'Where the hell is Kate?' he muttered irritably as he threw it open.

'Miriam!' he bellowed along the narrow corridor. There was no response. Sally padded from the office into the hall, sniffed about her uninterestedly and returned to doze at her favourite spot, beside Stone's desk. It was almost seven. Philippe supposed that Miriam was in the kitchen preparing supper. He bellowed her name again.

'Miriam!'

Slowly the scullery door opened as, at the very same moment across the hallway, Stone's office door slammed impatiently shut. Miriam strolled casually into distant view, characteristically wiping her hands on an apron reminding Philippe of *Gone with the Wind*.

'Have you seen my wife?' He spoke patiently.

'No.'

'Bring me a whisky please, Miriam, with lots of ice.'

'No ice. Generator broke down a while this afternoon and no ice is ready yet.'

'Well, just bring the whisky then, and a jug of water, please.'

Without waiting for a reply he closed the door and returned to his papers, deciding that he would be glad to get off the islands. God-forsaken place, he thought. Nothing ever works here.

He spent the next hour reading every contract, every one of Sam's letters filed with the land papers, scoured again the solicitor's copy of the will but found amongst them not even a fraction of a clue. There seemed to be no plausible reason for anyone to offer such a sum for the estate, freehold or otherwise, unless, he concluded, there was something that he had not yet discovered. Something about the place that he did not know.

After his second whisky he abandoned the oppressive living room, preferring to pace deliberately around the torchlit garden. It hadn't occurred to him to be worried by Kate's overdue absence although it was now a crow-black eight o'clock. As always here, after sundown, night fell speedily. His mind was caught up with another, more pressing detail: Danil, or – more specifically – the identity of the hungry, anonymous force behind Danil. Something must be decided before they left for England.

He strolled back to the round table on the porch where he had left his locked briefcase and the whisky bottle and wearily poured another much-needed Scotch.

Kate was exhausted, struggling to make her way up the uneven hill, cloaked in a bone-black light. All around her, nestling amongst distant waving palms, kerosene lamps glinted in the middle darkness while distant cries of native laughter screeched and hooted, incomprehensible language reverberating through the whistling fronds. Unknown villages and tiny settlements were preparing for their evening entertainments as she laboured with the gentle hillside wind biting into her burnt goose-pimpled flesh.

In the daylight the walk had seemed a comfortable, even inviting distance but now, shaken and sunburnt, every shadow remodelled itself into a rapacious enemy and every screeching insect or bird made her jump out of her terrified skin. She looked about her, constantly fearful of meeting any stranger yet yearning for assistance. She had no notion of the time, nor any certainty of the distance ahead of her. Feeling nauseous and unsure, she decided to pause for breath, steadying herself against a haglike flinty rock that jutted obscenely over the cliff face and glared down on to the lapping navy water.

She wiped her damp face with the hand towel from her swimming bag and stared out across the sea. The opaque lights of modest fishing vessels bobbed like beacons in the blackness.

129

Her dream was still disturbing her; as was her journey with Stone earlier in the afternoon. Something was being concealed, she feared, and the secrecy was tormenting her.

And she was furious with Philippe! He was betraying her! Why had he spoken to Stone about his plans for a holiday resort without discussing the idea with her first? She regretted visiting the island at all. What was the point? Philippe had, as usual, been right. 'Why dig up the past?' he had said. 'It will only make you miserable.'

Perhaps they should have returned directly to London, and simply put the Plantation on the market. Yet, even now, she longed to know more about Sam. His memory haunted her. It always had. But the memory that she had carried of him, the picture that her mother had painted of him seemed so alien, so out of tune with the generous man that both Stone and Khumar had known and cared for. She wondered again what had happened to him. Why had he changed his plans about selling the Plantation? What had possessed him suddenly to find her and write to her? Had he needed her help in some way? Had he known that he was dying? How had he found her? Perhaps he had always known where she was. Secretly watching over her while she had pined for him, believing that she had been left alone in the darkness?

She felt a surge of violent anger towards Philippe. He had no right to make plans without consulting her. After all, it was she who owned the place, not he. Sam had left his legacy to her. And she was not going to allow Philippe to turn her patrimony into a holiday resort!

With renewed energy she commenced her climb but, hearing the distant moan of an engine on the road above her, she stood still. It's Philippe looking for me, she thought with a sigh of relief. 'Philippe! I'm here! Down here!' she bellowed into the phosphorescent night. There was no response. Only the quiet whine of a motor drawing closer, wending its careful way down the narrow, potholed track. She leant back against the rock and waited, her heart thumping with relief. Logic told her that this was the only trackway and the driver could not fail to find her.

Actually she was mistaken. She herself had passed several inland slip-roads camouflaged in the darkness by clusters of trees, any of which led to concealed thatched bures and dwellings whose occupants would have welcomed her with water, or even pounded kava root to drink. Any one of these unseen lanes would normally have been the driver's destination, usually approached by him on foot, but not tonight. Tonight the sole purpose of his journey was his search for Kate.

When De Marly had enquired after his wife earlier, Stone had been very concerned that she had not yet returned. After hearing Philippe call out again he had discreetly enquired of Miriam and had learnt that Kate had not been seen all day. He was the last person to have seen or spoken to her. He feared that perhaps she had not listened to him, that she had been foolish enough to swim close to the mill and so he had decided to set off down the track to look for her, alone, without alerting Philippe.

Kate heard the jeep approaching and rushed forward from the pathway on to the car track to halt it. But before she was able to call out, dazzled by the headlights, she lost her footing and stumbled in the darkness on the loose stones. A pain shot up through her leg. She had twisted her ankle and could not move.

Stone drew closer. Kate cried out to him, fearful that he would not see her collapsed on the ground. He heard her cry and shoved his foot hard on to the brake. The jeep skidded for several feet, its tyres whirring on the loose shaly ground. Amidst the dusty spray Kate screamed out, 'Stop! For God's sake!' She flung herself on her side, dragging her twisted leg.

The jeep screeched to a halt inches in front of her.

'Jesus! Are you all right?' Stone called, seeing the outline of her outstretched frame illuminated by the headlights.

'Yes, I think so,' she wept.

'Need some help?'

She shook her head.

'You'd better get in.'

She tried to drag herself to her feet but found she couldn't move. 'I've hurt my ankle,' she whispered hoarsely.

Stone locked the handbrake on, threw the gearstick into

reverse, then climbed out and made his way around the front of the bonnet. He put his arms around her trembling waist and lifted her, carrying her to the passenger door, wrenching it open. 'It always sticks, this bloody thing!' And with one almighty heave he unfastened the door and helped her in, cautiously holding on to her elbow as she climbed unsteadily into the jalopy.

'I'll have to take her down the hill to turn her round. It's too narrow here. You better hold on tight. It's a bumpy ride,' he commanded, once back at the wheel.

Kate obeyed silently. The throbbing in her ankle was easing. She prayed it was not a sprain.

Stone slammed the gearstick into first and the battered vehicle lurched off down the hill, growling like a disgruntled beast. Kate scrutinised Stone's shadowed face in the darkness, realising for the first time that she had been expecting Philippe, not him, before turning her attention towards the ocean.

'Thank you,' she muttered softly.

Lights from the other tiny islands beamed and blinked in the black night. 'What made you look for me?' she asked.

'Your husband was asking for you.'

'Yes, I suppose he was. I thought you were him,' she explained. She heard him scoff in the darkness.

'Where d'you go?'

'Oh, nowhere special, just walking . . . thinking. Did you tell him you'd seen me?'

'No,' he replied.

She casually wondered why he hadn't mentioned it but thought better of asking.

'Mr Stone?'

'Yeah.'

'Do *you* think my father's death was an accident?'

'That's what they said.'

The jeep had reached the clearing in the road that led inland to Timi's village and then, a little further, became the beginnings of the asphalt road that led along the coast to Loquaqua. Stone knew every indentation, every boulder on this piece of coastland. He knew they were close to a drop where, yards beneath them, water lapped against a patch of shingled shore. He shoved the gearstick into reverse, it grated and the engine roared. They made the turn without difficulty.

He returned to first and they began labouring back up the hill, in silence. Kate surreptitiously watched him, never turning her head towards him. They passed the craggy rock where she had rested and fallen and where he had found her. Soon they would be at the house.

'Had he been drinking then?'

'Who?'

'Sam!' She was losing patience. 'Was he drunk when he fell and hit his head? She spoke every word emphatically, tersely.

'What the hell difference does it make whether he'd been drinking? He's dead, isn't he?'

'Mr Stone, I want to know what happened to him. Shyam Khumar said that it was suicide, or natural causes. You said it was an accident. Is that what you think? Was it an accident?' She was shouting, raising her voice hysterically above the slow groan of the engine.

He stopped the car, slamming on the footbrake, and stared towards the water, away from her. She waited patiently for him to turn, to say something. She longed to see his face but it was dark. No moon yet.

'He was murdered,' he whispered, almost inaudibly, not turning, keeping his gaze on the water. Her breath caught in her throat, her flesh shuddered.

'Leastways, that's what I believe. He must've been under some kinda pressure to sell the place. I suppose that's why he left it to you . . . family. Guess he thought you'd never come here. Leave me to run it without giving me the power to sell it. I dunno . . . dunno what he was afraid of . . . angry about. . . . Something though.'

She sat numbly. Having dreaded the truth, she was now stupefied. 'Have you talked to the police?'

'There was no inquest. Death by natural causes, they said. He'd been drinking. Stumbled in the dark. The fall killed him. There was no enquiry. There's nothing to tell the police.'

133

'I see.' Rage howled within her, uncoiling like a waking viper in her groin. Her mouth was dry. It smarted as if cut. 'Take me back, please.'

They climbed the hill, isolated by their separate memories of Sam. Neither spoke another word. Sam's house gleamed silently, lit by the sullied glow of burning kerosene lamps dirtied with the corpses of singed moths.

'I'll park the jeep round the back. You can go in through the kitchen. It's not so far to walk.'

With the exception of Miriam clattering plates and chattering noisily to herself, preparing a meal which tonight would never get eaten, the house appeared deserted.

'Why don't you take Miriam home,' Kate said to Stone as he supported her to the scullery. 'I'll be all right.'

She sat alone at a Formica-topped, chipped enamel table, staring sullenly, her ankle throbbing, with a tumbler of milk in her hand. Fragmented moments of her childhood with Sam slid through her head like split film rolls. Entertaining her friends at a party with Punch and Judy puppets, his foolish voices, Sam coming home late, sharing his bed when he and her mother were not speaking . . . Once she found him weeping, leaning over a punctured tyre. It had pained her to see him so vulnerable, so incapable. She had watched him from a corner, hiding like a guilty spy watching his bent back heave, until he, seeing her, had pulled her to him, hugging at her mercilessly.

Suddenly a shaft of light stole through the door. Someone had pushed it open. The light settled on the tiled floor and created an angle against the neglected, peeling wall. It was Philippe.

'How long have you been here, Petal? I've been waiting for you,' he quizzed, a hint of accusation in his voice.

She held her eyes averted, seemingly contemplating her glass. He remained in the doorway staring fixedly at her.

'Where've you been, darling?' he persisted, more persuasively and more gently, conscious now that something could be wrong.

'Mmm. I went for a walk. I . . . I felt a bit sick so I came

134

in the back way. Thought I'd get a glass of milk.' She caught his look, gazing at her uncomprehendingly.

'Are you all right? You look terrible.' He made his way to the fridge and opened the door, peered into the freezer compartment, saw that there was no ice and slammed the door again. 'Damn! I suppose this is the only icebox?' he enquired hopefully, momentarily forgetting his other more consequential question. 'Where's Miriam?'

'I sent her home.'

Philippe stared at his wife blankly, before understanding that she seemed ill, too long in the sun. 'You look a bit burnt, Petal.' He placed his tumbler of tepid Scotch next to her glass of half-consumed milk and pulled over a Formica chair from beside the dresser, scraping it noisily against the floor as he dragged it. He sat down beside her and lovingly caressed her sand-encrusted hair. 'Bit of a mess, eh? Too much sunbathing? I warned you how strong it would be. It's a bastard, gets you in a minute.'

'I'm fine, Philippe, bit of a headache, that's all. I'll have a shower and an early night.' She stood up, resting both her hands against the cool Formica surface to gain her balance.

'I've got some Queasies in my toilet bag in the bathroom. I'll come and look for them. You'll be fine after a couple of those,' he said encouragingly, watching her as she made her unsteady, deliberate way towards the door.

'Why are you limping?'

'It's nothing, I twisted my ankle on the hill.'

'Here, let me help you,' he offered, rising from his chair.

She shook her head. 'I'm fine.' Her emphasis caused him to sit again.

'Well, you go ahead then,' he added, sipping the warm Scotch. 'I'll grab my papers from the porch and join you in five minutes. Scrub your back!'

As she reached the doorway, holding on for support, she turned back towards him: 'Goddam you, Philippe! You have no right to turn my father's plantation into a bloody holiday resort!' she rounded on him forcefully before disappearing along the corridor, leaving him speechless with his mouth full of warm booze.

135

Kate climbed the stairs slowly, still reeling from the shock of what Stone had told her, and what she had just said. Clinging to the wooden bannisters as she ascended, she prayed that Philippe would not follow, that he would leave her in peace for a while. He did sometimes, when they had argued, stayed downstairs alone, reading. All night sometimes. She wanted time alone, now, to think things through. Things were changing. Perspectives altering. She was feeling isolated and longed to curl up and sleep.

Chapter 11

Kate was woken early by the sounds of natives shouting in the garden below her. The room was quiet. No breeze blew in through the windows to disturb the white, limply hanging curtains and there was no sign of Philippe. His pillows were uncreased. He must, after all, have slept downstairs. The door which she remembered closing tight was ajar now. It creaked open; Poncho peered in and padded to her bedside. He nudged at her with his damp nose and dribbled his expectant mouth against her arm until she stroked his soft honeyed skull. Encouraged, he settled himself on to the Indian rug and lay panting contentedly at her side. She peeled back the sheet and climbed out of bed, almost stepping on him as she did so. Remembering her fall, she placed her foot gingerly on to the floor. The night's rest had eased it. It no longer stung her. Moving carefully yet purposefully towards the bathroom she reminded herself of what she had decided, during the dawn hours, the hours of restless morbidity between waking and sleeping.

There would be no changes made, no sales agreed, without her consent.

She found Philippe downstairs, dressed, drinking tea on the porch and reading a paper. He glanced up briefly as she settled herself into the cane chair which he had placed opposite, ready for her.

'Feeling better?' he asked. Kate nodded.

It was still early, less than ten minutes after eight, and already she could feel the heat. The sunlight streamed on to the porch from around the side of the house. But at this time of day it was still shaded and cool enough. Kate poured herself some tea. 'Want some?' she proffered softly.

Philippe simply shook his head, without glancing towards her.

All around them were the muted sounds of household activity, Fijian natives casually tidying up fallen coconut husks, an Indian gardener hoeing weeds from the grass beds and the distant, constant generator, obviously repaired. Poncho wandered out from the house in search of her and, sighting life at the table, began to wag his tail in anticipation of breakfast. Neither paid him any attention. Kate stirred some milk into her tea and then lifted the cup to drink. 'I thought you might be interested in seeing this,' Philippe said, a touch incisively, as he handed her the local *Times*. The dog wandered off aimlessly into the garden, deciding that his errand had been fruitless.

Kate glanced at the headline: NO CONFIDENCE SAY THE OPPOSITION. Below, the paper carried a quarter-page photograph of Shyam Khumar. He looked tired and bleak.

'What is this?' she frowned, mumbling to herself.

'Read it.' He stood up and stepped off the porch on to the damp, already watered lawn. Close by, a sprinkler spun and whispered into the bright morning. Kate placed her cup back on to its saucer, took the paper in both hands and leant back into the chair which creaked as it received her light weight.

Shyam Khumar, she read, *respected Leader of the Opposition Party since its inception seventeen years ago, has been ousted by his own party.*

A vote of No Confidence was brought in last night at a referendum in Suva.

She flicked a glance at the date on the paper. November 25th. It was two days old.

Ashok Bhanjee, Deputy Leader of the Party and well-known duty-free emporia magnate, will replace Khumar. (See page 2, Col. 1.)

In a short statement by Khumar, she read on, mouthing the words like a child with a picture book, *he said that he hoped to continue to take an active role in the islands' politics but as an independent rather than party member.*

'He must be devastated,' she muttered.

Philippe stepped back on to the porch and sat down. 'Have you read it?'

She shook her head. 'I haven't finished yet.'

'Here.' He leant over and took the paper from her. 'Where did you get to?' She pressed her unpolished finger into the creased print as she passed the crumpled, yellowing pages back to him. He began to read aloud. His expression was grave, his voice concerned.

'He feels that, under the circumstances, the decision taken by his former Party was the appropriate one. They have been pushing for a direction that he could not condone, he stated. He believes that the party, the islands' majority Indian Party, is seeking rule without giving due regard to the differing races inhabiting the islands.

'Listen to this,' Philippe said as he read on: *'He fears that the shift in party line is in danger of becoming racist and that ignorance will cause bloodshed. He believes that the islands cannot survive in a modern world unless* – and they quote him here,' Philippe said – *'"unless we accept ourselves as multi-racial and unless we work together towards a Pacific identity we will not survive. Our danger is that we chase the dreams and idylls of Western Capitalism. We are no more than a Capitalists' satellite society. Racism," he stated, "is our supreme threat to a better way of life."'*

Philippe threw the paper on to the table where it lay fluttering between them. 'He's an idealist, uncompromising. He'll never change. But he's right about the bloodshed. If the Indians get too much power here, the Fijians will panic and retaliate . . . I'll call him later when I'm in town. I have to go to Suva again. Will you be all right here on your own?'

'I'm coming with you,' she stated firmly. 'Stone told me yesterday that you intend to turn this place into a holiday resort. Is that true?'

139

Philippe let out a patient whisper of a sigh but did not answer her, preferring to allow her the anger.

'Did you tell him that?' she persisted forcefully.

'Petal, when you heard in Sydney that your father had died, you asked me to look after things, right?'

'But not so that you can build a holiday resort! Is what Stone said true or not?'

'I have been considering it, yes. I was looking at all the options open to us,' he conceded wearily.

'You never mentioned it to me! You treat me as though I'm not capable of understanding your plans. It's always the same. "Don't bother yourself, Petal!" you say. "I'll tell you when it's settled." Philippe, this plantation was left to *me*! Sam left it to *me* because he believed that he could trust me to keep it the way that it is. He didn't want it sold or changed!'

'Did Stone tell you that, as well?'

'Yes!'

They were suddenly both aware that Stone might be in the office. He might be overhearing this minor outburst between them. Their voices were still heated but now, with an effort to keep them inaudible to any other listener, raw whispering.

'Don't be naïve, Petal. Of course he told you that because he's got a vested interest in it. Don't you see that?'

Kate remained silent.

'He and Timi glossed over the situation here, didn't they? You said yourself that the Indian boy, Ami, had been in a fight. Stone didn't tell me that! Look at what Shyam says in the papers. Why should this place be an exception?'

'Philippe, I do not –'

'Listen, Petal, why are you getting so upset? If you want to come with me today, then please do so. I thought that you might prefer to stay here, enjoy the beach and have a holiday. That was what you wanted before we arrived, "to see where he'd lived," you said. You said yourself that his death had shocked you. You asked me to take care of everything. Remember? When I suggested returning to London you said that you couldn't bear to come alone. "Come with me," you said. I have been attempting to manage the whole tedious business as swiftly and as smoothly as possible. So that we can both go home.'

'Philippe,' she began, more softly and certainly, 'I don't want Lesa sold and I don't want it turned into a resort or anything else. I want it left the way it is.'

Philippe crossed one leg over the other and his foot began twitching to and fro. One hand slipped inside his open-necked shirt and nervously patted his shoulder. They were gestures she recognised. He was getting very angry.

'And who is going to take responsibility for the place? Stone? Kate, you are being sentimental. Don't you see that this is the decision Stone wants you to make?'

'Perhaps . . . I might stay on for a while.'

'Oh, Kathy, for God's sake talk sense! I have meetings in New York at the end of next week . . . Listen, *chérie*, I have to get back to London! I want to have something settled before we leave. We have an offer for the place . . . an exceptionally good offer . . .'

He stopped, his thoughts drifted, or he changed his mind, she could not tell which. Instead he stood up and walked towards the interior of the house. 'I'm going to ask Stone to run me to Loquaqua. I want to take the nine o'clock ferry. We can call Shyam. Give the poor bugger dinner. Are you coming or not?'

'Yes, I am.'

Shyam was sitting in the front, Kate and Philippe in the rear, his torso swung round to face them as the taxi travelled west along the southern coast road towards the Botanical Gardens.

'They give a reception there every few months or so. It's an exquisite spot and it'll give you a chance to meet some of the Europeans living and working around Suva. Eric Peters is the fellow who owns the place. He says he's been here for "donkey's years". Since the British first arrived, I think,' he joked.

Kate watched him, admiring his composure. He appeared so unruffled by his recent defeat.

'He used to be a fairly high-ranking civil servant for the

141

British government before Independence but like so many of those old expatriates he didn't want to leave. Couldn't face England again after so many years in the tropics!'

Even before they had passed through the wrought-iron gates and entered the formal garden, Eric Peters had spied them. He walked with a silver-headed ivory stick, spoke with a gruff, over-articulated, clipped British accent, sported heavy darkened spectacles and a grey Montgomery moustache. He was a hardboiled late sixties.

'Shyam, my dear fellow, welcome!' Peters called out as he limped towards them. He shook hands energetically with all three and gestured them through the inner gate, out into a lawned garden which advertised 'This way for English cream tea.'

'Yes, I'd heard you two had arrived here. How are you enjoying Lesa?' he asked Kate, ushering her enthusiastically onwards, towards a white-clothed trestle table acting as bar. Philippe followed a few steps behind her talking to Shyam.

The two men wore cream lightweight suits. Philippe looked supremely elegant, a blue silk *mouchoir* in his breast pocket. He might as comfortably have been entering the Ritz Hotel in Paris. It was clear to Kate tonight, seeing him surrounded by strangers and guests, just how difficult these days at Lesa were for him, cut off from all that made him flourish. Within moments he was approached by an efficient Indian woman in a rich purple-and-yellow sari. 'Monsieur De Marly? Mrs Patachli. Shyam tells me you are in the City. I'm working for Reuters here, but I took my degree in London at the School of Economics there. Perhaps we could do an interview . . .'

Kate was separated from them, her two escorts, as they were led away and unknown guests swarmed into other groupings. Eric Peters remained loyally at her side, pouring her gin and talking about his passion for the islands. She glanced about her into the torchlit twilight. The moon, full soon, shone through the susurrating royal poinciana treetops.

Young round Fijian girls, hibiscus flowers adorning their crinkly black hair, mingled leisurely, giggling, serving drinks from small round trays, and sausages on sticks.

142

The noise of spirited chatter was overwhelming. It wafted between the meticulously cultivated tropical plants. Late birds sang. A parrot here and there; crowds of white Europeans, several in batik shirts; Indians in sober British suits, and Fijians in national skirts and Western jackets, or short-sleeved gaily printed shirts, bedecked the gardens. The night air was fragranced by a plenitude of blossoms.

'We are expecting our Prime Minister to drop in later,' Peters confided to her. 'He's promised to join us for a nightcap. Have you met him yet?'

Kate shook her head, gratefully accepting her cocktail.

'Bloody bad news about MacGuire,' he continued, raising his glass in a gesture of health. Kate nodded tightly, wincing at the mention of her father's name. Her conversation of the day before with Stone, the idea that Sam had been murdered, had left her feeling bruised and shocked. Coming to the mainland, and Shyam's invitation to this 'do', she thought, might put another perspective on things. She hadn't as yet mentioned to Philippe what Stone had told her. He was so clearly set against Stone, and she didn't think it would ease anything. No, for the moment she was guarding the information, keeping it to herself, as if in some way it acted as a mark of respect. A secret between her and her dead father.

'What are you going to do with the place? If you keep it you'll always have staff problems. It's the same as owning a farm in southern Spain. There, one's always worrying about lack of water for irrigation. Here, we worry about the stability of the staff. But there'll be plenty willing to buy the place from you. The main house needs a bit of money spent on it though, as I remember.'

'We haven't finally decided,' she smiled cagily.

They spied Shyam in the distance, weaving his way through numerous folk huddled together in laughter and conversation. He was smiling, speaking a word easily here and there as he travelled, cigarette always between his fingertips.

'Bad luck for old Shyam, eh? This change of leadership. There'll be a bloodbath here if the other fellow wins the elections. Fijians have got their troops at the ready. But don't say I said anything, for God's sake,' Peters whispered to her conspiratorially.

Kate gazed at him in horror. 'How do you know?' she asked.

'Shyam is more moderate. He understands that the British still support the Fijians. But Ashok Bhanjee, he wants Indian control here. If he gets the majority vote, which he might, he'll want to change the constitution in favour of the Indians as soon as he gets into power. The Fijians won't let him form a government, you see if I'm not right. All hell'll be let loose.'

Shyam was gesturing to her, negotiating a path towards her. Kate smiled gratefully, disturbed by what she was hearing.

'I'm afraid we've lost Philippe to admiring guests.' He smiled as he approached.

'I've just been telling Mrs De Marly what a fanatic old Bhanjee is, eh Shyam? If he gets in none of us'll have a look in.'

'Don't be gloomy, Eric. Now, will you allow me to show Mrs De Marly some of the exquisite gardens here?'

Shyam eased Kate towards him with a brushed touch on her shoulder. As the two slid from the spotlighted chatter Kate noticed for the first time, having missed it in the twilight and the reflection from his glasses, that Eric Peters was blind in his left eye.

They walked side by side in shadowed light, down a wide stairway of stone steps; on either side were banks of brilliant red flowers with aubergine-dark leaves. 'Glorious flowers. What are they called?' Kate asked.

'Those? Amaranthus. Or some call them "Love Lies Bleeding". Wonderful colour, the red.'

Love Lies Bleeding. How soulful, she thought.

They stepped towards a waterlilied lake located at the foot of the garden's incline. The silence was balming. Kate's wrist brushed against the blood-red flowers.

'Is it true what Eric Peters says?' she asked as they walked alongside one another. Being together seemed so natural, so much unspoken intimacy, a prized, fearful happiness.

'Did he tell you there would be a bloodbath?'

She nodded.

144

'He's been predicting that since the British announced they were leaving,' he laughed. 'His European comrades call him Cassandra.' She sensed in him a flippancy, a desire not to talk politics, not tonight. This is how he deals with his defeat, she mused.

'Did he tell you his story about the willow trees?' He pointed ahead of him to two weeping willows overhanging the still water.

She shook her head, smiling.

'He says his wife bought two willow trees for their garden but before she could plant them her Fijian housemaid ran into the garden shouting, "Stop! Mrs Peters, stop, stop!"' Kate watched as Shyam acted the parts of the maid and then of Mrs Peters. 'The maid explained to her that apparently there is a superstition here. If a wife plants a willow tree in the garden she will lose her husband. Mrs Peters, though not superstitious herself, never planted the trees. And now, when Peters is giving one of his tours around the gardens here, he asks every woman tourist in his audience to tell him what she would have done in the circumstances.'

'Is it a Fijian superstition?' she asked.

He shook his head and smiled. 'I don't know,' he answered softly.

They had reached the trees and were standing in dappled light, suddenly so alone, at the water's edge. Shadows danced like pleats on her white dress. The lake was larger than she had supposed from a distance.

'The lake seems larger than I'd realised from a distance,' she whispered awkwardly.

Kate glanced along the bank, up the small hillock, past the hedges of red Amaranthus flowers, towards the cocktail party. Slivers of laughter echoed in the night. She was thinking of Philippe, hurting, guilty, facing away from Khumar, feeling herself gauche. Her breath was catching in her stomach.

'Shall we sit for a while?'

'I'd better get back,' she said shyly.

She felt the warmth of his hand poised against the back of her neck, a tenderness in his voice.

145

She was burning.

'Please don't.' She spoke faintly. She felt impelled to move, to hurry back towards the others, almost running as she crossed the grass. Proceeding up the centre of the stone stairway she saw Philippe above her, on the terrace, surrounded by people. He waved and beckoned to her, lifting a glass. He was in his element. All his earlier anger and frustration had disappeared, forgotten in the hub of conversation and life. She glanced behind her and saw Shyam walking more slowly towards the light, away from the lake. He lifted his eyes, looking towards her, caught her gaze; she smiled wistfully and stepped on towards Philippe and his companions.

Chapter 12

The sea in front of them was calm, limpid as jellyfish. Kate sat idly watching a European child, blonde-haired, playing alone in the sand, talking to herself. The small girl had built herself a sandcastle and was now acting out, with various blue and red plastic spades as weapons, an invasion. Men – Tchung! – shot and then buried into the sand as they invisibly leapt the moat.

Behind them, around the kidney-shaped swimming pool, cries from tourists could be heard, ordering their first aperitifs of the tropical evening while two Fijian guitarists strummed popular local and European songs. A barbecue was being prepared and chairs laid out around the poolside of the exclusive Fijian Island Resort.

'Why have you invited him to stay with us?' Kate asked finally.

'Do you mind? I thought you rather liked Shyam?' Philippe was twisting in his chair in anticipation of attracting the languorous Fijian waiter.

'No, of course not. I do like him. I'm rather surprised, that's all. I got the impression that you thought he'd changed. You said he lacked a sense of humour.'

Kate had been disquieted by what had happened the previous evening. Khumar was preying on her mind. She was intrigued by him, deeply attracted to him and a little afraid. The very sorcery that drew her towards him also unsettled her. And now, Philippe's unexpected invitation had disconcerted her.

147

The waiter, acknowledging Philippe's wave, sauntered towards them, elegant in his calf-length sulu. Philippe gestured towards their two emptied glasses and the waiter, smiling and nodding, disappeared back towards the bar.

'Yes, I think he's rather too serious, he always was, but I think we might be needing a little local help. Frankly, I am not entirely sure who else I could turn to. I trust him. Shyam knows the islands well and, as far as I can see, if there is anything we haven't found about the place he's probably more likely to discover it . . . It's a delicate situation here . . . people seem very nervous about the upcoming elections. It's no time for someone to be offering such a sum for the Plantation. So there must be another reason . . .'

The waiter returned with their drinks, one tropical fruit punch laden with slices of pineapple and papaya and one whisky soda, plenty of ice.

'And yet when I mentioned Sam's death, the possibility that he was murdered, you accused me of being dramatic!' She agitated the plastic cocktail stick around the ice in her glass. 'If something is going on, if there is anything about the Plantation that makes it more valuable, then I have a right to know!'

'Kate, *chérie*, for the last time, if something is going on we both have a right to know! But he wasn't murdered. He got drunk, fell over in the dark and smashed the back of his head against a rock. It was an accident! Now, please, forget it. I spoke to Stone myself and he told me that the ol' boy's death was an accident.'

'That is not what he told me!'

Philippe took a swig of his whisky, ignoring her retort. 'I am just thinking,' he continued, overly patiently, 'that if, for example, Lesa has been given some special building rights or whatever . . . Khumar might know why this particular land is so valuable. Perhaps there is nothing, perhaps Danil is telling the truth. His "wage-payer" just wants the place. Who knows?'

'And perhaps he wants it badly enough to murder for it!'

'Oh, Kathy, for Christ's sake!'

They sat alongside one another in silence, both nursing an agitation, their painful inability to understand one another's point of view.

148

The afternoon before, when Philippe had suggested it, it had seemed a good idea to stay on the mainland, spend a couple of nights at a luxury resort, away from the Plantation, indulge Kate a little and ease the creeping tension between them. But they had been bickering all day, ever since she had told him Stone's story about Sam's death. Nothing was getting resolved. Her nerves were raw. This business about her father's death was wearing her down. Frankly it was wearing him down too – the whole damned place! He would be glad when they boarded their flight the following Tuesday for New York. Five more days.

He took another soothing mouthful of the Scotch and began to speak again, his tone more patient. 'I think our options are more limited than I had initially hoped. The Sugar Company has instructed me that we cannot break the Plantation's contract with them without giving two years' prior notice. They won't accept a settlement. That makes the idea of a holiday resort unviable. I had hoped that I could negotiate the right to turn the place into a resort and then sell the Plantation as it is, with the necessary planning permission, but we don't want the headache of hanging on to the place and running it as a plantation until that permission could be secured. Who knows what will happen to land rights if there's a change of government? And there's no real profit in the sugar industry. It's not a stable market and . . . I heard last night that the government is broke. If the sugar industry is not supported here, it will go bankrupt . . . No, we should sell now, as we had originally intended. Accept Danil's offer – unless we can find out why he is offering above the market value. But I can't hang on much longer. I've got to get back to work. If Shyam can enlighten us during the weekend, excellent, if not . . . we should sign the contract and get out.'

'Philippe, I won't sell now. Sam wouldn't and neither will I. I want to know *who* has made the offer and why.'

Kate rose nimbly from her seat, lifting her sunglasses from the table next to the fruit punch. She wandered off along the crisp, white sand and then up the steps towards the swimming pool. She was toying with the idea of a swim. Philippe watched her back moving away from him in the fading light. She was lean. Her slender light-skinned hips swung easily from side to side. He still

149

fancied her, surprisingly, after so long. There had been other women in his life, during his marriage, but they had almost always been merely business-trip distractions, and he had always been discreet, even with Susan. Kate had never known, or suspected. And eventually he had always been ready to return to her.

But now she was becoming irksome. This Plantation business was a real headache. They should never have come here, but he hadn't foreseen just how much the place and her father's death would unsettle her. They should accept Danil's offer, sign the contract, settle the money in Geneva and get out . . .

The islands reeked of racial unrest. He felt it smouldering beneath the surface. And who could know what did happen to Sam? Perhaps he was murdered, by some Indian-hating white, or a discontented employee, but it was better not to delve. . . . He would accept Danil's offer . . . they could agree the deal, draw up the outline of the papers before they left on Tuesday, secure a handsome deposit and the rest could be finalised long distance. Yet, it rankled! His instinct told him that there was something else, something that Danil's client wanted and would pay dearly to have, perhaps, as Kate had said, even kill for. Philippe hated the idea that some unidentified figure was stalking him and perhaps making a financial fool of him. Perhaps Shyam would know. If not, it was better to sell up and get out.

He picked up his book from the table next to his second, now empty Scotch glass, and headed towards Kate who was stretched out along the tiles, at the poolside, drifting one hand aimlessly through the water. 'I'm going for a shower. Are you coming?'

She shook her head effortlessly and dangled her wet fingers in and out of the water.

Philippe slapped his left hand against the back of his other arm. 'These mosquitoes are another reason to get out of the tropics and back to civilisation!' he joked. An attempt at lightheartedness. She said nothing.

'Right, I'll see you in the bure then. Don't be too long, Petal. They serve dinner early here.'

He disappeared amongst the bushes, vermilion red with aubergine leaves, planted either side of a narrow, pebbled pathway, neatly manicured and lit every six feet or so by flaming kerosene torchlights. The Fijian guitarists smiled contentedly as a few appreciative holidaymakers applauded their last medley. Thin, tin clapping. The crooners began again, strumming on their guitars at the same time. It was something Kate vaguely recognised. Was it a Crosby, Stills and Nash song? A melody from her past? She couldn't be sure. What did it matter?

She lifted her wet fingers out of the blue, pellucid water and stroked them sensuously against her thigh which responded to the cold, wetted touch with tiny goosebumps surfacing on her downy skin, like bubbles rising in liquid. She gazed at the tiny bumps and stroked them. Perhaps the gooseflesh had not been caused by her touch. Perhaps it was because she was feeling afraid, terribly afraid. Small shudders of fear crept through her skin. But perhaps that, too, was an illusion brought on by the heat. An overdose of sun. That's what Philippe would have told her. 'You're overwrought, Petal, too much sun.'

Why had he invited Shyam? Was he blind to what she was feeling? She could after all, she felt, guess his responses by now. They had been married for so many years. Years during which she had never betrayed that marriage. Of course, they had often disagreed or argued, ignored one another and taken one another for granted but fundamentally they had stepped together, simply moving onwards with the regularity and certainty of a travel timetable.

Philippe had given her everything. Their marriage was perfect, friends would tell her, although they still had no children. She had realised that she wasn't satisfied. Her girlfriends had families, children to care for. She had been aware of a loneliness, a sadness . . . One or two of the husbands had made passes at her, late at night in her kitchen, usually when they were a bit sozzled during dinner parties. But it had never really occurred to her to be unfaithful. Never, until now.

And now she wondered how she had so simply accepted her life.

She stared into the water at her own faceless, porcelain reflection, disbelieving her own thoughts. An oversized, pale-winged moth skimmed the surface of the pool, creating a ripple of neat

151

waves which distorted her own compact self image. She wondered vaguely if she had stopped loving Philippe. But she knew that she did still love him. The thought of not loving him alarmed her. She would be afraid to be without him, to be alone, after so long. Their lives were so intricately intertwined. She relied upon him. She had no one else. And he loved her . . .

Perhaps it had been easier for Sam to go away, never to return and never make contact again. Easier than occasional visits. The teas on Sundays with her, sitting opposite her in a Croydon cake shop, a Lyons Corner House, feeling guilt-ridden, forced to justify the unjustifiable when perhaps he had simply felt dissatisfied, craving something more intimate. Perhaps he had recognised, as she was now fearful of recognising, that the days were passing without a whisper of intimacy.

She saw herself now with Philippe, judging him, listening to him making decisions for the pair of them, for their lives as a couple. Which he had always done and she had never questioned. It was she who was at fault. She who had never looked after her own way of perceiving. Always allowing him to take the responsibility, believing that he was more capable . . .

The sun began to disappear behind the forested, distant mountains as the last dregs of gin aperitifs were downed and the last of the guests strolled towards their chalets to shower.

She sensed her isolation. The isolation that was growing between her and Philippe. Fresh days were being pasted on to stacked, bleak days.

She had been surprised by Philippe's intolerance towards Stone and Timi, and their working situation at Lesa, so unlike Sam who must have discovered, even created, an understanding of the way of life with its precarious melange of races living awkwardly side by side. Sam had obviously understood their suspicions created by their differences, and the balances that needed to be respected and maintained. She longed for Philippe to understand that, too.

She decided that she would leave him rather than allow him to sell the Plantation, or turn it into a holiday resort. He would say that she wasn't being reasonable. And yet, perhaps, Sam had died for that very thing . . .

It was dark now save for the torches burning all around her. She trembled as the evening air caught her skin, trembling at her own truths never fully faced. Deciding that it was time to dress, she lifted herself slowly from beside the unlit, still pool water, forgotten now until the morning, and strolled towards their bure.

Chairs were being scraped behind her as the first dinner guests settled down to enjoy their barbecue.

Her thoughts drifted back to Khumar and his forthcoming visit. She would look forward to enjoying time in his company, when he and Philippe had tired of business and plantation politics.

A party of middle-aged Americans were settling themselves at their table. The women chattered triumphantly about their shopping expedition to Suva earlier in the day while one of the husbands informed his companions, 'We come from California and I tell you I saw snow this year in Palm Springs! It snowed so damn hard we couldn't go on the golf course till nine-thirty in the morning. People talked about it for weeks.'

Kate smiled silently at their cooing concern and then hurried on towards her husband waiting in their bure. She glanced skywards. It was a splendid evening. Inside the bure Philippe was out of the shower and on the telephone. Kate clipped the latch softly, fearful of disturbing him.

He put his fingers over the mouthpiece and whispered to her. 'I'm ringing Stone,' he said. 'We're going back by seaplane with Khumar in the morning. I want him to pick us up at the bay.'

Stone had been working late when the radio phone sounded in the office with news of the De Marlys' return. Chores now concluded for the evening, he locked the front porch door, put the bunch of keys in his back jeans pocket and wandered on to the shaven lawn, heading towards the back of the house. It had been a while now since he had been obliged to lock the place up and he found the silence of it, deserted and darkened, surprisingly reassuring.

He paused for a moment beneath the whispering garden foliage, and decided not to leave yet, to stay awhile, sit on the porch step and smoke a cigarette. It was a fine, breezy evening on the

153

island, clear and light. He sat staring heavenwards at the brightly lit southern sky that winked at him from between the trees. He fancied he heard the ghost of a soft, whisky lilt. Was that his much-loved Irish companion whispering through the tall shimmering coconut fronds? Not that Stone believed in the afterlife. He was not a religious man at all. He never cared to ponder such matters. 'Time wasting,' he would have said, 'changes nothing.'

Nevertheless, he took a deep breath, laughed back at the mass of glinting, silver stars and decided he would take the old marmalade jalopy down to the bay, pick up the speedboat and head on round the island to Taqawari to find himself a woman, a hearty local creature he knew, for the night. In loving memory of Sam.

Mellow with anticipation, he began to make his way around the side of the house towards the parked jeep, boots crunching on the gravel, when he caught his shin against something sharp, lying discarded on the pathway, close to the open door of the generator shed. 'Shit!' He had stepped on the wooden handle of an abandoned scythe. Swearing again, gripping the smarting leg he had paused to rub, he noticed the unlocked door. 'Fuck that goddam Indian boy!' he swore under his breath.

Ami's chores included cleaning and locking away all tools used in the gardens and around the Plantation House. In an unaccounted-for absence, these had been forgotten. Stone guessed at once that Ami had been negligent and supposed that the wily youth had slipped away early, 'on business'.

He picked up the offending scythe and a rake, which he also found lying close by, and put them inside the shed in a corner behind the generator, and, as he slammed the door, made a mental note to give the boy a stern warning the following morning. But for now his mind was consumed with sweeter matters and he was not intending to allow the troublesome young Indian to trespass on the pleasures that lay ahead of him.

That was until he had walked around to the back of the house and realised that the battered, whining jeep was not parked in its usual spot. It was nowhere to be seen, leaving Stone, and everyone else, without access to the port. And no car to pick up the De Marlys in the morning!

He remembered that Ami had been asked to drive to Loquaqua

154

to collect provisions from the ferry and, as he tunnelled now into the recesses of his tired mind, he could not recall having seen the youth since. He set off on foot down the hill towards the village and his own bure. Timi might know where the boy had disappeared to and, more importantly, where he might have left the jeep.

Both Stone and Timi knew of Ami's 'business dealings', involving the disposal of pirated audio and visual cassettes, blue and otherwise, to various private outlets and small electronic dealers on the island, on behalf of an unknown source on the mainland; but it was an arrangement that both had chosen to ignore. In the course of their busy Plantation lives neither Timi nor Stone had time for moral judgements on such matters. As far as they knew it was harmless, simply a means by which the foxy youth augmented his fair though by no means abundant wage packet. In the past these private dealings had occasionally made him late for work, but, although he had never been exactly assiduous in his attention to punctuality, he had never before remained away an entire day without saying a word to anyone. And worse, he had taken the house vehicle! That, too, was a step further than he had ever dared venture before.

Unlike Timi, patient and understanding, Stone had never understood why Sam had taken the boy on. And it was merely as a mark of respect to his dead friend that he had not kicked the boy out sooner. And, perhaps, fear of an Indian strike. But certainly since Sam's death Ami had been worse, drinking more heavily, and less respectful. In Stone's mind Ami had always been a weasel, and a difficult, ambitious one at that. But now the boy had gone too far. Stone's evening had been ruined and Ami would have to pay.

While the bronzed glowing tourists surrounding Kate and Philippe chattered haphazardly, imbibing clinking drinks and tonic under the unfolding curtain of stars, while their less fortunate holiday companions showered and creamed their reddening, stinging skins, Ami Chand waited anxiously in the antiseptic-smooth ground-floor tea-rooms at the rear of Ashok Bhanjee's newest duty-free hypermarket. A recently acquired and refurbished shopping paradise laid out on three, musak-sweet floors, where smiling Indian women in dresses of man-made fibres waited eagerly to serve.

Ami had been summoned for seven o'clock. Raj had tele-phoned his parents, who, in turn, had contacted him at the Plantation. 'Ashok Bhanjee's cousin, Raj, has telephoned for you,' his mother told him. 'He wants you to telephone him.'

It had always been his arrangement with Raj when there were extra little duties for him. 'We won't telephone you at the Plantation, Ami. We'll leave a message with your family.' Ami's older brother Roshan had worked for Ashok Bhanjee. It had been he who had introduced his younger brother to the Bhanjee 'family'. He had always been the one to deliver the messages, but now he had made his fortune and left, with his wife and two small children, for a new life in Canada. It was what Ami dreamt of, too. But for that he needed a chance, a better job, more money.

It was now ten to eight. All around him chairs were being noiselessly stacked, sleek white laminated surfaces and plastic palm trees were being cleaned and he had missed his last ferry to Loquaqua.

It would mean an explanation to Timi, or worse, to Stone, in the morning. But he had sensed by the tone of Bhanjee's voice that this rendezvous could be worth the risk. His 'uncle' wanted to see him.

Ami pulled a chewed, damp straw from one of the two Coke bottles standing emptied on the table in front of him and twisted it between his delicate fingers.

His blood was racing. He felt ready for anything! No responsibility would be too much for him. It was time for him to be recognised, to be given his chance.

Why else would Ashok – newly appointed Opposition Leader and, perhaps within a few short months, the First Indian Prime Minister of the Islands – why else would he donate his precious time to seeking out his young relative? He was a busy man. Unless, as he had promised so many times in the past, Ami's chance had finally come!

Ami was getting nervous; clammy palms, tasteless over-chewed gum in his dry mouth and a racing heart. Two Cokes enjoyed within the cool oasis of air conditioning were beginning to lose their soporific effect. Alcohol was not sold in this tourists' tea-room and he did not smoke which left nothing for him to do but deflect the burdening time by chewing mindlessly. He watched the strolling shoppers, equipped with cameras and traveller's cheques, wandering through the freshly decorated, alpine-scented emporium.

To be Master here! How he dreamt of such a thing! A King among Businessmen. And a purring, sweet, leather-upholstered saloon car of his own, for him and Jal to ride in . . .

Outside in the dusty, humid city street, unseen by Ami, lost in his own fantastic dreams, Ashok Bhanjee's polished black Mercedes, sleek as wet liquorice, pulled up in front of his store. Amidst a cacophony of battered jeeps and bleating Diahatsus cursing their way through the bustling streets of Suva Port the newly appointed Opposition Leader stepped confidently from behind smoked glass windows. Gucci soft leather moccasins trod against dusty paving stones as he made his way through the revolving doors towards the bidden, expectant boy. He proceeded into the store, bowing his head to his staff, gliding with the ease of a man on castors pulled by a thread of nylon ambition so finely spun that only he perceived it.

Ashok paused to inspect the Dunhill for Men sports display. Ami watched with palpitating heart as he spied his rendezvous draw closer. He rose clumsily to greet his superior.

'Ami, *kaise hai?*' the older Indian enquired with a note of surprise which suggested, should anyone be inadvertently listening, that Ami was the last person on earth he had expected to find standing in his tea shop.

'*Accha*, uncle, *accha.*'

Bhanjee was not, in reality, his uncle. They were related, it was true, but only distantly so. It was as a mark of respect towards a celebrated family elder and as a bold step towards an anticipated, future familiarity that the boy dared now to address Ashok so.

157

'I've kept you waiting, Ami, my apologies,' the elder regretted before seating his linen-tailored, sprawling size opposite the nervous youth who took this as a sign to be seated himself. 'I have been engaged in discussions with the Fijian Army.' He grinned enticingly and Ami, following his lead, grinned too. 'The Colonel-in-Chief. Know thy enemy, Ami. Always an important lesson. When we win the elections, we will want the army on our side.'

Bhanjee waved his plump hand in the air, nimble, delicate gestures, surprising for a man of his size. He was beckoning attention from one of his loyal, attendant staff. His gold bracelet rolled against the monogrammed letters on his sharply pressed blue cuff. 'Please bring me some American filter cigarettes,' he purred at the dainty waitress. She disappeared, delighted to be of service.

Ashok Bhanjee fell silent, guarding his words until she was out of earshot, all the while locking his hooded, unblinking gaze on to his young nephew, hypnotising him like a snake with a mongoose.

'I hear from Raj that you have been working diligently, if, perhaps, a little over-enthusiastically,' he jested, or so Ami read it. 'I have high hopes for you, Ami.'

The boy's heart began to pound with pride and anticipation until, as if some hidden antenna had bleeped a warning, Bhanjee paused. Once more, he waited; this time while the cigarettes were carried the twenty feet from the counter behind him. He took the red and white packet, without looking at the waitress, and peeled off the cellophane. Ami watched. His poor young heart was racing.

'You are keen to follow your brother, eh Ami?'

Ami nodded vigorously.

'Have you ever asked yourself, Ami, what has made me the man I am today?' Bhanjee did not wait for Ami's reply, for his own was already prepared. 'Remaining loyal, Ami, to those who love me and are loyal to me. As I have been to your brother, Roshan. He served me well and now he has his reward.' Slowly, as he spoke, he drew a cigarette from the fliptop box, allowing time for the boy to drink in the weight of the words being generously donated to him, and more importantly, to prepare the already fallow soil for the next seed to be sown.

'I fear you may have been a little foolish, my boy. A little overzealous in your ideas of business, or so Raj has told me, for I knew nothing of these . . . "misunderstandings",' he confided as he tossed the cellophane on to the table. It landed and uncrinkled next to the Coke bottles and the chewed straws. 'Raj tells me that you have been complaining. That you say you cannot live on what you earn. He says that you have been renting out illegal movies. Cassettes, Ami, that Raj gave you! They were for you to borrow. You have been renting them out. That is impermissible. A man of my political standing cannot be involved in such underhand dealings.'

Ami was confused. He had earned good money for his work! 'But Ashok, you knew what I was doing! You were there sometimes when I got paid.'

'If Raj or I ever gave you money it was as a gesture of our support. You came to us saying that times were hard for you. That you had a son to bring up alone. We gave you money because you needed it. It was an offering of generosity, Ami, to family. Don't let it happen again, will you? I have always prided myself on running an honest business, you know that.'

Surely, Ashok must realise by now that Ami's silence was secured! Had he not already proved that! 'But what about my future, following Roshan, going to Canada? Me and Jal?' the boy demanded. 'You promised!' He was muddled, hurt, uncertain what was happening to him.

'One day. Ami, when you are ready we will find something very special for you, I promise . . . I hear that the new owners of Lesa want to make changes there . . .'

Kate lay drowsing, allowing her turbulent thoughts to drift about the unfamiliar room. She listened to the birds screeching discordantly into the clammy night air. Someone calling for help! She turned, sleepless and troubled.

Close by, sleeping yachts clinked faintly as they bobbed rhythmically on the gently undulating water and slowly she allowed herself to be lulled to sleep, secured for a while by the regularity of her husband's familiar breathing and light snoring.

Kate dreamt of England, of the distant forgotten scent of chrysanthemums and of winter smoke, burning leaves in darkening backyards. Smells reminding her of 'the young Katherine'; of cold November evenings with dusk falling early and abruptly; of her own young breath cutting against her cold cheeks as she hurried home from school in a bruised, ill-fitting uniform, weary from a day's tedious studies and remonstrations.

She dreamt of a man, a shadowy figure, waiting for her on the corner at the top of the lane that led to her home, a cramped and untidy flat, where she and her mother lived. The man sat in his smoky-blue car, a Morris Minor, watching her approaching through his rearview mirror. As she drew closer he leant towards the passenger seat and wound down the window.

'Katherine!' he called indistinctly. She thought she heard her name and turned, frightened by the unexpected beckoning. She knew him at once, although she had not seen him for five years. She remembered the tiredness in his baggy eyes, the bleary sadness. She ventured a nervous step and then paused but she could see his face more clearly now, lit by the street lamp close to where he had parked. He was unshaven, a crumpled face like a rubber mask.

'Come here, my darling,' he seduced with his whisky Irish lilt.

She obeyed, approaching tentatively, uncertainly, trembling with fear, awash with longing for his grown-up embrace. She had been forbidden to talk to strangers, and to him more than the others, should he ever appear. She was twelve years old, not yet quite tall enough for the length of her fast-sprouting, gangly legs which had grown on well ahead of her. She stood now, half leaning against the car door, unaware of herself, her undefined sexuality, staring through the window at this stranger, this forbidden father. Her legs, in short white cotton socks, were crossed over one another, burying her fear and attraction, embedding them tightly in her groin. She was willowy, thin, dainty like a cultivated bird, and with tiny buds for breasts.

'Where's your mother?' he asked her softly, after staring at her for some moments without speech.

160

She shook her head, fearful of telling, of betraying or angering her mother, her constant companion.

'Would you like some tea? Have you time? Shall I take you to Lyons Corner House and buy you an orangeade and a cream puff, like I used to?' He smiled enticingly. His damp eyes warmed her shivering features, poured over her like heated oil. She would have liked the trip to Lyons, for the outing and the chance to be with him – how she missed him! – but she was afraid, afraid of her mother's wrath.

She was leaning with her head bent low, staring at her feet, shy of meeting his gaze, but then her upturned face peered curiously into his car. It reeked of stale tobacco. On the back seat was a rug of dark, tartan wool covered in dog's hairs.

'I miss you, little Katherine. Do you sometimes think of me?' he asked, holding a hand towards her face.

She gazed uncertainly, huge nervous eyes seduced by him.

'I hate you!' She thrust the words vehemently and, turning her face from the car, her body following, she unexpectedly hurried on down the lane, tears burning into her cold cheeks, past the high bricked walls either side of her, towards the mean concreted quadrangle that led her to her block of flats. She could hear her name echoing through the bricks that lay behind her as she disappeared inside the tawdry, wintry building.

Kate was jolted from sleep by an eruption of salacious laughter followed by the sounds of a woman screaming lasciviously. She threw back the thin sheet, careful not to disturb Philippe who had obviously heard nothing, and crept over to the mosquito-screened balcony door. The drunken sounds of a woman's frightened shrieks pierced into the stillness of the bright, moonlit night. Silver shreds of fear were followed by a loud splash, much laughter and then applause. Kate attempted to draw back the screen but it had jammed and each time she pulled at it, or pushed, it slid from its base. She could hear sounds of more water splashing as others dived, jumped or fell drunkenly into the pool. Then silence, hushed murmurings.

She turned back towards Philippe, and considered waking him. She was feeling miserable. He was still sleeping soundly.

He was always sleeping soundly! She crept back to bed, curled up beside him and tried to sleep again, thinking of her dream. Sam had met her from school once. Waited for her in the lane and she had run away from him, shouting that she hated him. It had been the last time that she had ever seen him.

Chapter 13

Beyond the beach, along the dusty track that Kate had first travelled with Stone, the heat shimmered like corrugated glass. Shyam approached alone, walking from the lane. An hour from the main house. 'I thought it was you I could see, crouched in the sand.'

At the sound of his voice, Kate spun around on her haunches and found him, dust-stained, standing a short distance behind her. She was surprised not to have heard his approach. The stark light burnt down upon her, blinding her as she smiled awkwardly, discomforted at having been discovered here, even by him.

'I hope I'm not disturbing you,' he ventured graciously.

She shook her head and without speaking turned her attention back towards the glassy water, still as marble.

'May I sit with you for a while?'

She nodded warmly. 'Of course you may.' And he moved forward to crouch like a crab in the white sand, at her side.

Neither spoke, not from any sense of awkwardness, more from an ease that was growing naturally between them, the silence of an impending intimacy. They gazed impassively beyond the reef to where erratically shaped clouds were gathering on the horizon. A distant, unseen plane droned high above them, indifferent to their unspoken attraction on this deserted stretch of beach.

Kate idled the warm straw-coloured sand between her well-manicured fingers. The bareness of her light hands and arms caught his attention. She was wearing no jewellery, not even a wedding ring, and he wondered whether she had removed it or never worn one. He could not recollect having noticed it before.

He longed to touch her, to kiss her on the mouth.

He placed the palm of his hand against the flesh of her fingertips, felt the softness of her skin. Kate breathed as he touched her, an almost inaudible inhalation of breath. Her heart was beating fast and her eyes filled with tears – not sorrow; moistness of wanting, a forbidden euphoria.

'I was thinking about Sam,' she began clumsily, 'wondering what he might have been doing here that night. Stone says he loved this spot. It seems an odd place though, in the middle of the night, don't you think?'

As he watched her she gathered up a minute, striped shell between her fingers and threw it idly, mockingly, towards the decaying, uncaring, bleach-dried mill. 'I was wondering how long it is since anyone tried to go inside there.' She paused and sighed, dropping her gaze to the sand beside her. 'Stone says that he thinks my father was murdered.'

She turned to face him now, creasing her eyes in the light, to find his features. It made her look much older. 'I have to know,' she said firmly.

'Is that why you've decided to stay?' he asked, cautious of her apparent confusion.

She shrugged.

'Listen,' he began gently. 'His death was diagnosed by Patterson, a close friend of ours. I think I mentioned him to you before. He is a highly regarded English doctor. Of course, it's possible he may have been mistaken but if he was murdered, there would have to be a motive and your father was a well-loved and well-respected man. I don't think murder is very likely.'

'Someone jealous of his success? Another European, per-haps, who wanted his land? There are not many left who still do well here.'

164

'Kate, Lesa is the only plantation of any size on this island. He had no competition here, and I hardly think one of the smaller cane farmers . . . As you know, he worked well with the Indian community. There was no reason for anyone to kill him.'

She turned her gaze back towards the heat-misted horizon, quietened temporarily, accepting his reasoning, unwilling to challenge him further without argument. She had nothing except a harassing certainty brewing in her gut.

'Then why should Stone think such a thing?'

'He's probably upset, perhaps angered by the unexpected bereavement.'

The matter seemed to rest. Kate felt no further desire to discuss it with him. 'I've been reading in the papers about you. Speculations about your future. Might you decide to stand as an independent candidate?'

'I expect so.'

'I think it would be a pity if you don't. You seem so . . . committed.'

He laughed warmly, yet, unlike the evening of their first meeting when he had also laughed openly at her, she now sensed a hint of a rebuff which hurt her. 'That's kind of you, Kate. Yes, no doubt I'll stand again. Shall we walk back together, along the beach?'

Not waiting for her response he rose to his feet and held out a hand to help her which she accepted. Once on her feet, they stood facing one another. Kate, made self-conscious by his touch, let his hand fall again. 'Philippe will be waiting,' she whispered hoarsely.

'I know.'

They began to stroll at a leisurely pace in the direction of the house, high above them on the cliff-top.

Kate felt the sea air burn against her slowly tanning skin as she walked silently at his side.

'I was surprised by what you said during lunch. Obviously you enjoy it here. But I hope that your decision to stay is not because you believe that your father was murdered.'

'Are you mocking me, Shyam?! You agreed with Philippe

165

that the price that has been offered for the place is unrealistically high, beyond any recoupable market price. Why? There must be a reason for it. If someone wants the land badly enough to pay such a sum perhaps they also want it, or need it enough to kill for it!' She had stopped and stood, back to the water, facing him. Her upturned face was angry, passionate and he saw fleetingly a quality of the old man there, glimpsed his Celtic fervour, the determination to see things fair. It was a surprise to him. During their first meetings she had been less passionate, more reserved. He had not supposed that she possessed such anger and he warmed to her more for it.

'As you've already heard,' she continued, more in control now, 'I don't want to sell the Plantation and, yes, I would like to stay on here . . . just for a while . . . and help to run it as a sugar farm. I could use that time to find out who wants to buy Lesa and why.'

His eyes burned into her. 'And Philippe, what does he say?'

'He's leaving for Los Angeles after the weekend. He has business in New York. I'll meet up with him in London for Christmas.'

She had not answered his question. He supposed, as he would have felt, that Philippe was not happy with the arrangement although he had given little of his feelings away during their lunch together. But it would explain the tension that he had felt between them since his arrival.

They continued to walk. He speculated that his day ahead with them might prove uneasy, and there was nothing more he could tell Philippe to help him with his decision, but to leave now would be impolite and . . . he was not ready to leave.

They had reached the small rocky bay where Kate had fallen asleep in the sun a week or more earlier. Her dream that had so haunted her at the time felt vague and distant now. But as they reached the spot she felt a shiver as though something had stood between her and the sun. A shadow, a dark portent of something unaccountable.

'Did you and Philippe know one another well in Paris?' she asked suddenly, needing conversation.

'Not really. I was given an introduction to his family by the parents of a close friend of mine at Oxford. I wrote to them and they invited me to stay with them when I was in Paris. They assured me that they would look after me, which they did, more than generously. Philippe was home during the weekends. He had his own small apartment in Paris. We talked a little, not much. Later, when he was alone in London, I introduced him to a few friends, quite different to his rather elegant Paris circle.' He laughed. 'And . . . there was a girl – Rolande. She was Philippe's girlfriend in Paris. He brought her home for several weekends and I became rather foolishly infatuated with her. I fear she never cared for me.'

'Yes, Philippe mentioned her soon after we met in London. I think they were actually engaged for a while.'

They stood together, lost in their English pasts. A time, she reflected, when it might as easily have been he who had asked her to dance at that party and . . . fleetingly she wished that it had been. 'What happened? Why did you lose contact?'

'I think his parents rather disapproved of my part in the student demonstrations in Paris. They were a very conservative French family.'

She nodded, grinning. 'Don't I know,' she joked.

'Then, once we were in London, I think we just accepted that we had very little in common. He was still with Rolande when we last met . . . so . . .'

'But why England, why Oxford? Why not America, Harvard?'

'The Mother Country,' he replied with the merest hint of irony. 'In those days I dreamt of education, the finest. I worked hard to win a scholarship, to be the pride of my family and to . . . escape from my family. Indians, you see, believed, as my family did, that England ruled the world. And so for us, she did. I craved learning, a glut of it, the finest and the most renowned. I longed to break free from my bonds, my Asian culture, the island mentality born of living here, and the extended family mentality, even mine. A

167

highly regarded bunch!' He smiled. 'I wanted to be done with India or Fiji, my roots, and though I had not understood it then, even my skin, my colour.'

Without need of gesture or thought they sat together on the sand amongst a small cluster of rocks, damp at the core from the movement of the water. Kate said nothing, happy simply to listen to him talk, lost in his proximity.

'To be truthful, I had never considered my "colour", my difference, until I reached England. I knew that my family had fought hard to win Indian freedom here, on these islands, and I was passionate about it too, in an adolescent sort of way. I thought myself clever but truly I was very naïve.' He paused. 'But what about you?'

'Oh, brought up by my mother, after Sam left. No brothers or sisters . . . I met Philippe in '69. We married the next year . . . I don't work . . .' She shrugged. There seemed so little to tell in comparison.

'You have children?'

'No . . . No reason why not. We planned to have several but . . . not yet. . . . Were your family shipped here from India by the British?'

'Yes, my grandfather was a peasant from North India who had been brought here in 1910 as an indentured labourer, to work in the sugar fields . . . Why don't you work, Kate?'

'I was working when I met Philippe. My French was quite fluent, so I had a good job but we were going to have a family . . . He rather preferred that I didn't work, so I stopped . . . The French has been useful!' she quipped. 'What was it like when he first got here?'

'Who, my grandfather? Oh, the conditions were appalling for all the men and few women who came here. Things were so bad that the anti-slavery movement had been alerted. They had been fighting against the indentured labour system for several years, long before my grandfather. After his arrival he became one of the most audible voices in the struggle against the system. I knew this. As a child I used to listen to his stories about those desolate days. I knew, also, that my father had worked hard using the land that my grandfather had eventually

168

acquired. He had struggled to win a position here. He was the first-born and inherited everything that the old man had bought and maintained. My family earned money from the land, growing cane. Eventually they became a well-respected, powerful voice here. They encouraged me to study, to use the wealth such as it was to win a place at university. I accepted their encouragement, worked constantly, but it was towards my own dream. To escape, to gain knowledge – I was greedy for it – and then, once educated, to rid myself of my roots. I wanted to live in England and become British! In those days as a student I had no interest in bringing the islanders, Fijians and Indians, together. I had given no thought to Independence, except my own! Ironically, all that was bred in England! . . . and in Paris . . . I discovered the reverse of what I had expected. I discovered that I could not just rid myself of my roots and my skin like some local lizard! My cultures, both Indian and Fijian, were inseparable from me. And Independence was imminent here. I felt I had to return. Eventually I gave up all my dreams of practising law in England and I came home, to play my part in the struggle for freedom. And that's where I am today . . .'

Silently, as though he had entirely forgotten her, he began to walk, looking neither right nor left, slowly yet determinedly making his way back towards the Plantation House.

Kate chose not to follow him. She allowed him the exquisite pleasure of his own privacy, feeling that she had perhaps delved too deep, encroached too far. She dangled her toes and the soles of her feet into the water which had crept up around the base of the rock on which she was now perched. It felt cool and inviting. She decided to stay for a swim. It would allow Shyam the time to arrive back at the house ahead of her, giving him an opportunity to talk further with Philippe.

Her thoughts drifted towards the future, to the solitary days that were waiting for her. It would be the first time since she and Philippe had become engaged that she would be alone for more than a few days. The idea tantalised her and, at the same time, filled her with concern. For the first time in her adult life, it seemed, the future held no perceivable shape.

169

She thought of Philippe, and felt saddened, knowing that he was burying his anger and hurt. She desperately wanted this separation, albeit a temporary one, but she wanted it to be painless. He had, after all, honoured her wish and made this journey with her and she knew he was not finding it easy now to accept the idea of leaving without her, leaving her so far from home with only a vague promise about when she would be returning.

That evening, as the dusk brushed blood red across the sky, Ashok Bhanjee stepped hurriedly from his parked Mercedes and crossed the last two or three strides of the gravelled driveway that led to his front porch. The door was opened in advance of him by an impeccably dressed, elderly Indian in starched white, who stepped back from the door, bowing his head deferentially as Bhanjee swept through into the air-conditioned hallway.

'Is my wife upstairs?' He spoke to the servant in Hindi.

'Yessir. And your guests are expected.'

'Good. Serve my whisky in the drawing room, please Jay.'

Bhanjee climbed the stairs and pushed the door that opened on to the family drawing room. There he found his wife, dressed in a traditional sari, seated, waiting obediently with his four children, all of whom looked up from their homework as he entered. Each spoke a polite greeting but none rose to embrace him. It was not the habit here.

'Where is the tutor?' he enquired of his wife in their own southern Indian dialect.

'He left almost two hours ago. It's already late, Ashok,' she replied defensively.

They had three sons, eleven, nine and eight, and one younger daughter, six. The three boys were expected by Bhanjee to study for several additional hours each day with a private tutor. All had places waiting for them at a private school in Sydney. The first-born, Sami, would begin his overseas education in a matter of weeks, when the new school year began in late January.

Paying for the private education of his offspring was one of

170

the privileges Bhanjee cherished. Privileges derived from his hard-earned success. He could afford the best for his family and he intended that they should have it. In most cases Bhanjee perceived the best as the most expensive. Each of his three sons was being prepared for university in Australia or New Zealand or, with application and extra pressure, America. He intended that they should have the opportunities and qualifications that he himself had never been given. He intended that they should have every chance to win in life.

'You don't realise, Ashok, the children need time for leisure,' his wife continued as the four youngsters gathered around her like chicks with their hen. 'Now they are going to read to you. Each one a page at a time, including little Lela.'

'Splendid!' Ashok applauded as he walked to the closed window and peered out towards the horizon, across the dirtied, tanker-slicked water.

Lela beamed self-consciously and nestled her shy, almond features into the folds of her mother's sheeny silk robe. The girl was barely able to read but longed to fit the jumble of letters into a pattern than would make her father roar with pleasure and her mother stroke her with loving, patient acknowledgement.

The eldest son, Sami, not the brightest of the three, began. Bhanjee, at the window, clasped his hands behind his back, listening without turning. To the right of him, if he strained hard, was Suva Port where tourist liners and freight ships could be seen setting sail for the open waters, onwards towards exotic destinations. Frequently from this chosen window he watched the cargo ships idling, waiting for clearance to dock and to disgorge themselves of their precious loads. Silently he would gaze, content in the knowledge that unknown foreign crews were preparing to disembark their wares and flood his duty-free emporiums with ever more luxury goods, pumping consumer hardware and perishables into his ever-expanding companies. Just as he, as a child, had wanted to fill his garden sandpit with more and more buckets of sea water, knowing it would never be replete yet unable to withstand the challenge, so now, he too would never feel replete. He believed there

171

was no end to his potential, to the commercial paradise that he intended to create here in the South Pacific, this gloriously untapped water belt of the world.

'You are not saying the word correctly, Sami,' he interrupted brusquely as his dull son stuttered and stumbled over a phrase.

The Bhanjee Empire had an annual turnover of approximately thirty million local dollars. His family of Suva Bay were one of the fortunate minorities. Bhanjee never lost sight of that fact. Daily he gave thanks to his now deceased father whose determination, perseverance and courage had built the family business. In the twenties, after Indian labour had been freed from the indentured system, Ashok's father, always a man with a keen eye for a lucrative deal, had foreseen the possibilities of inestimable financial rewards in the distant land of Fiji, and had paid his own passage by steamer from Gujarat, northern Bombay, to begin a life of trading in Fiji.

During those first solitary years here on the islands, he had saved prudently and used the money that he was earning as a market-stall holder to acquire a smallholding. On that modest piece of Fijian land he built his first store, the seed of his empire, the sapling fruit of the Bhanjee Emporia.

Once that had begun to flourish he had returned home to India for his mother and two younger brothers – his own father was dead – and to persuade his betrothed, Bhanjee's mother, to marry him and return with him to Fiji. It had been a humble yet courageous beginning, travelling as a family back to Fiji with the young Bhanjee senior, still in his early twenties, as head of the family.

Ashok never allowed himself to forget his father's accomplishments. It was in honour of his father that he now forged onwards, pushing himself to ever greater achievements in business, the community and now politics. What pride the old man would have known to see his eldest son Prime Minister of the islands – Ashok's dearest ambition – and to see his grandchildren formally educated, a privilege that even Ashok himself had only scantily known.

Although his own family had never known the suffering of

172

the indentured labour system – he was a Gujarati and few had been labourers – he was an Indian. That was his cultural identity, even here in the South Pacific, on the islands that he knew as home, and he could never forget that heritage. He despised Khumar for his liberal thinking. He longed to see these islands ruled by Indians with himself at the helm. Let the Fijians fend for themselves, his were the majority race now. They were the workforce. And he would lead them to power, whatever the cost . . .

'Jay tells us you have guests for dinner, Ashok?' The musical lilt of his wife's question interrupted his imaginings. 'Would you like Sami to continue reading or shall we leave you in peace now?'

'You will be joining us for dinner this evening,' he announced good-humouredly to his wife and family as he turned back towards them, wrenching himself from his distant dreams born of cargo boats. 'It will be nothing elaborate. A simple family meal in true Gujarati fashion. But I want you all on your best behaviour.'

The boys regarded him silently with their books still open on their laps.

'You are not to speak out like any street beggars. You will make your points only when asked to do so.'

They stared as a family, wide-eyed and uncomprehending.

'These men are journalists from New Zealand and America,' he added as an explanation. 'They want to interview me, to see our family life here. But we will be discussing politics, the future of the islands. These are not subjects you know anything about, so best to keep silent.' He smiled ebulliently, lightening the overly respectful mood in the room. The children smiled coyly in response to him, nestling closer to their mother and watching as he walked briskly from the window towards the door.

'These journalists, they speak only English. Hindi is forbidden tonight.' He opened the door. 'Where is Jay with my whisky?' he boomed contentedly, in warm round tones like an opera singer preparing for a performance. He left the room, hurrying proudly towards the shower to work

173

quietly through his thoughts in preparation for his overseas guests.

Minutes later the telephone began to ring but Bhanjee, sodden and soaped, did not hear it. It pealed helplessly for several minutes until finally Jay approached mistrustfully from the downstairs back kitchen. His English was imperfect and the intrusive apparatus was an anathema to him. With disgusted features he picked up the black receiver and, holding it in his awkward hands, bellowed into the mouthpiece.

'Yes, hello? Hello!' he cried in uncertain English.

Only a crackling silence answered his efforts. He tried again, this time yelling louder. The receiver at the other end was mysteriously replaced, leaving Jay to contemplate the burring dialling tone before recradling the hateful object. He returned to the kitchen, muttering foully.

Across the water, on the isle of Lesa, Ami recradled the receiver and dialled another number. It was still early, not yet half past seven. Perhaps if he caught him now, before the gin had taken its evening hold, Doctor Patterson might still be sober and would agree to see him. Ami, if he sprinted, would just be able to make the last ferry to the mainland.

Unless Patterson's houseboy had received instructions. Ami recalled them from his own days as Patterson's houseboy. 'No more calls for tonight,' Patterson would have said, retiring to the garden verandah, content in the company of his bottle.

Ami left the phone to ring several times but no one answered. He replaced the receiver and slouched miserably out on to the muggy, busy Loquaqua street, kicked at a stone and watched it coast several yards along the shabbily paved sideway. He set off in the direction away from the bus station, idling his way towards the water, to sit awhile at the dockside, watching tankers creep slowly towards their destinations.

Here, he could dream of other continents, worlds unknown to him. Worlds that he could escape to with Jal. Bombay perhaps – The Land of Films and Filmstars . . . or America – where Rambo ruled the universe. But instead he was in Loquaqua, dejected, standing like a small thin post on the

174

edge of the world, watching jagged rainbow slicks colour the thick, mud-brown water. He despised his life and he longed to escape.

Stone had taken away his job! He had stared at him with cold, misunderstanding eyes and told him to pack up and be out by the following Saturday. Why had Bhanjee not offered him that long-promised employment?

He sat mindlessly staring at a sign which read: 'Boats for Hire'. The sign at the end of the narrow jetty to the left of him read, 'Journeys around the Island. Discover our Unknown Forest Jungles and Volcanic Rock Paths'. It was written in untidy, hand-painted, English lettering.

Loquaqua, the most southern point on the island, scathingly referred to as the end of the world, was quite literally the end of the road. Only a sketchy dust track extended around the eastern belt of the island. This other, less inhabited shoreline possessed only isolated settlements nestling in amongst the coconut trees, where shy clusters of natives forced a living out of fishing and matmaking.

It was Fijian land. No Indians had settled in this littoral setting because sugar did not grow there, the climate was too damp, and no town for commerce had grown up. Occasionally American or Australian helicopter traffic landed to drop geologists in search of rich mineral sources but few other white men visited there.

This eastern belt possessed only one town. A tiny fishing port called Taqawari, with a single, mud-tracked, rutted street and two whitewashed churches, one Catholic and one Seventh-Day Adventist, sitting at either end of the street. Its hotel, a woodboarded construction, was laughingly named The Great Southern Hotel and housed to its rear a whorehouse. Taqawari was almost inaccessible. To reach this isolated strand it was necessary to hire a small outboard-motored dinghy in Loquaqua and navigate a route around this rocky side of the island. A small deposit was required and a promise to return the boat before ten o'clock. That would give Ami more than two hours. Plenty of time. He would go tonight and it would be early enough to hitch himself a

Saturday night ride back along the road towards the Plantation.

Alone in their room, unheard by Khumar, Kate and Philippe argued violently about the Plantation. She had told him that nothing he said would change her mind and that she would remain on at the house after Tuesday. They had fallen asleep in anger and silence.

She woke in the night and crept out on to the terrace, conscious that somewhere, to the rear of her, Khumar lay sleeping. Perhaps he had been right, perhaps he and Philippe were both right. Perhaps, as Philippe had accused in the hours before sleeping, she was being foolish and headstrong. Was she lying to herself? Was her reason for wanting to stay nothing to do with Sam at all?

There was only Stone's word that Sam had been murdered . . .

Ami, wretchedly drunk, swivelled awkwardly on his stool in the kerosene-lit bar of The Great Southern Hotel, and ordered himself another drink. The place was empty save for one woman, a heavily painted sweetheart sitting alone drinking gin in a spill of light at the far end of the bar. Her large, tired breasts heaved dispassionately against a white sweater. She ignored Ami as he ignored her. Their business was not with one another. Behind him, across the gloomy room, he saw the outline of a Fijian couple locked together in animated conversation. Holding hands, they giggled like children. He watched them for a time with unfocused, abstracted eyes but their companionship began to rankle. Caused him to remember Jal's mother.

He faced back towards the bar and took an unsteady swig from his refilled glass. The locally distilled liquid burnt into his unaccustomed gut and set his muddled head reeling. He felt himself about to puke and staggered from the stool, groping for balance. Hastily and with what pitiable dignity he could muster, watched by the meretricious doxy, he made his way out of the back door towards the cubicled lavatory in the

176

yard. His hand lurched against the wall and his stomach retched its confusion.

Wearily, he stood again to his full height, resting his sleek black head against the rusty bracket on the lopsided door. Breathing deeply, he closed his eyes and let his mind slip backwards. Stone's angry eyes burnt into his memory.

He swung himself, in one exerting movement, from the lavatory on to the damp terrain. It had started to rain. No surprise on this side of the island where the climate was wetter and the vegetation lusher. It would be impossible now, even had he been sober, to take the small dinghy back to Loquaqua. He would have to spend the night in the Fijian village. Possibly take a bed here at this hotel, or sleep out in the rain. He hurried back inside, out of the damp, misty weather into the unwelcoming refuge of the foreign bar.

When Ami returned Stone was at the bar, drinking with a woman, his favourite whore, the doxy Felise. He spotted the distraught Indian boy immediately, assessed his drunkenness, mouthed a word to the barman, slipped his arm around Felise's waist and led her from the bar through to the back of the hotel. There was no way he was going to allow Ami to ruin another night. Ami bought himself another large whisky. Perhaps even two, he could no longer remember. Then he asked to be given a room at the hotel. The barman shook his head. 'We have no rooms. Full up. Sorry.' Ami persisted with his drunken request, insisting that he was being refused because he was an Indian. The continued refusals and the liquor made him bellicose.

'You're a liar,' he shouted, flailing himself across the shabby bar, knocking his empty glass to the floor where it shattered into tiny pieces at his feet.

'You're from Lesa, right?'

'Yes! Sam MacGuire was my friend!'

At this point Stone was called out, Felise at his side, wrapped in a sulu. Another white man, ruffled from sleep, ordered himself a beer and stopped to watch the incident.

Stone paid for the broken glass. 'You better get yourself somewhere safe, Ami, before you cause real trouble. I've paid for the glass, now get outa here before you get real hurt,' he warned, setting off with his woman into the late-night rain, to the warmth of her tin-room companionship.

Ami still cussedly refused to leave until finally the stoic barman, with the aid of several bullish Taqawarian locals, carted him by the back of his shirt collar and the seat of his jeans and threw him out into the wet, muddied main street. He lay there, semi-conscious, until at some drizzling miserable hour before dawn he managed to crawl to the beach and drag himself into his small boat to sleep. When he woke mid-morning, hung-over and aching, damp and shivering, his raw skin chafed and the pain from his bloodied, closed eye gnawed into him.

By noon on Sunday it was sweltering at the beach. The welcome light breeze of the morning had entirely disappeared. After a swim, Khumar, Kate and Philippe returned to the house. They picnicked in the shade of several magnificently scented frangipani bushes in full white and rose bloom. Kate prepared the lunch and Khumar assisted her. She seemed more brittle than she had been the afternoon before. Yet he found himself even more drawn to her, more attracted by her vulnerability. Warmed by her beauty, he longed for her.

After lunch Philippe went inside to work in the shade and they were left alone together, seated on the terrace, cooled by the long shadows, staring into the afternoon heat.

'Shall we walk in the garden?' he suggested.

She nodded silently.

'What is the matter?' he quizzed. 'You seem upset.'

'I've changed my mind about staying on. I'm leaving with Philippe on Tuesday. Did he tell you?'

He shook his head. The news disquieted and saddened him. 'Why?' he asked her.

'I think he's right.'

'What about your father, and the Plantation?' he queried.

'Both you and Philippe agree that my fears about his death are groundless . . . and Philippe is right. We can't run the place from London. It has to be sold.'

178

By two o'clock it was time for him to leave.

'I'll take you,' she proffered.

He said his farewells to Philippe and she drove him in the jeep to the ferry at Loquaqua. He felt joyless yet calmed to be going on his way home. His solitary existence had numbed his sociability. Home, work, would tranquillise him. He was pained by his attraction to Kate . . . he felt a cruel irony. First there had been Rolande, and now Kate.

They arrived at Loquaqua early. 'Will you wait with me until I go on board?' he asked.

They decided to cherish the unexpected half-hour by strolling peacefully along the wharf and through its surrounding shacked lanes. It was an indulgence soon to be denied them both. Silently, as he lit a cigarette, Khumar chided himself for allowing such a situation to have arisen between them.

They set off side by side along the garbage-ridden quayside. Several Indians working, gathering scrap metal or sea-drift from around the waterside, recognised him and waved warm greetings. He smiled in acknowledgement, feeling championed by their enthusiasm.

'Isn't that Ami over there?' Kate said with sudden surprise, and a certain anxiety. It was the boy's appearance that had initially drawn her attention. Without knowing why, she felt inexplicably alarmed. Ami was looking unkempt, tattered even, but there was something else which from the twenty yards or so distance between them she could not make out. 'Is he in trouble? Shall I call him?'

Khumar stood hesitating for a moment, deciding whether they should call out to the boy who was tying up a small motorboat alongside a narrow wooden jetty.

'No, don't,' he said finally.

There was a sign above it which read, 'Boats For Hire', and then in smaller lettering, 'by the hour or the day'. Beside Ami was another Indian, sulued, naked from his waist upwards. The two figures appeared to be in the midst of a disagreement. Khumar stepped back a pace or two, taking Kate with him with a touch on her arm, to the rear of a wooden-planked walkway. He wanted to observe the scene but was diffident about spying.

179

The other Indian, Khumar supposed the hirer of the boat, had grabbed Ami by the arm and was shouting into the boy's face. Ami turned his head away from his angry companion and stood stock still, staring weakly out towards the ocean.

Finally Ami must have conceded because he dug deep into his muddied, jeaned pocket in search of dollars and begrudgingly handed a retrieved bundle to the victorious boatman. Apparently their dispute had been a financial one. Then the boy shook his arm free and strode away from the water towards where Khumar and Kate were standing.

Khumar, caught between a desire to assist and a sense of guilt at having spied upon the boy, finally called out to him. 'Ami, over here!' he shouted. Ami looked up and saw Kate and Khumar watching him.

'What's happened to his face?' Kate asked. His left cheek had been bloodied and the eye above it was darkened and misshapen.

'He must 've been in an accident.'

Without waiting for another word from Khumar, and before they could move forward to help him, Ami turned on his heels and fled, heading inland towards a maze of jumbled, narrow shanty streets, in search of refuge from the gazing eyes of judgement.

Khumar, without moving or attempting to follow him, watched the boy disappear before turning in the opposite direction with Kate, heading back along the quayside towards the jetty to where his ferry would be boarding. 'Better leave him alone, eh?'

He felt himself strangely unsettled by the incident but attempted to brush it aside, telling himself that the irascible youth had no doubt been caught up in a fight and had not wished to be seen in the face of such evidence. Kate and Khumar approached the precariously timbered jetty and caught sight of the ferry boat. It had already begun boarding. Their own predicament had been temporarily overshadowed by the sight of Ami.

'I better let you go.' Kate smiled spiritlessly.

Cargo and Sunday passengers, for the mainland, organised

by a Fijian crew shouting merrily at everyone, were being hauled aboard.

'I've got a few moments.' He took her hand, and stroked it lightly. 'Take care of yourself,' he whispered.

The boat hooted its bull-like cry of departure. Khumar stepped aboard. He glanced about him, in seach of Ami. Perhaps the boy was heading for the mainland, but there was no sign of him. He had disappeared into the bulging shanty streets built at the edge of the sea's grimy banks.

Kate waved as she stood watching from the dockside. The ferry drew away from the reeking port. Khumar watched her silhouette fade to pinpoint as the outline of the coast took shape. To the left of him were sugar plains, Lesa Plantation land, Sam's land, Kate's land, green, fresh and thriving; and to the right, unlaboured land, swamp land, overrun with teeming, infested mangrove swamps.

Somewhere in the midst of all this Ami was running. Kate was leaving. And he was left to fight alone.

Ami's shame, the cause of his fight, was born of his present distress. He paused now, panting, to draw breath. Thankfully they had not followed him. He could not have borne to face them, tormented as he was by his present circumstances.

He set off towards the bus station, dragging himself miserably towards the square, remembering that little Jal would have been on his own now for almost twenty-four hours. Stone had given him one week to pack up his belongings, which were few, and leave his hut on the Plantation.

Perhaps he could persuade Raj, Ashok's manager, to allow him to continue selling the pirated cassettes. After all, he told himself, they had always been friends. And Ashok need never know. His position as future Prime Minister would not be jeopardised. He thought back again to his meeting with Ashok Bhanjee. Why had Ashok not understood that he was willing to take on any position that might be offered to him in the emporiums business? He would start anywhere. But Ashok had not even wanted to discuss it.

'I hear, Ami, that the new owners want to make changes to

181

your plantation,' Ashok had confided. 'It will mean no more work for Indians. Someone should stop them, don't you agree? . . .' What difference did it make to him now? He no longer cared.

But perhaps it would make a difference to Ashok if he could see that Ami was capable of taking action independently. That would prove irrefutably that he was worthy of a responsible role, ready to take on any challenge that might be handed to him . . .

The turbulent youth sat shoved against a window on the teeming, airless bus. A cambered road, potholes and no suspension exacerbated the discomfort and length of the journey. The antiquated bus stopped in every village, and several times in between each of them, to deposit and transport Indians and Fijians with their kava root for pounding grog, their cock-a-doodle-dooing chickens, their radios, their children and occasionally even their furniture. Once or twice the entire Fijian busload poured off to load, and later unload, a mattress, table and several chairs which, after much discussion and riotous giggling, were tied precariously to the already bulging open boot. On weekdays the bus made this winding journey hourly but this was Sunday and the service was limited. Ami was sitting on the only bus leaving before seven o'clock. To a stranger, it would have seemed that the entire population of Loquaqua was on the move.

He gazed out of the window without noticing the green cane of the Lesa Plantation passing alongside them, nor the interior of the crowded bus where Fijian sat beside Fijian and Indian with Indian, wherever possible avoiding direct contact with one another. He thought only of his miserable future and what was to be done with it.

In the distance, as the rickety bus began to moan its way up the incline towards Lesa Plantation House, he saw the dusky-grey pillars of the smoking canefields. Pockets of dark, sweet smoke were rising into the sweltering afternoon heat as the stubbled cane was burnt. He watched it, quietly burning with tears, filled with hatred for his lost labours.

On his walk up the hill towards his hut he saw Stone.

182

Briskly he stepped from the track in an attempt to avoid him but Stone had already seen his approaching silhouette.

'Ami,' he called to him. 'You make sure you're packed and gone by Saturday. Do you hear me?'

Ami glowered in silent rage.

'And Ami, I'm taking last night's damages out of your money. Any more trouble and I won't give you a week to get out. You'll be on the next ferry, kid an' all.'

Ami stalked his unspoken anger into the fresh living canefields. Silently, in the late afternoon heat, he sat watching fellow Indians, canecutters, burning the chopped residue. He calmed himself, dreaming alone, breathing the scent of charred, black, angry smoke.

And then his task became clear . . . He was determined.

That night with the agility of a snake his dark figure slithered through the tall, ripe, tussocked sugar grass. Stealthily he scurried to vantage points, longing to witness the labours of Stone and his team disappear into threatening, brutal columns of navy-grey heat and to savour the aroma of that revenge. As he lit the first of many matches, he felt satisfied knowing that he would upset the balance here, he would stop them, and he would prove to Ashok that he, too, could take responsibility.

Ami set the Plantation alight.

Chapter 14

'*Kama! Kama!*'

Stone rolled over in his sleep. Some disturbance jerked him awake. Someone belting down the dusty street, yowling his name. 'Stooone! Fiirre!' He sat bolt upright, bleary-eyed, flinging himself from the bed as Timi, sweating, heavy sandals thudding against his wooden floor, came pounding into his room.

'Cane's burning. Faster than the plague.'

'Jesus Christ!' Stone grabbed for his jeans, pushing Timi aside. Outside the light was fretted. Vermilion flames swirling like firecrackers ascended into a roaring sky. Panic was spreading through the terrified village. People milling to and fro, children crying, dogs barking, babies nestled at breasts screaming blankly. No one slept. Everyone running crazy.

'God damn it! Let's get moving!' he shouted. Stone headed on up the hill. They would need the jeep, which he had left parked at the house. Without pausing he shouted to one of the neighbours, 'Bruno! Gather up all the able men. Send one man on to the next village and from there someone on to the next. Get help. All the help you can! Get every one of them to bring hoses, buckets, blankets. Anything they can lay their goddam hands on. And Bruno, no women. No kids. Get moving!'

'How the fuck did it happen?' he yelled after Timi, who was striding in sturdy brown leather sandals behind him.

'Notta clue!'

They reached the jalopy, keys in the contact point and, losing no time, set off again down towards the valley below. Ahead of them, inland as they descended, the flames were leaping like gymnasts into the southern midnight sky.

'There's no one here! Timi! Get back to the village. Organise them! Get the men out here as quick as you can. I want someone on ahead cutting back the cane. Some cuttin' back in the valley and others working over to the east. I want everyone soaking the fields. Wind's movin' it south. I want nothing left dry, d'you hear me!'

Timi leapt obediently from the jeep, already shouting the alarm in his native tongue as Stone turned the vehicle around, spinning in the dark dust. He headed inland, uncertain whether he could stop the fire before everything was destroyed. Behind him the danger signal was being shouted into the roaring night air.

'*Kama! Kama!* Fire!'

Big-boned Fijians were arriving from everywhere. Word had spread through the neighbouring settlements. Trucks were arriving bulging with able-bodied men.

'We gotta first stop the fire and next, save everything we can! Right, let's get you guys into teams. Divide yourselves into groups of five and six. Make sure you got loadsa water with you. I want the guys who can drive to chauffeur the water to and fro. No slacking. No time for talking. We gotta get ahead o' the flames. Jump to it!' Stone's face was alight from the burning sky above him, sweating and charring his features, and his eyes were ablaze with determination.

They were gonna beat this!

Men were running backwards and forwards carting buckets, slipping on muddied patches of brown cut cane. The sky reeked of molasses.

''I'll get back to the main house and wake De Marly,' Timi called to him from across a dampened stretch of cane.

'Leave the bastard,' Stone cried hoarsely. His voice blotted with smoke.

Philippe was woken by the distant cries in the valley and

185

hurried to the window to see what the noise was about. There was something strange about the light. He stumbled down-stairs, blindly alarmed, but careful not to wake Kate. She turned in her sleep but was not roused.

Outside, there was a silence. Deadness. No birds screeched or moved. No sounds of life, at all. Like the end of the world. He looked skywards. It hovered above him, low, smutted black, eerily so, not a pre-dawn light but a threatening inkiness. And then he realised, no stars. They were obscured by blankets of thick smoke moving like metallic waves above him. The air about stank. A sweet, cloying smoke.

'*Qu'est-ce que se passe!*' he mouthed, swinging about him in search of the fire. Flames were roaring and blazing in the valley below. He hurried back inside, staggered up the stairs to dress and then, in sneakers and jeans, ran on down the hill towards the burning sky looming horrifically in front of him.

His step had woken Kate. She saw the empty place beside her, the darkening ominous light without and leapt fearfully from her bed. Beneath her, in the valley, the hellish fire, the *kama*, raged on, roaring through the night like a starved jungle beast tormenting those who worked defiantly against it.

Stone and Timi were battling against exhaustion. Organised parties of able, fearless Fijians, wearied and smoked out, were being bolstered by others from farther afield. Someone had driven to Loquaqua and woken up the local, inadequately equipped fire brigade. A long hard drive in the dark but they were expected any time. Thank God. The roasting flames were beating back those who struggled hard against them with nothing more than water buckets and inefficient hoses. As one field burnt itself out the flames continued to leap dart-like in search of other virgin cane.

'What can I do?' Philippe shouted, gasping as he approached.

'Get into one o' the gangs and take orders from the leader,' Stone bellowed at him. The entire area was a raging furnace.

'I'll stay and help you. Has someone woken up the canecut-ters? Lets get the Indians down here!' Philippe retorted.

'Listen . . . If you wanna help, see Timi. Just keep outa

186

my way. You hear me?' A young Indian ran to Stone's side, grabbing at his naked blackened torso, begging attention for advice. Stone's eyes dismissed Philippe who turned in search of Timi. It was no time for their personal hatred. He would fight in the line.

Nearby, in his small corrugated hut, Ami lay beside his sleeping son listening to the extent of his work. Little of the uncut crop would have been saved. He was satisfied. His honour had been vindicated. He closed his eyes, weary at last, and dreamed of Ashok's face. The pleasure he would see there, when he gave him the news. He would be rewarded for his ingenuity.

By dawn the flames had begun to fracture, thus making it easier to combat the wall that had blazed on through the night and razed the rich, green crop to the ground. Little, if any, of the cane would be saved. But no villages had burnt, and, mercifully, no one had been hurt. The small lorry that represented the fire brigade arrived towards dawn. It was almost too late. The fire was abating and there was little left to burn.

'Lets get some of these guys home,' Stone suggested to Timi, drained and disappointed.

They packed off most of the exhausted men, back to their villages to sleep. Throughout the night there had been others who had volunteered, arriving in dribs and drabs to join the firefighters as the news reached them in their various homes closer to Loquaqua. They stayed on for a while to help with the clearing. They had arrived willing to take the places of the tired men but by then the worst was over.

'Looks like we beat it, but there ain't much of it left, boyo,' Stone said to Timi, sadly imitating Sam, as the pair stood alone watching the fire engine begin its journey back to Loquaqua. The beaten men were drifting slowly into the morning. 'You better get some shut-eye, mate.' He slapped his comrade on the shoulder with gratitude and respect. The two men stood helplessly, side by side. 'An' I better get the boss back up the hill, eh?' he muttered bleakly.

Stone drove Philippe back to the Plantation House. Their

187

faces were smeared with charcoal and sweat and their exhausted bodies ached, too drained to speak or sleep. Stone was too broken even to dislike him.

'Use the downstairs bathroom and get cleaned up. I'll make some coffee. I don't suppose Miriam's here yet,' Philippe offered as they pulled up in the jeep.

They sat drinking locally roasted instant coffee, already made by Kate, who had been waiting anxiously on the verandah. 'I thought I better keep out of the way. Stay up here,' she explained when they found her, sitting alone. 'How did it happen?'

'We ain't sure but I got a damn good idea,' Stone said and went inside to wash.

The sun crept up from behind the mountains. The coffee tasted foul and was only lukewarm. Philippe remembered having tried it the first morning or so after his arrival and had vowed never to touch the stuff again. This morning he was too tired to care. When Stone returned he sat exhausted, seething with regret, his eyes firmly shut. They were not comfortable in one another's company but the struggle had given them a point of contact for the first time, like two strangers side by side in war.

'Thank you for your help. I would never have heard it in time, up here,' Philippe proffered.

'In time!' Stone retorted bitterly. He shrugged and shook his bowed head. 'We didn't catch it in time.' He looked scrubbed now and tousled but strained and wrecked. He ached with sadness. 'How can you say that! We'll have to lay the men off. Poor bastards,' he said painfully. 'I'll get Timi to pay them off later this morning. They'll have a pretty lean Christmas.'

Kate watched his anguished beaten face as he slurped at the warm liquid, wishing she could help him.

'This coffee's piss. Got any beer?' he asked, getting up to look for it himself without waiting for a reply.

Philippe blanched at his companion's Australian manners and looked at his watch. Almost seven-thirty. He stretched out a hand to Kate. He felt in need of her, wanted her warmth, her reassurance close to him. It had been a while, he thought. And he knew for certain now they should both get the hell out.

The shadow of Stone's body standing at the unevenly hung, open wooden doorway passed across the beaten face of Jal's sleeping father. Jal watched apprehensively. He was seated on the floor close to the foot of the camp bed, gazing anxiously at the white boss who had stepped inside their impoverished home. Stone ignored Jal and shook brusquely at his father's shoulder.

'Get up, Chand,' the white man ordered.

Ami's eyes opened slowly, as if he had not been sleeping at all but simply thinking, concentrating with closed lids. He expressed no surprise at such an intrusion but he made no effort to move.

'I said, get up, Chand. De Marly wants to see you up at the house in twenty minutes and I mean twenty minutes, or I'll wring your fuckin' neck. There's men down there, your kind, queuing to get paid off. Those guys worked almost a whole goddam season and now we gotta pay the poor buggers off, on account o' you. You selfish little bastard!'

Stone turned without waiting for a reply and strode out into the morning sun. He took in a deep unsteady breath. The air he breathed was acrid, sooted. Small flakes of cindered vegetation drifted deliberately on the almost imperceptible wind.

Further down the hill, the sky was overcast with bruised, smudged markings. Bands of dark smoke rose in sheets towards the sky like thunderous rain falling in the long distance. Little had been salvaged of the remaining uncut crop and Stone knew it now. He was dearly glad that Sam was not alive to witness all this.

Earlier he had called the Indian canecutters together, over a hundred men, many fatigued from firefighting, and had told them they better pack up their belongings and go back to their families in Loquaqua, the mainland or wherever the hell they had travelled from.

189

'There's gonna be no more cutting this season,' he had announced. 'No more work for you here. Get your stuff together. They'll be buses laid on from later this afternoon. Timi'll see ya all. And, fellas, thanks for your help.'

Not for several seasons would things be running smoothly again. The poor bastards will be lucky to find work canecutting, now, he thought to himself, too late in the season. Only a coupla weeks left to Christmas. One or two might get a break, and he would keep a dozen or so of them here until the end of the year, to help clean up the place, sort things out. But for the rest?

It would have broken ol' Sam's heart to see Timi paying them all off. Weary men in worn sulus queuing like ants for their due. They would have their ferry passage and a bit more but that was about it. By the end of the week the Plantation would be pretty dead. The place was broke. No insurance would cover all this. A pittance only.

He turned his gaze away from the smouldering valley; he was so dog-tired he thought he would weep. He hurried back through the forest path to the main house.

So the De Marlys would be forced to sell, after all. Not that they had mentioned their plans to him. He had overheard Philippe on the radio telephone about half an hour earlier calling a number in Suva and he had been asked to drive them to Loquaqua for the early afternoon ferry. He idly wondered if they were selling 'the farm' to planters or resort owners. Christ knows what he was going to do, he thought. But then he had been asking himself that for weeks now. Anyways, he decided, it was about time to get the hell out. Move on someplace else.

'But it is true, Ami, that Mr Stone had given you the sack only a couple of days ago?'

'Yessir.'

Kate leant back in the cushioned, wicker sofa and closed her eyes. This could be a migraine! She detested listening to Philippe grilling the boy like this. For it was grilling. Nailing him into a confession.

190

'And you still hold that you had nothing to do with the fire? That you were sleeping and heard absolutely nothing?'

For a moment the boy made no response. Kate listened to the silence then turned her head, opening one eye to regard him. He was certainly nervous, wet with sweat. But that could be Philippe and Stone sitting in front of him in angry judgement. Inexplicably she remembered the poor fellow at the port on the morning of their arrival. He had looked so guilty too, even before the customs officials had found the cassettes hidden beneath his pyjamas.

Deftly, with forefinger and thumb, as she watched him, Ami picked individual beads of sweat from his beaten face, from where they sat like irritating pimples or flies.

Stone, seated beside Philippe, lit another cigarette and exhaled pensively. The smoke annoyed Philippe. But he said nothing. Both studied the boy. 'I think you're lying, Chand,' Philippe accused.

The boy shook his head vigorously and the sweat sprayed his interrogators. 'No sir, I'm not lying,' he lied. His words were hoarse, strangled. Either side of his slender hips his hands hung, clenched into tight, wet fists.

Did it matter now? Kate asked herself angrily. She had agreed to sell the place. Perhaps the boy was guilty. *Probably* the boy was guilty, but she wished they would just let him go. They had no proof, nor it seemed would they be able to prove anything. Philippe had refused to call the police when Stone suggested it earlier. He was fearful they might lose their offer. So why torture the boy for a confession if he would not allow the police to punish him justly?

'We'll keep all this quiet,' Philippe had said. 'Everyone will know about the fire, of course, but we'll claim it was an accident. There's enough uncertainty and unrest here as it is. Let's get the contract and deposit agreed and get out of here.'

She ran her fingers through her hair, stood up and went inside to shower. It must be nearly eleven and she hadn't even washed yet. Stone's eyes, unnoticed by Kate, briefly wandered from Ami as they followed her sauntering into the house.

'I think you should let him go,' she announced defiantly as

191

she stepped across the verandah into the inner cool hallway. Philippe sighed loudly, articulating his irritation at her remark. Stone noted it, and so did she as she disappeared inside.

I don't care! she mouthed furiously to herself, wondering what Sam would have done under these circumstances. The truth is, it would never have reached this bloody mess if Sam had been here, she thought.

She untied the sulu knotted around her breast, letting it fall loosely about her feet, leaving her body naked. She stretched to turn on the shower taps. They had an afternoon appointment with Danil. She had agreed with Philippe that she would sell the Plantation and he was keen to settle and sign the deal that day, fearful that any delay would lose him his flight.

'Oh, God, Sam, I'm sorry!' she wailed audibly, as the hot water flowed on to her upturned face and cascaded down around her sunburnt flesh. 'What can I do?' Her eyes felt puffy and tired, her whole body saddened and weary. The warm water was only a temporary respite. She would sign the damned papers but she wasn't leaving with Philippe . . . not yet!

The next morning feathery twists of grey-blue smoke were still drifting from the cindered landscape. But it was an assuaged anger, the day after the massacre. There was nothing left to gut.

The office door was closed, no activity within. Timi had not been seen this morning and Stone was nowhere to be found. The place was like an emptied school at the beginning of summer when all life but oneself has departed. Kate was sitting pouring a cup of tea from the lukewarm pot, her hair still ruffled and uncombed. The cicadas were already sizzling like a chain saw into the melancholic air. These days before Christmas were the hottest. Thickly sliced, factory-processed bread lay on a chipped, cream-coloured plate in front of her. She stirred the tea and pushed the unappetising breakfast across to the other side of the table, where Philippe's dirtied plate had been discarded.

She rarely ate in the mornings, even in England. Back at home – London seemed so distant to her now – she was usually out of bed before Philippe, preparing his breakfast. Here in Fiji the heat, combined with the recent circumstances (though she preferred to blame the heat), had shrivelled her appetite and she had become noticeably thinner these last few weeks. She found it attractive. She enjoyed the feel of her bones rubbing tight against her light skin but Philippe would, no doubt, soon start to complain. He had always preferred her with slightly more flesh. 'I'm not fond of an anorexic woman,' he would tease.

There had been little physical contact between them since they had arrived here, at her father's home. She had not intended her refusals as rejections but . . . she supposed he must be feeling miserable about that as well as everything else. Sex had always been a regular event in their well-structured married lives.

She sipped her tea. It was going to be a difficult day. Philippe was furious that she had changed her mind.

A gull screeched overhead, a raucous piercing cry. She watched the approach of two barefooted Indians, trousers rolled to just below their knees, wandering languorously to and fro. They carried their gardening hoes against their shoulders, like rifles, and she quickly averted her gaze for fear of catching one or other's glance. Such mysterious eyes! She could not bear just to smile and say good morning, as though nothing had happened. But these were the lucky ones, the ones that still possessed work.

Would the new owners, whoever they might be, rebuild the Plantation and keep on the remaining staff?

Kate was never very mellow in the mornings and today she was feeling particularly bloody. These last few days had been taxing. Her thoughts returned to Khumar; she dismissed him directly. She ran her unvarnished fingers through her hair and leant her weight back into the raffia chair. She was feeling desolate. Bidding Khumar farewell; and wishing more than anything in the world that she had not agreed to the sale of the Plantation.

Philippe rounded the wooden verandah corner and stepped up on to the porch. He was slickly dressed, in an ivory-coloured suit, ready for his departure, unlike Kate who was still wearing her sulu. She busied her fingers, retying the knot around her breast; she had bought it in the local village the afternoon that she had visited Sam's grave.

Philippe looked grim. In a hopeless moment of panic she wondered if it was perhaps not too late to put a stop to the proceedings.

'I've just spoken to Stone,' he began, as her moment of illogical fear subsided. 'I've paid him up to the end of January. He's agreed to stay on here for the time being. Look after the place, clear up the mess. I told him you'd be staying here . . . for a bit . . . couple of weeks at the outside, I thought.' He fell silent and regarded her. From his considerable height he scrutinised the tired features of her upturned face. His disquiet was undisguised.

So that's how long he's giving me, she thought, but said nothing. Nothing had been mentioned before, by either of them, about a couple of weeks. She could not promise two weeks. She perceived a vulnerability in his features; deep blue eyes strangely saddened. It was an expression that she had rarely, if ever, read in his face. It surprised her, caused her a pang of guilt.

'You're certain about this. You're not going to regret this, change your mind again when I've gone? I can still radio across to the airport and get you a seat.'

She shook her head quickly and averted her gaze.

'Christ, Petal! Are you going to be all right?' he asked again. His voice was nervous, almost petulant, like a child not winning his own way.

'Of course I shall. Please Philippe, don't make such a fuss. It's only till the contract's settled.'

Stone approached from around the corner of the terrace, from where he had been talking to Philippe, finalising details. He stepped up alongside them on to the verandah, mumbling an almost inaudible good morning to Kate, and strode purposefully towards his office. Kate lowered her unscrubbed face, mouthing a response, waiting for him to pass.

The two mongrels trailed obediently behind him but as Stone disappeared Poncho turned and padded back, deciding to settle at Kate's bare feet.

'I need it, Philippe,' she continued softly. 'A short time here alone. I'll sign the papers, close up the house and . . . It won't take long.'

'Yes, yes, I know. It's just that I think it's dangerous here. Why don't you come back with me, and then, if you really feel you need a break, you can go down to Antibes, stay with my parents or rent a villa in the village there. At least I'd know you were safe, but here . . .'

'Philippe, please try to understand . . . it's here that I want to be. Sam's house . . .' she sighed.

'Is there any more tea in the pot?' he enquired abruptly, clumsily changing the subject, feeling at a loss.

'It's not very warm.'

'Doesn't really matter.'

She drew his soiled cup towards her and began silently to pour the barely warm liquid followed by two heaped teaspoonfuls of sugar and his dash of milk. He pulled one of the wicker chairs closer, so that it was beside her, and folded himself down into it.

'Here,' she said gently, handing him the cup.

'I'm not happy about it, Kate. You know that, don't you? I can't think why it's necessary. Your father's dead and buried. The place is burnt to hell. There's nothing here now. We can settle everything else quite easily from London,' he began, placing the untouched cup back amongst the breakfast plates. 'And I don't believe it's safe here. This fire . . .'

'Philippe, we've been through all this last night. Nothing's changed. I am not coming with you. I want to stay on here.'

'Yes, I realise that but . . .'

'Just stop, please,' she began forcefully and then rubbed her hands across her bare, crumpled face and sighed impatiently. They sat close to one another, in silence. She just didn't want to fight about it any more. They had been through the same

195

argument endlessly during the past twelve hours. Round in circles, since she had first told him conclusively that she had decided to stay. She felt foolish, changing her mind again, but it was what she wanted.

'All our married life I've stayed beside you. Done what you wanted, folllowed your advice. But this is for me. Me and my father . . . I've agreed to sell, against my better judgement. Now please, let me see it through. Let's not keep going on and on about it.'

Philippe took a deep, pinched breath. His thoughts drifted back to the meeting the day before in Danil's office. It had been tense but the fire had not been an obstacle. . . . He had feared it might ruin the deal but, curiously, Danil had still been satisfied with the price. Philippe had also been fearing that at any moment Kate might change her mind and withdraw from the agreement, but she had accepted it. That, at least, was settled. They would have their *handsel* in Switzerland. He had been expecting that once the Plantation was no longer 'hers' she would feel less emotional about the place, that she would be happy to leave with him, but she was still being difficult. At first he had shouted, lost his temper with her, told her he wouldn't hear of such rash decisions but once he had understood the depth of her resolve he had withdrawn and left her alone. Nonetheless, he feared for her, her safety here alone. He realised that he had probably overreacted with her but that did not change his concern. She was behaving irresponsibly. It was simply foolish to put herself unnecessarily at risk.

The place was rife with racial hatred. Any fool could see that. Fiji reeked of dissension. It felt like living inside a volcano that was about to erupt. Not here on the Plantation, perhaps, but . . . the fire at the weekend had confirmed his worst fears about the underlying disharmony. The fire was an act of arson, vandalism, an expression of the tensions on the island. Kate was unwilling to accept that but he would say no more. Anything else would only alienate her further and cause a deeper friction between them. Philippe stretched out his arm and touched her unscrubbed delicate face. She smiled disheartenedly and rose from him, leaning out over the timbered porch. Bougainvillaea petals brushed lightly against her arm and cheek. He considered her shoulders, her body naked beneath her sulu. It was painful for him.

'It's so beautiful here, tranquil,' she said. 'I hadn't realised before. It's a pity that we haven't had a chance to enjoy it.'

If Sam had been alive we would have had the holiday we'd planned, she thought, resolving to relish the short time that she had left to her here. She was allowing it to be sold. She felt she had betrayed his memory.

The radio telephone in the office began to ring. Philippe, still seated behind her, stood up and walked through into the house, calling out to Stone. Poncho stood too, stretched and yawned and wandered towards Kate, a few steps to be at her side. He whined for attention and she stroked at the soft hair on his skull.

She was feeling guilty about Philippe. Part of her longed to reassure him, to tell him that her behaviour was foolish and sentimental and that, of course, she would be leaving with him. But she knew she could no longer do that. She had to stay. Somehow, though how she could not yet say, she felt her destiny lay here. For a short while, at least. Just as if Sam were calling her, beckoning to her. And what of his death? She was still not satisfied . . . But how could she say that to Philippe? Her thoughts were interrupted by his return to the verandah.

'I'm going to have to change my connection in Los Angeles. The airline have just radioed across. Apparently there's been a delay. We won't be leaving until eleven-thirty tonight,' he said as he arrived at her side, clearly aggravated. 'I can't charter the seaplane. They're full this afternoon, so I've asked Stone to take me over in the speedboat before dark. It'll take longer but I can't face that damned ferry, not with the luggage . . . Will you come too?' he whispered, caressing the back of her turned head. 'To see me off? Or would you prefer to stay here?'

She turned her face towards him, smiling warmly. 'Of course I'll come, silly,' she reassured him. He had taken off his jacket.

'I'll book you a hotel then, in Suva. It'll be too late to return

197

here tonight. I'd better book Stone into the same place. I suppose he'll know where you can both stay.'

'Yes, if you like. I'd better get dressed.'

Alone in their upstairs bedroom Kate lay against the rumpled, unmade sheets and stared listlessly at the ceiling fan. During these last few weeks it had become a source of comfort to her. Its regular creaking as it wound its way, cooling and soothing her. Fans. They served a dual purpose in this climate, she thought, like listening to the certain ticking of one's own heart. She had still not bothered to dress, preferring to gaze, if not at the fan, then out of the window across to the distant islands. She closed her eyes and listened to the cicadas screeching amongst the trees. What would become of her here alone, she wondered? Blaming her inertia, once more, on the heat.

'I've booked you a room at the Grand Ocean. I thought you were going to dress?'

She turned her head towards the door and opened her eyes. 'Yes, I am.' He seemed about to say something but clearly thought better of it.

'Here.' He crossed into the room and placed a page torn from his meticulously maintained diary on to the dressing table, littered with her jars of skin cream. 'I've scribbled down a few telephone numbers. Just in case you need anything.'

'What numbers?' she asked languidly, rubbing her right hand through her still tousled hair and marvelling at the idea of Philippe 'scribbling' anything.

'Mine in New York. I'll be at the Meridian until Friday night then I'm on the British Airways flight to London. It's written down. The BA 176 which gets me in at eight-thirty a.m. Saturday. Unless there's a hiccup I'll be at the house by ten-thirty on Saturday morning. Then there's Khumar's, the British Embassy over on the mainland, American Express and Susan's. She'll be at the office all week and will know my schedule in New York. I'm sure you have hers somewhere but it can't hurt to have it again. You might need something in a hurry.' His thoughts drifted somewhere as she watched him

198

walk towards her. He seemed ill at ease as he perched himself gingerly on the border of the mattress and dared his hand to stroke her ankle upwards to her calf. The ring that she had bought him on their tenth wedding anniversary felt hard against her ankle bone.

'You're losing weight, Petal,' he whispered, his head bent, staring only at her leg. 'I love you, you know that, don't you?'

She nodded awkwardly.

'For Christ's sake, take care!'

Suddenly she felt angry. It shot through her like a knife searing into her stomach. What for? His unexpected helplessness? This man that she had married, she neither knew now nor understood him. Was that her fault? This man, that only weeks ago she had perceived as brutish beside his Indian university companion, Khumar, of whom she could not bear to think. This man, her husband, who only yesterday she had witnessed relentlessly cross-examining a frightened Indian boy. She had grown so far away from him and she blamed him for it! And she felt such a weight of confusion and guilt. He tortured her now with his vulnerability, his weakness. She did not want to hurt him and yet . . .

'Stop it, Philippe! Jesus! You're making it so difficult. What's the point?' And she lifted her naked body from the bed. Fearful of weeping or, worse, hitting him, she walked to the armoire and opened a drawer in search of what . . . shorts! Found buried beneath an untidy clutter of lace briefs.

'You carry on as if it's forever!' She hated herself for saying this because in her heart she feared it might be forever. She felt as though her very thoughts were betraying him. She could see no way back and that was what pained her. 'Let's go for a swim,' she begged, wanting to get out of this oppressive room. His hurt trapped her, made her feel intensely claustrophobic.

She grabbed a beachrobe and swept impatiently from the room, leaving him alone on the edge of the dishevelled bed.

PART
2

Chapter 1

The sun beat down against the Pacific Ocean, reflecting its burning light with streams of amber ribbons. Outside the reef, where the ocean plummeted hundreds of feet to its sandy depth, the water was glaucous, glistening with shimmering silver refracted patterns. The speedboat bobbed to and fro, safely anchored, like a cradle being sensuously lapped by the waves.

Stone had been right. There was no immediate reason to hurry back to the Plantation. 'You should see something of the place. Get out on the water, do some swimming, mebbe a bit of diving,' he had suggested earlier in the day, when they had breakfasted together at the Grand Ocean Hotel in Suva.

She had accepted his offer of an afternoon tour around the island hoping that it would ease her into the prospect of time alone, although she knew these were not to be idle days. It was a little more than a week to Christmas now. She felt the pressure of the short time left to her weighing upon her, if, as she had reluctantly promised Philippe at the airport, she was to be home in England in time for their holiday. 'Hurry back, Petal, and we'll rent a house in the Alps. Spend an extra week, perhaps.'

It was half past four, Wednesday afternoon, and still burning hot. Philippe would be in Los Angeles by now, still Tuesday evening for him. He had crossed the date line, gone backwards in time. He would be waiting, no doubt, for his connection on to New York, stepping even further back into yesterday.

It was a strange concept for her. They had separated until Christmas, and now she felt him slipping away from her, moving into another time zone. Different days, different nights. It made him seem all the more remote to her, all the more part of yesterday's life. It felt frighteningly liberating.

Only she had reached Wednesday! Everyone else, the people in her 'real life', friends in England, in-laws in France, were still living Tuesday. But she was here alone, living on the islands closest to the first sunrise on earth. It seemed to give her a strange, inexplicable sense of courage, of adventure and of liberation. To be ahead of time, beyond it!

All those years that she had spent wondering about Sam, wondering where he was and what might be happening to him, all those questions about him, all those questions while he had been here. Living ahead of her. In time ahead of her!

It felt like a death.

Or another more liberated form of life.

'You all right?' Stone supposed that she was thinking about Philippe, missing him already. He did not know that she had chosen to stay on here alone. She nodded and smiled freely. Her face lit up.

She looked different, he observed, since her arrival here. Her skin had lost its pallid city texture. It was golden now. It glowed more, too. Her hair, bleached by the sun, was like chamomile. He had seen it happen before, to people in the heat, people from cities and northern lives. They loosened up. Not De Marly though, he thought scathingly. Take an earthquake to loosen him up!

'I was thinking about Sam,' she replied, without looking at him.

He had forgotten that he had asked her a question. 'Oh, yeah,' he responded, taking a shot from his cold beer bottle. He wiped the glass lips and held it in her direction. Kate shook her head, and then changed her mind.

'OK, why not?' She gurgled like a naughty child.

204

'It's cold,' he encouraged as she took the brown-glass, stumped bottle and swallowed from it. Indeed it was cold and tasted sharp, pleasingly so, against her chapped, slightly salted lips.

'You all right there? Not getting too burnt?' he asked warmly. She was looking pretty rouged, kept covering herself with cream which, as far as he could see, was making little difference. Nothing he knew could protect against this burning sun, if you couldn't take it. And no white man really could. He rarely let it get to his skin for any length of time. Even now he wore shorts over his trunks and a shirt.

'I'm gonna go down and get some lobsters for supper. You wanna come too, or just wait here? We're just into open sea here. Reckon you could handle it?'

She shook her head and handed him back the bottle. 'I'm not a very strong swimmer and I don't know how to dive. I'll just wait here.'

Kate watched fascinated as Stone slipped off his shirt and shorts and began preparing his diving equipment. Buckles and straps were clipped together with the ease of one who has performed this routine many times before. It was new to her. She knew nothing about diving and had never seen anyone put on the apparently cumbersome equipment. He clad himself in a life jacket and weight belt and then slung the iron lung over his smooth-skinned, brown shoulders. Once this was in place he leant his weight over the side of the launch, ducked his plastic and glass mask into the salt water then lifted it to his mouth and spat into it before rubbing it with his fingers. She was intrigued.

'Why are you doing that?'

'Mmm. Stops it fogging up when you're down there. Gotta see your way around the sharks!' he kidded, grinning at her apprehension. 'Here. These'd be about your size.' He threw a pair of flippers towards her which landed at her feet on the puddled, wooden deck. 'There's another snorkel and mask under my T-shirt, there. Just in case you wanna get in the water and take a look around. The coral's superb, but stay close to the anchor rope. Don't go wandering off. I'll be about half an hour, maximum.'

She glanced at his watch. She had noticed it before when

205

they had been driving together in the jeep. But only now did she realise that it was a diving watch, thick and heavy, silver framed, with several smaller dials within the clock face. Must be like wearing pebbled glasses, she thought as it gleamed in the sun, spotted with water. His arm was wet, from ducking the mask, and the blonded hairs stuck flat against his skin almost to his elbow. His arms were strong, solid.

He sat on the edge of the boat, held his hand over his face, covering the mask and regulator now in his mouth, fell backwards into the open sea and disappeared beneath the rolling water leaving a trail of air bubbles above him.

Kate was left alone on the open sea. She picked up Stone's T-shirt and placed it around her shoulders which were beginning to sting. She leant over the side of the launch, basking in her own idleness and the sight of living things she had never seen before. Transfixed by the moving aquamarine water she watched the floating nekton and gloriously coloured, tropical marine creatures scuttle playfully past her, oblivious to her curiosity. A World without Man. She envied Stone his liberty to explore it. It thrilled and seduced her with its silence, its unrevealed and as yet unspoiled life and its awesomeness. She lay back into the boat and felt its rhythm beneath her. The sky above her reclining form was an empty mass of clear blue. She felt glad to be here, to be so alone.

The boat rocked idly.

Stone returned with his catch, slung the beast on board and unhitched his diving lung. The newly arrived lobster, melon-toned and armoured, pounded his pincers against the slatted deck, struggling miserably for his life. Kate watched its battle, horrified, as Stone, pleased with his catch, steered the launch alongside the reef, keeping an eye out for the break.

He held a lit cigarette between his wet fingers. Damp crept along the white paper casing towards the burning tip but he didn't notice or, if he did, it made little difference. His hair, peroxided by his Pacific life, was now matted with deep-sea salt and the shirt that he had flung on after stripping himself of his diving equipment clung to his wet, easy-muscled flesh. He was in his element, an amphibian master. Unlike the lobster,

Kate judged. Suddenly she was reminded of Ami standing in front of Philippe, the master, sweating and afraid. He had been fighting for his life too. Chosen as a victim and accused by the powerful animal. It was no different. She wanted to fling the crustacean back into the sea.

'Open up that icebox and grab me another beer, will ya?' His voice boomed its Australian drawl so as to be heard above the sounds of both the diesel engine and the spray. She turned to the icebox. The lobster was wedged up against it, between that and Stone's diving lung lying on the deck. She felt afraid to go near it, lest it should nip her.

'What about the lobster?' she cried out, more to be heard than out of fear. Stone had his back to her at the wheel.

'Tell him to behave himself or you'll pick the bugger up and sling him outa the way!'

She couldn't see Stone's face but she knew he was laughing, revelling in her squeamishness. She had already begged him once to throw the poor creature back but he had only joked at her foolishness. 'Not much like your ol' man, are ya?' he had teased cheerfully.

She took a deep breath now, determined not to be made a fool of, and bent forwards towards the clawing, disoriented sea beast. As she lifted him at the centre of his back, as she had seen Stone do, his feelers and talons began flailing at her from every direction. She closed her eyes, breathed deeply to ease her pounding heart and flung him, ever so gently, overboard, back into the open sea.

Stone had not heard the splash, drowned as it was by the constant sound of the spray washing against the hull. He was singing quietly to himself, dragging on his damp cigarette.

Her hands delved in amongst the ice cubes and brought out a bottle, and then on reflection, two bottles. She was feeling triumphant, her spirits soaring with independence!

'Here!' she called blithely, having unscrewed the cap of one bottle on the base of the other. Stone had shown her how earlier. An Australian method, he had boasted. 'They're called stubbies.'

'Thanks,' he yelled now and stretched back for the bottle

207

and threw a mouthful of beer into his parched, salted gullet, without turning back. His concentration was with the launch.

They were approaching a break in the reef. 'Here we go, baby!' he called, almost crooning as he turned the launch and they sped past the broken coral wall into the shallow waters, inside the reef, that led them towards Lesa Bay.

The sun, preparing to set and sink behind them now, slipping lissomly beneath the ocean horizon, flooded the colours of the landscape ahead of her. She remembered her first sight of this island with its dusky mountains towering in the central belt against a celestial-blue sky. They no longer appeared alien or fearful to her. She exhaled deeply, cushioned and bolstered by their dignity and their pleasing familiarity. This was not uncharted terrain to her now, with its palm trees and sandied beaches. She felt at home here, enveloped by its abundance.

She caught sight of the charred, blackened land ahead of her. Her land. She thought of the destruction and of Sam. She was beginning to feel that this journey, a well-thought-through, cleanly prepared voyage, a simple answer to a call from her past, had shifted. It was taking an unexpected route. It was digging into ruins of remorse that she had long since buried, leaking muddied rivulets of doubt that she had packed safely away beneath her role of housemaker and wife. And the mountains ahead, indistinct in the sun's rays, suddenly took on a life. The shadow of a dead man heaved its fury all around her, nudging at her remorselessly, threatening never to give her peace until she found the courage to face its restless, beckoning umbra. His soul, trapped in limbo, cried out, calling for justice to be meted.

'Are you all right?' Stone took the power out of the engine, threw his cigarette butt overboard and began to idle the boat towards the shore, a calm meandering towards land. 'You look a bit freaked.'

'What's going to happen to Ami?' Kate asked suddenly.

He rubbed his free hand across his stubbled chin and turned to face her. 'Whaddya mean?'

'About the fire?'

'Nothing, unfortunately. Your husband said he didn't want any talk about arson, said he wanted it hushed up. Thought it might kill your sale. Nothing more I can do. The little bastard'll get away with it.'

'I don't know how you can be so certain that he's guilty.'

'Of course he's guilty. He was about the only guy who didn't come out to help. Said he heard nothing. He's paying me back for kicking him out.'

'Why did you kick him out? He seemed all right to me.'

'I told you weeks ago. He's a troublemaker, always fighting with someone. And he's not reliable. He's only interested in getting into business and making a buck. Bloody little fool. He's bein' used to run some small-time racket. Black-market videos for some big shot on the mainland.'

'Who?'

'I dunno. Some crook.'

'Why haven't you sacked him before?'

'Sam took him on board.'

He lifted the flap on the chest pocket of his shirt and drew out his cigarette packet, offering the box to Kate who shook her head. He put one between his lips and then replaced the carton.

'What do you care what happens to him? He just destroyed your ol' man's plantation crop,' he asked, with the unlit cigarette still in his mouth. He lit up before she replied.

'I don't . . . I was just wondering what will happen . . . with the son. He has no wife, has he?'

'She's dead. Died in childbirth. Sixteen years old.'

'Why did Sam bring him over here in the first place?'

'I dunno. Help out the guy Ami was workin' for, I think.'

They were approaching the bay. Stone turned back to the wheel and began to negotiate the shallow water.

'Mr Stone . . .'

'Call me Rob.'

'All right. Who found my father's body?'

The old vessel bobbed in the water lapping on to the bay as Stone leapt out over the side to secure the anchor in the sand higher up the beach. He strolled back towards the boat and offered Kate a helping hand to climb overboard.

209

'Hey, what the hell's happened to my lobster?' he protested, looking back inside the launch.

'I threw him back.' Kate was still gathering up her small overnight bag and sandals. 'Who found Sam's body that morning at the sugar mill?' she asked again as she jumped over the side into the ankle-deep, crystal ocean, letting out a small yelp as her feet splashed the water against her burning skin.

'Ami did. Jesus, Kate, that bugger was my supper!'

Kate helped Stone secure the speedboat and they trudged along the sand towards the jeep.

'I was gonna cook us all something on an open fire, invite you down to eat with us. But now we'll have to go beggin' for it. Get Miriam to rustle up something. You wanna come anyway?'

Kate shook her head, feeling penitent about the lobster. 'I want to go back to the house. Do a few chores.'

'I'll take you back up there. Check the office. I'll leave the jeep outside the house. Just in case you need anything. Or if you get hungry you can come and find me. You know your way about now, eh?'

'Thanks.'

'You sure you're gonna be all right, up here on your own?' he asked her as the jeep pulled up at the back of the house. 'Sure you won't come on down to the village?'

But she insisted, nodding affectionately, 'I'll be fine. Good night, Mr Stone.'

'Rob.'

'Yes, Rob. Thanks for today. I really enjoyed it,' she smiled.

'Keep the hounds in your room,' he volunteered, wandering off reluctantly along the gravelled path still joking loudly about his lost supper.

Kate felt lighter than she had for several days. Her isolation was balming. It was the first time that she had been entirely alone in the house. It felt liberating. She wandered idly, as she had in the days soon after her arrival, but more freely now, strolling from room to room, searching for trivia, anything that might tell her something about Sam. Except the office, that she respected as Stone and Timi's territory. But for the

210

rest, she moved about as though she were really taking possession of the place for the first time. An irony considering she had just agreed the sale. Like the bedroom above, the house was strangely lacking in personal knick-knacks. It told little of the man. Perhaps the two faithful mongrels, ever at her side, said more of Sam than any possessions.

Later she decided that she would find Ami's hut and pay him a visit. She took the jeep, and made her way several miles inland towards the rain forest. There, she discovered the path, signposted to the workers' settlement. It was cut through a jungle overrun with burgeoning breadfruit trees, moss-covered coconut palms, gnarled and malformed like shadowed spirits in the evening light, as well as glorious rain-forest trees known locally, Timi had told her a few days earlier, as *mbaka* trees.

A burnished umber trackway led inland above the highest point of her Lesa sugar fields. It was the uppermost limit of her property. Beyond this lay only impassable stretches of overgrowth leading towards the volcanoes. Here there were no signs of the fire. She drove for almost a mile, occasionally catching sight of floridly plumed squawking kula birds, collared lories, fluttering noisily amongst the towering vegetation. Finally as she approached the labour settlement the vegetation became less dense and the birds were nowhere to be seen. It was no longer a sunless wilderness. The path became bordered by banana trees, yellow with ripe fingers of fruit, papayas and mangoes.

In a powdery clearing beside what was now, in high summer, no more than a dribble of river, fed by a mountain ravine several miles further inland towards the mountainous interior, she found the canecutters' settlement. A cluster of rickety corrugated iron shacks haphazardly built were perched on the banks of the dusty rivulet, like an ageing patchwork quilt. This was the base for the canecutters. From here they could more easily find access down the hillside towards the ripening sugar fields. The casual labourers, the Indian canecutters, journeyed from the mainland every June or July and worked on the estate throughout the cutting season, until Christmas.

Kate drove stealthily, scanning the commune in search of Ami. There was an air of gloom about the place, silent and bleak, like a gritty ghost town en route to nowhere. A few chickens and one dust-caked pig were the only signs of life that she immediately spotted. Perhaps Ami had already left? Normally in the season upwards of a hundred men lived here. Two, and sometimes three, space permitting, shared a hut but many had already packed up and left, returning to their homes in the hope of finding several more weeks of work somewhere else. They had claimed their outstanding dollars from Timi, boarded the buses hired to transport them to Loquaqua and taken one of the ferries to the mainland. But it was nearly Christmas, the season for canecutting was almost at an end. The fire had cheated them of their last days of employment and those that still remained here were despairing and resentful. The hopefuls had fled.

In a few days the place would be almost entirely deserted, save for those that Stone was keeping to help clear up and those working in the gardens. The camp would then be left empty for months at the mercy of the rains and cyclones, flooding and regenerating it.

Kate spied a group of six or seven men with cracked, stained bare feet, sitting crosslegged, or lounging together, smoking, circled on the ground, like a python in repose. They turned at the sound of the arriving jeep. It was a vehicle they would have recognised, both Ami and Stone would have driven here many times, but Kate was an unexpected visitor and, she sensed by their expressions, one perceived as an intruder. Perhaps they feared that she had come to hasten their expulsion? She looked swiftly about her. Not a woman in sight. She pulled on the brake and stepped uncertainly from the jeep. 'I'm looking for Ami Chand. Do you know which is his hut?' Easier to visit the hut, she felt, and find out for herself if he had already left.

One man, the eldest of the bunch, a gaunt, hoary-headed fellow, pointed to a shack set higher than the rest, away from the manky riverbed. Kate shaded her eyes from the glare and stared back behind her, to where the man was pointing. She spotted a shack set apart from the others and supposed that was

212

the one. Nodding a thank you, she set off. The men continued to stare after her as she picked her way along the track winding between several unevenly built rows of dwellings.

The pathway was cluttered with buckets, filled with what she supposed by its colour was dirtied washing water. Lines of washworn garments were drying in the still open air. She had to stoop to avoid these. Small bundles of kindling sticks, old abandoned tyres securing lengths of blue plastic sheeting to the ground and several rusted petrol drums and aluminium cooking utensils lay scattered apparently randomly. As far as she could detect in the fast-dwindling evening light the cooking and eating in this deserted, beggarly place seemed to take place communally and out of doors.

It was airless here, still and malodorous. Mosquitoes thrived. She passed one solitary Indian crouched on the ground dicing a root vegetable that she could not recognise. His fingers were like chopsticks, thin as bones. Close to his side stood a much-used blackened pot containing dal and water. It was gently heating on an open fire. He peered at her mistrustfully and then, as if recognising her, smiled a warm welcome. Worn brown teeth and deep secret eyes.

She enquired again for Ami. He nodded enthusiastically and then pointed her on in the direction that she was already heading.

The door of Ami's hut was open and swung unevenly from its hinges like an oversized threadbare coat hanging uselessly from a dead man. As with all the others this hut was built from rusted sheets of corrugated iron attached to a timber skeleton. Kate approached the open door gingerly.

Ami was there, inside, lying on his bed with Jal sitting crosslegged at his feet. It was both dark and cool. There was a sweetish smell of burning spices which, although it deadened the putrid river stench, she found unpleasant, and supposed it was its unfamiliarity. A swarm of flies hovered noiselessly about the doorway. The seated Indians had had flies circling across their hands and faces, she now realised. They were everywhere.

213

As she peered uncertainly into the interior of his home she spoke his name softly, to ease the possible shock of her intrusion. 'Ami,' she said.

Both he and the boy threw a glance towards the door and recognised her. Neither moved, apparently unsurprised by her arrival. 'Hello, missus,' he replied, without stirring from the bed.

She dared a step indoors. There was no electricity inside. An unlit kerosene lamp, perhaps a storm lamp, stood on a naked wooden table at the far end of the single room. A black-and-white photo of a young Indian girl smiling was Sellotaped to one of the wooden timbers above it. One solitary chair stood alongside the table. It faced outwards, towards the open door like a third, immobile member of the household. Above the chair a small square had been cut out of the corrugated iron and draped with a fraying rice sack. This hessian sack was stamped with black lettering and served as a curtain. It was a plain rectangular space, his home; simple but surprisingly clean, serving only for sleeping and seeking refuge from the glare and heat of the sun.

Father and son must have slept huddled together in the one single bed with its lean, sunken mattress. For meals they would either have sat side by side on the dust-packed floor decorated with rush mats of vivid yellows and pinks or simply eaten outside. It had evidently never been thought of as a dwelling for more than one person and certainly not a child, as far as Kate's eye could judge. She wondered if the photo was of his young wife.

'May I come in?' she enquired.

He made no gesture either to invite or rebuff her but merely lay contemplating the ceiling with his arms folded behind his head in the manner of a pillow.

'Sure. You want something to drink, Mrs De Marly?' He sat up, rousing himself quite suddenly, coming to life as if some switch had been pressed on. He was wearing only a white sulu wrapped around his waist like a towel and around his dark-skinned shoulders hung his gold chain.

214

'No thank you, Ami. I just wanted to talk to you, if I may?'

He leapt up from the bed and pulled over the chair, carefully, almost defiantly, placing it close to him and gestured her to sit. She did so.

The three of them faced one another, in a circle. Father and son crosslegged on the bed and she, legs crossed, on the wooden chair. Now that she had arrived here and had found him she was feeling uncertain about where to begin, and glanced about her, rallying her thoughts, her courage.

On the floor at the foot of the bed in a small brass holder, like a decorated miniature candlestick, a joss stick burnt. She recognised now the sweet cloying smell that had initially repelled her. Beside it was Jal's silent, oversized radio cassette player, strangely out of place in this austere setting.

'I feared you might have already packed up and left,' she began.

'Saturday,' he answered confidently, without hesitation, undaunted by the future.

'I haven't come about the fire,' she assured him.

He made no response.

'Where will you go? Do you know?'

His small son, seemingly already bored with the English conversation, shuffled down from the bed and hurried out into the darkening evening light. In the distance voices could be heard, Hindi, echoing towards the sky, picked out against the descending blackness. Lamps were being lit, glowing and winking at her across the tinted pathway. Ami paid the disappearing boy no attention.

'To Suva. I start work there on Monday.' He became animated by his own good news.

'Really, where?' she asked incredulously, realising that she too had believed him guilty of the arson and therefore unemployable.

'Good friend of mine. Important man. I told him what Mr Stone has done to me and he gave me a job. Better job than here.'

She wondered whether his boast was a lie and watched him carefully, his body moving, as he slithered proudly from the

bed and glided towards the table. Beneath it, a plastic covering
hid a bottle of whisky and, it seemed, a motley assortment of
basic kitchen utensils which fell clattering as he scooped up
two white enamel mugs, handed one to her and returned to
his original berth, offering her a shot as he poured his own.

She accepted, as a gesture of comradeship or out of an
unwillingness to refuse him, and to conceal her guilt at being
ill at ease and just a little repelled by the basic nature of his
lifestyle. They clinked mugs in a maty fashion as he said: 'To
my new job!'

'Yes, of course! Good luck, Ami!' she toasted, sipping the
tepid liquor. He stood again, this time to light the lamp. It was
becoming impossibly dark now.

The undiluted liquor scorched her throat, causing her to
cough explosively as it burnt its way down towards her
stomach. She had never swallowed anything quite so lethal! It
must have been a rough local brew or simply her inability to
drink it neat. He slapped her lightly on the back, offered to get
water for her, which she refused, fearing for the village
hygiene, so he sat back on the bed. She shook her head and
spluttered, embarrassed, doing her best to minimise the
coughing and the smarting eyes.

The room flickered and glowed now with a serene, diapha-
nous light. Suddenly it made her unconventional surroundings appear quite welcoming. He leant back towards the floor,
stretching his naked torso sensuously like a whore, and flipped
on a tape of Indian sitar music.

'What's the job?' she asked hurriedly, to cover her embar-
rassment, both about the drink and his physical seductiveness.

'Business, missus,' he announced triumphantly. She could
tell now that he had not lied. His features shone proudly
amber in the light, beaming like a milk-bottle top.

She was reminded of Stone's remark earlier in the afternoon, out on the launch. Silly little fool's mixed up with some
black-market video deal. Some big shot on the mainland.
Wasn't that what Stone had said to her?

'What sort of work?' she pried cunningly, having recovered
her equilibrium.

216

'Manager of a store. A bit small but plenty of prospects. The company have plenty of opportunities for those who work hard and commit themselves.'

She watched him fascinated as he slugged his whisky and described the shop in Suva. He spoke as if he were reading from a pamphlet in an unemployment bureau. For several minutes he ran on, elucidating on the dream opportunities that were to become available to him. His plans reached as far as travels to Japan and the United States. He was to be the business representative for the company with, later, deals to be made in Europe, contracts to be signed in Paris and London. He was flying and, as far as she could tell, had temporarily forgotten her existence. She had merely been the trigger.

She waited patiently for him to draw breath and then interrupted him. 'Ami, is it true that you found my father's body?'

He sucked in his breath. The light had gone out of his features. His face fell as if being dragged back to a reality that he no longer recognised and perhaps despised. He stared at her uncomprehendingly.

'Is it true, Ami? Did you find Sam's body?'

'Yes, missus. Poor ol' Sam.' He poured himself another drink, a generous measure. She covered her own mug to prevent him offering her any more, while he drank, gulping at it, expressing his blatant discomfort.

Kate held her breath, willing herself not to speak, keen to observe his reactions and curious to know why he should suddenly be so ill at ease. She had not anticipated this reaction.

'What time was it, Ami, when you found him?'

'Early.' He stood up and restlessly paced his way to the open door, looked out into the early night, sipping his whisky as his furtive eyes scoured the surrounding terrain.

'What do you mean by early? Six o'clock? That sort of time?' She persisted, determined to regain his attention.

'Bit later, maybe.'

'What was he doing down there at that hour, do you know, Ami?'

'Not sure, missus.'

'Tell me what happened when you found him. Was he already dead? Were you by yourself? Did you call Stone? What were you doing at the mill at that time in the morning?'

'It's weeks ago, missus! I can't remember the details now.' She felt his resistance. He was squirming away from her questions and searching for a reason to be rid of her.

She was pushing too hard, she thought, driving him away from her. She would never win his confidence now unless she drew him more cunningly. 'I'm sorry to press you, Ami. I hadn't realised until this afternoon that it was you who had found my father and I . . . just wanted to know for sure what happened to him. You told me that he had had an accident, had fallen over because he'd been drinking. Did you see him fall over? It's just that . . . there seem to be several different opinions and as you were the last to see him alive, I thou –'

'I didn't see him alive, Mrs De Marly!' He rounded on her defensively. 'He was already dead by the time I got to him . . . That's all I know, missus, honest. Then Mr Stone came. He took care of him. That's all I know. I must take care of Jal now. It's suppertime. Sorry, Mrs De Marly.' And with his mug still in one hand and the bottle in the other he disappeared out into the still, navy night, heading towards the flushed flames of the camp fire where a spattering of men sat waiting for their supper under the stars.

'Ami,' she called, before he was out of earshot. His white cloth wrapped about him like a skirt stood out in the darkness, like teeth against black skin. 'When you told me the way to his grave why didn't you tell me that it was you who found him?'

'You didn't ask me,' he answered simply.

'Yes, of course. What's the name of your employer?'

He hesitated uncertainly before answering, curious to know the reason for her question but too proud of his triumph to resist the boast. 'Ashok Bhanjee, missus. Duty-free King.' With the answer still winging towards her, he was gone, heading towards his fellow Indians, freed from the cage of her questions.

218

She called after him, 'In case I don't see you again, Ami, good luck with your new job!'

Ami had not lied to Kate about the job waiting for him in Suva, although he had exaggerated the position that he was being offered. But that was no more than a mere detail, he felt certain, a matter of time only. It would take him no more than a few weeks to rise to the role of shop manager and then . . .! He exhaled contentedly. Bhanjee had, after all, come to his rescue, as Ami had always believed he would.

He had made a phone call to Bhanjee's office the previous afternoon. At first he had had difficulties getting through to the man himself but once he had loosely explained his reason for calling he was connected directly to Bhanjee and was able proudly to confide what he had achieved. Even now as he thought of it he conjured the flames roaring in the night and the excited, terrified Fijian voices, and later, Indians crying orders to one another.

'Yes, I heard about it, Ami,' Bhanjee had replied to him. 'Such bad news. I wondered what you knew about the incident, if anything . . . I also heard that the Plantation has finally been sold. So, I suppose you will be needing a job.'

And so the hungry boy's instinct had been accurate. He had finally proved himself. And now, after what had seemed to him such an interminable wait, his loyalty, service and silence were to be rewarded. His initiative had earned him his step into the world of commerce.

He sat quiescent and contented now, under the starry darkness, his young son at his side, and watched his crouching Indian companions grasping their meagre bowls of supper, scooping their hungry fingers into their waiting mouths. Not one of them had a future to look forward to. Probably they would remain unemployed until the next caning season. Six months of emptiness! How he despised their lack of ambition! Just as they covertly loathed his apparently unquenchable cupidity. Who amongst them, he asked himself, could understand his dreams, his fervent longing to better himself, make good for his son, and escape this beggarly existence?

219

He had told no one, excepting Kate, about his change of fortunes. Not even Jal, for fear his son would chatter amongst the labourers and create discontent. Didn't they despise him enough already for his solitariness and his independence? And for what they read as aloofness, which was simply time alone needed to formulate his plans. He supposed that no one this side of the island knew of his connection with Bhanjee. Nor about his part in the fire. And better so.

These men were casual labourers while he, and a handful of the house gardeners, were permanently employed at the Plantation. His role, given to him by Sam, had been a more responsible one, keeping order in the gardens, cleaning and putting away the tools, errands for the house, running guests and main staff to and from the ferry at Loquaqua. There was no reason why these men should know anything about his private life, or secret ambitions.

Jal collected his bowl of food from the Indian whom Kate had seen earlier chopping the vegetables and sat happily munching at his father's side, while Ami poured himself another whisky. He winked contentedly at his son but he had no appetite himself.

Stone's jeep could be heard chugging into the distant nightfall. He turned vaguely to look at Mrs De Marly on her way back to the main house. He liked her, she was a nice lady like her father, but he felt no guilt towards her about the fire. It had been a necessary action. He did not allow himself to consider his feelings towards Sam. Sam was dead now.

He felt it would have been better for her if she had gone away with her husband. He wondered why she continued to ask questions about Sam, and wondered what she might already know. It made him uncomfortable. He took a long slug of whisky and scratched at his bare skin. Mosquitoes! Damn this detested place!

Saturday morning he would leave, bright and early. Friday night, his last here, would be time enough to tell those still left about his good fortune, and any that had secretly clapped jubilant hands about his dismissal, they could weep into their plates. He would sing his success.

220

Chapter 2

The radio crackled and Philippe's voice came through as if from a ventriloquist's case. 'I've had a hell of a job trying to get through to you! What time is it there?' he continued.

'Nearly half past four, Friday afternoon! How are you?' Kate spoke slowly, enunciating the syllables to facilitate his understanding. He sounded so distant!

'It's still Thursday here!'

'Yes, I know.'

'How are you, all right? No hiccups?'

'No hiccups,' she affirmed, wondering if she felt pleased that he had called. It was reassuring to know that he was safe.

'Have you heard anything . . . Dan . . . said he . . .' The radio hummed, buzzed and then fizzled. They had been disconnected or the lines to the island had gone dead.

'Philippe! Philippe! Hello?'

'Can you hear me?' his tiny alien voice cried. 'Danil? Have you heard from Danil about the papers? He was supposed to be in touch today.'

'He rang this morning.' She was almost shouting now. It felt such an effort to communicate. 'He said the papers were still with the lawyers in Suva but he was expecting they'd be ready by Monday. I said that I'd go over to the mainland and sign them in his office on Monday afternoon. He agreed to call me over the weekend if there were any more delays.'

'Good. I might give him another ring tonight. Put the pressure on. Have you booked a flight yet?' The echo and crackling on the line had disappeared and she could hear him clearly now, just as if he had suddenly travelled distances towards her. She sighed, feeling his question pressure her.

'Not yet,' she replied.

'I see.' In the silence she felt she could hear his uncertainty, and a buried anger. She hated these long-distance calls. There was either nothing to say or it was too difficult to speak easily.

'I might call you back later, after I've spoken to Danil.'

'No, listen, Philippe. I won't be here. I'm going to a wedding this evening. With Stone . . . with Timi and Stone. In Timi's village. Some relatives of his. Call me tomorrow.' She fancied she had heard footsteps on the porch in front of her but no one walked past the office window. One of the dogs whimpered half-heartedly from the kitchen at the rear of the house. 'Call tomorrow, Philippe,' she reiterated, more hastily.

'All right, Petal. Go carefully at the wedding. Watch what you eat or you'll get food poisoning. Might not be well enough to travel. I'll talk to you tomorrow. Call Shyam if you have any problems.'

'Yes, all right.' But she knew that she wouldn't call Shyam. She had promised herself.

'I love you.'

How long was it since they had talked of love on the telephone? Normally these business calls were more perfunctory. She felt his need for her commitment, her reassurance that all was well and she would soon be on her way home. But she wasn't ready to give it to him. Not yet.

'Yes, I love you, too. Take care of yourself. Bye.' It was true. She did still love him . . . She replaced the handset and walked through from the office on to the verandah. Stone was there, sitting in the rocking chair. He smiled as she approached.

'Oh, sorry. I hadn't realised you were already here!'

'Heard you talking on the radio so I thought I'd wait out here for you. How're you doing?'

He had shaved, she noticed. He looked all spruced up.

222

Clean denims this afternoon, clean shirt. It made her smile silently. It almost felt like a date. She wondered if he had overheard her conversation with Philippe.

'I'm nearly ready. I was interrupted by the call. That was Philippe, from New York.'

'Yeah,' he said, looking at her. Her dress was flimsy, perfect for the climate. Light blue, with a loose skirt, delicately transparent, no sleeves, thin shoulder straps. She was wearing open, low, slingback sandals and a pearl necklace which sat easily against her collar bone. She had dressed for a conventional wedding. Very European. She looked very beautiful. He noticed her skin. It was delicately tanned now, there were freckles on her face where the sun had caught her.

'I'll need my hat. It's on the bed. I'll be back in a tick.' She disappeared back inside the cool house and hurried up the stairs feeling unreasonably excited, like a child on her way to her first party. Within moments she was back, flushed and eager, but he was still sitting rocking to and fro, enjoying a cigarette.

'Listen, there's no hurry,' he drawled as she returned to the verandah. 'Wedding's at five. That means nothing'll happen before six. We call it "Fiji time" here! We've got time for a drink.' He grinned.

Feeling a little discomfited by his ease and familiarity she settled herself into one of the wicker chairs and fanned herself with her beaten straw hat. 'I'm so used to being on time . . . what with Philippe's business and . . .' She apologised uneasily, feeling foolish.

'There's a bottle of Scotch in my office. We'll have one for the road. How do you take it? With ice?'

'And water, please. But not too strong.'

'Don't wanna get drunk, eh?' Stone teased.

He rose and drifted lazily into the house. The two dogs, whom Kate had closed into the kitchen thinking that her departure was fairly imminent, recognised his footsteps and began a chorus of welcome. She heard the office door close after him as he headed down the hallway towards the scullery, his voice humming as he prepared the two drinks and crooned

223

phrases of affection for the overexcited animals who, freed, came bounding out on to the porchway, tails wagging, tongues panting, nuzzling and collapsing at her feet.

'There ya go,' he announced, returning, as he handed her the glass. She was surprised that it had been he who had prepared the drinks. She had judged him as less chivalrous. They sat for a few moments, drinks in hand. Strangers.

'What will you do now, Rob, when the Plantation is sold?' It was the first time she had actually used his name without him reminding her.

He shrugged lazily. 'Same as before I got here, I guess. I'll drift for a bit, see what turns up. Might even go back to ol' Oz, pay a visit. 'S been a while since I was there.' He rocked languidly to and fro in the chair, seemingly undisturbed by the approaching uncertainty of his life, and then added, more pensively, 'Sam's gone. Cane's burnt. Take a year or so to get this place on its feet again. Good time to move.'

'What about your family? Will you spend some time with them?' On their first trip to the canefields, the day that he had shown her where Sam had been killed, he had mentioned to her that he had family.

Stone regarded her, scrutinising her, surprised that she had remembered such a thing. 'I haven't seen them in sixteen years. Kids'll be grown and gone now.'

'Where are they, Australia?' she probed.

'Samoa. Western Samoa. The kids' mother . . . my wife . . . she's a native. Met her soon after I started travelling. Settled down too young.'

'Do you think of them sometimes? Wonder about the children?'

'Sure, but they're native kids, brought up in the village, by the family. They'd be all right.'

It occurred to Kate how similar Sam and Stone must have been. 'I've been going through the cupboards and drawers. There's not much here. Is that all Sam left or is there more stowed away somewhere?'

'Uhuh. That's pretty much it.' He took a sip. 'Bit more locked in the office. His passport. Wallet of photos. Not

224

much. Travelled pretty light, ol' Sam did. You looking for something in particular?'

She shook her head. 'I would have liked something, one small thing, to take with me when I leave next week, that's all.'

He turned to regard her for a moment. His steel-blue-grey eyes, brilliant against his weatherbeaten, shaven face, bored indomitably into her, then he set his Scotch on the table between them and ambled into the house. The mongrels were disturbed but neither bothered to move, preferring to doze peacefully, heads resting on their front paws. She heard Stone rummaging through a box or drawer in the only part of the house that she hadn't made her terrain.

'Here,' he said as he returned to the porch and handed her a worn, black leather wallet, the size of a passport holder. 'A few of your dad's memories. You might as well have them. Not much good to me.'

She took the wallet and stared at it, without opening it, turning it over in the palms of her hands. It felt almost more precious to her than the entire estate as she placed it lovingly on the table and let it sit there, undisturbed. 'Thank you,' she said softly.

'Finish your drink and we'll get going. Or they'll be married before we get there.' He threw the remaining liquid down his throat in one gulp and stood up. 'Want me to put this back inside?' he asked, pointing with a nod of his head towards Sam's wallet.

'I'll do it.' She drank one more sip and then abandoned the glass on the table.

'I'll see you in the jeep,' he shouted after her as she went back into the house. She called the two dogs who stood, staring at her, unwilling to follow, suspecting that they were about to be returned to the empty kitchen while the partying took place elsewhere.

'Listen!' he shouted after her, from outside. 'You don't need to lock up the pooches. They take care of themselves.'

The ceremony did not after all take place in Timi's village. There had been a change of plan, earlier in the day, Stone explained as they turned off the road, rumbling inland over a potholed track, past tapioca plants and split-leaved banana trees towards a village situated at the edge of a narrow stream. There, they found the local children splashing, screaming and larking about in muddied water no more than fifteen inches deep. This airy village was surrounded by a blaze of full-blooming deep-vermilion ginger flowers. How different, Kate thought, to the spot where Ami lived, with its sombre note of fatality.

The priest, Father Dooley, who was to conduct the short ceremony, arrived caked in dust, minutes after Kate and Stone, in a decaying Suzuki jeep that rattled and shimmied like a worn-out washing machine. He had driven some distance, from his mission house close to Loquaqua. A shabbily dressed, quiet, unassuming Dubliner whose arrival was greeted and cheered by the fullhearted, big-boned Fijians with the enthusiasm of the coming of a Messiah! He held hands with the children skipping cheerfully at his side, drank yangona with the elders under the shade of a feathery flame tree, and once refreshed heard the confessions of those who felt in need of absolution before the wedding ceremony commenced.

'They'll be wanting to take communion, and for that they need clean souls,' he explained patiently to Kate, as she looked on, astonished, at the queue of pious Fijians all waiting to unburden themselves of their misdemeanours. This unexpected priest, Father Dooley, was a worn-out-looking fellow with gentle, patient eyes and a rasping cough that he was doing his utmost to conceal. He greeted Kate with the affection due to a long-lost daughter, shaking her hand warmly and speaking fondly of her father.

'That old Irish reprobate from County Leix! I knew and loved him well. Even though the fella never darkened a church door in all the years he lived here!'

That, at least, had not changed. That was how she remembered Sam. It was her mother who had hauled her to Mass each Sunday morning, calling to Sam as they left that his heathen ways would catch up with him one day. Dooley insisted that she attend Mass in his humble parish the following Sunday morning and she hadn't the heart to tell him that she hadn't stepped inside a church since she was sixteen – except for her own wedding in Philippe's family Catholic chapel!

Stone explained to her later that the village was divided, like many of the Fijian villages, between Seventh-Day Adventists, such as Timi and his family, and Catholics. This wedding came from the Catholic contingent. But no matter. This evening everyone celebrated.

The entire village, whatever their faith, and numerous other neighbouring settlement families, arriving on foot, carrying wedding gifts of woven palm mats and yangona root, had gathered together to enjoy the promised party. A village 'hall' had been erected for the festivities the previous evening after the location of the wedding had finally been agreed upon. It was a seemingly arid plot, but for a few tufts of tussocked grass growing haphazardly, shaded by a hastily constructed corrugated iron roof held in place by numerous wooden poles dug into the dry earth. These supports were decorated with palm leaves, twined and twisted into intricate shapes and patterns.

The bride and groom, Kate observed, a young couple in their mid-teens, spent the entire ceremony looking mystified and uncertain; he, with his head bowed guiltily like an adolescent who has been caught stealing apples.

Later, when Kate asked Father Dooley the reason for his apparent spiritlessness he explained that the young couple had run off and spent an illicit night together. They were being married now because the bride's family had insisted that the boy make an honest woman of their daughter. 'She was head girl at my mission school, this year past. The poor child's just sixteen,' Dooley confided. Kate wondered why no one had put a stop to such a ceremony but she said nothing.

Females, of all ages, crowded into the open 'hallway' in readiness for the feast. They sat close to one another on the ground now covered with rush matting, crosslegged and gossiping, or stood packed into the open palm-decorated entrance ways. An amazonian regiment of women they were, resplendent in their richly coloured dresses, with hibiscus flowers resting against their ears to decorate their tightly curled jet-black hair. Yet they giggled and grinned like naughty schoolchildren when amused, covering their wide, teeth-spilling mouths with large, strong, working hands and leaning and lolling against one another in high-pitched laughter like sailors in a brothel.

'They love a party. Any excuse for a celebration, or a feast,' Stone explained admiringly. He seemed to Kate to be exhibiting a similar enthusiasm. She felt envious of his winning ease and watched furtively as large-eyed girls with ample breasts flirted skittishly with him and he, in turn, bewitched them with his smile and his charm, but no woman in particular, as far as she could see, won his attentions.

It was the first time that she had felt curious about his more personal life. She knew nothing about him, had never visited him in his bure, home. Perhaps there was a woman in his life. Another native woman, as his wife had been. Why not? Although she had never sensed it. She had simply assumed that he was a loner, that there was no one. Yet she doubted his celibacy. She knew that he had 'whored together' with her father. He had told her so himself. It unsettled her to realise that the idea caused her a certain passing jealousy but she dismissed it swiftly as foolish, telling herself that it was his openness and the Fijians' love and acceptance of him that she envied.

'Feeling a bit lost?' Stone whispered, leaning towards her.

She nodded readily.

'Have you tried the local firewater?' he asked, mischievously winking. The present-giving rituals had ended and preparations for the feast were beginning.

'The yangona? No, I haven't.' She was shouting to be heard above the din of natives rolling out their dusky brown laughter and giggling disorganised instructions at one another as they laid lengths of sulu cloth on to the matting, making colourful tablecloths which they decorated with more twined palm leaves. It seemed to Kate they were preparing a monster picnic!

'Follow me. It'll be a while before things start hotting up here,' he said, leading Kate out across the cracked, sun-dried earth and into a neighbouring thatched bure.

Inside, in cooling semi-darkness, a group of village men and elders sat poised tranquilly around a large circular wooden bowl. Stone, speaking fluently to them in their local tongue, presented Kate before telling her to make herself comfortable. She sat crosslegged, following the local example, on the rush matting and looked about her, feeling a certain fear of the dozen or so men with their eyes red-stained and lugubrious. There were no other women present.

She spotted Timi who seemed to be presiding over the proceedings and she felt a little easier. He was spooning liquid from the circular bowl into a half coconut shell which he then carried carefully across the hut and held in front of her. It resembled diluted mushroom soup. All eyes turned to her as Timi intoned something entirely incomprehensible to her. As he finished, the men, in rippled unison, clapped three times.

'It tastes bloody awful the first time!' Stone warned, after explaining to her that she was obliged to clap once, accept the grog-filled shell, down the liquid in one gulp, return the shell to Timi and then clap once more in thanks.

Kate stared at the liquid and felt her stomach somersault. It reminded her of dirtied washing-up water!

'Go for your life. You'll feel terrific,' Stone encouraged. She hesitated. 'Go on. They're all waiting,' he persisted.

She saw his face. He's bloody well enjoying this, she thought, feeling peeved. She looked about her, saw their expectant faces, reluctantly clapped once, took the shell and swallowed hard, managing the entire bowlful. Stone hadn't lied. It did taste bloody awful! Lukewarm and acrid. But he had lied about her feeling terrific. She didn't!

Stone, Timi and the entire assembly nodded and clapped approvingly. She was uncertain whether their clapping was a final stage of the ceremony or merely an expression of their approval. Timi took the shell from her limp hand, she clapped once more, and the whole process was repeated again. This time for Stone.

Time seemed to have no meaning here. While the women, outside, giggled and played, these men sat motionless. Save for the lighting of cigarettes, the stubbing out of burnt butts, and the preserving of half-smoked filtered lengths, no one moved and no one spoke.

She found it curious. The inactivity and the silence. She supposed that the feast had begun and was being eaten without them but she began to feel no concern. Instead she stayed to drink another bowlful of the soporific root liquid and found that she too no longer cared about when the meal would take place. It would happen in its own time, she told herself philosophically.

Her focus was beginning to alter. She felt easy and light-headed, as she sat staring curiously at the men scattered around her, seated in silence. Many of them had open, ulcerous sores on their crossed legs. All were shabbily dressed in extraordinary combinations of Western and Fijian garments. The elders wore sulus and short-sleeved shirts and ties while the younger men, cheaply fibred, threadbare trousers rolled to their knees and either T-shirts or bare upper torsos. The T-shirts bore such incongruous messages as 'Life is a Beach' or 'Jogging for Jesus'. One young, one-eyed fellow as raggedy and limp as a Guy Fawkes dummy had written across his polyester-clad breast 'God makes me Sing', which, sported by one so utterly mournful, made Kate giggle helplessly, almost uncontrollably.

She caught Timi's eye, watching her. He nodded and giggled a response though he could not have known what was making her laugh. She was beginning to feel less of an intruder and less uneasy about herself. It seemed to have a purpose, after all, she reflected, this Sitting Doing Nothing! Stone turned to her and winked, a warm statement of encouragement. And, she hoped, friendship.

Father Dooley wandered in to join them and sat beside her. The yangona ritual was repeated once more in his honour. He drank easily and clapped his thanks with the authority of one who had furnished his response many times before.

After Dooley's yangona had been drunk Stone signalled to her that they would go. She crept stealthily towards the door, fearful of disturbing the mood. It was unnecessary. No one gestured more than a gracious nod of the head and few responded to, or even noticed, their exit.

Back across the dusty track the feasting had begun. Women and children were eating heartily: curry, earth-baked pig, and root vegetables. Everyone was screeching gleefully. The energy here was lively and cacophonous. Quite in contrast to the small bure where the soporific men remained seated in silence, careless of the feasting.

They squeezed themselves places and settled on to the ground in between several shrill gaggles of women. Kate had Dooley on her right and Stone to the left of her. Timi wandered in and joined them. On all sides, ample women ate heartily with their fingers, holding palm fans in their unoccupied hands to shoo away the flies. Father Dooley ate little, one small plateful only, and then prepared to leave. 'I'll be on my way,' he whispered to Kate. 'It's a long drive back to Loquaqua and I've a mission meeting later tonight. I don't suppose I'll be seein' ya at Mass so come and see me before you leave for England. And watch out for that yangona!' he teased. He shook hands with Stone, spoke a few grave words to the terrified groom and his new bride and set off, wading across the stream to where his Suzuki jeep was waiting in the shade.

All about her Kate saw poverty, flies and generosity. She had been welcomed with the exuberance offered to a long-absent relative and she realised that she was beginning to feel a sense of liberation. She was floating! Thousands of miles from her comfortable home, her life and her friends and it seemed to her, from such a distance, a sterile existence. Here she felt close to the people and villages that her father had known and loved . . . perhaps died for . . . and she enjoyed their generosity, their sense of plenty.

She asked herself if this feeling was light-headedness or was

231

she being romantic? Or was it simply, as Father Dooley had warned her, that she had not 'watched out for the yangona'?

Night fell. Kerosene lamps were lit. Rob Stone, drenched in euphoria, lifted another half coconut shell to his lips and downed the misty-coloured juice. He smiled at Kate, winked and exhaled contentedly. 'She's really a good-looker,' he mused approvingly.

A few guests were still gorging themselves on the remains of the supper. A locally caught, glaze-eyed bonito lay fleshy, still sizzling from the fire. But most were replete and entertained themselves with servings from the wooden kava bowl which had been placed now in the centre of the wedding picnic table.

Somewhere outside a thatched hut, higher up the hill, a youth strummed languorously on a guitar. Several companions hummed and crooned at his side.

Rob Stone leaned back against the palm-decorated support behind him and turned his head towards Kate, brushing his hand against her arm. Behind her, across the stream gulley, he saw an Indian pounding towards them.

'Mr Stone!' the breathless Indian heaved as he approached.

Stone, disturbed by the sweating, bleating messenger, let out a troubled sigh. 'Hey, Timi. We got company,' he exhaled.

Timi, crouching over the sacred wooden bowl and holding a bag of pounded yangona root in his powerful hand, straightened his heavy frame and gazed towards the other side of the stream. Both men silently regarded the approaching leathery worker. Kate, inebriated and replete, caught their expressions and with stupefied curiosity followed their gaze until she, too, spotted the gatecrasher belting along. The barefooted Indian, splashing his way through the shallow water, had silenced all merrymaking.

'Fight broke out, mister! Man dead!' the frightened fellow confessed to his boss as he panted to a halt.

'What the fuck!' Stone and Timi leapt to their feet. 'OK. Let's go!'

Kate rose, preparing to accompany them. Stone wheeled round on her. 'You wait here!' he ordered curtly.

Without staying to argue the point the two men, sombre and humourless now, followed the Indian back over the stream,

232

picked up the jeep and roared off down the track, lost in a cloud of dust and banana trees.

Moments later, Kate set off after them on foot, calling for a lift. Two natives went in search of a truck. 'Hurry please, or we'll lose them!' she cried.

Stone halted the jeep amongst the long shadows of the starlit palm trees and they followed the jogging Indian the last few yards on foot along the beach to where they found three more Indians mindlessly babbling over a knifed body.

The Indians fell silent as they recognised the approaching trio. Trembling, they shuffled aside to allow the bleeding body to be examined. One stepped backwards on to a plate. It cracked beneath his slight weight. The debris of a forgotten supper lay untidily in the sand.

'You want me to take a look?' Timi whispered to Stone as they approached. Timi was a better man to handle this. No white man was welcome at this scene. Stone nodded and held back whilst Timi stepped on forward, watched by the Indians, their fearful white eyes bulging.

Timi reached the body and paused, staring down on to it, sickened by what he saw. He glanced towards Stone who was lighting a cigarette and hadn't recognised the dead man. Timi rubbed his concerned features with his strong palm and crouched at the dead man's side, touched the bleeding, lacerated flesh, listened for the youth's heartbeat and then delicately closed the petrified eyes with his powerful brown fingers, surreptitiously turning the face in Stone's direction. He stood up.

The two men exchanged a worried look.

Stone addressed the waiting men in their Hindi mother tongue. He could have spoken in English. They would have understood that, also. 'Who did this?' he asked.

No one answered. White conspiratorial glances darting from one to the other.

'All right then, who found him?' he persisted patiently.

The four stood dumbly, quaking with fright.

'I said who found him!' he shouted. Stone turned uneasily towards Timi. 'I don't want that body left here.'

Timi nodded. 'You two,' he said softly, 'carry the boy's body back up to the main house.'

The two bidden figures bent obediently over the body and began, with some difficulty due to their shaking and lack of co-ordination, to hoist the corpse on to their shoulders before carrying it away from the water.

'And you guys,' Timi persisted, more forcefully now, 'get some sleep. We'll discuss this in the morning. Don't go anywhere.'

As the men turned facing inland, ready to move slowly away from the scene, Kate came pounding towards them. She was breathless and fatigued. Her two Fijian drivers pounded at her side. She saw the body balanced precariously on the wizened Indians' shoulders and ran directly towards it.

'Kate, get away from there!' Stone called to her. Kate ignored him. 'I thought I told you to wait back there!' He was standing under a swaying palm, inhaling a cigarette. He stepped towards her and grabbed her roughly by the arm, halting her.

She stared into his angry face. The swaying leaves created ominous shadows across his features. 'I was not aware, Mr Stone, that it is your place to tell me what to do!' she replied tersely.

'Well then you better take a look, ma'am,' he answered sarcastically, seething with anger, still gripping on to her arm.

The sombre procession of Indians, those carrying the youth's body followed by those without, passed alongside her, allowing her to see clearly the identity of the knifed figure. She retched as she caught sight of the corpse, grotesque with its make-up of congealing blood and head swinging loosely. A gold chain glinted in the occasional moonlight.

'Oh my God!' she yelped softly. 'It's Ami!' She stated the name as though no one but she had discovered his identity.

'Listen, if you want to help,' said Stone, more kindly now, and releasing his grip on her arm, 'get someone to take you to his hut and look after the kid. All right?'

Kate nodded, keeping her head bowed low, feeling shame and disgust.

234

'Walk back to Timi's village and find someone to show you the way. Don't ask these guys to take you. I don't want them in the settlement. Not tonight. I want no trouble between the Fijians and Indians tonight,' he repeated emphatically, uncertain whether she had heard him.

'I know where his shack is,' she answered faintly.

'Then take our jeep. Go steady.'

She turned and walked obediently back towards the parked car, her sandals crunching beneath her into the white creeping sand. She cursed her footsteps. They sounded indecently loud.

Stone, already regretting his harsh words, watched her small figure disappear into the cocoterie. He stepped forward, towards Timi who was facing the ocean. He looked bleak, one hand partially covering his face. Stone lit another cigarette and handed it to his companion.

'I'm gonna have to call the police in. I better get up to the house, radio across to the mainland. Get them to send someone in the morning. They can bring a doctor, too.' Stone flicked his own, almost untouched cigarette into the sand. It glowed in the darkness. 'I mighta guessed it was him. What a stinking mess!'

'He's been asking for it,' Timi conceded.

'It's revenge. For their lost jobs, I betcha. You're a prayin' man, Timi. Pray it's just an incident.'

The two men walked heavily beside one another along the beach towards the hill, ignoring the ocean as she rolled sensuously on to the damp shore. Close by, unnoticed by them, a coconut fell to the ground. It thudded and bounced its way on to a stray tuft of grass growing in the sand. Here and there several more coconuts fell, thudding like muted shots. A wind was beginning to pick up as the rain fell.

Chapter 3

The waves were breaking forcefully against the reef and, like listening to music, Kate found it balming. It made her feel more quiet. She had been crying. She leant, tired and motionless, against the bedroom window frame, staring out across the water, blindly hypnotised by it. It was still too dark to see clearly but she felt drawn by its immensity, seeking as she was to overwhelm and flood her own sense of emptiness.

Below her, in the garden, frogs were croaking. For about an hour the heavens had opened and gushed rain. She and the child had got soaked in the open jeep, but now it had stopped. Raindrops were falling rapidly from the tall, leafy trees and the sky still looked furious, scribbled with inky patterns of more heavy rain clouds.

It was almost the beginning of the rainy season, or more precisely, the cyclone season. Somehow, it seemed fitting that it should begin now. That it should flood the charcoaled, scarred landscape that she was about to abandon. Sold off for a bank account in Switzerland! Sam's anger, his retribution! His curse on their indifference to all that he had worked for.

She felt numb and tired. Only a few hours earlier she had been asking herself if all this was the answer to her happiness. It seemed so ludicrous now. She turned and glanced back towards the bed, Sam's bed. Ami's boy lay sleeping peacefully. No one had told him, Your father's dead, been murdered. She supposed the task would be left to her. But not now. Later, after sunrise, when he had woken. For now it was better just to let him sleep.

She wondered what would become of him, where he would go. To Ami's family? There was a soft tapping on the closed door. She glanced back briefly out of the window. One more consoling sight of the early morning horizon, and then the door. She supposed it must be the police.

It was Stone. 'Saw you at the window. Wondered if you were all right?' he asked. His voice was raspy, tired, tobacco-ridden. He looked worn and depleted.

'I'm fine. The boy's in the bed so . . . I couldn't sleep anyway,' she whispered, fearful of disturbing the child and bringing her unwanted task closer.

'There's the spare room downstairs. Lie down there. At least, get some rest,' he said.

She looked damp and drawn, like a small dog lost in the rain. She shook her head. 'Thanks, I'll stay here with the boy. In case he wakes.'

He leant back against the wooden, apple-green door frame. His blue-, now weary-grey eyes watching her. Her thin, frightened face. His hand moved up towards her cheek and lightly brushed it.

'Sorry I shouted at you, back there,' he muttered softly. 'Didn't want you to see it.'

She sensed he was about to kiss her but changed his mind. And she realised that she longed for him to do so, not because it was him, simply because she needed . . . someone, and that need was torturing. She wanted to hold her head against him, to feel his strength beating, to bruise away her fear, her sadness and failure. Swiftly she dropped her eyes, guessing that he might read what she was feeling, that he might see the need within her. She felt so weak.

'Listen,' he said soberly, 'it's five a.m. The police'll be here about seven. I'm going to sit downstairs on the porch, pour myself a large neat Scotch and wait for the dawn. It that suits you, join me.'

Her head still lowered, she watched his dustied, muddied

leather boots, his denim jeans move away towards the stairs and then his back, his earlier freshly laundered shirt that had made her smile like a teenager, disappear out of sight. And she started to weep, dumbly. It all felt such a mess.

Across the room, on the dressing table, was the page torn from Philippe's diary. If you need anything, just call Shyam, he had told her. She walked to the dresser and turned the paper on its back. He must still suppose that she had left with Philippe.

Before going downstairs she towel-dried her frizzed, damp hair and washed her face. Fearful of rousing the sleeping boy, wanting to give him a few more hours of sweet dreams, she decided against changing her damp clothes, even though they felt like orange peel suctioned around her.

Stone was reclining in the rocking chair on the porch, glass in hand, one boot crossed over the other thigh. He rocked rhythmically to and fro, gazing at the horizon, seeming not to notice her approach. There was no sign of Timi or anyone else. The stillness was as if the entire island, save for them, had been evacuated. She wondered where they had laid Ami's body but decided not to ask.

As she sat in one of the wicker chairs it creaked. Stone turned his head one hour of a clock towards her. Without speaking he lifted a bottle, ready on the ground at the side of his rocker, and handed it to her. She took it numbly, though the thought of whisky made her want to retch, and held it stupidly for a moment.

'No . . . no. I don't want any whisky, thanks. I might make some tea in a moment. Would you like some?'

She placed the bottle on the small table between them. He shook his head. 'Tea? Nah, thanks,' he said.

As dawn began so too did the birds, ringing like sleigh bells in old American films. Curiously mellisonant in the purpled morning light.

An hour or so later Stone heard and then spotted the seaplane heading from the left, across the horizon in front of them towards its landing destination at Lesa Bay.

238

'That'll be the police. I'll head down to the bay in the jeep and pick them up. You be all right here, on your own?' he asked as he rose. She nodded and smiled softly, looking tired. 'I'll make some fresh tea and change my dress.'

'Listen, we'll be a while. I'll show them about a bit. Where it happened, the body etc. They'll wanna talk to the three guys who were with him. Find out what their story is. Then we'll pick up Timi at his place and I'll bring them back up here. OK?'

She nodded. 'Rob, he was murdered, wasn't he?'

'Looks that way,' he drawled, and wandered off towards the jeep still parked where Kate had left it, round the back of the house close to the generator shed. The first of the early morning gardeners arrived, wandering aimlessly, like some lone straggler, amongst the full-blossomed oleander bushes. His clay-stained feet squelched and sank into the sodden earth. Kate caught his nervous glance. She smiled and called out an encouraging 'good morning' before disappearing inside to change her dress.

No doubt the news of Ami's death had already spread across the Plantation and into the neighbouring Fijian villages, she thought as she stealthily climbed the stairs, considering the fear in the gardener's eyes. . . . Or had they all conspired to kill him?

It was a sultry, heavy morning. A stormy sort of day. Stone's head ached, he'd been up all night, and he'd drunk one hell of a lot of grog at the wedding. He knew Kate wasn't going to like the news and he wasn't looking forward to telling her. He returned to the main house alone. Timi was still with the police and the three Indian witnesses. Kate was in the kitchen, making breakfast. She had been expecting them anxiously for several hours.

'Where are the police?' she asked, confused.

Dispassionately he relayed the result of Patterson's diagnosis.

'But that's ludicrous! It's a lie. You know that as well as I do! Suicide! Jesus! Where is this Doctor Patterson?'

'He's with Leger, the Chief of Police. They're loading the body on to the plane. Taking it back to the mainland with them. I said I'd get the kid. He's going with them. Is he still sleeping?' Stone could understand her bitter discontent, her disillusionment. He had felt the same after Sam had been found. It had been the same doctor. That time Patterson had stated the death as a drunken accident and later, natural causes.

Stone had been up against this kind of 'island justice' before.

But in this instance there was a certain reasoning behind it. If it leaked out that there had been a fight and a young Indian murdered on the Plantation there would be many willing to make trouble, particularly now, a few days after the fire, after the entire canecutting staff had been made redundant. There could be strikes, uprisings, riots, who could tell? Others would use it against the Indians. Cite their irascibility as a stumbling block in their bid for leadership. It was just two months before the general election. There was too much to lose. Or for some, too much to gain.

People turned their backs on justice. He had learnt to understand that. But how could she? And would she under-stand even if he explained . . .?

'Doesn't this Mr Leger want to interview me, as a witness, as the property owner here?' she persisted. Her face was seething with recrimination, burning with the raw whiplash of injustice.

'Sure. He'll be up shortly. I said I'd drive the boy down to the plane.'

'He's still sleeping.' She spoke the words challengingly. Change the verdict or I will not hand over the child, she seemed to be saying. But she knew she could not win. And anyway, Stone was not her enemy.

'Shall I get him?' Stone persisted, 'or would you rather go?'

'Where are they taking him?'

'To his grandparents. Ami's family.'

She cast her eyes downwards, towards the weatherbeaten wooden verandah deck and she sighed. A slow, weary exhala-tion. At least, the child was to have a home.

240

'I'll go,' she conceded. And without looking up at him again she turned and walked back into the house and up the stairs. It was a heavy movement. A weary, hopeless step.

Upstairs the door was unlocked and opened just a tiny crack. She had left it that way on purpose, in case the child had woken, had been afraid to find himself away from his hut, and had needed her. She pushed the frame gently and the door creaked open. Her gaze fell on to the rumpled double bed. It was empty. The boy was not there. Jal was no longer sleeping. She discovered him on tiptoes, leaning over her dressing table, ransacking several of her drawers. All had been opened and untidied.

Clusters of dress jewellery, not worn since the cruise, tweezers, nail files, cuticle sticks and English coins were scattered in disarray across the dressing-table surface. The boy turned in surprise at having been disturbed. Kate gasped in horror at the sight of him. He looked grotesque! wearing a pair of her pearl earrings, drop style. His mouth was smeared with lipstick which against his dark, Indian skin glared a livid fuchsia.

His eyes widened with fear and guilt when he saw her, just as they had done that first evening when she had found him in the kitchen with the stolen biscuits. He stood motionless now, doe-eyed, like a guilty puppy waiting to be reprimanded.

'Don't you know that it's stealing to take someone else's property?' she asked as she moved slowly towards him.

'I wasn't stealing! I was playing,' he replied sulkily.

'Well you'd better put them all back now and wash your face.'

He shook his head defiantly. The earrings tinkled. 'Don't want to,' he said.

'Jal, put the earrings back and wash your face! We have to leave now.' She was feeling inadequate. No child of her own to refer to.

Slowly, under the power of her gaze, which was more distressed at the prospect of what lay ahead for him than anger at his disobedience, he pulled the clip-on earrings from the

241

lobes of his reddened ears and threw them crossly on to the dressing table. They clattered like paste, sending a five-pence piece scuttling to the ground as they settled.

'Now wash your face. There's a good boy.'

He glared at her and then made his unwilling way towards the bathroom. While she waited for him, hearing the ancient plumbing gurgling and belching, she quickly threw her various possessions back into her jewellery box, checking that everything of value, watch, engagement and wedding rings, pieces that she had stopped wearing because of discomfort in the heat, were still there. Nothing appeared to be missing.

She walked towards the window, heard him peeing. She was searching for Leger, or indeed, the doctor, Patterson. It was still outside, hot and overcast. A blanket-grey sky sat low on the horizon. The loo flushed. She turned back expectantly, towards the bathroom. He was standing in the open doorway. His mouth had been carelessly wiped. Remains of her lipstick were streaked across his left cheek. She smiled approvingly and held out a hand to him.

'OK. Let's go,' she encouraged. He stared wilfully at her, ignoring her hand, thudding on ahead, down the stairs to where Stone was waiting. As she approached she heard voices drifting in from the porch, but not what was being said. Her heart began to beat faster. Was it Stone and Jal, or had Leger finally arrived?

She hurried through the living room. As she reached the open doorway Stone was disappearing around the corner of the wooden porchway, towards the jeep, the boy in his arms. She had not even had a chance to say goodbye. And the child still did not know about his father.

Kate sat alone, waiting for what seemed an eternity, having showered and washed her previously limp hair. No one came. She considered walking down to Lesa Bay, to where the boy would be taking the plane, but decided that she must be patient. What if Leger should arrive and she had gone? No, she must stay at the house as Stone had advised her.

Sitting idly on the porch was making her restless so she

returned upstairs to tidy the drawers that Jal had earlier foraged. She heard a plane flying low almost over her head and ran to the window. It was the seaplane circling the bay before heading back towards the mainland, buzzing like a wasp replete with pollen. She glanced down on to the flower-filled garden. There was no sign of Stone. One solitary Indian was hoeing at the bed edges. And she had neither met nor spoken to Leger or Patterson.

'Jesus!' Anger rose within her like a fire.

She glanced at her watch still lying on the now ordered dressing-table top. Quarter past eleven. Her mind began to whirr, thoughts rushing out of control. Something had to be done. If Philippe were here he would know exactly what to do. He was always so level-headed and concise about decisions, so unlike her! She calculated that it would be Friday evening in New York, or perhaps late afternoon. She had lost count of the exact time difference.

Philippe would be making his way through the weekend rush-hour traffic towards Kennedy airport. She could not remember which of the evening flights he had told her he was taking but, no doubt, he would have checked out of the Meridian by now. It would be impossible to reach him until London. And what if he should try to contact her as she had told him? She would be gone. Yes, she would go to the mainland herself . . . and get help. She would ring Philippe herself tomorrow, and explain.

She needed the page he had torn from his neatly maintained diary. She tried to remember where she had left it. Perhaps it was in her handbag? She glanced about the room. Hadn't she taken the bag with her to the wedding the evening before? That seemed a lifetime ago now. Eventually she found it on the floor, at the side of the bed, where it had been discarded while caring for the sleeping boy. Philippe's note was not inside it.

Hurriedly she returned to the dressing table and rummaged untidily through the previously arranged jars of skin creams and perfumes. She had moved it, turned it face downwards, she remembered, earlier this morning, the scribbled note. She smiled when she recollected Philippe's use of the word scribbled. She stood back for a moment and stared at the crowded surface in front of her. It must be there. But she had not noticed it when tidying earlier.

Then her heart began to sink. The slip of paper with his phone number had gone but also, more importantly, the wallet.

Sam's wallet was missing

She had definitely left it there before hurrying off to the wedding. Her mind had been so saddened, so troubled by Ami's death that she had forgotten all about it. And now it was missing! And she had never even opened it.

She cursed herself for such thoughtlessness, furiously, flinging open all the drawers, pulling at their laminated handles and dragging them to the floor. One after another she emptied them on to the rug, turning out and untidying all that she had painstakingly put back in place. Pearls dropped noiselessly on to the rug, her fountain pen fell open spilling a word of ink, followed by her Cartier leather purse, her passport in its leather wallet, her leather address book. Everything was there except Philippe's note and the stained, dog-eared black wallet. Her only remaining souvenir of her father.

'You look like you mighta been fossickin' down there?' Stone was standing in the open doorway.

'What?' His voice had jolted her.

'Prospecting. Digging for gold.' He laughed, cracks around his eyes, looking exhausted. Neither of them had slept.

'I'm looking for something. I've lost Sa – something. Where's Leger? He never came to talk to me.' She lifted herself from her knees but remained squatting.

'Headed on back to the mainland with Patterson and the boy. Said to tell you he'd be in touch if he needed anything. Didn't want to distress you any more. I told him you were pretty upset. What've you lost?'

'Mmm. Oh, Philippe left me a slip of paper with some numbers on it,' she bluffed, too ashamed to tell him about the wallet. 'I put it away somewhere safe and I can't remember where.' She began clumsily gathering together the assortment of possessions scattered around her feet. He watched for a moment from the open doorway and then moved in to crouch at her side.

'Here, let me help,' he said, as he scooped up a handful of scissors, emery boards, purses and jewellery with one hand. 'You should get some rest.' His free hand tenderly touched her cheek, brushing his thumb against her eyelash.

'Rob, I'm going over to the mainland for a few days. If Philippe rings will you tell him I'll phone him tomorrow, in London.'

Still crouching, they faced one another. He dropped the retrieved articles back on to the floor and put his arms around her shoulders. Kate dropped her gaze, not able to look at him, staring deliberately at the collection of belongings, possessions from another life. She was feeling raw, with herself for misplacing Sam's wallet and with him for allowing Ami's death to be so easily dismissed.

'Listen,' he began, 'if you're going over there because of Chand, you're wasting your time. He's dead. Believe me, it's better just to accept it.' He cupped her chin in his hand, lifting her face, forcing her to look at him. 'You can't help him, Kate. They've said suicide because it saves a lot of hassle.'

'Was that what happened with Sam? Did everyone just agree that it was easier? It would save a lot of hassle just to settle on "an accident" and say no more?' she accused bitterly, tears burning her enraged cheeks.

'That was different. All the evidence actually pointed to an accident. The ol' bugger was loaded. He tripped in the dark and hit his head. It was obvious. It's only me that thinks it was something else. I have no proof. Just a gut feeling, that's all. He wouldn't sell the land. Someone wanted it. Maybe he knew something. Jesus, I don't know! I'm just guessing. Either way it won't bring him back. And you, rushing off to the mainland, crusadin' for that Indian kid won't bring him back either. Anyway, he was askin' for it. If it hadn't been here, yesterday . . . it would've been tomorrow, someplace else. Kate, just sign the contract, sell the place and go home.'

'I thought you were the one who didn't want it sold?'

245

'That was before. There's nothing left now. Just the land. Or a year's work, with good men, to put the place back on its feet.'

'And you?'

'Me? Nah. I told you I'm on my way. It's time for me to move on.'

'What if I decided not to sell? If I asked you to run it for me, you and Timi? What would you say? Would you stay then?'

His steel-blue eyes, lined and tired, his unshaven up-all-night face looked at her hard then crinkled, dissolving with laughter. It was disconcerting to watch him.

'Sister, you beat your ol' man! Do you have any idea how much that crop was worth? We're broke. The insurance money won't cover it. We don't have enough to buy new sugar plants. Anyway, what would your husband have to say about it?'

'Does that mean that the contract with the Sugar Company is null and void? I mean, when whoever is buying the Plantation . . . could they use the land for whatever they wanted . . .?'

He thought for a moment. She watched him puzzle and search for the answer before finally shaking his head. 'I dunno. I guess it depends what they want to do with it. And who they are . . . Yeah, mebbe the Sugar Company would cancel the contract.'

'Do you really believe that Ami burnt the crop?' she asked, getting to her feet and moving towards the bed, sitting down on it.

'Sure as hell, I do.'

'Yes, but, just because you fired him? Or might someone have put him up to it? To defeat us, make us sell? . . . Or, I don't know, just to have the land available, not contracted to the Fijian Sugar Company?'

'Listen, he was a wild kid. He could've done it just for the hell of it. He drank too much whisky and he had big dreams. I gave him a bashing and he kicked back. And the other guys slit his throat 'cos he burnt the crop and ruined their work prospects and because he was a big mouth. Talked a lotta shit. No one liked him. Except mebbe Sam.'

'Why did Sam like him, if he was that bad? That unpopular?'

246

'He thought the kid had energy. Just runnin' along the wrong track. Said he used to be the same. Ami and kids like him were screwed up by everything around them. It made them losers, he said. Give everyone a chance, he used to say. Never turn others into losers, or you end up losing the whole damn game yourself. That's why they loved him and why they worked so hard for him. He gave them all a shot.'

'I still don't understand what Sam was doing at the old mill.'

Kate took the ferry across to Suva early on the Sunday morning. Stone drove her to the port at Loquaqua.

'Why don't you let me come with you? I'll take you over in the speedboat. Help you find your way around. Timi can handle things here. Anyway I gotta see the insurance guys in Suva. Might as well do it now as later,' he offered, but she had refused.

'I'll call if I need anything. Thanks.'

She gazed idly into the pellucid, lapis lazuli waters and then stared curiously at her gaily attired fellow passengers, day trippers en route to the mainland to visit families, friends and relatives. She needed time alone. Time to consider what she was about to do.

She had arrived early, and was almost the first to board. She found herself an empty bench on the still deserted top deck. Within minutes the crowds began pouring on to the humming diesel ferry, no one empty handed. All were laden with variously sized parcels, bundles of sered kava roots carelessly wrapped in newspaper, or plastic bags bursting with outsized root vegetables.

Loping Fijian women, the circumferences of car tyres yet with the lightness of pencil drawings, jabbered loquaciously, screeching merrily at one another, all the while yelling discordant instructions at their ever-mischievous children. Close by, seated saried Indian women sat with their silent offspring hugged close to their sides and impoverishedly dressed Indian workmen, carrying disintegrating suitcases, smoked incessantly and stared meditatively out of darkly ringed eyes on to the passing coral beds.

The stench of rancid coconut oil on skins and plastic bags filled with dead fish was overwhelming. Kate turned her head towards the water and looked out on to the passing atolls with their uninhabited white beaches and their solitary palm trees. Sketches from childhood books of Robinson Crusoe!

'Merry Christmas!' an ebullient Fijian shouted across the deck to all fellow passengers. People responded, giggling with glee like children let out of school, and Kate was reminded that it was indeed the Sunday before Christmas. She had promised Philippe that she would be home for the holiday and here she was, on a crowded ferry, with no thoughts of leaving, heading towards the mainland in search of justice.

A Fijian woman began to sing, someone produced a guitar to accompany her and suddenly a flock had gathered about them to sing their beloved Christian tunes. 'Silent night, Holy night . . .' Ambrosial voices drifting from the deck, celebrating under the burning sun.

She could still sign the papers with Danil the following afternoon in Suva, as arranged, and then take the early evening ferry back to Lesa, pack up her several cases and return to the mainland on Tuesday for a late-night flight that evening, to Los Angeles. She would be crossing the date line, travelling backwards in time so, with a direct flight from Los Angeles to London, she could be home by Wednesday afternoon, Christmas Eve.

Shopping, bustling crazily through the damp, English streets and then on to their rented chalet in the Alps. She and Philippe, and the same gang who arrived every year in Courcheval from various parts of Europe. They knew one another well now, after several years of sharing Christmases, late nights and skiing together. It was all quite lively, in a raucous, holiday sort of way.

Or she could stay. Break her promise, and stay.

She could phone Danil's office the following morning and explain that something had come up requiring her immediate attention and that, unfortunately, she would be unable to keep their three o'clock appointment. Business language. She had

248

heard Philippe speak it often enough. It would give her a little more time.

She glanced about her. The vocalists had moved on to 'White Christmas'! One or two were now beating the flats of their hands against the deck floor like a spreading kettle drum. Others tapped their broad, clay-encrusted, bare feet in time to the music.

She needed more time.

She decided that she would phone Philippe that afternoon from her hotel in Suva and warn him that it was unlikely that she would be home before Christmas. And then what? She knew that Stone was right. There was nothing that she could do now for Ami. He was dead and the reason for that death was almost irrelevant. And yet it rankled with her. It had been settled so easily, dismissed so conveniently, causing her to wonder, yet again, about Sam. She could not alter the fact of his death either but if there were a reason for it, if the facts had been buried beneath some lie . . . what then? Perhaps, knowing that, would alter her decision about selling the Plantation.

If Stone was right, if Sam had not wished that sale to take place, who was she to scoff at that last gesture?

Suva sported a choice of two large hotels. One was a modern, motel-styled lodge which Kate rejected and the other, its neighbour, where she had stayed with Stone, one of the majestic remnants of Fiji's British colonial past. The Grand Ocean Hotel was a magnificent edifice built in the Art Nouveau style and reminiscent of a glorious pre-war liner. Erected in 1914 by the Union Steam Ship Company it overlooked the Pacific Ocean and the eructating, silted and sewaged port of Suva, originally sited there to benefit from the cooling trade winds. Kate gratefully installed herself, for now it was nearly midday and the city was noisy and stifling, in a dingy mouldering suite overlooking the ocean. 'It's the best we have available due to refurbishment in progress,' she was assured.

At her bedside sat a black upright telephone that might have been designed for the original opening of the hotel! Outside her window, tankers sat waiting, rusting on the horizon. Above her an antiquated fan wobbled like a roulette ball giddy on its wheel. She plumped herself on to the faded floral bedspread and scrutinised the bare, impersonal space. A weathered room that someone had left around 1950, and had never returned to.

But Kate was content. It was the first time that she had ever, in her life, been entirely alone, and, besides, she had other thoughts on her mind. In the base of a bleached-out bedside cupboard she found the local directory, stretched herself comfortably across the bed, took a long deep breath to stop her palpitating heart and began turning its damply scented pages. She found a choice of KHUMARs and ran her finger down the list until she reached S. KHUMAR, SHYAM. Suva 309.

She picked up the telephone earpiece, held it against her blonded hair and asked the obliging Fijian receptionist to connect her. Then she lay back, staring at the peeling ceiling, and waited sanguinely for the call to be put through.

250

Chapter 4

Two cornets caressed their way on to the terrace, mellifluous and lithe, rubbing notes with the piano and bass, while Khumar's crystal eyes glowed like black marble in the early afternoon heat.

She was seduced by his mesmerising eyes.

He was dressed more informally than she had previously seen him. An open-necked, short-sleeved sports shirt and lightweight slacks spoke of Sunday at home. He was not as slender as she had remembered. These easy clothes revealed a more comfortable waistline. And he was more formal with her than she had expected. She felt confused by his distance.

'I won't forgive you for not phoning sooner,' he smiled. But surely that was not it.

The jazz rhythm moved up tempo and swung into a popular tune. She recognised it but could not put a name to it. The 'St Louis Blues'. She was sublimely content to be at his side again, yearning for him to feel the same.

They were standing on the terrace of his home, set in the palm of the hills, overlooking a flawless tropical garden. This was one of Suva's more elegant residential areas, Wavumea Heights, judiciously situated outside the grinding, restless pulse of the cosmopolitan city.

'Were you working?'

'Some notes, for a rally later. Nothing that I can't catch up on.'

251

She spied several Indian gardeners working, antlike in the shade. Sunday was not an Indian sabbath. The spacious lawns were bordered by a profusion of redolently perfumed plants, frangipani, beds of butterfly orchids, red ginger, hibiscus, bougainvillaea, king's mantle, birds of paradise and other exotica that she had never seen before and could not put a name to. Behind her, within a cool, darkened room whose walls were lined with shelves of books and ageing law journals, she heard the automatic arm on a dated hi-fi system lift itself from the long-playing record and switch itself off, leaving them both, outside, conversationless. Only the calming sounds of insects humming in the garden broke the silence.

'Duke Ellington and Johnny Hodges. It's called "Back to Back",' he explained casually, after a moment. 'An old favourite of mine.'

She smiled but said nothing. Her knowledge of jazz was pitifully limited and she was already feeling herself an intruder. Perhaps there was someone else, or had he only been playing with her? His delicate, though not impolite silences intrigued her. Always, she felt, he was listening to a language, musing with a universe that she was not party to.

'I could give you Patterson's address,' he continued after another few moments. 'That might help you. He will certainly know where you can contact them.'

Patterson's address. Yes, she had certainly intended to seek him out! 'Thank you.'

He picked up his glass and drained the last of the beer. 'I'd heard about Ami's death. Leger contacted me yesterday afternoon. He wanted me to prepare something, a statement just in case there should be any difficulties with the local press. People are very sensitive here at the moment. We have a general election in the New Year. No one wants trouble. Particularly the ruling Fijian Party. The killing of an Indian on the Lesa Plantation could incite unrest, violence . . . It wouldn't look good for them.'

'Are you going to stand again?' she asked. Her tone was formal, almost cautiously polite. She was feeling ill at ease, fearing she had intruded in his private world.

'Yes,' he said, rubbing his eyes with his forefinger and thumb, a gesture of tiredness or impatience. 'I spoke to the papers this morning. I'll stand as an independent. Opposing all ideas of either Indian or Fijian supremacy. Many will find that unpopular but that is not new to me . . .'

He turned his regard away from her and looked out across the kaleidoscopic display of blossoms growing beneath them. The cicadas started up, shrill and piercing, after a temporary respite, while the gardeners glided noiselessly between one shaded corner and the next. The heat, the balmy fragrances and perhaps the afternoon beer made her head swim. In his company she felt light-headed.

She was so attracted to him and wanted so vigorously to understand him. She dared to venture closer, tempted to inhabit his stillness. Fumbling, she searched for a question, lost for words, desiring to reach him and yet fearing to appear foolish in his eyes. She had never particularly cared for politics, or jazz, but . . .

'When you led your own party did you have dreams of becoming Prime Minister here?' she asked finally, wanting to regather the lost intimacy between them.

Without turning to look at her he smiled at the question. She saw it in his creased features. She watched his profile, hungry for his reaction, and saw, relieved, that his dark eyes, crinkling in the sunlight, were laughing. He was surprised that she should ask him.

'Yes, I did! Of course I did! You know, if you believe in something you want to lead people towards it. Otherwise what's the point? Kate, if Ami had not been killed would you have just left, never letting me know that you'd stayed on?'

'No, of course not . . . I have to see the lawyer tomorrow. I would have called when I got here,' she lied. She had promised herself that she would not call. For her own sake, she had wanted to leave Fiji without seeing him again. And that too she knew was a lie.

'You know what I most fear, here, on these islands, Kate, is the bloody narrow-mindedness!' She looked bemused. 'I've missed you! When I read about the fire I wanted to call, to

253

know you were safe but . . . you were already on your way home. Or so I thought. You've let me believe for a whole damn week that you'd gone!'

Kate was taken aback by his intensity, the suddenness with which he expressed it. He grabbed her by the shoulders and dragged her tenderly towards him. She laughed, cracking in relief. Her breath caught in her throat.

'Why did you do that?' he begged, caressing her, leaning his lower back against the stone-balustraded terrace wall, pulling her ever closer to him.

'I don't know. Fear! My fear! Philippe! . . .' she exclaimed. 'Tell me about your work, the narrow-mindedness that you fear here on the islands. I want to hear!' she whispered forcefully.

'You really want to hear?' he said.

'Mmm. Talk to me. Tell me things. Let me listen . . . what narrow-mindedness?'

'The belief that we can only be governed by one race or the other,' he continued, stroking her hair, holding her face pressed against him. 'We are fearful of losing our cultural identity to the other when all the time it's the damned Western culture creeping up behind us, unseen, that will swamp us! I missed you!' His eyes were gleaming. He was speaking softly as if confiding a secretly cherished dream. 'I dream of a Pacific Identity, not pockets of people fighting for their own petty racial identities. You understand me, Kate?'

She shook her head. Truthfully, she could not say that she did. He led her by the hand and guided her inside, seated her, out of the daylight. 'I dream of making love to you,' he laughed delightedly. He took her arm and held her, almost with the patience of one talking to a child. 'Will you let me love you?'

There was a light rapping on the door. Khumar started, sighed and stood away from the chair where he had been kneeling at Kate's side. He glanced at his watch. 'Yes?' he called. An Indian servant entered, and handed him a note, which he unfolded and read. 'Thank you,' he said. 'I'm on my way.' The servant disappeared.

254

'I'll have to leave, Kate. We can give you a lift part of the way and then we'll find you a taxi.'

In the rear of his car, sitting together, skin occasionally brushing, he was already preoccupied, talking again of his plans.

'What's the rally about?' she asked. He was stepping back into another zone. One that did not include her.

'It's a warm-up for the elections. I'll talk a little about why I'm standing independently, what my aims are. Why I am not with, nor for, Bhanjee and his policy.'

His passions had been transformed to other more pressing concerns. She feared losing him. 'What sort of things will you say?'

'That we must learn to live together, Fijian and Indian alike. The rule of one race over the other can't serve us. We're a small multi-racial nation, a Third World nation. We are dependent for our survival on major overseas investors, for example the British. As long as we fight between ourselves and contort ourselves with dreams of dominating one another, we will never be strong enough to free ourselves from the international economies that have ransomed us. We will never join forces as Pacific Islanders and create our own policies. I dream of that!' He paused, smiling. 'Kate, an economically sound, nuclear-free South Pacific State! Think of it! That is why that damned Ashok Bhanjee and I could no longer see eye to eye. He dreams of more overseas investment, more foreign support. He wants to turn us into a group of duty-free islands backed by Western powers. We will be supported by overseas capital and produce. But that will not save us. We have to grow up, learn to live with one another. Take responsibility for ourselves, whatever our colour. These islands have been weaned on racism, on mistrust of one another. Pockets of people fighting for their racial identity. You cannot build a society on that structure.'

His words were simple, yet she was drawn by his vision. She saw him as an alchemist, bewitching her, turning base metal into gold. In his commitment to his subject she had been forgotten. She watched him in the beams of afternoon

255

sunlight, glancing animatedly about him, smoking cigarettes, leaning out of the window, sitting close to her, touching her skin, drawing diagrams into space with his hands.

Shyam talked to her of his dreams, wooed her with plans of multi-racial schools where children would learn to grow in harmony, naturally accepting one another. He excited her with his vision of all Fijian islands co-operating with every other South Pacific nation and building a Pacific Community. He understood the Fijians' fear for their loss of their lands and culture, like the Maoris and the Aborigines.

His subjects came alive for her. His eyes, tortoiseshell now out of the sunlight, burned with a fervour that made her jealous and, at the same time, inspired her. She longed, too, for him to feel such a passion towards her, and she longed to possess him, for him to possess her, to be fired by such a commitment. And to be loved by such a man.

It was almost sunset as she rode through the winding, manicured residential streets back down towards the city. She had been intending to return directly to the hotel but decided, suddenly, to seek out Patterson.

'Do you know this address?' she asked the until now mute Indian driver, handing him the sheet of paper upon which Khumar had written, in bold striking letters, Patterson's address.

'Different way,' the Indian said after staring at the paper for several moments.

'Could we go there from here, please?' she insisted.

'We go towards the city and then when we reach Suva Way we turn in other direction. OK?' he explained helpfully.

'Thank you.'

She leant back against the fraying upholstered seat and gazed at the passing hillside homes but saw nothing, staring into space, thinking only of all that had been told to her, and of the man with whom she had passed the afternoon. She wondered where Sam might have fitted into Shyam's vision, searching back, trying to remember clearly what Stone had told her. Giving everyone a chance to play. No such thing as

256

losers. That's what Sam had believed. Was that not also what Khumar was fighting for with his talk of Pacific Identity?

How alien to her comfortable life with Philippe where personal gain was the goal. Philippe. The very thought of him and their life together filled her with sadness.

The taxi wound down the hill until they reached the junction that led out on to the main city road, Suva Way. A mackerel sky streaked red above the harbour as they descended.

'Can't go that way,' the driver informed her as the taxi came to a stop at the junction. 'Can't turn right.'

Kate was about to disagree with him, to insist that he followed her instructions when she saw for herself that the road had been blocked off. During the course of the afternoon rusted chains and naïvely drawn NO ENTRY signs had been mounted, closing off the right-hand entrance to the road.

Confusion was gathering all around them. Drivers sat hooting helplessly, packed alongside one another like animals herded into a pen. A broad-boned Fijian policeman, in native uniform with a sharply cut, white sulu-skirt stood, vaguely signalling to confused drivers and appearing equally bemused himself. Kate leant out of the open window and called out to him. He burst out laughing and made a gesture towards the accumulating traffic, telling them to wait, before wandering lazily towards her.

'We need to turn right. Is the road blocked off entirely?' she demanded with a winning smile.

He beamed broadly and said, 'One bridge down at exit to the city. Best to go back up, or turn left into Suva. There's no way through. Where are you from, madam?'

'England. But there must be some way out of the city,' she protested.

He nodded while cars hooted impatiently behind him. He disregarded them. 'Back up and down the other side. Do you know the Queen of England? Fiji's Queen?'

She shook her head. 'Not personally,' she said.

'Good lady,' he said, and, seeming cheered by her response, he smiled broadly displaying an array of large white teeth.

257

Happy to have been of assistance he bowed his head graciously and wandered back towards the impatient cars, waving them chaotically in an assortment of directions.

'I'll go back to the hotel, please,' she sighed as the taxi crept, behind queuing cars, towards the junction. The driver seemed satisfied. It was the simplest solution.

They turned left and headed towards the port, through blocked lanes of traffic bleating angry horns, under a darkening sky, past occasional cows adding to the confusion by wandering aimlessly across the already overcrowded street.

The receptionist inside the high-ceilinged, airy reception hall smiled warmly when Kate arrived at her hotel, exhausted from the fumes and heat. She welcomed her by her Christian name which she had learnt from Kate's passport.

'Any messages for me?' Kate enquired, not really expecting any, ready for a swim.

'No calls, Kate, but boy came with one envelope,' the young girl replied familiarly.

'Envelope? What boy?'

The girl shook her pretty, curled dark head and beamed happily. 'He didn't say, Kate. Just left one envelope and said it was for you.' She turned away from the desk in search of the unexpected delivery and having located it in Kate's box, handed the slenderly packed, ten by eight brown Manilla package to Kate, who turned it over. Nothing was written on it, not even her name.

'The boy didn't say who this is from, did he?' she asked, puzzled.

Once again the girl blithely shook her head.

Upstairs in her fusty, portside suite Kate sat quietly to open the envelope. Inside, wrapped in a blank sheet of white paper, was Sam's much-travelled wallet. She held it between the palms of both hands for a moment and smiled thankfully. There was no note accompanying it but, whoever the sender, she was grateful. She had no way of telling where it had come from or even if it still contained everything that had been there previously. It felt the same, as far as she could remember.

258

She laid it beside her on the discoloured bedspread and opened it, with the delicacy and care given to a precious manuscript. Inside on a faded slip of scissored-cut card, protected beneath a slither of transparent plastic, was Sam's name and address.

> Samuel MacGuire,
> Lesa House,
> Lesa Plantation Estate,
> Lesa.

and beneath, the radio phone number, Lesa 19.

The handwriting was slanted, inclining a degree or so to the right. It was neatly printed and evenly spaced. The tail of the letter G curved elegantly, like a cat's tail in repose. She realised that she had no recollection of ever having seen anything written by her father before. It was a stranger's script but one that she responded to and, though she possessed no knowledge of graphology, she liked the style, found it well balanced and thought him quite a calligrapher!

The wallet contained two pockets, one on the left, the other on the right. Both contained something. She began with the left side, pulling out a small wad and found, on a folded sheet of lined exercise-book paper, an address. It was written in the same hand, his hand, but more hurriedly. There was no name with the address, nor any telephone number. Simply an address situated on the mainland. Beneath the torn exercise sheet were several photographs including, to her astonishment, a ragged photograph of herself, sepiaed with age.

Her young self wore a white cotton sunbonnet tied in rather too large a bow beneath her chin and a frilled apron-styled sundress. She was laughing and pointing towards the camera. She could not have been older than three, perhaps four, and recognised herself by the one large curl that crossed like a hair roller from one side of her forehead to the other. This curl, she remembered now, had inspired her nickname, taken from a popular song of the time, she had been assured. It was bestowed upon her by her grandparents, The-Girl-with-the-Curl-in-the-Middle-of-her-Forehead! At her side, lying carelessly asleep, was a shaggy, king-sized animal, bulkier even than the small girl grinning proudly at its side. This leviathan companion resembled a huge Angora cat but was in fact a chow.

Kate stared incredulously at the ageing, creased snapshot. She had never seen it before nor any that might have been taken from the same roll of film. She had no memory of the occasion or, indeed, of the dog. Had he been hers? She supposed not, for how could she have forgotten such a fellow? The picture had been taken as a close-up, thereby excluding most of the surrounding landscape, but they must have been in a garden for there was lawn beneath them – heath or field? Her family garden? They had lived in a house before Sam left home which had possessed a small garden but she could no longer recall it.

It had been later, when she and her mother had been alone and times were hard, that they had moved to the flat. Their concrete existence in Croydon. No, she neither recognised the animal, the dress, nor the location. She turned the photo on to its back. There, in her mother's hand, was written: 'Katherine, four years, with Zambia'.

Zambia! He was gone from her memory, erased, buried in a past that, it seemed, she was unable to recall.

The next photograph, according to the writing on its back, had been taken in July 1950. One month after Kate had been born. This, too, was of child Kate though barely visible, swathed in a cream crocheted shawl and held in the loving arms of her proud mother. The photograph had a period quality about it, post-war, tailored, black and white. As she sat now in her unfamiliar hotel suite, musty and outdated like the photo, she was struck by the unfamiliarity of her young mother's expression. It was a face that she would hardly have recognised.

Mary MacGuire was wearing a formal, grey, worsted suit that gave her the appearance, not of a young mother, but of a widow. Her pose, unaccustomed to being photographed, was awkward. She was obviously ill at ease with the moment, hoping that it might soon be over; but then she had always possessed that same awkward stance towards Life, as if it were intruding upon her, taking up too much of her time. Kate always knew her that way. But here, in this photo, she was seeing someone else. Here was a softness that Kate never remembered having seen. Her mother was smiling, poised like a shy, self-conscious squirrel in her fitted suit. It was the face of a young woman, a mature girl, who had not yet found reason, as later she believed she had, to berate Life for its harsh dealings with her. The weary brooding creature that Kate had shared her childhood with had not yet existed.

Kate wondered if it had been Sam who had taken the photo. Was it he standing behind the lens, calling to Mary, making her smile shyly? Was it he who had caught this moment, so precious, before her face had cast off its softness, trading it for anger and accusation? She wondered if that was why Sam had kept the photo all these years. Why else should he?

The last photo amongst this slim collection, this mosaic from the past, was of Sam himself. Not the man that she had carried in her imagination for almost thirty years. No, he had long since gone, but another, older man with bleached beard and baggy philanthropic eyes, with wrinkled face, tanned and creased from the climate, and pot-bellied though not obesely so. This fellow struck her as sturdy and comfortable like some old, long-favoured piece of furniture. Aged with time and mellow as mahogany though not overly cared for.

He was wearing soggy, patterned swimming trunks which clung precariously to his skin but failed to reach his well-fed waist. Closer observation showed her that his whole body was dripping wet. In his left hand was a fish which he was holding towards the camera, a triumphant, warmly ostentatious gesture. Its colours glinted in the sunlight. She supposed that this silver-scaled, rainbow-coloured, heavy pounder had just been caught by him. His right arm, which sported a diving watch similar to the one Stone wore, was slung around the naked brown shoulders of a woman, also in swimming costume. She was Fijian, with a keyboard of gleaming white teeth and frizzy jet hair, but otherwise more Westernised than the average native woman. Kate assessed her to be considerably younger than Sam, perhaps mid-thirties, probably the same age as Kate herself. Her body, unlike most Fijian women, was lithe and slender. Her eyes, black and walnut, sparkled with jocosity. Both she and Sam were convulsed with laughter. This laughter, their gestures and their body language spoke of an intimacy between them that took Kate by surprise, even caused her a moment of searing jealousy.

Her thoughts fled back to the sounds of his laughter echoing still through chinks of a distanced childhood.

She flipped the photo on to its back. Nothing had been written there to mark the occasion.

So, there had been a woman. And apparently not so very long before his death. Had she been living with Sam at the Plantation? If so, she wondered why Stone had not mentioned her. He must have known about her. She glanced at the woman's fingers in search of a sign. The left hand was out of sight wrapped behind Sam's waist and the right, held against her collar bone as if to support her body's reaction to the laughter, was bare. She was beautiful, this woman. A sensual vibrant creature. How different from the shy, grey squirrel that he had left behind in England!

She laid the three photos and the scribbled exercise sheet aside and picked up the wallet, opening up the right-hand pocket, pulling out its contents and setting it back on to the bedspread, glancing once more at the last photo. She wondered where the woman might be now. It could not, after all, have been taken so very long ago. No signs of ageing coloured or marked the print and the scanty clothes the couple were wearing were not outmoded. She had not noticed any signs of her about the house but it was almost six weeks now since his death.

The right-hand pocket: Sam's international driving licence. Born December 6th 1929. She calculated then that he had died, or been killed, just weeks before his fifty-seventh birthday.

Had this woman been in his life at the time of his death? Ami, she recalled, had told her that Stone had been the first, after him, at the scene of Sam's death. No one had mentioned any woman.

262

Other odd scraps of paper with notes scribbled illegibly lay buried amongst several business cards and one or two other snapshots. Shyam Khumar. President of the Fijian Sugar Company. Underneath an address. Not the private address that she had visited. Another. She supposed a company address. She recollected that Shyam had told her, after supper that first evening on the terrace at Lesa, that he had hardly known Sam, that they had been introduced to one another at a dinner party given by Patterson. And yet, that seemed unlikely. If Shyam had been the President of the Sugar Company, surely Sam would have met and dealt with him on a regular basis?

Her heart began to beat heavily. A percussive striking inside, pounding at her system. She could not believe that Shyam had lied to her. She glanced anxiously at her watch. Half past seven. She decided that it was time to contact Patterson.

Impatiently she shifted through the remaining cluster of cards, papers and photographs still held in her hand. A letter from a London lawyer: 'Dear Mr MacGuire, We are happy to inform you . . .'. And there was her married name and address. So, that was how he had found her again. The letter was dated July 13th. A month before she had heard from him.

A business card. Robert S. Danil. And the address that she had written in her diary along with her appointment with him for the following afternoon. She turned the card on to its back and found written there, 'Tuesday 2 p.m'. No date. No year. It was Sam's writing as far as she could tell. It had been carelessly scribbled as if resting on an uneven surface. And underneath the time, a name, scribbled by Sam, almost illegible . . . 'Rob Waskill'? . . . Too scribbled to read. Perhaps it was 'Rob Danil'? Strange, though, to write Danil's own name on the back of his business card. Misspelt. With what looked like two looped ls.

It must have been Danil who had made the original offer to Sam. The offer that he had spoken of with such enthusiasm. She rummaged hastily through a number of remaining, meaningless scraps of messages scribbled on torn slips of paper

– salmagundi in a lucky dip – until she came across a passport photo, black and white, quite dated. Was this the same woman that was in the other photo? She could not be certain. She stared hard at the tiny representation. The hair was less groomed, lacking style, and the face was a little plumper. Here, the woman was wearing make-up, gauchely applied and very old-fashioned in its lines. Her expression was serious, almost fearful of the camera, but, yes, it was the same woman. The same dark animated eyes, several years younger. And again nothing written on the empty reverse of the cheap booth photo.

She slipped it back amongst the potpourri of Sam's presumably cherished farrago and stuffed the handful back into the wallet. She was feeling restless and uneasy. It was just after half past seven. Deciding to telephone she leant forward towards the stark, wooden chair where she had left her handbag and dug for the handwritten address that Shyam had noted for her. Patterson first, and then Philippe.

She lifted the black receiver and was answered by the same willing receptionist.

'Yes, Kate?' the warm brown voice responded.

'I would like to make two phone calls, please. One local and one international, to London, please.'

'Can you give me the international number first because that will take longer. Then I dial the other.'

Kate painstakingly dictated the numbers and then replaced the receiver. She lay back against the musty pillowcases and watched a cockroach head steadily towards a chink in the sill beside the closed window. Outside, lights from the liners anchored in the harbour shone in the darkness like strings of paste necklaces. She closed her eyes and prayed that Patterson was home.

It was several minutes before the bell on the heavy black telephone brayed into the settling night light and dragged her back from her heavy drowsing.

'Yes?' she drawled.

'I'm getting no answer on your local call, Kate,' the chirruping voice announced.

264

'Can you try it again, please,' she asked, rousing herself and leaning on her elbows. Her limbs stung with sleeping circulation. Pins and needles, she used to call it.

'I've rung several times already, Kate.'

'Please keep trying. It's important.' Without waiting for any further response she replaced the receiver and lay back into the blackness cracked with lights beaming and throbbing in the port. In the silence, somewhere beneath her window, she could hear a gang of local boys giggling drunkenly. She closed her eyes, her thoughts drifting easily towards Shyam and their afternoon on the terrace, before she fell asleep.

It was almost midnight when the insolent bell broke into her sleep once more. She woke, opened her eyes and panicked, unable to recognise her surroundings. The phone clanged on, brazenly pealing for attention.

'Yes, hello?' she stammered. Her mouth was dry, her voice raspy.

'Your call to London, Kate.' The same chirrupy tone but this time a man's voice. The Fijian night porter.

In the distance she heard an English ringing tone. It remained unanswered. It seemed he was not at home. She was about to replace the receiver when a woman's voice, distant and reverberating, said hello.

Kate said nothing, stunned and confused. It must be a wrong number. She dragged her dulled thoughts together and repeated her own home number. The woman confirmed it. 'I'd like to speak to Philippe,' she demanded, rather more firmly than she would have expected.

'I'm sorry he's not here at the moment. Can I take a message?'

'Yes,' she replied curtly. 'This is his wife. I'm telephoning him from Fiji.' She could hear her own note of accusation.

'Oh, Kate. It's Susan. He's only popped out to buy a paper. Can I get him to call you back?'

Susan! Wasn't it Saturday evening, or afternoon in London? Unless she had completely confused the days Philippe had only arrived back from New York that same morning.

'Hello, Kate, are you still there?' Susan's purring voice enquired efficiently.

'Yes, I'm still here. No, listen, it's the middle of the night here. I'll ring again. Just tell him that I telephoned, please.' She didn't wait for Susan's smooth, well-presented response or request for any further message, just replaced the receiver and lay back on to the bedspread. She was still fully clothed. It was hot and sticky. No air conditioning and she had fallen asleep without turning on the fan. She felt terrible and the room smelt damp and sordid. She picked up the receiver, once more.

'Yes, Kate?'

'What's the time difference between here and England, please?'

'Twelve hours, Kate. It's half past midday there.'

'Thanks.'

What the hell was Philippe's secretary doing at the house on Sunday morning? Had she been entirely blind, naïvely foolish? Her mind raced back to the many occasions when she had rung Susan at the office to discuss surprise birthday suppers for him, confirm travel arrangements, enquire about his plans, all of which Susan had always known better than Kate herself. Jesus!

She sat up and pulled her cotton shirt over her head, fumbling for the light switch placed somewhere on the wooden bedhead.

The phone rang again. The light went on, blinding her and making her realise that she had a pounding headache.

'Kate, this is the night porter. Have you finished your call to London?'

'Of course I've finished! I'm off the phone, aren't I?' She held the shirt over her face to ease the callous white light.

'Thank you.' The bewildered porter replied before hastily hanging up. Instantly she regretted her sharp tongue, tossed her shirt on to the chair still holding her bag, turned out the light and, with the help of occasional lights flashing in the darkness from the harbour, groped her way towards the bathroom.

266

Chapter 5

'I'd like to send a telex, please, to London.' Kate was handed a form by the receptionist who then silently returned to her work.

'Thank you.' She pulled her diary from her handbag and searched for the telex number of Philippe's London office. 'Can you send it immediately, please?'

The girl nodded. She was Indian, this taciturn receptionist. Heartbreakingly thin, possessing the body of a fragile undernourished child. Arms like walking sticks yet with shy, languorous eyes overflowing with female omniscience. Her full mouth was painted a cherry-rich red and a circular dot of the same colour decorated that spot between her dark, unplucked brows. The Hindi third eye. Cascading coarse black hair had been neatly plaited and hung sensuously over her left shoulder covering a finely cut strap on her cheap cotton sundress.

Kate smiled warmly at the delicate creature and walked towards a small writing desk hidden in a shadowed corner of the stone-flagged floor of the lobby entrance. She slipped her hand into her white cotton skirt pocket, pulled out the message that she had painstakingly composed upstairs in the privacy of her room and copied it in bold capital letters on to the form.

SPOKE TO DANIL AN HOUR AGO STOP SALE
DELAYED STOP WILL KEEP YOU INFORMED

She read it over and decided that it had been cleverly phrased.
It did not exactly lie, only by implication. She had spoken to
Danil an hour ago almost as soon as his office opened.
Philippe would not receive this message for another twelve
hours. By then it would be night here and Danil's office would
be closed. Too late to telephone from England. Philippe
would have to wait until the office reopened the following
morning. That would give her a few hours' grace. Should
Philippe decide to telephone Danil, which she was sure he
would, he would learn that it had been she who had delayed
the signing of the contract, not Danil. Danil would be unable
to explain to Philippe for what reason because she had not told
him. If, however, Philippe did not check or was unable to get
through he would assume that it was Danil who had delayed
the contract.

'Actually, there's no hurry. As long as it goes today,' she
said, handing the completed form back to the receptionist
before making her way towards the front entrance.

It had started to rain. A heavily moustached gentleman in a
dark red uniform and pristine white turban nodded politely as
Kate asked him to find her a taxi. And perhaps an umbrella.
He beckoned to a waiting barefooted youth who hurried inside
in search of umbrellas. These formalities seemed to her
absurdly out of place in a hotel so run-down but, nevertheless,
she found it appealing. A misguided attempt to recreate a
glorious colonial past amidst peeling, stuccoed walls and
mouldering furnishings. Certainly she preferred this to the
American-style lodge next door with its anaesthetising musak
and sanitised breakfasts. Businessman's fodder! She was done
with it!

The bellboy returned with a miserable example of an
umbrella, definitely the last one in the cupboard. He handed
her a message.

'Just came for you, Mrs De Marly,' he announced proudly.

'Mrs De Marly. Room 21. 10.24 a.m.', she read on the

folded slip of paper. The telephonist must have taken it whilst she was standing at the reception desk!

'Thank you.' She fumbled in her handbag in search of loose coins which she shared between them, the turbaned doorman and the bellboy. Both seemed content so she scrambled into the back of a jalopy masquerading as a taxi, handing the driver the address that Shyam had given to her for Patterson. If she could get no response on the telephone she would have to find him in person. 'Will you take me to that address, please?' she asked, carefully avoiding mentioning the possibility of a roadblock.

The driver nodded and the old car lurched heavily forward.

She settled back to read her message. It was from Stone. 'Your husband called here this morning. Wants to talk to you urgently. Please call Plantation. Lesa 19.'

She smiled contentedly. She had not spoken to Philippe before leaving the Plantation and had not given Susan any idea of her whereabouts so Philippe would not be able to find her, unless Stone had told him, but somehow she doubted that.

She was feeling more optimistic this morning as the taxi trundled through the teeming city streets towards the bridge and yesterday's roadblock. In her handbag was Sam's wallet. Patterson had been his close friend. She felt certain that she would hear the truth from him. Finally. About her father's death and perhaps about the Plantation, too. Maybe she would decide never to sell it. Susan would be welcome to Philippe. Her freedom was beginning to feel invigorating.

The road had been cleared. Yesterday's chains and hand-printed signs lay abandoned on a grassy bank at one corner of the T-junction. There were no more traffic jams and no smiling policeman to bar their way. The antiquated taxi sailed on, out of the city.

Patterson's home was situated on a modern housing estate. Directly outside in the stark asphalted road sat a pale green, time-worn Morris Minor probably built in the mid fifties. Otherwise the road was empty, virtually treeless, wintry and

269

lifeless. Its bleak setting was accentuated by the now blustering rain. As the driver pulled up alongside the Morris Kate asked him to re-check the address. 'Are you sure,' she asked incredulously, 'that this is right?'

She had expected something entirely different, though what, she could not say, had not even considered. Something more in keeping with an expatriate?

The driver stared hard at the sheet of paper before assuring her that this was indeed the address.

Could Shyam have been mistaken? she considered. 'Well, will you wait here for me, then?' She was afraid that she might never find her way back from this barren concrete desert. They bartered until an acceptable waiting fee had been agreed upon and then the driver, satisfied, pulled in next to the kerb.

'I'd like to speak to Doctor Patterson, please.'

The boy held himself firmly against the almost closed door, as if fearing that Kate might spy something forbidden within. 'Not here, sorry.'

She felt certain from the expression in the youth's secretive eyes that he was lying but she had no idea how to find out. 'Do you work for the doctor?' she persisted.

'Patterson not here, missus.' He averted his face, unable to hold her questioning gaze. His accent and language made him sound like Ami. An echo of the dead boy, this youth of probably no more than eighteen, younger than Ami, more beautiful, more finely chiselled, less vulpine.

'I need to speak to him urgently. Can you please tell me what time he'll be back?'

The boy shook his head. Fear shone in his amber eyes. 'Not coming back, missus,' he stated uncertainly.

The rain was dripping like a pencil stabbing into Kate's unprotected shoulders. She felt cold from the damp and fearful that something ominous might have happened to Patterson.

'What do you mean he's not coming back? Do you mean for lunch or has something happe – ?'

'Gone away, missus. To another part of the island. He's

working far away, the outer end of the island,' he interrupted smartly.

'When did he go?'

'Yesterday, missus.'

She swung her torso away from the boy, turning her back on him, and stared out hopelessly, through a fine sheet of rain, along the dampened, miserable street. Not a soul in sight on the lifeless estate. No one to help her. An underfed beige and muddied mongrel, hair tufted and patchy, barked insanely at her from across the street. No one to pay the mangy creature any attention. Probably a starving stray who had wandered in on to the estate. She could believe that it always rained here.

She stared at Patterson's car. She supposed it was his car, standing unused, left to rust in the relentless rain. 'Listen,' she said, rounding on him, this time more forcefully. 'I want to leave a message. Have you got something I can write on, please?' But the door had been closed. Silently, while her back had been turned, the youth had shut the door and disappeared inside the house.

'Jesus!'

She stepped down from the open porchway and stood in the mud-sodden pathway searching hopelessly for a clue. Patterson had seemed like her last hope. She glanced about her looking for a gate or some sort of entrance to the rear of the house. But there seemed to be no way through. Bricked walls either side. All the windows were darkened and she felt fearful about peering into them.

It seemed impossible that this doctor lived here, in this uninviting bungalow. She retraced her sodden steps and banged forcefully against the wooden door, calling out his name. There was no reply.

'Please open the door. I need to leave a message. I'm Sam's daughter!' But the silence was unrelenting. Nothing or no one stirred within and the door remained closed.

She set off back along the pathway towards her taxi, hurrying in the rain. Her driver watched her as she made her way towards the old beaten Morris parked behind him. The chrome was rusted. She peered nervously through the

271

window, conscious that someone might be watching her. The inner driving mirror was cracked, a zigzag splintering it. Papers, empty cigarette packets and oddments of clothing were strewn across the seats, save for the driving place. She toyed with the idea of trying to open the door, glanced furtively about her, catching the eye of the Indian waiting in her taxi. With an anticipating inquisitive gaze he watched her. Stealthily she lifted her hand, clasped the handle and pressed hard on the chromed button. Surprisingly, it was locked.

She took a step towards her taxi and then, noticing a copy of the *Fiji Times* on the passenger's seat, she hurried on around the bonnet of the car. It was a photograph of Shyam Khumar that had attracted her attention. The heading read: 'KHUMAR TO STAND ALONE.

At a rally late yesterday afternoon . . .

She pressed her face close against the dust-smeared window and read the date at the top of the incomplete page – someone had torn away a section from the lower part of the page. It read: *Monday December 22nd 1986*. Today's date.

Hurriedly she glanced back towards the house and then ran through the rain the few yards towards her waiting taxi and climbed into the rear of it. The driver turned towards her, cheerfully waiting for instruction, knowing that if she had completed her visit his waiting time had been generously rewarded.

'Drive down to the end of the street, turn right and come back around the block, please.'

This command seemed to please him less but he obeyed without argument. He had still negotiated a good deal.

Each of the streets, dripping and miserable, was identical to the last. And there was not a breath of life to be seen about the place. Obviously the rain had driven these occupants into their homes.

Why was Patterson living out here? she wondered yet again. She wondered too, who else had driven that little car. If Patterson was away who else had bought this morning's paper?

She stared out through the windows distorted with dribbling raindrops, listening to the wipers whining and slapping to and

272

fro like women heaving sopping laundry against rocks at a riverbed. And she had been feeling so optimistic! So certain that Patterson would answer her questions.

She sighed, feeling defeated and disappointed, and pressed her cheek against the glass in an attempt to seek out the angry, navy sky. The weather was getting worse.

Or perhaps it was simply her mood.

They turned the corner and were again approaching the Morris Minor, having completed their tour around the desultory block.

'Pull up here, please,' she requested, on an impulse.

With only a whisper of impatience the driver followed her instructions. His money had not, after all, been so easily earned. They sat, two strangers, staring into the distressed morning listening to the rain scuttling like rats' paws across the roof.

Nothing stirred within the house.

Her driver coughed impatiently and lit himself another cigarette.

'I think we'd better get back to the hotel before it gets any worse,' she sighed, slumping back miserably against the rug-covered upholstery and staring stupidly at the hotel umbrella lying on the seat beside her, dry and unused, realising that she had forgotten to take it with her.

They journeyed through a blanket of lashing rain, like driving through a metallic-sheeted tunnel. To the right of them, could they have seen it, the sea was the colour of soggy hay, its waves churning and whirling on to the drift-dirtied sand, oblivious of them beating a hazardous path towards the city, along a now deserted coastal road.

It was almost half past three when her weary driver finally delivered her, safely, into the entrance way of her hotel, now a mass of whirring, puddled stones. It had been an enervating journey. No doubt, worse for him. He insisted on a large tip, stating clearly the exact amount he had in mind. Kate paid him and he hurried off, leaving her defeated, with her broken umbrella in the rain!

A handwritten note from Shyam Khumar was waiting for

273

her at the hotel desk. Recognising the bold lettering, she tore it open and read it through damp lashes and feverish gaze. 'From the desk of Shyam Khumar,' she read. 'December 22nd.'

Dear Kate,

An unexpected meeting has come up for early this evening which, alas, prevents me from making the invitation that I had originally intended. I had visualised driving down into the city, collecting you from your hotel, taking you on a short tour of Suva and persuading you to join me in a delicious supper. If, of course, you are free and the idea entices!

If supper does appeal and you can face the idea of repeating yesterday's taxi journey up here into the hills of Wavumea, I would be delighted to prepare you something myself. I cannot promise the same standard! As I shall be absent from my desk almost the entire day will you leave an answer with my secretary, please?

Much looking forward to seeing you again this evening. About 8 p.m.?

Shyam.

One raindrop fell from her wet head on to the page clutched between her trembling fingers. It blotted the ink, misshaping the words 'hills of Wavumea'. She re-read the letter before folding it meticulously on to its previous creases and placing it back into its envelope.

Her flustered heart was thudding against her damp, flimsy clothing. He must have left it earlier, before the rain had really begun. 'What time was this letter delivered?' she asked. The words were out before she could restrain an appearance of over-concern about what must have seemed such an unimportant detail.

The receptionist, now another Fijian girl, frowned and shook her bemused head. She could not think how she could answer such a question. Then brightly she announced, 'Before I arrived. And I work afternoons only.'

'Do you think this weather will clear today?' Kate continued, though she felt there was little hope of it. The sky

274

outside was black and thunderous, like a wintry northern European evening, though it was still before four.

'Should be clear shortly now, Kate.' The frothy-haired native girl beamed. Kate saw little reason to share her optimism but was obliged for it just the same. Her thoughts soaring she made her sodden way up the once elegant stairway along the sombrely lit, one electric light bulb of minimal wattage, narrow, flaking corridor towards Room 21, cherishing the note sitting in her damp skirt-pocket.

She was in need of a very hot shower and a short rest and then she would telephone to accept his invitation.

She stretched back, naked and steamy, creamed and damp, against a towel that she had earlier flung across the hideous bedspread, and picked up the receiver.

'Lesa 19, please.' First Stone, she thought, and then Shyam's secretary. She was drawing out her moment of acceptance, savouring the invitation, like preserving the very favourite food until the last.

'I thought we'd lost you on the high seas!' Stone kidded. 'What the hell are you up to? You'll never get back tonight. I hear the weather's filthy that side of the mainland.'

'Yes, I've had to change my plans. Thanks for the message from Philippe. What time did he call?'

'This morning . . . earlyish. I didn't really notice . . . He doesn't seem to know where you are.'

He's fishing, she thought, wondering what he had told her husband and feeling an inexplicable pang of guilt towards him. 'What did you tell him?' she asked cautiously. She heard him drag deeply on a cigarette, imagined that she heard him smiling wryly, and felt the exhalation of smoke before he spoke.

'Said I wasn't too sure,' he drawled. 'Thought you were on the mainland, in the city, signing the contracts. Said I'd pass the message on to you, if you called in. But said I wasn't expecting to hear from you.' He paused, knowing it was all right, before adding, 'That OK?'

She laughed with relief, almost openly, at his complicity.

'Thanks,' she said, realising how much more relaxed she felt knowing that Philippe could not get hold of her. And yet that duplicity, paradoxically, made her feel uneasy.

'So you haven't sold the old farm, yet?'

Her breath caught, audibly, and a shiver ran up the back of her wet naked skin. She sat slowly upright, swung her legs from the bed and placed her undried feet on to the stained, worn carpet. How could he know that? she thought. Philippe would still not have received her telex. She had purposely sent it to his office, not their home fax number. Stone must have spoken to Danil, she surmised hurriedly. But why?

'It's been pouring here since this morning. I couldn't get a taxi to Danil's office. I'll probably try and make the appointment for tomorrow morning.' She was almost stammering and felt sure that he would be able to detect the trembling in her voice. It was a stupid lie, she judged. If Stone had spoken to Danil he would know that she was lying. And as she had been out of the hotel earlier, when he had telephoned, did he suppose she had walked all day in the rain? Where did he suppose she had been?

And, anyway, why was she lying to him?

She remembered the snapshots of Sam and the woman in the bathing costume. They were still sitting in her handbag. Stone had not told her about the woman. He must have known. She groped for a straw. Something to give her faith again. Stone had been the only one that she had trusted, in spite of Philippe's misgivings about him. But perhaps Philippe had been right!

'How did you know?' she ventured. She knew she might be stepping on to ice. He could tell her anything.

'I spoke to Patterson at midday. Timi had asked Leger to get hold of Chand's family address. Apparently we owed him some money. Timi wanted to send it on to his family and to check that his son had arrived safely. You know Timi.'

'Yes, but why Patterson?' Her voice was shaking and her mind was whirring back to the lunchtime rain. It must have been about noon when she had been standing at Patterson's door. Was he inside then? Had he already spoken to Stone?

276

Did Stone know that she had been to visit him? Her instinct had been accurate, she felt sure. Patterson's guarded youth had been lying.

'Leger asked Patterson for their family address and Patterson telephoned us here himself. They were pretty close, Patterson and Chand. He knew the boy's family.'

'Where was he phoning from, do you know?' She hardly dared the question.

'God knows. Didn't ask. His place, I suppose.'

'And did he tell you that the contract signing had been delayed?'

'Yeah. Asked me if I knew anything about it. I said it was news to me.'

'How did he know about it?'

'Haven't got a clue . . . wh –'

'I see. OK. Thanks.' Kate replaced the receiver without even saying goodbye, without even hearing that Stone was still speaking, asking her about her return to the Plantation. She sat back against the crumpled pillow trying to gather her thoughts. In a growing world of uncertainty she trusted Stone, whatever Philippe might have thought about him. Almost like a brother. He and she, Sam's adopted ones. She had to trust him, she told herself.

Chapter 6

The overcrowded room smelt of jasmine. It was an enveloping perfume, soporific and inviting, seducing her weary senses, saturating her with a heat, like flames blazing from a log fire on a miserable winter's night.

In spite of his company she had been feeling subdued, drugged with a damp tiredness. Once or twice she had remembered his card tucked amongst the potpourri of Sam's wallet.

'Are you President of the Sugar Company here?'

'Used to be,' he laughed in surprise. 'I never had time to do a great deal for them. How did you know?'

'I found your card in my father's wallet.'

'Are you suspicious of me, Kate?' He laughed loudly.

'No, of course not. I was surprised. You said you hardly knew him.'

'I must have given it to him at Patterson's.'

Outside the rain was finally stopping, but not for long. They had listened to it all evening long, lashing at the walls around them, beating them closer together.

It was getting late, close to midnight. Time to leave. Call a taxi while the rain has stopped. I'd better go, she thought, but spoke no words. They were both hypnotised, close to one another, listening to Glenn Gould, Bach's Goldberg Variations. It felt uncanny to be so familiar with someone who was

278

so unknown. What did she know about him, save for his work, and moments of his past? Was there a woman, a wife, children? She glanced about his room, his world of politics, law, music, books. There were no photos. Like Sam, a man with so few signs of a past.

Kate listened to the silence. A short respite only from the thunderous storms whiplashing across the sky. The music had stopped. 'Are you married?' she ventured softly.

'Once, yes.'

She stared through the tall windows in search of the balustraded terrace of yesterday but could see nothing now, except their own reflections in the glass.

'She died some years ago.'

On a less bleak, mist-ridden night the room looked out over the garden towards the hills and on, further, towards the distant mainland volcanoes. She watched him silently, in the glass, longing to touch him.

'No one since.' He rolled his torso towards her. His hand slipped towards her ankle, caressing it.

They had crossed through here the day before, on their way to the terrace. Then, jazz had been playing and he had talked passionately, and about his future. Now, they sat quietly, at ease in one another's company, replete from an almost untouched meal that she had mirthfully helped him prepare. They were finishing the last half-glass of a bottle of Australian wine, unfamiliar to her, red and heavy, and were slumped untidily, close to one another across two cushioned cane chairs. She was feeling stoned now as well as tired. It made her loose-limbed and alluring.

'Will you stay?' he asked, peeling the question from the silence that hung, hungrily, between them.

She heard her breath quicken, felt her nipples tauten. It was like the first time. She felt afraid. She was a married woman locked within the confines of regularity, the inexperience of one well-trodden relationship. She was inept, clumsy, yet flushed with desire, suffused with it. Next door, cutlery clattered and fell into dishes. Someone was collecting the debris from their table and carrying it through into the

279

kitchen. They were not alone in the house, as she had supposed. This embarrassed her. A witness to her unskilled adultery.

She nodded a yes.

She longed to tell more, to mouth her desire for him, her burning thoughts of him, but nothing else was possible.

Smiling, he leant towards her shy, bent face and cupped her chin in the heart of his warm, dark palm, drawing her towards him, dragging her from her chair on to the floor.

Beneath them was marble, Persian rugged but unyielding. She felt its cool hardness beneath her and his heat above her. He was not as gentle as she had fantasised in her secret moments. His passion was forceful. It overpowered her, almost frightened her.

Once naked, he knelt above her, regarding her, proud and certain of his prowess. His gestures seemed a mockery to her coyness. After such longing for him she felt herself beginning to close, unable to respond to him, overwhelmed by his sinewy brown form stalking her. She felt crippled by her own apprehension and her fear of wanting him too much. She closed her eyes, shutting away his image.

'I can't,' she whispered inaudibly.

His slender finger stopped her frightened mouth and slid across her soft flushed skin as she felt his weight lower itself tenderly upon her. Instinctively she turned her torso on to its side away from him, momentarily resisting him until his determined hand gripped at her thigh and eased her perplexed pelvis hard against the glassy floor beneath her.

Delicately he pressed himself against her, wooing her dry, trembling lips until her thighs slid open and rested unresisting against the frozen surface beneath her. Once scissored apart he entered her. A considerate journey and he was inside her. At last!

His flesh was upon her, submerging her, his powerful breath alongside her. Her weight sank into the floor beneath her, limbs sprawling freely, falling away from her, lost to his motion.

Slowly he moved, rhythmically, mellifluous as his jazz,

surely ignoring any weakening fear until her lower mouth accepted him willingly and she felt a single salted tear of joy topple from her cheek on to her bare shoulder.

It was two in the morning when they ascended the stairs, hands held, naked and exquisitely aching from the floor. She slid beside him into the unfamiliar darkened room and tumbled drowsily at his side.

Heavy rain had begun to fall again during the night, beating relentlessly against the roof above them as they had lain, intertwined and satisfied. Now it had ceased.

Kate opened an eye, inched her arm towards him. The expanse of white sheet at her side was creased, still mildly damp, yet cool and empty. It smelt of him but Shyam had disappeared. All around was still and silent.

She peered about the unfamiliar room in seach of an alarm clock and found one sitting crooked on a small lace-covered table adjoining his side of the double bed. It was quarter to nine. She lay motionless, listening for signs of life in the surrounding rooms, but they too were silent. Abandoned for the day. And then beneath her she heard muffled sounds of activity. A radio playing faintly, doors opening and closing. She supposed it was Shyam downstairs, eating his breakfast and, at the thought of this, she stretched her limbs sensuously. Silky as a cat she felt, rolling on to her side, touching the forgotten sheet once more before climbing from the bed.

Her clothes were nowhere to be found. She assumed they were still in the downstairs drawing room where she had abandoned them in the small hours of the morning and was concerned about what she might do until she discovered a cotton kimono hanging from the foot of the bed. She wrapped it about her naked sleepy skin, ran her fingers through her matted hair and went in search of a shower, following an indistinct aroma of after shave, essence of verbena.

In the bathroom her clothes were hanging, pressed and waiting for her.

Downstairs a servant began silently to prepare breakfast.

281

'No, thank you, just coffee will be fine,' she requested. 'Is Mr Khumar in his study?'

He told her that Khumar had left before eight, and handed her an envelope. She drank her coffee, staring at the white envelope without opening it, waiting until the Indian servant had cleared her cup and retreated discreetly from the room. The envelope was still moist where someone – he? – had sealed it. The short message read:

Away for the day, across the island. A court case at Nandi. Talk to you later.

Shyam.

And then underneath his signature as if as an afterthought: 'Stay for Christmas.'

She felt a wave of pleasure surge and soar within her. It was bone bare the note, shaped with his bold ebony ink, but it held a promise of another time.

Ecstatically she called to the servant, asking him to order her a taxi, and she set off into the milky-thin morning sunlight towards her hotel at the port. Everywhere along her route the vegetation was bruised and misshapen, saturated by the previous night's deluge. The steamy air oozed drenched mud and roots. They drove alongside solitary Fijian labourers or groups of workers clearing debris from the waterlogged roads. They seemed unperturbed by the damage.

It was the beginning of the cyclone season. The islanders had known more serious weather. Today their homes were still standing. Another time, when the cyclones came, everything could be destroyed.

She contemplated her next few days, her next decisions. Tomorrow would be Christmas Eve. Philippe would have received her telex by now. He would know that the contract had not yet been signed. She blenched at the thought of how angry he would be when he read it, and then realised that, at this moment, she really did not care. She warned herself against foolhardiness and then smiled at her own light-headed happiness.

But there was still Sam's death to unravel, and the future of the Plantation to be considered. Patterson still had to be found. And Danil? She would stall him until she had spoken to Patterson. She must find Patterson. And she would stay for Christmas! She relished the thought of it. She remembered the newspaper cutting that Shyam had given her early the evening before. She unzipped her handbag and pulled out the torn section from yesterday's paper. He had circled one small column, no more than an inch and a half long, with red Biro.

The heading read: GUJARATI YOUTH COMMITS SUICIDE.

Twenty-four-year-old Ami Chand, originally from Suva, committed a violent suicide last Friday evening on the sprawling, European-owned estate, Lesa Sugar Plantation. Although no written statement has been found confirming the reason for the youth's action it is reported that he took his life in a state of despair. He is believed to have been responsible for a fire which destroyed the Plantation's entire uncut sugar crop several days earlier. He had recently been fired from his post as garden manager on the estate. The estimated value of the damage has not been given.

Doctor J. Patterson, also of Suva, a previous employer and close friend of the dead boy, confirmed, after examining the body, that Chand had taken his own life. The suicide had been carried out with a kitchen knife.

Patterson also confirmed that Chand had telephoned him that same evening. During the telephone conversation Chand had confided in Patterson that he was tortured with guilt. He had apparently wept and said that he had no hope of future employment and could see no alternative but to take his own life. Patterson stated later: 'I did not take the boy seriously. I believed his words were simply the voice of depression. Nor did I believe he would kill himself.' Chand's parents were not available for comment at their home outside Suva. He leaves one son, aged five.

Kate folded the clipping of newspaper and sighed loudly. She thought back to the last evening that she had seen Ami alive, lying untidily, naked but for his white sulu, across his narrow bed. She had genuinely believed his story. Got good job, missus. Start on Monday, he had announced proudly. All the dreams he had spoken of, of travel and success. He had convinced her that someone, this important friend, was going to give him another chance. If what she now read was accurate she had completely misunderstood his despair. But she still did not believe in his suicide.

Chapter 7

'Stay for Christmas,' Shyam had suggested. 'Spend it here with me. There's nothing else you can do now.' And she had gladly accepted his invitation.

She telephoned Philippe and explained that she would not be leaving. That she still needed more time. He was furious with her, as she had feared he would be, insisting that she return.

'Kate, please, just sign the papers and come home,' he begged impatiently.

'I can't, Philippe, not yet. I need more time. Please try to understand,' she told him. She felt unprincipled. She had wondered about Susan but had said nothing. It no longer seemed important.

'Listen, Kate . . .' He had stopped calling her by her nickname, Petal, and she felt a sense of relief about that. Like a caterpillar finally shedding its dead skin. 'You said you wanted to stay until the contract was signed, and I accepted that, and now you say that you are still not ready to leave. What's going on? I don't understand. What do you want? I'd come back for you but I can't leave London now. There's a merger mooted from Switzerland and I have to be here, and I want you with me.'

She heard his anger, his frustration stung her, but there was nothing she could say to him. At this moment her marriage, her other life in London as Mrs De Marly, Philippe's hostess and elegant wife, seemed so unreal to her, so insubstantial, and the painful part was that Philippe was the last person she could explain that to.

'Kate? Are you still there?'

'Yes, I'm here.'

'Listen, The Associated Banks of Switzerland group want to buy our merchant banking and securities group. Shares are rocketing sky high and the newspapers are talking about nothing else. The proposals for the shareholders are being drawn up now. They'll present them today latest, Christmas Eve. I can't just up and leave, can't you understand that?'

'I'm not asking you to. I want to be here alone. I'll call you after Christmas,' she replied.

'Jesus, Kate! What the hell is going on?' The line began to crackle. He sounded exhausted. It must be around two in the morning in London, she realised.

'Philippe, I hope it goes well for you today . . . really I do. Get some sleep. I'll talk to you soon,' she said finally, replacing the receiver. She had not mentioned to him where she was phoning from. She sat quietly for a moment or two before preparing to leave, considering their brief conversation, feeling saddened by what was happening between them but sensing that it was somehow inevitable. Her marriage, it was dawning on her now, had not existed for some years. She had been inhabiting a shell that was not her own. If she had never heard from her father, never visited Lesa, would she have gone on forever living out empty postures? Whatever her feelings for Shyam . . . it had nothing to do with him.

Before going out she decided to ring the Plantation, make contact with Stone. Timi answered and told her that Stone had left for the mainland. 'He's got an important meeting with the insurance company later and has been trying to contact you.'

She wondered why there had been no message waiting for her at the hotel. Timi gave her the address of Ami's family. She asked him about Patterson. He told her that he hardly knew the fellow. 'You doing all right there, Mrs De Marly?' he enquired kindly.

286

She smiled at his consideration. 'Yes, I'm fine. Thanks, Timi. Have a good holiday. I'll see you after Christmas.'

'Yes, indeedy. Stone tells me we're not selling the old farm, after all?'

Did he, she thought! 'I'm not sure yet, Timi. It's possible. I won't know until . . . Timi, you know Sam's woman? What was her name?'

There was a silence. No disturbance on the line. He was still there. He must have been thinking, recollecting or deciding what to tell her.

'Which woman you mean, Mrs De Marly?'

'Dark hair. Fijian. In her thirties. Very pretty lady.'

'You mean Nancy?' he posed, after a moment's pause.

'Yes, that's her. Nancy,' she bluffed. 'I need to have a talk with her. Do you know where she is now?'

'Listen, we haven't seen her since she left here.'

'You don't know where she went?' she pressed, groping in the dark.

'She's not here any more. I think they left the islands.'

'They?' she prompted, wary of pushing him too far.

'Her and the American.'

'The American. What was his name?' She was hedging her bets about the sex.

'I don't remember. Talk to Stone.' She noticed a coolness set into his voice. He had become wary or suspicious. Must have guessed that she had been bluffing him.

'Yes, thanks, Timi, I'll do that. Merry Christmas.'

Shyam was still working. They had arranged to meet later that evening, Christmas Eve, at his home. She had originally suggested that they spend Christmas together at the Plantation but he had rejected the idea. His work, he had said, at this time required him to stay on the mainland. It was getting too close to the New Year elections. And, upon reflection, she had agreed. Better to stay alone with him at his home. It would be more discreet.

She had been intending to take a taxi back to the estate where Patterson lived. To try once more to see him to ask him

287

for the address of Ami's family but now that Timi had given her the address she changed her plans. Instead she rang Patterson's number. The same youth answered the telephone. He told her that the doctor was still away and he had no idea when he would be back.

She was convinced now that the boy was lying. He also refused to give her any contact number, saying that he had none, so she left her room number and a message asking Patterson to call her urgently. She was baffled to know why the doctor, Sam's close friend, would be so loath to see her. But, at least, she had Ami's address now and could visit his family. That much she had achieved.

As she set off along the narrow, faded corridor the telephone in her suite began to ring. She was engrossed in trying to decide what she might buy Jal, and perhaps Shyam, too, for Christmas and she did not hear it, hurrying on down the stairs, deciding whether to visit one of the rather old-fashioned-looking department stores. She could buy herself a present, too. A raincoat! Christmas Eve. The shops would be bursting with locals shopping for their families. Normally, in England, she would detest such a prospect but, somehow, here the novelty appealed to her.

Carols were being sung in the hotel foyer by scantily dressed Fijian children. It made Kate laugh to see the cotton wool glued in decoration around their tin collecting boxes. Not one of them would ever have seen snow, these small wide-eyed children. Perhaps in photographs or newspapers but not on television. They had none.

Rummaging happily through her purse in search of coins she found several dollars which they accepted gratefully, beaming and giggling as they whispered and debated what hymn they should sing next. She smiled warmly at them, wished them a Merry Christmas and hastened towards the entrance doors. The sky outside was looking ominous. She would definitely search for a raincoat!

'Mrs De Marly!' The voice behind her, for no apparent reason, panicked her. Her attentions previously given to the carol singers and her concern about the weather were abruptly interrupted. She swung round towards the measured voice and as she turned, before meeting the face, recognised the accent and realised why she had felt a stab of fear.

It was Danil, standing uncomfortably, ill at ease without a chair on which to rest his obscene size. Her heart began to pound anxiously as she stared into his watery, bloated face. She was feeling inexplicably threatened by his presence here at her hotel.

'I was about to leave a message for you, Mrs De Marly.'

A cigarette was burning between his fingers. She noticed a ring, a diamond set in gold, wedged on to a corpulent little finger.

'Really, why?' she asked innocently, knowing exactly why. She had been avoiding his calls.

'I rang your room. And they told me you had left.'

'I am . . . just about to leave. Now,' she stammered.

'Not checking out of the hotel, I trust?'

'No, of course not.'

'Because I think we need to have a little talk,' he droned, dragging on the smoking cigarette. His voice was thick with rasping breath and smoke. She sensed a threat in his statement, a hint of menace.

'Excuse me, Mr Danil, I have a meeting and I am already late,' she lied, surprising herself, gaining in confidence as she did so.

'Mrs De Marly, let me remind you, we have a contract to complete and we are now two days behind our agreed signing date. Tomorrow is a holiday. I think we need to have that talk now.' He swayed as he finished his sentence. Clearly the effort to remain standing and the acid-sweet tone of his civility were a burden to his constitution. 'Why don't we go to the bar where we can talk more comfortably over a drink?' he added more sweetly. Like saccharin, she found him.

The carols had started up again behind them. Crisp accurate notes drifting past her and wafting heavenwards, towards an elegant chandelier reminding one of past decades, of long-forgotten, glorious glowing-hot British Christmases. 'Ding dong, merrily on high . . .' and so incongruous to her, here.

289

She had to think smartly. She felt a ridiculous urge to cry out for help! Several guests, onlookers or visitors, brushed against her shirt sleeve as they stretched to throw coins into the choristers' collecting boxes.

'It's too early for the bar and as I have already told you I have an appointment. I will ring you later. Now if you'll excuse me, Mr Danil,' she bluffed, speaking firmly, resisting any attempt by him to threaten or intimidate her. His eyes narrowed and he snorted impatiently.

But her courage was up and riding on a newly discovered confidence now. She longed to tell him that the deal was off, that she had changed her mind and no longer intended to sell the land, to let him know in no uncertain terms that she suspected him a crook and loathed the very sight of him, but her thoughts briefly flashed to Philippe, to the delicacy and sangfroid he brought to his business negotiations and she decided that for the moment, until she had found and spoken to Patterson, she would say nothing. Let him sweat it out. Until she could be sure.

Until then she would play the game her own way. 'One question, Mr Danil,' she dared.

Danil glowered at her with livid, lizard hooded eyes.

'Did you ever meet my father, Sam MacGuire?'

He dragged on his cigarette, considering his response. Lengthened ash spilt on to his tie and slid to the ground. 'On several occasions,' he replied cautiously.

'In connection with the sale of the estate?'

'Yes.'

'You made him an offer for the Plantation?'

'A generous one.'

'Which he refused?'

'No, Mrs De Marly. He had accepted our offer . . . Unfortunately his untoward death prevented the deal being completed.'

'Do you have anything from him in writing, confirming his acceptance of your offer?'

'We had only got as far as a verbal acceptance, Mrs De Marly.'

290

'Really. How unfortunate for you, Mr Danil.' She turned from him and strode purposefully towards the hotel exit, fleetingly fearless in her triumph.

He watched her, his breath heaving, as she disappeared into the heavy morning light.

This was the coastal road that she and Philippe had travelled together, weeks ago now, on that first tired morning before their arrival at the Plantation. Ami had been driving. She sighed now at the thought of him and glanced at Jal's Christmas present cradled in her lap. It had been raining that morning too, but the inky overcast sky today gave the majestic tropical surroundings a more menacing feel. Or perhaps it was her own growing sense of foreboding. Meeting Danil at the hotel had unsettled her, left her agitated. Perhaps she had goaded him too far.

She glanced anxiously out of the rear window. Butterflies turned in her stomach. For the last several miles she had felt a nagging dread that someone was following her. In a pale blue car. Several times already she had stared hard out of the taxi's rear window, straining to read the licence plate or to identify who the driver might be. At first she had supposed that it was her imagination or her growing uncertainty but once out of the city, travelling along the almost deserted coastal road, she had realised there was a car, the same blue car, travelling at a constant speed, keeping the same distance behind her. Just far enough behind to be unrecognisable.

'How much further is it?' she enquired anxiously of her driver.

'About another mile along on the right, there's a small Indian settlement. It's there.'

She turned back to look behind her once more. Could it be Danil? His story conflicted with Stone's. Stone had said that Sam had rejected the offer. One of them was lying. This same thought kept churning in her head. The car had fallen behind about a quarter of a mile. She watched anxiously. It was slowing down, as though searching for a house or slip road. And then it pulled off the road and parked on a grass verge close to a tiny settlement of no more than half a dozen shacks.

291

'Could you please slow down, just for a moment?' she demanded of the driver. She watched the distant parked car. As far a she could see, no one got out of it. There was no movement at all around the vehicle and then it seemed that someone was approaching it from one of the shacks.

'It's all right, you can keep going now.'

The blue car remained stationary, disappearing from her view, a diminishing speck on her horizon. Unseen by Kate, the stranger that she had observed approaching the car had strode on past it, oblivious to its presence.

They must have been collecting someone, she thought. She had been mistaken. She exhaled deeply and settled back comfortably into her seat to enjoy the lush beauty growing all around her.

They journeyed onwards, she threw one last glance behind her. The car had entirely disappeared from sight. So, it had been her own foolish anxiety. She stared down at her gift for Jal. The jolly wrapping paper was creased, sticky at either of the corners from where she had been grasping it too tightly in her clammy hands. Unthinkingly she unpeeled a sticky label stuck there by the storekeeper who had wrapped the gift. She had always possessed an aversion to such advertisings but had not noticed it until this moment. She screwed the small rectangle of sticky paper into a ball less than a thimbleful in size and flicked the paper into an ashtray laden with cigarette butts, hoping that Jal would enjoy his gift and wondering what she might learn from Ami's parents.

The words *Merry Christmas from Bhanjee's Duty-Free Stores. Gifts for all the Family* had disappeared and lay, amongst the butts, gathering ash.

They arrived at the settlement and she was immediately pointed towards the Chands' bungalow.

'I've brought a Christmas present for your grandson,' she explained shyly to a lean, bedraggled Indian who opened the door and leant out on to the front porchway. He regarded her with mistrust, screwing up his eyes. He seemed to have emerged from sleep, disturbed, and dragged himself unwillingly from his

292

bed. His eyes were bloodshot, troubled by the light. His face, worn and bleary. He was wearing a frayed, soiled sulu wrapped about his waist in the local style. Around his forehead was a strip of soiled material taken from the same print as the sulu. Its ragged ends brushed against his naked, bony shoulders.

'What you want?' he said, dragging hard on his hand-rolled cigarette and inhaling deeply. The tobacco smelt aromatic like some sweetly perfumed exotic tea. The hand holding the cigarette was rested against his dusky smooth-skinned breast while the other stroked at his unshaven chin as he tried to comprehend what it was she wanted. His English was poor.

'Are you Ami's father?' she quizzed, and then, realising her thoughtless error, added hastily, 'I mean . . . Ami, was he your son?' She was still clutching the gift-wrapped Walkman, worrying now that the present was too extravagant. Tawdry of her, she thought, to have assumed that it would assure her of a welcome and a little information. But too late now to turn back. The fellow shook his matted head.

'Listen,' she began rather more patiently, speaking the words more slowly to assist his comprehension. Was he shaking his head because he had understood or because he had not understood?

'My name is Katherine De Marly. Ami might have mentioned me?' The fellow made no response. She still could not tell if he had even understood her. 'I'm the owner of the Lesa Sugar Plantation . . . where Ami worked. I've brought this present for his son, a Christmas present. And I was wondering if I could have a word with Ami's father. Please.'

She stepped forward, self-consciously thrusting the Walkman at the unwilling, curiously taciturn fellow.

'Not here,' he replied, tucking the gift into the waist of his sulu.

'Who, Jal? Is he here? Is he living here?' She wanted to scream with frustration. So many closed doors on the islands!

He nodded his head, raising her hopes momentarily before adding, 'Not here now. Gone to market with his grandparents.'

'Ah! You're not his grandfather . . . Right. Will they be back soon?' she persisted hopefully.

293

'Back tonight.' He dragged hard on his pungent reefer, speaking through the exhaling smoke.

'Tonight! Are they shopping or . . .'

'Working.'

'I see,' she sighed. 'Then could you write down the address, please, of where I can find them?'

He looked bemused by such a request. Stupid of her, she thought. Perhaps he was unable to write English.

'Chand's Handicraft Store. Suva Market.' He spoke the words blandly, as if she were indeed foolish. Foolish for not realising the location.

'Thank you very much!' she called out after her, already heading away from the house, hurrying back across the softly muddied grass, passing other newly built prefabricated homes. Several amongst this settlement had been revamped, rebuilt or modernised, like the Chands' more comfortable home, designed with curtains, windows, porchways while others were still constructed from the rusted and occasionally buckled, familiar sheets of ageing corrugated iron.

Close by a group of Indian women, maiden girls and older wives, sat together, squatting in the stormy, muggy morning. They worked without speaking, chopping vegetables laid out on rush matting under the protective arm of a spreading flame tree. As Kate passed by them they stopped their work and stared after her; she called hello, they giggled awkwardly, watching shyly as she walked quickly onwards towards the mud track that led back to the road.

At the corner of the path a corrugated iron lavatory, open doorway swarming with flies, gave off an odour so insalubrious it made her want to retch. Her driver had unlocked the door for her; as she stepped inside the taxi she glanced back to smile once more at the working women. Their shy faces still watching curiously and their brightly coloured saris, light as air, brought a life to the otherwise leaden, depressed surroundings. She closed the door and settled back into her seat with a sigh.

'I'd like to go back to Suva please. Drop me somewhere near the market.'

294

Without speaking he reversed on to the deserted road and began hurtling back towards the city. A mile or so along, ahead of her, she spotted the blue car, still parked, waiting like a beast of prey on the opposite side of the road. They sailed past it. As they did so it pulled out from the grass verge and within seconds had disappeared from view, heading on speedily away from the city in the direction from which she had just come.

She laid her head back against the seat and closed her eyes, feeling fearful. Had it simply been waiting for her there? She could not bear to open her eyes and turn around.

It was the sounds of the approaching city that roused her from her drowsing. Overheating cars hooting impatiently, belching excesses of black burnt oil, oxen being led or stubbornly chivvied in and out of traffic queues, weaving their way at an exasperating pace, stray dogs barking neurotically at uncaring pedestrians crossing the streets, oblivious to the lorries and trucks raging and cursing around them. Muggy city days.

She caught sight of her reflection in the driver's mirror and was surprised to see how drawn she was looking. In spite of Shyam. Soon, she thought as she fumbled into her handbag in search of a comb, she would have to make a decision about the Plantation. Her sun-blonded mane, grown longer now, was falling on to her face. She brushed the hair away from her features and there, creeping up behind her own reflection, was the dusty blue car. It was gaining speed, closing up behind them. The same car. Her stomach churned. She was definitely being followed!

But why had the car pulled up in advance of her destination, unless he had known where she was going? If so, how? Only Timi knew that she had Chand's address . . . unless he had spoken to Stone and told him . . . even so, neither could have known that she would visit there immediately. She did not want to believe that it was something to do with Stone. Sam's right-hand man! But who else could know?

'Listen,' she said hastily with drying mouth and heavy pacing heart. 'As soon as we're within walking distance of the

295

market, drop me. But choose somewhere busy, please. How much do I owe you? I'll pay now.'

He pulled an exorbitantly high figure from his head, she knew it, but not wanting to waste time with argument, she dived into her purse, drew out several bills, tossed the dollars on to the seat in front of her and told him to keep the change.

'Just make sure you leave me somewhere crowded,' she reiterated nervousely.

She could see the market, bustling and brilliantly coloured, from where the driver pulled up. A barrage of florid fruits or sun-ripened vegetables were laid out in heaps spilling from the pavements on to the streets. Through the crowded entrances she could see into the inner market, covered lanes humming with noisy, bleating vendors.

Pushing vigorously at the taxi door, she stepped out on to the street squelching with rotting fruit, cautiously scanned the traffic, spotted no blue car or other signs of danger and so hurried across the honking, squawking, full-throated city street in search of Chand's Handicraft Store.

Within a market teeming with Christmas shoppers she found the stall with ease. Above it, in bold lapis lazuli lettering, was written: 'CHAND'S HANDICRAFT STORE . . . VISIT US FIRST. VERY BEST PRICES.' And underneath, as she drew closer, in smaller hand-painted white letters, the words: 'All our handicrafts are fumigated for your convenience. Shop in a friendly environment.'

She pushed her way through the bustling hive of market life until she reached their roughly assembled, timbered, skeletal stall, laden with variously sized carved ebony handicrafts. Jal, almost hidden behind the crammed counter, was seated beside his grandmother. A slight woman with creased delicate features, grey-black hair, probably in her late forties, enveloped in mourning – black sari trimmed with gold. The child was chewing a stick of sugar cane, sucking at it like a lolly. He caught Kate's approaching eye, recognised her, stopped his sucking for a few seconds, stared at her with bold boyish eyes and then turned away uninterestedly, distracted by the richness of the market theatre. Her presence had apparently made no impact upon him. She had hoped, expected even, that it might. Undaunted she pressed on towards the grandfather, Ami's father, engrossed in rearranging the layout of his carvings while waiting patiently for the next customer to appear.

On a normal day he would have been more active, standing watchfully, hawklike, in front of his display, beckoning potential buyers; but today his mood was sober and he preferred to occupy himself more privately. But when he spotted Kate struggling through the crowds to reach him, his face lit up. His previously concerned features began to glow a little and, assuming her a customer, he welcomed her warmly.

Kate introduced herself, explaining briefly who she was, that she needed help and that she had just returned from his home. And just as moments earlier his expression had lit up now he became sullen, his tussore-brown eyes stared at her with a cold angry silence.

'Our son is dead,' he began. 'He brought disgrace upon his family. We want to forget that he ever existed.'

'But, Mr Chand . . .'

'There is nothing more to say. Thank you.'

Horrified and speechless, Kate glanced towards the elder Chand's wife. Her doleful, lamenting eyes told another tale, a woman's story. Clothed in her mass of swarming black cloth she mourned her lost son. Weeping unseen tears for her disgraced boy. Her tired, pallid skin, the bags beneath her eyes, and the wisps of greying disordered hair betrayed her outlawed dolour. Feeling no courage to argue, less to intrude still further, Kate mumbled an apology, throwing a glance at Jal who was huddled at his grandmother's side, hiding from her gaze. Hurriedly she turned and pushed her way back through the humming, surging stream of perspiring life, retracing her bemused steps from yet another cul-de-sac.

Chapter 8

Robert Danil finished his gin and rose from Ashok Bhanjee's side. He waved his thick fingers in a gesture of reassurance. 'It's late. I'll show myself out,' he wheezed.

'I'll walk with you to the stairs,' Bhanjee insisted.

Once outside the room brimming with Ashok's party guests, Danil's host confronted him. 'You've disappointed me again, Robert. Time is short. I must have control before the elections. After, it won't look healthy,' Ashok stressed.

'She's resistant, but she'll sign.'

'Are you certain?'

'Give her time, she'll sign.'

'I don't have time, Robert! Listen to me, I have been patient, very patient with you. You made me look a fool already and I don't like that. I want that contract signed before the New Year. Am I making myself clear?'

Danil bowed his head and glanced sheepishly back towards the party, breathing asthmatically, 'I'll get your contract, Ashok.'

'It's your arse if you don't. I'll make sure you never work on any of these islands again. Merry Christmas.'

Danil nodded towards a white man, a solid-looking fellow leaning against a wall across the room, barely visible amidst the partygoers, and then stepped his lumbering way towards the stairs.

Ashok Bhanjee strummed his fingers against the bannisters, watching Danil disappear. He took a deep breath before returning to his seat, smiling benevolently.

He loved Christmas. For him it was a tradition. And every Christmas Eve, another tradition was his party given for chosen members of his extended 'family' gathered about him at his luxurious home in Suva Bay; family members who had worked loyally for his company throughout the year and lesser staff members, also in his mind part of his greater family. Tonight, as every year, they were being repaid for their services with the fruits of his bountiful generosity, which they accepted with lashings of the gratitude due to him.

Ashok rapped his glass against the small table at his side and flashed his heavy hooded eyes around the room, smiling appreciatively, considering his assembled gathering of family and loyal friends. All eyes turned to him. Someone toasted his longevity. Others followed the lead. With a gesture of false modesty he raised his glass to silence them.

Few realised the depths of his ambition and what he might sacrifice to acquire that dream. He shot a glance towards the white man, watching him now.

'Our party, this year,' he announced to his attentive listeners, 'is something a little special. This party tonight is in honour of Sami, my eldest son, who will be leaving soon to start school in Australia. I said to my dear wife, "I want our son to be given an occasion he will never forget. Something that he will talk about proudly amongst his new friends, when he's away from us, suffering the pangs of homesickness." Of course, I know Sami will be returning at the end of each term but that does not alter in my mind the importance of these festivities. I want to make tonight a shining landmark in my boy's childhood.' Sami bowed his thick head in awkwardness.

Unlike the previous years Ashok had taken excessive personal delight in the preparations, thrilling at their extravagances, gloating for his dull-witted Sami (who appeared to be only obediently rapt himself); but in reality Ashok had his own private cause for celebration and that he kept a darkly cherished secret.

And now while his guests stood by, attentively listening, enjoying the fruits of his hospitality, he swelled silently with joy at his own private reason for jubilation. A reason nourished and loved voraciously like the unknown stash of dollar bills that he had kept hidden as a child, and had counted in secret when alone in a household that contained no room for privacy.

Ashok was Party Leader now. And soon, within months, he would be Prime Minister, the first Indian Prime Minister in Fiji. The climate was ready and there was little, soon no one, to stand in his historic path.

'My friends, this is the end of another year when I want to thank you for your support, and to say that now more than at any other time in our pasts I shall call on you, my family, for that support, unquestioned.' A voice here and there about the room mumbled undying loyalty. 'We are living in the South Pacific. An untapped Paradise. There are vast sums of money waiting to be earned here by those with the tenacity and vision.

'And it will be us! Me, and you, my family, who will give these opportunities to the children of our families and their children's children.'

Various listening guests clapped, or called a cheer as Bhanjee paused for breath and theatrical effect. He appeared not to have heard them.

'Within a few months of power I will change the tax laws, declaring Fiji a duty-free port. Such a move will boost tourism beyond our wildest dreams. Our chain will build new hotels for all our cities creating a stopover ideally designed for the international businessman crossing the Pacific. We will create incentive schemes for foreign investors. For example, our friends the Americans!

'I have been promised American expertise and finance to build our industry. Isn't that so, Bob? Anyone in doubt can enquire of my American colleague there, in the corner.' Dark eyes turned towards the white man, a tall blond American standing discreetly to one side. The American smiled in acknowledgement of Ashok's words.

300

'In return,' Ashok continued, drawing the attention back towards him, 'we will take American merchandise, electrical goods, cosmetics, whatever, and we will sell them in every duty-free outlet on the islands.' Bhanjee drained the last few dregs of whisky from his glass. 'My friends, my brothers,' he cooed, 'we have cause for celebration! Merry Christmas to you all!'

Guests and family members applauded, toasted him and drank up. Like every other year the final words of Ashok's Christmas speech were a cue. It was time to leave.

'Sami,' Ashok called ostentatiously towards his son, smiling benignly at a gathering of lesser guests departing obediently. The eldest boy hastily shook hands with a young cousin and bid the leaving child a 'Merry Christmas'. He moved swiftly across the room towards his father. Bhanjee pinched his son roughly on the cheek. 'All this, what I'm building here, is for you, Sami.'

The dull-spirited, uninterested boy nodded his pallid gratitude, supposing that his father was referring to the party.

'Get someone to pour me another Scotch, there's my boy,' Ashok commanded gustily, waving his glass towards his son standing at his side. The obedient boy disappeared carrying the empty crystal tumbler. Alone once again, Ashok glanced at his Dunhill watch. It was quarter past ten. He was feeling tired.

Danil had not delivered.

Land. That was what he needed . . . But land on these islands was not easy to come by. Little of it was freehold. And to gain access to the eighty-seven per cent owned by the Fijian Native Land Trust Board he would need to change the constitution, thereby parting company with the British and withdrawing Fiji from the Commonwealth. That would cost the islands economic stability. But, if, as he was determined, he secured Lesa for the US Government, his position would be guaranteed.

The clean-cut American and his companion, a beautiful Fijian woman in her mid thirties, crossed the room, shook hands with Bhanjee, bid their farewells and left.

All around the spacious room small pockets of relatives and

friends were preparing to leave, to set off into the still muggy pitch-black night. They wanted for nothing, Ashjok had seen to that. Not one of them, immediate family nor more distant relatives. They could go to their beds and sleep soundly. Dreaming the dreams of security, of lack of poverty.

Ashok's attention was drawn towards Raj, his first cousin and much-prized business associate. Raj's son was standing patiently at his side clutching a computer given to him by his uncle Ashok. Each boy had received one. Toys for education. A much-prized notion of Ashok's. Raj's wife, a shy, slight creature from another well-regarded Gujarati family, was busy gathering up their gifts and putting them into plastic bags. Each bag, doled out by the servants, bore the family motif in navy and red. And then: 'Bhanjee's Duty-free Stores. Gifts for all the Family.'

Tomorrow, when his own family were gathered together for reading (even at Christmas Ashok insisted on this discipline), he would slip off for a short while, down to his penthouse office overlooking the port. There, in his sumptuous surroundings filled with polished mahogany desks, cut-glass decanters, gold-plated palm trees, and bars laden with every conceivable form of alcohol, he would switch on his computer system and pore contentedly over the latest figures. He was a rich man and soon he would be a very powerful one.

A silent barefooted servant glided up beside him and placed his refilled whisky glass on the coffee table at his side. Bhanjee ignored it, his concentration was elsewhere.

Raj was crossing the room, followed by his wife and child. His arms were outstretched, in full flight, preparing to embrace his cousin and benefactor. His gesture was unctuous, ostentatious.

'Ashok,' he gushed loudly, 'as always you have been too generous!' Indistinct murmurs of agreement resounded throughout the party. 'My wife,' Raj continued, 'is thrilled with her gifts.' His wife smiled compliantly. 'And so is the boy.'

Gratified, Ashok lifted himself awkwardly from the velour-covered chair to accept his cousin's embrace and to accompany him out of the drawing room, down the stairs to the door. Several partygoers turned to bid the parting family good night.

'I will need you tomorrow,' the political leader murmured to his cousin as, side by side, they strode on, one pace ahead. 'That is if you can drag yourself away from your delightful family, for a couple of hours,' he cooed, within earshot now of Raj's wife, certain of her loyalty. She nodded submissively.

'Whatever time suits you, I am willing,' Raj assured.

Ashok slapped his lighter-weight cousin magnanimously across his silk-shirted back and the two men descended the stairs arm in arm. A servant stood below, patiently waiting by the front door.

'What news of Mrs De Marly?' Ashok quizzed discreetly.

'She bought gifts from us . . .'

'Good, good,' he interjected. 'Robert says she will sign.'

Raj waggled his head from side to side, Indian-style. A ruminative gesture. He was less certain. 'She gave me an address. It was the Chands' family address. Asked me if it was within walking distance. I told her no. She left the shop, took a taxi. I followed and waited. She spoke to that dim-witted uncle. The stupid fellow was stoned. He swore he'd told her nothing. But she left the Walkman that she'd purchased from me with him. I threatened him but he assured me it was a gift for Ami's boy. I caught up with her near the city but lost her in the centre. She got back to the hotel about six o'clock.'

'Mmm. That's all?' Ashok probed in hushed tone.

'She's been spending time with Shyam Khumar . . .'

Bhanjee caught his breath and frowned thoughtfully. 'That is unfortunate.'

Several departing guests prattled and trilled their way down the stairs, approaching the two men. Raj smiled at his host and announced loudly: 'Good night Ashok. A delightful evening. And for Sami, your best ever.'

Many thank yous were spoken as other guests and children hurried out into the dark night, clutching newly acquired gifts. Ashok bid each a benign good night and a happy holiday. He was agitated, concerned, ready to be rid of his tiresome guests.

'These social occasions wear me down,' he remarked tetchily. 'Keep behind Danil. Don't let him go soft on this.

303

Time is running out, my friend.' Ashok stepped from the porchway after Raj, into the late evening air.

'Sleep. We'll discuss her tomorrow,' Raj assured him, noting that his older cousin was tiring more easily these days. He shook Ashok's hand before chivvying his wife and son towards the car.

Ashok glanced heavenwards. Not a star in sight. A heavy sky, low dark clouds. Rain for Christmas, he fancied.

The shimmying of a heavy diesel engine brought his attention back towards his departing guests. It was Raj, reversing a Mercedes 220 in the driveway. He honked the mellow horn, proudly, his wife lightly chiding him for the disturbance at this hour. The car had originally been owned by Ashok but had been given to him. He honked again. A final reassuring good night.

It had been a pleasant evening and tomorrow he and Ashok would work quietly while others celebrated. That suited him. He had ambitions of his own. When Ashok was Prime Minister who would run the Emporiums? He would do everything to assist Ashok and then . . .

His family waved good night. A perfect end to the year, he mused as his powder-blue Mercedes crept like a hush-boat from the crowded, chattering driveway into the deserted tree-lined avenue. He glanced in his rear-view mirror and saw Ashok stepping wearily back into his home.

Elsewhere, within the celebrating drunken city, Stone sat alone. He was in the lobby of the Grand Pacific Hotel patiently awaiting Kate's return. Too drunk to be restless.

Mrs De Marly, they had told him at the reception desk, had left no message. She had gone out in a taxi during the late evening, saying nothing about the expected time of her return.

'Well, I guess, I'll just have to wait then.'

He slouched impassively, watching as parties of guests hurried in and out of the hotel, in search of late-night entertainment. There was an air of festivity and craziness about the place. Throughout the city, discos were packed with celebrating tourists and locals.

As the night crept towards the small hours he began to feel uncharacteristically anxious, in a bleary kind of way, thinking about Kate, worrying that something might have happened to her. Unable to think where she might have got to. Insensible. Unable to think . . .

He finished his Scotch and left the glass on the round corner table where he had been sitting patiently for several hours, removed from the general flow of revellers. Life at Lesa had killed his tolerance for city folk. He ambled towards the reception desk. A smiling Fijian porter greeted him.

'*Bula!*' the cheerful fellow welcomed him.

'*Bula!* You gotta n'empty room here, mate?' Stone's words – he spoke in Fijian – were perceptibly slurred. But who would notice or care tonight?

A room was offered. Nothing fancy, he had insisted, a deal made and Stone was given the key. He had been expecting to return to Lesa before the holiday.

'Listen, you working all night?' he enquired unsteadily.

'Yessir.'

'You got something to write on? I wanna leave a note for Kate . . . I mean, Mrs De Marly. She's in Room . . . Jesus.'

'Room 21, sir.'

'Yeah, Room 21.'

Stone took the coarsely made paper and the borrowed Biro back to his former seat. A waiter sauntered lazily by him. He ordered himself another double Scotch and settled to the note.

'KATE,' he wrote; 'Where the hell've you bin? Tomorrow's Christmas.' He crossed out the word 'tomorrow' and changed it to 'today'.

I promised Timi I'd spend it with him 'n his family and thought you might like to join us. I'm staying here tonight. Will leave about 8 in the morning to get back to Lesa. I'll call you before I go. Sleep tight.

Rob.

P.S. Spoke to Patterson. What the fuck's going on?

He scratched out the last two sentences then tore up the note and rewrote it without the P.S.

305

The Scotch arrived. He downed it in one gulp and left the note at the reception desk. 'Now, you make sure she gets this, eh?' he asserted and headed unsteadily up the stairs, ready to fall into bed.

In the late-night darkness of his room Shyam whispered words of love to Kate in a strange, delicate tongue. Words which teased her but which she could not understand while, at the foot of the bed from a portable cassette machine, Dexter Gordon played 'Weep for Me Willow' and 'Stairway to the Stars'.

They made love again, learning each other, tracing themselves along the geography of the other's desiring limbs.

Later, they lay exhausted, enveloped in one another's dampened flesh. He slept while she lay listening to the sounds of night creeping into the silence that contained them. Shafts of white street-light crept in through the windows, trespassing on their intimacy, making slatted shapes on the plain, night ceiling.

She heard voices singing softly in the tranquil residential street. Then high-pitched ululations in expectation of the fast-approaching Christmas dawn. She wanted to wake him, ask him to talk to her, tell her everything about himself. She loved the sound of his voice. She loved him.

'I love you,' she mouthed, knowing he could not hear her, daring the slatted darkness to wake him and let him know.

She stroked her dampened hair away from her clammy face with the inside of her upper arm and pressed her teeth into her own viscid flesh. Her skin tasted pleasantly salted from her exertions while the aroma of his sandalwood oil seeped into her.

Her juice secreted itself. Like sap from her source it trickled down her inert inner thigh. She was feeling full, throbbing from him, and yet wanting him still, at peace with the man sleeping soundlessly at her side and longing to wake him, to possess him once more.

Unable to sleep she lay, waiting for the rain.

Her thoughts began to meander from her happiness, to race

uncomfortably once more, travelling towards Danil and his blue car, wondering why he might have been following her. She saw his weak venomous face, his tightly curled blond hair cropped close against his skull, the sweat beads lacing his florid features. He frightened her, haunted her. She wondered again who he was working for and what they might do to her if she refused to sell the Plantation. Would they kill her too as they must have killed Sam? How was she going to find Patterson? And would he help her when she had found him?

She mourned her loss of Sam, wishing that he were alive now to guide her, and she mourned the death of poor Ami, pitying him his father's heartlessness.

The dawn was beginning to break, creeping through the shuttered windows. It felt muggy. She rose and crept silently through into the bathroom in search of water. Shyam turned over on to his side, murmuring as he resettled himself and then fell silent.

Kate took the glass of water to the window, peering through the crack of the scarcely opened shutters. Still no sign of rain. She glanced round to Shyam, sleeping peacefully, and then back to the window. Once the Plantation was sold, she mused, she would have no reason to stay. There would be no place for her here. Her life with Philippe was over. Of that she was certain. She was on her own now, untethered and placeless.

Suddenly the thought frightened and saddened her, causing her to sigh.

'Are you all right?' he whispered from behind her. She turned towards him and saw him lying in shadow, watching her. She smiled and nodded. 'Come back to bed.' He spoke the words under his breath.

Silently she crept towards him, sliding herself beneath the sheet and beneath his expectant body.

Stone woke with a bruising headache just before eight. He had intended to be gone by then but figured that as he was already late he would take it easy. They would all still be there, Timi's family waiting to welcome him for Christmas, offering him the warmth given to one of their own.

307

He showered and dressed cautiously, fearful of aggravating the thumping in his head, and made his way downstairs in search of coffee. But this was Christmas morning. The dimly lit dining room was closed, not a soul in sight. He muttered expletives under his breath, lit a cigarette which made him feel worse and slouched over towards the reception.

One of several chirpy Fijian staff greeted him with a Good Morning and a Merry Christmas. He asked to be put through to Mrs De Marly. The phone rang in her room as the receiver was handed to him, piercing into his thudding head. There was no response.

'You sure you got the right room?' he enquired after a few moments. The girl nodded. He finished his cigarette and ground the stub into an ashtray on the desk. 'Has Mrs De Marly gone out already?' he asked. Although where she might be spending Christmas he had no idea, unless she'd headed back to the Plantation.

The girl smiled brightly, on another day he might have found her rather attractive. She assured him that since she had been on duty, half past six, Mrs De Marly had not passed by.

'Did she get my note?' he asked, lighting up another cigarette, and considering whether he should put a call through to Lesa House, although unless Kate were already there, it would be empty. And how would she have got there? No ferries ran on Christmas Day.

The girl searched the square wooden box containing one room key and an envelope. She pulled out the note. It was Stone's handwriting. Either the porter had forgotten to give it to her, or Kate had not returned. He took the creased, forgotten envelope and tapped it against the desk.

'Is that the only key to the room?' he quizzed, dragging hard on his cigarette. The girl nodded. 'OK. Listen, I've gotta get myself some breakfast. I'll call back in about an hour,' he drawled, eyes creased with his aching head. He stared at the envelope and then stuffed it into his back pocket. 'If she comes in, tell her Rob Stone's looking for her and ask her to wait for me. OK?'

The girl nodded, smiled coquettishly at Stone who, not in

the mood, made his way out of the hotel into the vaporous morning air. Across the port bay, deserted for the holiday, the horizon was blurred, misted white like transparent plastic wet with condensation. He wondered if Kate was all right, vaguely considered contacting Leger who would swear at him for the inconvenience, particularly today, rejected the idea and then cursed himself for giving a damn about her.

Shyam and Kate left his home late on Christmas morning and drove down into the city. 'Christmas is not my holiday,' he explained, 'I'm an agnostic Muslim!' He laughed. 'But I enjoy wandering through the deserted holiday streets, watching the handful of passers-by. It gives me an opportunity to reflect upon the islands, watch them in their stillness, consider the blend of peoples and cultures that make up this hybrid mosaic called Fiji.'

They parked his car outside her hotel and, without going inside, walked slowly through the deserted streets, passing an occasional soul with nowhere to celebrate the festivities. Unnoticed by them a taxi hurtled past, on its way towards the coast road, to where the Lesa speedboat was moored. Inside was Stone. He sat with his head slumped back and his eyes tightly shut, nursing his bruising hangover. He had still found no breakfast, nor any trace of Kate.

Kate asked Khumar about his work, and about his future.

'I know that I can't beat Bhanjee,' he reflected, 'but I could possibly divide his vote and stop him. Save these islands from his greed.'

Several cars, ancient Australian rusted carcasses bulging with families, hurtled past them, heading towards their next holiday destination, enjoying the luxury of the deserted streets.

'Later,' he continued as they crossed a small bridge, pausing to glance into the oil-slicked waters and across the port, out towards the open silent sea, 'I will form a splinter party and fight for leadership; but for now, standing independently, I just aim to stop him. And that is what he fears. I am his obstacle. He knows that there are those who remain loyal

309

to me. With those votes, as well as a few far-sighted Fijians, I could bore a damn great hole in his campaign . . .'

They strolled past a cinema plastered with posters for forthcoming war films. From the outside it appeared no bigger than a small grocery store. Two Hindi war films and an American picture starring Chuck Norris were advertised. Programmes were scheduled to commence later in the day. For now, the doors were closed. There was no sign of life within but several patient Indians sat huddled together on the pavements, waiting for the first screening of the day.

'Wouldn't it be better not to split the Indian vote, to help him into power and then try and win back the leadership of your party?' she asked, as he brushed his hand through her hair and caressed her softly downed neck.

'Not at all!' He spun swiftly towards her, gripping her by the shoulders. 'It's no longer my party, Kate, nor ever will be again. And that has given me a freedom. A new lease of life! The time has come for me to encourage a thinking that embraces all peoples. Listen to me, Kate.' He grabbed her by the hand and they headed off across the road away from the heart of the small city. 'If we are fighting to see one race win and rule over another we are moving backwards in time.'

It began to drizzle.

They hurried hand in hand along the streets towards Government Square. He was talking passionately as they hastened onwards or paused to admire the architecture. 'The Fijians fear being overrun by Indians. They fear being dominated on their own islands, so they have given the Indians no land rights. That causes the Indians to fear that one day a bill will be passed that will kick them off the islands and leave them stateless, or the constitution will be changed, denying them rights to gain political power. And so, they say, we must protect ourselves. Make money, become the strongest, the richest and gain power.'

They stood now, arm in arm, regarding the palatial home of the governor. 'And so, each struggles blindly, sometimes corruptly, towards power. To gain a place from where they can dominate, protect their own. But you can't build a society on those fears, that lack of understanding of another's ways. You've seen how it is here, Kate. It doesn't work. There's too much poverty, hatred and mistrust. And that will lead to bloodshed.'

Across the street from the elegantly lush gardens of the Governor's House, the khaki, silted Pacific Ocean lapped.

They crossed the street hand in hand towards the low stone wall that separated the roadside from the water's edge and sat. Not a single tanker adorned the horizon as they stared out towards the clouded distance. An empty picture, desolate even, daubed only with ash clouds.

'Bhanjee and I separated,' he explained, 'because he wouldn't accept that. He wants Indian domination here. I do not. He wants winning and materialistic gain. A Western concept, Kate, and I believe, an outmoded one. To accomplish it he will seek support from one of the Western Alliances by offering them access here. For example, a duty-free port where they can offload their stocks. Attractive overseas investment returns. Perhaps, although I dread to conceive it, he will offer more. These islands will be bought again, ransomed.'

They sat for a while in silence. Kate pondering his words. He, lost in his own purpose.

She felt impassioned by him and yet serene in his company. His ideas broadened her. She trembled as she brushed against his hand resting on the moss-covered stone wall. Dark smooth skin, damp from the light rain, against green and granite. His passion had penetrated her fears and touched her.

'We're five minutes from your hotel and it looks like rain,' he said. 'How about a drink and some lunch?'

He took her hand and they ran happily back along the expansive deserted avenue. Silence and stillness hung around them but for the mute lap of the water alongside them.

Above them a blackening nebulous sky loomed. A cyclone had been forecast, moving southeast towards the islands. Behind them, unseen by either, the blue Mercedes.

The overcrowded dimly lit bar was noisy and thick with tobacco smoke. Cheaply manufactured air conditioning roared helplessly while guests clinked glasses, desperately celebrating their holiday. Days before a cyclone could be unsettling.

Kate and Khumar gathered up their drinks and went in search of a spot outside in the garden. 'It might be quieter there,' Shyam suggested.

A party of Europeans, jabbering raucously, dressed in dripping swimwear, drank Australian champagne under the thick, steamy weather. Shyam pointed towards an empty weatherbeaten lounger. They wandered over hand in hand, stood their glasses on the flagstoned surround and sat down.

'Ashok Bhanjee. Is he the same man who owns the duty-free shops?' she asked after a moment's deliberation.

'Yes, that's him. The family have many interests. Business first, and now politics.' Shyam bent to lift his glass, glancing about him. His eyes rested on a group seated by the swimming pool, facing the roughening ocean. A straw-haired man, with his back to Shyam and Kate, in a tobacco-stained cream suit, was perching on a beach chair. His ivory-headed walking stick rested against his hip while three or four mettlesome young Indian boys dressed in jeans and short-sleeved shirts surrounded him, giggling girlishly, listening intently to the older man. The scene caught Shyam's attention.

'See the fellow seated over there,' he announced to Kate, with pleasured surprise. 'That's Jo Patterson.'

He took her by the hand and walked her towards Patterson and his vital young companions.

'Hey, Jo!' Shyam exclaimed warmly as they approached. The elusive doctor turned in his chair, to search out who was calling his name. He spotted Shyam and hollered at him irreverently, turning the head of every guest in the garden while his young Indian companions hooted with gales of inebriated, coquettish laughter.

Chapter 9

Kate beat her fist hard against the door.

The crisp wind had unsettled her hair and was blowing her flimsy skirt towards her waist, revealing bare thighs. She pressed her anxious fingers against the cotton material to keep it in place, and waited, her heart thumping in her throat, fearing to knock a second time.

Behind the closed door she could hear the sounds of muted voices. Leaning against the portico she turned her back to the closed door and passed her gaze up and down the barren windy avenue. Her taxi stood waiting further back along the street, several yards behind Patterson's Morris Minor which seemed to be parked in exactly the same spot as the last time she had visited. Probably doesn't work, she thought.

The estate appeared equally bleak without the rain. It looked as though it had been thoughtlessly erected and then hastily abandoned. A post-nuclear town.

Behind her, she heard a key turning and the door being unbolted. She swung round hopefully. It was the same youth that she had spoken with briefly before Christmas and had encountered, even more briefly, with Patterson at her hotel the day before, Christmas Day.

'I've come to see Doctor Patterson. He's expecting me,' she announced defiantly, fearing that Patterson might have changed his mind about seeing her or that the tiger-eyed youth would

313

once again refuse her entry. The boy disappeared without speaking, leaving the door barely open, impossible for her to peer beyond. She waited patiently, fearfully apprehensive about what she might discover here.

Moments later, he returned, opening the door wide and beckoning her gracefully inside. She stepped into a long corridor with two closed doors to the left of her and another at the far end of the passageway. There were no windows, which gave the place a sombre feel. The walls were covered in a patterned paper. Quite out of place in this country, this climate. It reminded her of a semi-detached in a London suburb. She breathed a familiar smell, musty, rather like ageing newspapers and noticed on the ground, outside the first door, an untidy pile of yellowing magazines and journals tied into loose bundles with fraying string. The boy opened this first door and showed her into the living room.

'He's coming now,' he announced softly in his alluring Asian accent. He was dressed in white. It enhanced his lean chiselled features and nut-brown skin. She smiled a thank you, recalling Ami lying on his narrow bed dressed only in a white sulu. The youth disappeared, gliding silently out of sight, closing the door behind him. She remained standing in the centre of the room, turning awkwardly about her, surrounded by mountains of newspapers and magazines stacked against the walls, causing the square cramped space to appear even smaller.

The room smelt like a soft, ageing cheese. Everything stood in shadowed light. Curtains were drawn. A cracked table lamp rested precariously on one of the stacks of papers. Its bulb glowed dimly leaving most of the room in semi-darkness. Close by the window stood an open bureau brimming with letters, bills and clippings. Either side of her, piled high with junk, were two tall-backed armchairs carved from a dark wood, with woven rattan as decoration. He must have brought them from Malaysia, Kate guessed, remembering that Patterson and Sam had met there.

Two dead gin bottles lay on the floor beside one of the two chairs. She stood patiently, waiting, surveying the bleak scene.

314

Sounds of movement, scuffling and mumbled voices could be heard in the adjacent room. The door opened, a stark overhead light was switched on, and Patterson, followed by the youth, shuffled in. His ivory-tipped cane tapped against the ground as he moved towards her muttering something incomprehensible to the boy in Hindi. The boy nodded and disappeared, closing the door behind him and leaving Kate face to face with the old doctor at last.

Patterson's pebbled features glared at her. Rheumy eyes regarded her fiercely. He was more sober now than when they had first met. 'You got here, then?' he announced sarcastically, waving his free hand towards one of the two chairs whilst heaving copies of the English *Times* to the ground with his cane. His stance was uncertain, swaying even in stillness.

Kate seated herself obediently on to the semi-cleared chair, discreetly shoving the discarded papers away from her feet. He sat opposite, with difficulty, lowering arthritic joints into place.

'I apologise for the chaos in here. Everyone tells me I should. But after all these years away from England I still can't break the blasted habit of having my papers posted to me and I wait so long for the damned things to arrive that I can't bear to throw them away. My boys have all despaired of me.' She watched as with wrinkled hands he placed his walking stick against the arm of his chair and stared nostalgically at the accumulated debris surrounding him.

'Some of these articles must have been written before our Independence,' he muttered pensively and then, abruptly, he quizzed: 'So, you've been spending time with Shyam?' He was still regarding his treasured literary hoard.

She found herself feeling affronted, sensing an accusation in his question.

'Yes, I've . . .'

'You've fallen in love . . . with the islands, decided to keep the old farm and settle here, right?' he stated wryly, turning his ravaged wintered features towards her. A hint of a twinkle in his bleary eyes betrayed him and eased her discomfort. He was not so fierce as he pretended. The melancholic face spoke more of despair, of bluff, lost in its own ambiguity.

315

'Not exactly . . . I wanted to talk to you about my father, about Sam,' she dared.

'Sam! He was my dearest friend, you know.' He looked squarely into her face and she saw his loss in the moistness in his eyes. 'I miss the old bugger.' Fumbling around the foot of his chair he grappled with papers and debris and produced a gin bottle which he held towards her.

'Will you join me?' he appealed.

She felt unable to refuse. 'Thank you,' she whispered kindly.

He grabbed ferociously at his stick and rapped it against a previously unnoticed piano concealed beneath lengths of ancient curtaining draped close behind him. Within seconds the door had opened, his boy's face had appeared, and disappeared at the order of two glasses.

'We'll have two glasses, Ahmed, and make sure they are clean. We have a guest.' He spoke distantly to the boy. A sahib ordering his servant which Ahmed seemed to accept without resentment. Kate noticed, too, that he had spoken in English this time, not Hindi, and supposed it had been a gesture made for her.

'I tried to see you just before Christmas . . .' she began as soon as the door had closed.

'Yes, I was away,' he lied audaciously.

She saw quite clearly that he was lying, trying to hide something, but felt no anger towards him, only compassion. She had been fearing that she might dislike him, mistrust him, in spite of his friendship with Sam, yet surprisingly she found him appealing. His florid, bespeckled face was vulnerable and beaten, an aged, ill-fitting mask. Tragic was the word she would have used to describe the expression in his watery-blue eyes.

'Sam's wallet arrive safely, did it?' His face broke into a tiny smile. Kate stared at him uncomprehending.

'I saw Ami's boy playing with it on the plane. Realised where he had taken it from. He's always been light-fingered.'

Their conversation was halted until the drinks had been poured and they were, once more, on their own. He downed

316

his gin in one gulp, poured himself another and sat cradling it in wrinkled bronzed hands, resting them on the chair in front of his groin.

'What is it you want to know, then?' he asked challengingly.

'About his death. There seem to be varying reports about it. I fear he might have been murdered.'

He lifted one of his hands and waved it impatiently about him, signalling her to stop, screwing up his features as though she were banging too loudly against a drum.

'Heart attack,' he stated simply and curtly.

Kate was taken aback. She had, after all this time, been expecting something more. She felt deflated by such a response, the wind gone from her sails, and she stared hard at him, searching for the truth in his face. Could it be that even now he was lying? He returned her scrutiny and then: 'What difference does it make how he died?' He looked bleak, dropped his gaze, staring into his glass, downed the second gin and shuffled for the bottle. His wild, straw-white hair stared back at her; she spotted the tell-tale signs of peroxide, as he leant forward, face averted, unwilling to tell more.

'But the Plantation . . . Danil! He is threatening me. He left a note. I found it at my hotel this afternoon,' she appealed. He remained with head bent, silent, and heaved a sigh.

'Doctor Patterson, listen to me. I thought Sam had been murdered because he had refused to sell the Plantation. Sacrificed himself . . .' she persisted softly.

'And what? Are you to be his Nemesis? You take after him, with your wild Irish romanticism!' he upbraided loudly, and then more softly. 'Listen to me. How he died, that's the past. It no longer matters. Why he died? That's a different story.' He leant towards her aiming to refill her glass. She refused with an abrupt wave of her hand. Close proximity showed her that his bulbous nose was covered with small broken veins which bled into his reddened cheeks. The face of an excessive drinker borne out by his present behaviour. He finished his third gin and poured another, refilling more than half of the tumbler.

'Sam had a good offer for the place. Better than good. He decided he would sell. Talked of travelling. I'll be off roaming

317

the world again, Jo, he'd say. Maybe see Australia again. He liked the idea of Australia, a wild untamed land. Good farming country. Thought he might settle there. He talked the idea over with Stone. And there was a woman, too . . .'

'Nancy?'

Patterson peered at her in surprise. His eyes told her that she had learnt more than he would have expected.

'Yes, Nancy. You're a clever little thing. He'd have been proud of you. He talked about you from time to time. Said that he had a little girl back home. And a wife. Pretty little thing, he said you were. He hadn't told his Irish tales about that.' His words were slurring now and his mind was beginning to drift. The bottle was starting to take hold of him. She saw in his face an abstracted look. Eyes averted and thoughts somewhere before her time. He downed another slug of the gin. Fanciful words, but his face told a maudlin story.

'What about Nancy?' she coaxed.

'Nancy wanted to go with him. Tried to persuade him to marry her. He said he was too old for that nonsense and anyway he had a wife back home. He was lying, of course. Your mother was long since dead. Blamed himself over her. Said that she'd consumed her passion in hatred of him. Finally killed herself with it.'

'What about Nancy?' Kate pressed again.

'You know these Fijian girls, all they dream of is marrying a foreigner. Australian, New Zealander, even an Irishman. To get a passport. An opportunity to get off the islands and see a bit of the world, feel some solid currency in their pretty little fingers. Same as all women,' he baited. 'He told her there'd be plenty of money for everyone but he wasn't marrying her. Nancy got upset. Started playing about, trying to make him jealous. There was an American. She'd met him on the Plantation. He'd been working there earlier this year. She met up with him again, went off with him. Sam was pretty lonely for a bit, I guess, but he got over it. Went back to his old wild ways.' Patterson fell silent. 'Women!' he murmured. 'I'd never have stood them.'

'I don't understand. You were telling me about Sam, why

he died,' she persisted, fearful of losing him to the imaginings of the bottle before she had gleaned all that she needed.

'I don't know why!' he yawled. 'He wouldn't tell me why. Let them blow up the whole goddam world, Jo. It's a corrupt old party anyhow but it'll be over my dead body they'll take my sugar land to do it. That's all he'd say. I don't know *why* they killed him.'

'Killed him! So "they" did kill him. Who?' she pressed. He did not answer.

'Who, Doctor Patterson?' she begged. 'Who killed Sam?'

'Listen, I've talked enough,' he began again restlessly. 'I'm weary. I need time on my own.' He lowered his right arm in search of his wooden cane which had slipped to the floor and lay carelessly across a batch of well-thumbed English magazines.

'If you won't talk to me about Sam, talk to me about Ami. Why did you lie, why did you say that his death was a suicide?' she entreated accusingly.

'Ami,' he moaned. 'I could have saved him.' He downed the last dregs from his glass. 'If he had only allowed me. And I didn't say it was suicide. I said "Self-inflicted". That's different. He brought it upon himself. That's what I meant.' Patterson leant his shambling frail frame back into the chair, letting the loosely rescued cane slide to the floor once again.

He closed his eyes and began to speak; slow empty sentences. 'Sam took him. He saw that Ami was destroying me. I loved the boy. He tried to use it. He was ambitious, even with his friends. Too blind to know a real friend. His ambition was restless, claustrophobic, foolish. He had an older brother, Roshan. He lives in Canada now. He worked for a man called Ashok Bhanjee. Bhanjee's a scrofulous bastard who'd stop at nothing to feed his own ambition. Roshan earned his living doing Bhanjee's dirty work. And then he made a tidy sum and left for Canada. That suited Ashok. He'd used him for what he'd needed. Ami idolised the brother, wanted to be like him, succeed like him.'

Kate smiled sadly, remembering her last conversation with Ami. How he had talked of his glittering future.

319

'Ami felt trapped here, wanted to get out, see the world, find work abroad, a new life, away from his family, the community. He was a dreamer, a bragger, full of naïve boasting, and he believed money would change the world. That was part of his downfall. He wanted to take his brother's place, started pushing Ashok, saying he knew something, stupidly pressing him for work, all but blackmailing him. I warned him but he wouldn't listen. Stifled by his own ambition. He caused himself to become a far greater threat than he could ever have realised. Ashok feared that. Feared that he would interfere, unwittingly, in a far more complex scheme of things. So, the poor stupid boy had to go. Blinded by his own overwhelming desire to better himself, to be rich, to be like his unscrupulous brother. His death was "self-inflicted".'

They sat moments together in silence, facing one another. So, it had been for Patterson, his friend, that Sam had taken the boy.

'Very kind man, missus,' Ami had said of Sam. Had he understood that?

Unheard and unseen by Kate the door had been opened and Ahmed had crept in, carrying another full bottle of gin. She saw in him, in his gestures and patience, the compassion of a companion and watched as, silently, he glided towards his beloved doctor, unscrewed the bottle cap, poured a measured shot into the empty glass still carelessly balanced in Patterson's limp hand and then turned towards her.

'Doctor likes to be alone now,' he whispered.

Kate nodded, smiling at the boy who had so loyally barred her entry, thankful that Patterson had found a more compassionate companion than poor Ami. 'I know. Just two more minutes,' she entreated.

The boy consented. Before leaving the room he switched off the stark overhead bulb and then disappeared. She sat silently a few moments in the semi-darkness perched at the old man's side, watching his loneliness.

'Jo.' She ventured to call him by his Christian name, as Sam would have done. 'Why was Ami blackmailing Ashok? Was it something to do with his brother's activities?'

320

He made no response.

'Does Robert Danil work for Bhanjee?' she asked, knowing almost certainly that he did.

'Everybody works for Bhanjee, except thee and me,' he droned almost incoherently, lifting the refilled glass to his lips to drink. The liquid slopped on to his cream batik shirt. He hadn't noticed. 'I wanted to help Ami but he wouldn't let me, said he didn't need me. He had something on Bhanjee that would make him rich.'

'What, Jo? Tell me what it was!' she beseeched.

'He could never have gone to the police because it was his brother. Ashok Bhanjee paid Roshan to kill Sam and then got the kid out of the country.'

'Why?'

'I don't know.'

'But you told me it was Sam's heart that killed him.'

'The shock of the blow caused his heart to give up. He would have died anyway.'

'But why didn't you agree to see me and tell me all this before?'

It was too late. He could no longer hear her. If he had he might have said, Because I'm weary. I lack the strength of Sam's indignation, his rage. But he hadn't heard. He was gone, sleeping, the prayed-for sleep of a tormented soul.

The glass resting on his damp, gin-reeking chest moved up and down marking the rhythm of his low, drunken snores like a metronome. Kate stood, slipped the glass from between his loose fingers and placed it on the floor, beside his cane. She rubbed the palm of her hand tenderly against his clammy perspiring forehead, bent to kiss his head and crept silently from the room.

Chapter 10

She asked the taxi from Patterson's to drop her in the city. It was later than she had realised and hellishly windy but she needed to stroll a bit, needed time to think. Time alone to decide what she must do.

Everywhere around her people were in the street, whooping, partying, celebrating in brightly lit, overcrowded bars and pavements. She had forgotten that, of course, it was still Christmas, Boxing Day night. She had promised to spend the evening with Shyam but first, somehow, she had to contact Stone. She would be needing his help. Whatever the reason Ashok Bhanjee had for wanting Sam's estate she felt certain that he would not let her stand in his way. Danil had made that terrifyingly clear. Her own life was now in danger.

If, as Timi had suggested, Stone had come to the mainland and wanted to see her, why had he left no message?

The wind was building, whisking lightly through the peopled streets. Bunting waved in the darkly lit streets, clinking like sails rolled against a mast. She found a telephone box, rang her hotel. There was a message from Stone. At last! It said he would call later but left no contact number. The message had been taken several hours earlier. It was almost nine p.m. She called Shyam, told him that she had been delayed but would be with him as soon as she could. He was worried. Was anything wrong, he asked. Nothing, she assured. She had been to visit Patterson.

'I'll wait here for you,' he said.

She considered phoning the police, trying to contact Leger, but then decided against it. What could he do? Patterson had confirmed the two deaths as natural causes and suicide. There was no case against Ashok Bhanjee. And the threat from Danil that she had found earlier in the day at the hotel? How could she prove it was him?

She was on her own. She had to find out why Bhanjee wanted the Plantation. And clearly, her time was running out. But whatever the reason she would never sell the Plantation to him. Not now. It was for Stone and Timi and the others who had worked it with Sam. Unless she stayed, unless . . .

She decided to go back to the hotel and searched about seeking a taxi but could find nothing. Strangers approached good-humouredly, offering her beer, invitations, wishing her a happy holiday. She pushed her way through the swarming pockets of people, wondering how much time she had before Danil delivered his promise. Every moment she feared he was watching her, waiting to make a move.

She decided to hurry back to the hotel; never mind a taxi, she would walk, and she would stay there until she heard from Stone.

Alone in her room she put through a call to the Plantation. There was no reply. Stone must either be in the village with Timi and family or, she prayed, he was on the mainland. His message simply read, 'will call later'. She could do nothing except wait for him.

Sam's wallet was tucked beneath her pillow, with her passport. She slid it from between the polyester sheets and spread its contents idly across the bed. Somewhere there must be a clue, or a direction for her. Amongst the very first photographs and papers she had searched, she had found an address. She rummaged desperately through the possessions once more until she found the scribbled exercise sheet. No name. No telephone. Just an address written hurriedly in Sam's scrawl.

What could she lose?

She wrote a note for Stone, and hurried off, leaving the message with reception.

Kate's wristwatch read almost ten o'clock when the taxi pulled up close to the isolated architect-designed bungalow. The address, approached by a narrow, winding, recently constructed private track, was situated on a steeply elevated peninsula which jutted into the ocean like a giant horizontal lighthouse. Adjacent on either side were glorious sandy bays. An idyllic position, this spot, several miles out of the city, southwest of Suva.

'Park here and wait for me,' she told her driver, adding as she emerged from the taxi, 'I may be a while. Just don't go.'

The climb to the door was fifty or so yards. She began it briskly, trudging on ground that was shaly and slippery underfoot. It had been raining here, she noted. Her shoe slid on something soft; she bent down and saw, in the starry darkness, that she had stepped on the remains of a dead toad, squashed by a truck. Its entrails lay splattered, embedded like raspberry jam in the solid tyre tracks.

The wind was really beginning to pick up, cutting through her light clothes, more biting because of the height and the open position. A few yards in front of the bungalow she paused for breath and to take in the surroundings.

A soft-hued light shone from one of the many windows of the glass and redwood home creating tufted shadows like black rags waving at the feet of the tussock grasses; an as yet untamed craggy terrain spilling out into the reefed ocean. The sound of waves slapping against the sand reverberated in the clear air around her. Kate breathed in the forceful, briny ozone and paused to look out across the water towards the coral islands. The bungalow, newly constructed – she could smell the fresh wood – faced south. Stupendous views, whoever owned the place.

It was Boxing Day night and she had no idea who, if anyone, would open the door.

A stranger, a good-looking athletic man, answered the door and stood in the shadowed light holding a Budweiser in his left hand. Somewhere in the background a female voice, Nina Simone, crooned melancholic notes. He was wearing jeans, an open-necked denim shirt; was probably in his late thirties. Rugged, tanned, well exercised and clean cut. Kate had no idea who he might be . . . and he screwed up his face, puzzled by her appearance.

'I'm sorry to trouble you. My name is Kate De Marly.' She was treading cagily, searching for a clue. If this was not another cul-de-sac . . .

'Uhuh. What can I do for you?' He nodded without recognition. Her name clearly meant nothing to him but his accent was thick American! Kate hastily recollected her conversation on the telephone with Timi. 'Her and the American,' Timi had said . . . Sam's ex-girlfriend . . .

'I'm looking for . . . Nancy.' It was a gamble. What other address might she have turned up, written shakily in Sam's hand, where an American answered the door?

'Oh, sure. Who did ya say it was?'

'Tell her . . . Kate De Marly.' She toyed with the idea of offering her maiden name, Sam's name, but feared she might not be received.

She was shown in to an open-plan home where one entire wall, straight ahead of her, was a window facing out on to the ocean. A sandy-haired mulatto child, dapple-skinned, with Betty Boop saucer eyes, sat watching an American video on an oversized television screen.

'Where's your mum, honey?' the blond American asked the child.

'Don't know.'

'I'll be right back.' He disappeared, wandering off through an open door.

'Hey, Nance,' she heard, muffled through several rooms. 'There's a woman here to see ya. Says she's Kate De Marly.'

He reappeared, smiling easily. 'She'll be right out. You want something to drink. Tequila? Beer?'

'Beer. Thank you.'

He strode through into a kitchen punctuated by a breakfast bar and opened a tall refrigerator, humming as he did so, throwing an appraising, unobserved glance back towards Kate. 'You're a long

way from home, I'd say. English ain't ya?' he called through to
her.

'Yes,' she replied uncertainly. 'And you?'

'Me? Wichita Falls, Texas. The name's Bob Maskell. Nance's
fella . . . There ya go. Real American beer. Hard to get over
here.' He headed back towards her and handed her the steaming
cold glass. 'Make yourself comfortable. She'll be right out.
Rough weather, huh? Radio says on accounta the cyclone.'

Kate perched herself on a multi-floral cushioned arrangement
running alongside a spacious whitewashed wall decorated with
brilliantly coloured primitive paintings. 'It's certainly very windy
out there.' She sipped the beer, hastily taking in the room and
adding, 'Happy New Year. Have you been on the islands long?'
she asked casually.

"Bout a year, on and off. I go to and fro. Working for the US
Government. We're doing some research here. Lookin' into
using sugar as an alternative source of energy.'

Moments later Nancy appeared. Barefooted and silent, wearing a blue and gold embossed kaftan. Her entrance was as sleek as
a well-groomed Persian cat.

She beamed broadly as Kate rose to shake her hand. The hand
of the woman that she recognised instantly from the photograph,
giggling triumphantly with Sam and his sweetlip catch. The
fingers that in the photograph had been naked were now
bejewelled with clusters of diamonds and Cartier gold. Her manner, though poised, was as open and welcoming as any Fijian
and, for the briefest of moments, Kate supposed that she knew
her.

'Bob got you a drink then?'

'Yes. Thanks.'

There was an uncomfortable silence. Both strangers waited
expectantly for Kate to speak.

'Forgive me intruding,' she began awkwardly. 'I believe you
were a friend of my late father's. I found your address amongst his
belongings and thought I would introduce myself.'

The minutest of glances darted between the couple.

Suddenly, her lie seemed absurd. Christmas. Boxing Day.
Late at night, such a distance from the city, this woman living

with another man . . . it became almost impossible to pretend a casual air.

Nancy intervened. 'Listen honey,' she seduced, stroking her American's strong hirsute arm. 'How about you get us both another beer? And Lela,' she cooed to her huge-eyed daughter, 'get ready for bed, honey.' The fair-skinned child opened her mouth preparing a protestation. 'Bob'll get your things together and then, when you're washed, you can come back, ready for a story.' The girl, no more than six or seven, accepted the deal, obediently disappearing through the open door, shortly followed by Bob who had already served the two fresh beers on to the breakfast bar.

Nancy, red-nailed and coiffured, glided to the bar and collected the drinks. Kate hurriedly downed her first, barely touched.

'You look a bit like Sam, you know that?'

Kate shook her head and smiled, accepting her drink. 'Thanks.'

They sat beside one another, two women almost identical in age, and smiled uncertainly at one another.

'So you found this address amongst his things, huh?' Her accent and language had become Americanised. 'Well, fancy that!' She twisted her diamond ring, turning it around her finger delicately. 'I never gave it to him. He must've got hold of it. Found it out from somewhere.' She dropped her gaze, stared at her fingers.

'Have you lived here long?'

'Less than three months. Had the place built on my family land. Moved in only a short while before Sam's death. He must've been planning to come over and visit me.' She smiled a saccharin-sweet smile at Kate. A winning, contented face, secure with her swag. 'What did you want to know?' she continued, just a touch defensively.

'What happened?'

'Between Sam and me? He had a good offer for the Plantation. Talked of leaving the islands. Moving on with Stone.' There was a bitterness in her voice despite the constant smile. 'Would've left us here, I guess.'

'What made him change his mind, do you know?'

Nancy's feline eyes bore into Kate. A dormant anger lay resting, reflected there. 'He found out where the money was coming from,' she replied tersely.

'Where?'

'Listen honey, what's it to me? He just didn't want to get married. I had to think of Lela. I decided it was time to move on, that's all.' She rose, preparing herself for Kate's exit. 'I've got to see to the kid. Thanks for coming.'

Kate set her glass on the polished cedar-wood floor and took a reluctant step after her hostess.

'You met Bob at Lesa, didn't you?'

'That's right. He was working over there for a while.' Nancy had already reached the door. She unfastened the lock and held it waiting for Kate who stepped out on to the porch and was blasted once more by the wind and the comforting roar of the ocean. She turned back towards the light spilling through from the open door and looked at Nancy.

'I'm sorry to have intruded. It's just that he was my father and . . . I didn't really know him. He left my mother and me too, you know . . .'

'It makes no difference now. As soon as Bob finishes his work here, we'll move to the States. We're gonna get married. He's bought a big ranch in Texas.'

Kate stared hard at Nancy, more poised now than in the photos with Sam. 'What is Bob's work here?'

'I'm not sure, honey. Something to do with sugar,' she bluffed uncomfortably.

'I see.' Kate stepped back down on to the flinty ground and took a step before turning back to Nancy who was still watching her from the light.

'Nancy, did you know that Sam was murdered?'

Kate could see from the expression on Nancy's face that she had touched home. The news had caught her in the gut. 'Where did you hear that?' she murmured.

'A friend. Nancy, one last question. Lela, is she Sam's?' Kate was guessing.

'No, honey,' the woman replied tersely, shutting the door.

*

It was after midnight. The silent roadsides were speckled with barefooted Fijians and Indians walking silently in the moonlight, impassively striding, journeying back towards their villages after celebrating their Boxing Day with friends and family. Coconut palms, black against the brilliant navy sky, shivered in the light wind, twisting and turning like the fingers of a Balinese dancer. Concrete pylons jutted darkly from the damp rich earth, stretching skywards like creatures from another life. In the city itself debris everywhere, straggled bunting hanging like discarded rag dolls, litter strewn about the streets, the bones of a celebration.

She and her driver rode on in silence, up out of the city, as Kate sat considering all that she had learnt. And what she must do. Nothing stirred in the quiet residential area of Wavumea Heights. People lay sleeping as the taxi climbed lazily, a weary mountain goat, winding its way along the roads towards morning, towards Khumar who, she hoped, was still awake and waiting for her. She longed for him.

Houses were in darkness and not a soul was in sight but as Kate stepped from the taxi and stretched, breathing in the clear air, a movement caught her attention. Another vehicle was pulling up at the corner of the street. She felt a stab in her gut as though she had been punched. Her heart began to race, chugging the blood anxiously through her veins.

It was the blue Mercedes, indistinct in the dimly lit street, creeping to a standstill. Danil's car or the car that had followed her a couple of days ago to Chand's. She was certain. She threw a glance towards the upstairs window and saw a light burning on the stairway. She hurried on into the house, fumbling with the key Shyam had given her only a day or so earlier, unlocking the door. The Mercedes inched a little closer along the road and began to make a U-turn. Her heart was beating like a grandfather clock.

'Dear God, is this it?' she begged, closing her eyes with fear.

A voice called to her from upstairs, it made her jump with fear and then relief, and outside the Mercedes slipped away.

But her destination had been noted.

Chapter 11

She found him seated by a partially open window, staring out towards the mountains. The wind had cleared the view, polished it like gleaming glass while the overhead moon shot shafts of light across the bulging, erupting elevations, creating a softness, an illusion of towering tufts of bluish-green moss. There was nothing savage or sinister about these volcanic giants in this light. The distance created a stillness and peace.

Khumar was smoking a cigarette. He turned as she entered his room, extending a hand to her.

'I'm sorry to be so late. I was afraid you might be sleeping,' she whispered.

'I couldn't sleep. Thought I'd wait up for you. How was your evening?'

She crept towards him and sat at his side, wrapping an arm around his torso, kissing him forcefully on the cheek, holding him tightly.

'I'm so glad to see you! I went to see Patterson, and then on to visit an old girlfriend of my father's. I've been followed here. And this was left for me at the hotel. I found it earlier this afternoon.'

He took the crumpled, overly fingered note and unfolded it, reading the bold letters: 'IT WOULD BE SAFER FOR YOU TO SIGN THE PAPERS. HOW MANY LIVES IS LESA WORTH?'

He turned to regard her, caressed her face. Her skin was almost translucent in the moonlight. She was looking tired and terrified.

'Do you know who left this?'

She shook her head. 'I thought it might have been Danil,' she began breathlessly. 'Christmas Eve a car followed me to Ami's family. Danil had been waiting for me at my hotel . . . and just now, the same car was outside . . . but . . . I'm not sure . . . Perhaps it's not Danil. I'm going to call him in the morning and tell him the deal is off. I'm not selling and I'm going to take the Plantation out of my name.'

'Stone telephoned.' He saw the incredulity in her face. 'Patterson's boy told him he thought he might find you here,' he explained and she nodded, comprehending. 'He said he'll come over to your hotel in the morning.'

They walked through into the bedroom, holding hands; both were tired. They lay, fully clothed, beside one another in the moonlight.

'Ami was working for Ashok Bhanjee. I think he's Danil's boss, too. He had Sam killed. And Ami. And I can't go to the police because I have no proof. Two death certificates. Neither of them stating murder. Bhanjee wants Lesa. But I don't know why.'

Shyam turned towards her. His eyes shone in the darkness. He paused. An angry silence. 'Bhanjee was here tonight,' he stated. 'There's an article in last night's evening paper. Quotes him as saying that I'm a spent force. That all I will do is divide the Indian vote and destroy the power of our people. He warned me to step down, for my own sake. Said it would be very unpleasant for me if I didn't.'

'And will you?'

'I won't be threatened by him. More so now than ever. I will denounce him. Tomorrow, there's a Christmas Parade, out near Albert Park. There'll be floats and a carnival. A pageant is planned, mass celebrations. This coming year is the centenary of the islands' sugar industry. I'm speaking at the rally. It'll provide me with a chance to speak to many of

331

the Fijians present and the Indians working in the sugar industry. I'll beat him yet, Kathy.'

He edged towards her and kissed her tenderly. She smelt the sweet tobacco on his breath and felt the softness of his dark skin close to her; soft, like the flesh of a ripe woman. His fingers ran against the contours of her slender opaque form. Touching her sexuality he peeled away her clothes, enjoying her latent desire rising like discovered power.

And later he asked her, 'Will you stay here with me? I love you.'

'Yes,' she promised.

Kate lay awake thinking about his words, her own happiness, their future together and she feared for them both. If Ashok Bhanjee had killed Sam what would stop him from killing her too? She rose silently soon after dawn to return to her hotel. Shyam was still sleeping. Not wanting to wake him, she scribbled him a note.

> Gone to the hotel to meet Stone. Will find you later at the centenary celebrations, or back here later.
> I love you so much.
>
> Kate

Kate's room at the hotel was as untidy as when she had left it, save for towels and the like which had been taken away and replaced. The bed, which she had not been sleeping in, was still creased from where she had sat the previous afternoon reading Danil's note. Everywhere was still strewn with her possessions. In her panic to get away from the hotel and its threat she had left everything scattered about the place.

The contents of Sam's wallet lay forgotten on the floral coverlet. In her haste she had not bothered to gather the various cards and photos together. She began now to scoop them into her travelling bag which she was packing. From now on she would be staying at Shyam's. She paused in her tidying to study again the photo of Sam with Nancy, recalling her meeting of the previous night with this now city-elegant woman and the small daughter that Sam might have fathered. She idly wondered why Sam had not left the Plantation to them.

If, after all these years, he had remembered her, his first daughter, why then not Nancy and Lela? It suddenly struck her as curious.

She slid the photos, including the ones of herself and her mother, back into the wallet pocket and began gathering together the various business cards. Danil's card, bunched in amongst the rest, fell from the assortment and landed back on the bed. She picked it up, considered tearing it up, and turned it on to its back.

'Tuesday 2 p.m.' she read, and then underneath, the illegible scribbled letters of Danil's name, written in Sam's hand. Or was it Danil's name? She stared hard at the loopings and realised, like the last piece of the jigsaw puzzle suddenly slipping neatly into place, that the letters did not spell R. Danil. It was suddenly so clear that she marvelled at how she might have missed it. R. Maskell; Bob, who had worked on the estate and had met Nancy there. Was it then he, and not Ashok Bhanjee, who, on behalf of an American sugar firm, was bidding for the estate?

But why would Sam feel so enraged by such an offer that he would want to withdraw from the deal? Surely not because of Nancy?

Kate laid the card beside the telephone on the bedside table and sat back on the bed, trying systematically to recall what had been told to her the previous evening. Voices rang in her head.

Bob was from Wichita Falls. Alternative forms of energy, he had said. Nancy, charming and self-assured, had been uncertain, vague even about her lover's work and profoundly shocked by the news that Sam had been murdered. And Patterson, what had he, in his lonely drunkenness, said? 'Over my dead body they'll take my sugar land.'

Something felt very wrong.

Almost without thought, she picked up the telephone receiver.

'Yes, Kate?' one of her chirrupy friends enquired.

'I have the name and address of someone here on the

mainland. Would you find me their phone number please, and ring me back?'

Nancy answered the telephone. She agreed to meet Kate in town. They rendezvoused in the café of the adjacent hotel. It was an antiseptic sort of place, as Kate had originally judged, filled with breakfasting guests and Europeans living in Fiji. The expatriates met together for lunch, to drink French wine at exorbitant prices and to remind themselves from time to time of their roots, though truth to tell the place was entirely Americanised.

Nancy was late. Pretty late. Kate was just beginning to despair, thinking that she might have been deceived, when finally she appeared. Her entrance was statuesque and assured. She was electrically dressed in American slacks and a carmine silk shirt tied with a bow at the neck. The image was alien to the woman who had giggled at Sam's side in the photos, but she had adopted it with confidence. She was open and warm, effusively apologetic, but when she sat down Kate saw that she looked terrible. She was heavily made-up, far more so than she had been the previous evening, particularly around the contours of her eyes. Kate deduced that she had been crying.

The two women were ill at ease in one another's company. Kate had not given away a great deal on the phone, insinuating only that she 'had found something of interest relating to Maskell, amongst Sam's papers', preferring to listen rather than talk.

Philippe, she considered silently during her two-coffee wait, would have been proud of her. Ah, Philippe, she sighed and dismissed him from her mind. It seemed a less pressing problem.

Nancy ordered coffee and lit herself a cigarette. A slim elegant thing with a white filter. It hung between her slender fingers like another piece of jewellery complementing her red nails.

'Thank you for coming.'

'I've got to get back. Bob doesn't know I'm here. I told him I'd be shopping,' Nancy explained. She dragged on her cigarette and sipped at her coffee, speaking with her eyes partially lowered, as if fearing to face Kate directly. It made Kate uncomfortable as though she were hunting some defenceless animal.

'How did Sam find out where the offer for the Plantation was coming from? Was it from Maskell?' she demanded.

'I told him. Bob told me. Or rather Bob told me some of it. But I don't believe he had anything to do with Sam's death.'

'He hasn't,' Kate reassured her.

Nancy lifted her eyes, and Kate saw the anguish. 'Are you sure?' she whispered.

Kate nodded. In fact she had no idea if there were others involved, apart from Bhanjee. 'Will you help me find out what's going on?'

'What do you want to know?'

'What happened between you and Sam?'

'Sam and I were goin' through a rough time. We had been for a while.'

'Did you leave him for Maskell?'

Nancy nodded, scratching her long nails against the table-cloth. Kate waited for her to speak, anxious not to push her. Clearly the woman was in distress. She glanced surreptitiously at a clock face on the wall. It was twenty to twelve. She was meeting Stone in just under an hour.

'I'd been with Sam a long time,' the woman began, 'but nothing was ever settled between us . . . it was never official. I suggested to Sam that we get married . . . but he always said no . . . I said I needed some security for Lela. He promised me he'd bring her up. Promised he'd never let her down, nor me, but he said he just didn't want to be married. Said he could never go through all that again. Told me about your mother. Knocked her against a wall, cut her head and nearly killed her. He said they were just kids when they met. Irish Catholic kids. And she got pregnant. So they married.' Nancy pressed the butt of her cigarette, stained red with lipstick, into a glass ashtray, pushing at it as she remembered. 'I'm not Catholic. I don't understand that stuff. I brought Lela up on my own.'

335

Kate said nothing, listening silently. She had never known all this. But there was no need to say so.

'Then, he got this offer for Lesa. Talked of moving on. With Stone and me, and Lela. Said he wouldn't leave us behind but . . . I got scared, frightened that if we were someplace else, Australia, wherever, and things went bad between us, what would Lela and I do? . . . I got pretty unhappy . . . Mack was out at the Plantation a lot – '

'Mack?' Kate intervened.

'Bob Maskell. I could see he liked me . . . I started flirting with him. Initially it was just to make Sam jealous. Make him see my worth. Make him marry me . . .' She lit another cigarette and inhaled deeply.

'Bob asked me to come and stay with him over on the mainland. I didn't really want to, at first . . . I stayed over a night here and there. Sam was mad as hell, started drinking, getting angry. It was pretty stupid. I really loved your dad but . . . I told him Bob wanted to marry me . . . He told me to get out. That he was selling up and leaving anyway . . .'

'What did you tell him about the Plantation that made him change his mind?'

'Bob was working for the US Government . . .'

'In alternative energy?'

She shook her head. 'He's in special operations. A South Pacific Task Force. They're looking for land for a Nuclear Missile Base . . . Someone promised them Lesa . . . But I don't believe Mack was involved in Sam's murder.'

Stone and Kate were sitting together in the lobby bar of her hotel. Both looked as though they could use a stiff drink but it was too early for the bar.

Kate was whispering, spitting out the words too fast, fearful of being overheard, fearful of who might be approaching, conscious of time running away, yet anxious that Stone should understand everything before she went in search of Khumar.

'I want you and Timi to take Lesa from me, run it as your own. Later, we can decide what to do. Here, I've written this

336

letter. It explains everything.' And then hastily, nervously, she added, 'It's in case anything should happen to me.'

Stone looked quizzical, sceptical.

'Someone threatened me.'

He took the hurriedly pasted envelope, his name scrawled across it, and held it between his work-beaten fingers. He was frowning, staring at the letter, looking weary and aghast.

'Listen Kate, I think we should get hold of Leger,' he murmured firmly.

'No, Rob, please don't do that . . . Later, before I leave the islands – if I do – I'm going to change the ownership officially, but for now, it belongs to all of three of us. You and Timi and me. It's all written in there.'

He said nothing, only gawped at the rough envelope.

'I've left a message at Danil's office saying that the deal is off, that the Plantation is no longer for sale. I've explained that it no longer belongs to me. But just in case . . . it's safer if we all own it.'

'Right. I'll take it with me then. You . . . staying here or . . . ?'

She nodded.

'Cyclone's comin'. It's gonna get rough.'

'I've got to find Khumar. He's speaking at a rally in Albert Park. I have to let him know what I've found out . . . he may be able to stop Bhanjee.'

'Shouldn't you go to the police? Why don't you let me call Leger?'

'It'll take time and I have no proof. Listen, Patterson signed the death certificates. Neither are declared as murder. Maskell is covered. He's here on official government business. All I've got is a note in capital letters, warning me that I should sign. Anyone could have written it. But if I can get to Khumar . . . He's speaking today . . .'

'Why don't you let me come with you?'

'No, it's easier if I'm by myself.' The feebleness of her reason seemed appallingly apparent to her.

He lifted his bowed head. Tired, wrinkled eyes peered hard at her. Days of heavy drinking told in his face.

'You look terrible, you know that?' she whispered softly. Kate turned away from him unable to bear his gaze, suddenly aware of him and of her own blindness towards him, her own heedlessness.

'Listen, Rob, I'm going to stay on the mainland for a while . . . with Shyam.' Aware of the pressure of time, she began babbling awkwardly. 'He's asked me to and . . . I'm going to write to Philippe, telling him that I want a divorce. Not because of Shyam . . . I don't know if I shall stay here or . . . but now I must find Shyam. Whatever happens, I want you and Timi to have the Plantation. It's yours, by rights, anyway.'

Kate made an uncertain gesture towards his hand clutching at her letter, thought better of it and withdrew her touch.

'I must go, Rob. I'm sorry. I must find Shyam.'

He nodded and tapped his empty hand with her letter. 'Sure, thanks. Right then,' he said, rising from the bar table. 'You better bloody take care of yourself, eh! See you later,' and without turning back he disappeared from the deserted bar-room.

Kate banged her wrist against the now vacated stool beside her, cursing her own insensitivity. And then she hurried back up to her room to collect her packed bag.

Chapter 12

Kate arrived at Victoria Avenue, the location for the holiday celebrations and centenary rally. Here, close to Albert Park, on the outskirts of the city, flocks of people were already assembled, lining the streets, pushing one another, jostling for key positions.

'They love a party,' Stone had said to her, on the night of the wedding. Weeks ago it seemed now. She was feeling sick for hurting him. From all that she was witnessing around her, this carnival promised to be a colourful affair. Occasionally, as she pushed by, she heard richly timbred voices shouting to friends. 'Happy New Year,' they boomed across the crowded street, picked out above the general anticipatory cries of glee.

Parents chivvied youngsters, encouraging them to 'push forward'. Some carried bundles of sleeping babies oblivious to the occasion. Everyone was vying to find themselves a better standpoint. She remembered as a tiny child being taken by her mother and father to the Queen's Coronation in London and how excited she had been.

Only the weather seemed to dampen the party mood. The light was dull and bleak, like her spirits. Overhead rain clouds hung low in the sky and the wind was chilling. The cyclone was advancing. Kate, still carting her bag from the hotel, pushed and shoved, searching for Khumar. It seemed impossible that she would ever find her way through the swarms of

339

people. But she pressed determinedly onwards towards Albert Square, where soon he would be speaking.

From somewhere behind her, a jubilant cheer burst out, drowning all other sounds. It was followed by the vigorous pounding of a drum battering steely notes towards an ever-darkening sky.

Still moving onwards she glanced in the direction of the outburst and saw the first of the day's floats ploughing its way towards her. In reality it was an ageing rusted truck but today, decorated with crimson hibiscus flowers and loosely disguised for the carnival, it carried the first of several Fijian bands playing locally known tunes. Many of the crowd began to sing exuberantly, or clap to the approaching music.

Next, another van, jollied up with tattered Christmas tinsel and palm leaves. Bold lettering in Hindi and English, advertising the family business, had been stippled unevenly across the driver's door. The Indian family travelled together in the open back save for the eldest son who was in the cab, driving. They wore the costumes of indentured labourers working the sugar fields. Theirs was a sober tableau, without music.

A procession of vans and lorries followed, at a snail's pace. Disguised as floats, each one had been splashed with colour. Some sported brilliantly arranged flowers and plants; others, painted banners waving carelessly in the blustery afternoon wind. Each presented its own tableau, its own story. It was a homespun, unsophisticated pageant with, now and then, delicate vignettes telling of moving moments in the torrid history of the islands' hundred years of sugar growing.

Kate pushed on through the crowds, following one of the lorries as passage. It was almost three o'clock. Khumar was scheduled to speak at three o'clock. She prayed not to be too late. The crowds thickened as she drew closer to the main square, the heart of the rally.

Banks of people forming a human wall impeded her progress and she held back for a few minutes, searching anxiously about her for an easier route, despairing that she would ever get through.

Beyond the sea of dark Melanesian and Asian heads, twenty

340

yards or so in front of her, was the square. In its centre she could see a hastily erected wooden platform' empty but for two microphones and several plastic chairs arranged in a straight line. Two shabbily dressed Indians stood shyly on the wooden steps to the left of the platform. They gazed about uncertainly, looking confused about their roles. But the speeches had not begun. It would seem she still had time.

The roads around the square had been closed off. Fijian police clad in their elegant navy-and-white uniforms barred the way of the seething mass. Kate, slender and determined, following the advice of the mothers she had spied earlier bullying and chivvying their children to find themselves better stations, took a deep breath and soldiered on, scoring with determination where others were happy to stand and party.

She spied Shyam! He was in conversation with a Fijian statesman, a venerable-looking elder. They were standing to the side of an antiquated government limousine. The two men joked together, at ease and respectful in one another's company. She watched him from her distance, enjoying him inhabiting his world, a world that she could not yet know; calmed that he had not yet mounted the stage. She wondered if he would be the first to speak. From somewhere beyond the carelessly parked black limousine an Indian emerged carrying notes on a clipboard. He hurried the two or three steps to the side of the platform, past the two waiting men and on to the stage, striding busily towards the microphones. It seemed he was to be the first.

This promise of activity caused the still gathering onlookers to pay vague attention, noises of 'shush' and 'quiet' were being muttered all around her. Kate grabbed her chance. She shoved herself forward but to no avail. Her path was still blocked by the clusters of bodies kept in check by police. There was simply no way through.

How could she make Shyam know how fiercely she needed him to spot her! Jostled by people, Kate impatiently resigned herself to waiting a few moments longer, hidden within the crowds. She could merely observe Shyam for a while, enjoy his quixotic charm as he waited stoicly, smiling and joking with his companion. Later, after this speaker had completed his address, she would seize her chance.

The speaker began his piece. Unheard. Discovering then that the microphones were not relaying his words he beckoned furiously to the two, until now, redundant Indians, still waiting on the steps. They leapt into action, jettisoned their cigarettes and clambered forward, scrambling about at the foot of the two microphone stands, bemusedly investigating various cables draped across the stage. Finally, defeated, they yelled out instructions to three electricians, barely visible to Kate, who were working from a van parked behind the stage. They hurried purposefully to the rescue. This little interlude caused much amusement amongst the crowds. Shakespeare's mechanicals, thought Kate, still searching out a route onwards. Within the crowd, intermittent cheering began, others jeered or broke into raucous outbursts of laughter or encouraged neighbouring friends to do the same, some lost attention or simply drank another beer. Eventually the problem seemed to be resolved and the speaker stepped forward once again. Gathering his dignity and gripping his clipboard tightly, he began his address. He spoke in English. Incomprehensible monotonous words drowned by the amplified wind roaring like a lioness through the speakers. Few paid him any attention.

Beyond the wooden temporary dais, unseen by Kate, Ashok Bhanjee had arrived. He emerged, slickly besuited, from his black Mercedes accompanied by a lesser politician, and his wife. They strolled confidently towards the side of the stage. He, too, was scheduled to speak later in the afternoon. Catching sight of Shyam and his venerable companion Ashok nodded benignly, but kept his distance.

Kate, spying him, propelled herself urgently forward. The sheer boredom generated by the present speaker made her task easier. No one was paying too much attention, including the police. She shoved her way to within several yards of the government car that stood between her and Shyam. Ropes cordoned off the crowd and she could move no further.

342

'Shyam! Shyam!' she yelled, but her call was lost, simply drowned by the amplified weather and a spattering of applause that marked the end of the first speaker's time.

Ashok Bhanjee stepped forward and glided his large frame easily towards the stage, his lustreless companion accompanying him, keeping a pace or two to the rear of him, a shadow of a man, with Mrs Bhanjee at his side. Shyam stopped speaking, watching Ashok's approach to the microphones. He began looking about him as if searching for Kate.

She bellowed his name again and again, 'Shyam! Shyam!' waving frantically, but he neither heard nor saw her.

Members of the audience, notably Indians, were cheering loudly, enthusiastically welcoming the arrival of their promised new leader. Centre stage now, Ashok held his thick arms in the air, gesticulating triumphantly, like a prizefighter at the end of a victorious match. He did nothing to quell his audience's enthusiasm. On the contrary he encouraged their loud appreciation. Kate saw him, smiling smugly, glance imperceptibly towards Khumar. A glimpse only.

She turned to note Shyam's reactions and saw that he was now standing alone. His erstwhile companion had stepped forward a pace or two, the better to view Bhanjee. Shyam was leaning slightly, bent forward, coughing. The curiosity of the small crowd immediately surrounding him was momentarily drawn towards him.

Ashok began to speak, drawing all eyes towards him. His voice boomed and echoed, reverberating throughout the avenue while the wind, as if at his holy bidding, had ceased to yowl through the loudspeakers. His audience, both Indian and Fijian, had grown attentive, listening with delighted anticipation or sinking hearts to his words of promise and change. He offered work for everyone, opportunities for the islands, growing industry. He spoke with confidence and certainty, wooing his audience with the affection and understanding bestowed upon a child mistress.

Kate could not deny his charisma, his power. He performed with the boldness of an Edwardian actor-manager and the deftness of a Kathakali dancer. Had she not known who he was

343

and all that he had done to reach this place she, too, might have been seduced. As it was she loathed him.

The man who had murdered her father, standing like a diva for all to adulate. His words rang out. All around her, bursts of applause, choruses of cheers, hibiscus blossoms thrown heavenwards, whoopings, more applause, and less audible, a spattering of booings. The noise seemed to lift even the rain clouds and in the midst of all this she turned to Khumar.

He was staggering towards the black limousine, apparently in pain, groping for balance.

'What is happening?' she murmured fearfully. Her heart stopped a beat. She shoved at her neighbour, feverishly rooting for space. Shyam stumbled like a drunk man, inches from the car, and then fell to his knees as if in prayer.

No one, except the few immediately about him, had noticed. Kate screamed out. Heads turned towards her. She beat the bodies out of her way.

Shyam was now crumpled forward, balanced on his knees, struggling to stand again. His former companion sped to his side. Frenzied with alarm, Kate was propelling her travel bag against the legs of her neighbours, beating and raging a path. Someone's careless overexcited arm knocked against her face, slapping her lip against her teeth. She might have tasted a spattering of blood but her heart was convulsed with fear. She saw and felt nothing except her driving madness to get through to Shyam.

'Jesus! Let me through!' she bawled at all around her but her voice was lost in the heat and chaos of Ashok's speech. She reached the roped-off area facing the limousine as Shyam slumped and fell to the ground, face downwards. He was clutching at his torso as though he had been poisoned.

'Christ! No!' she wailed. 'Let me through!'

Two burly policemen were hovering uncomprehendingly while the Fijian statesman, kneeling at his side, desperately turned about him, seeking help. Finding none he beat his firm palm against the naked calf of one of the two men, bellowing some order in their native tongue. The confused policeman pounded off behind the stage.

344

Kate crouched at the rope, onlookers' knees kicking in her back. She slid and grappled her way beneath it. No one to obstruct her now. The policeman who had guarded that patch was now at Shyam's side. All others were entranced by Ashok Bhanjee or confused by the drama surrounding Shyam.

Stumbling blindly, tears scorching her cheeks, she hurled herself towards him, gasping and spewing his name, dribbling spit and blood. Her mouth had been cut. The acidity of her own saliva stung into her wound. Her head was spinning. She reached Shyam, flung herself at his coiled figure. He lay insensible on the ground. His body still warm.

Across the back of his oat-coloured jacket were tracings of fresh blood where a bullet had pierced. Kate scratched at the limp body, heaving it towards her, thumping at it, desperate to make him talk. Her sex was pulsating with terror. 'Speak, for God's sake, speak!' she screeched. Ugly disconcerting sounds.

Someone behind her grabbed her by her elbows, dragging her away from him, pulling her to her feet, wrapping her in their arms.

'He's dead, Kate, come away,' she heard, spoken softly in her ear.

Her blood turned to ice.

She howled Shyam's name, screaming into the wind with rage. Inside, she felt dead.

And then she passed out in Stone's arms.

Chapter 13

At its height the winds of the cyclone reached almost 150 miles an hour. Several of the smaller atolls and islands were badly hit. Mainland Fiji was seriously damaged. Homes were devastated. Some were lost entirely, simply blown out to sea like weightless rags; but the eye of the cyclone, mercifully, never reached Lesa. Only its surrounding winds swirled about her, tearing and ravaging everything in its path.

Kate climbed from her bed and stared numbly through the cracks of the barred windows.

She bore witness to the brute force of the weather, screaming outside the house. Palm trees were sprawled against the earth. Their tall, giraffe-like trunks were pliable so few were splintered apart. Most suffered only the loss of their fanned fronds, unlike many of the smaller plants which were uprooted, ripped to shreds and hurled, swirling directionless into space like brush in a desert storm.

She said it was the soul of Khumar making its final circle around the earth, striding like a Colossus and treading with avenging steps.

The wind outside howled like a tormented banshee. It mourned Kate's loss. It rattled at the windows like a crazed, accusing animal screaming for entry, screaming for revenge.

And then, for a while, she would sleep again.

She dreamt that the roof above them was torn from its eaves while the rain battered against it.

She was blinded by grief, by the loss of Shyam, by the senselessness of his death. She wished only that she too could be disembowelled by the hurricane's fury.

Stone stayed up at the house with her, caring for her, and feeding her when she would eat anything.

It was five days now since the death of Shyam. The papers had carried the story and the islands were still reeling from the shock of such a crime. An unnamed suspect had been arrested and charged. But neither Stone nor Kate knew anything of these events. The islands had been cut off from the mainland.

Stone had managed to bring Kate back to Lesa before the cyclone had gained strength. He carried her home on the last ferry that had dared to make the choppy crossing.

With the help of pills she had slept for the first thirty hours. He had stayed close by her, sleeping irregularly on a chair at her side or downstairs in the spare room. Sam's two mongrels kept watch with him. Neither could leave the house. Once the wind began to rage, no one stirred. It carried everything mobile in its wake. All life on the island went underground. They were stowed away together, they and the two dogs, like creatures on Noah's Ark, waiting for Nature to abate her fury and leave them to live in peace again. Until the next time.

On the second evening the electricity cables were damaged by the storm leaving them with only candlelight. They spoke little but stayed close beside one another in a dreadful, or perhaps welcome, obscurity. Occasionally, while she slept, he stroked her head, checking her for fever but she had none.

On the third evening, dog-tired, unshaven, queasy as though he had not rested for weeks, he decided that she would be fine without him and he headed downstairs to sleep, to stretch his limbs in the spare room. He found the letter that she had given to him at the Grand Pacific Hotel, on the day of the Parade. It was still lying carelessly with his discarded clothes on his unmade bed.

He opened it and read it once again. He had scanned it briefly that morning at the hotel, before he had decided to

347

follow her. Had she supposed that he would have taken her letter and simply returned to the island, knowing that her life might be in danger? Her life had been threatened, she had told him that herself, and she had asked him not to contact Leger. What alternative had been left to him? Someone had to watch over her.

He had lost Sam. This time he wasn't going to turn his back so easily. She had, as she had promised, given the Plantation to Timi and himself. He understood why Sam had rejected the offer and for that reason, for Sam, he would stay on and rebuild the place. And when she was well again he would ask Kate to stay on with him.

He put the letter on to the bare dresser and lay down, exhausted, to sleep. The next morning, when he woke, the wind had died down. The cyclone had abated. He strolled through to the front of the house, to the verandah, and found Kate seated there, dressed in a T-shirt and a sarong tied around her waist like a skirt. She looked rested, almost at peace, but much thinner and frailer. Her lip was still slightly swollen and purpled from the bruise.

'I was listening to the birds singing,' she said, 'returning from their hiding places.'

'Yeah,' he said yawning, breathing in the fresh air, stretching sensuously, like a caged animal freed at last. 'It's great to hear them again, eh?' He smiled at her, regarding her. 'How are you feeling?'

Everywhere around them there was devastation. The garden was deluged.

'Bit battered,' she replied timidly.

Scatters of blossoms lay drowning in puddles of rainwater. Like abandoned confetti they formed patterns of bleeding colours in the muddy sand. The previously manicured lawn was now coated with a thin layer of branches and tobacco-stained water. Much of the gravelled path had been washed away.

'I thought I'd walk down to the beach. Get some air. Do you want to come?' he invited.

She smiled tenderly and nodded. 'Sure, why not?'

'Let's get these poor ol' hounds a bit o' exercise,' he encouraged.

The muddied turquoise ocean was flecked with white foamy waves. It was still rough and unsettled and the sand was too damp to sit on so they walked for a couple of miles, invigorated by the strong blustering breeze, for that was all that remained of the force of the cyclone. The two honey mongrels leapt playfully about their feet, panting gleefully, celebrating their freedom. The beach was entirely deserted. No human life, only driftwood and occasional gulls screeching, sailing freely on the strong wind.

They came across an uprooted palm tree lying like an extended elephant's trunk. Stone suggested that they turn it around, which they did, dragging it in the sand so that it faced out towards the horizon, and they could sit down on it. A giant bench of damp mossed coconut wood.

'Will you take the Plantation?' she asked him, after a while.

'Sure,' he said. 'What else could I do? Timi doesn't know yet. He'll be pretty happy. I'll drive down later 'n tell him.' And then after a pause, 'What 'bout you?'

She bowed her head. 'I'll leave in a few days. Go back to England first, I suppose . . . I don't know yet. It's too soon . . . I have to consider what to do about Shyam's death . . . about Ashok Bhanjee.'

'Listen, Kate. Let it go. There's nothing you can do. They'll arrest some poor unsuspecting sod and charge him and you'd never be able to prove it was otherwise. Bhanjee hasn't got the Plantation. He's got nothing to barter with. You beat him there. There isn't another single freehold piece of land this size on any of the islands. If he wants missile stations he'll have to take the bloody land by force. And they'll never let him get away with that. The army is Fijian and that's where their loyalties lie. If he gets into power they'll be waiting for him. The army would be on the streets within the first weeks. They'll never accept Indian leadership here. And they'd never let him take their land or change their constitution. And that's what he'd have to do. No matter who was behind him. There'd be a riot first.'

349

Kate listened to what Stone was saying without answering. Perhaps he was making sense.

Further along the drift-cluttered beach a black heron stalked, peering out towards the ineluctable horizon. Its silhouette was revealed against the stark, bruised landscape like a Japanese ink drawing. A second heron approached, flying past Kate, skimming gracefully across the surface of the churned water towards its attendant mate. They stood beside one another, picking their way along the edge of the waves.

Kate thought of Khumar. She turned her gaze away from the birds, aching for him, feeling her loss like schist breaking apart within her, splintering her.

'Why don't you stay here?' Stone asked her.

She shook her bowed head. 'I couldn't.'

And then without speaking she stood up, walking a few purposeful strides back along the flour-white coastline. 'I'm going back to the house,' she urged, projecting her voice economically against the wind.

'Kate, wait!' Stone called after her.

'I want to go back,' she called without turning.

'If you want to destroy Bhanjee why don't you think about Sam? This Plantation was somewhere for everyone to work. He gave everyone a go, remember? Stop feeling sorry for yourself.'

Kate returned the following evening on the late ferry from the mainland. She sat alone on the upper deck in the cool darkness, listening to the boat plough through the still uneven water, breathing the strong fresh air, while she gazed up at the clear heavenly sky.

She had been to Shyam's funeral.

Had walked inconspicuously through the city streets just a few feet behind his coffin. So close she felt she could stretch out her hand and touch him, could bring him back to life again by the sheer power of wanting him, could hear him call her name. Memories echoed every footstep. Her emptiness gnawed at her, sucking at her inside.

Hundreds of people, many openly weeping, had lined the

streets: Indians, Fijians, Europeans; a motley bunch. As he would have wished it. All lamenting their private loss of him. She was one amongst many.

Signs of the recent cyclone were everywhere to be seen. A city at war. Windows had been blown from their frames, telephone boxes uprooted, shop fronts blown apart, Nature's vengeance.

After, she had sat alone in a deserted café on the outskirts of the city, a solitary mourning, thinking about Shyam and all that he had given her, about her future.

She decided to telephone Patterson. Jo was her only evidence. If she could only persuade him to go to the police, change the verdict of Ami's death . . . His boy, Ahmed, answered the phone. Kate recognised his sultry voice.

'Doctor not here,' he said.

'I want to leave a message for him, Ahmed. It's Kate De Marly.'

'He's left for England,' he told her. 'I'm closing up the house.'

She walked aimlessly for a while, not ready to take her afternoon ferry, and then went to see Leger. She told him everything, gave him Danil's note and begged him to do something. Something to vindicate Shyam's death.

'You have no evidence, Mrs De Marly,' Leger said to her. I cannot help you. Listen to me. You are new to the islands. You know nothing of the ways here. Like our cyclones, tragedies cause a little havoc but everyone knows it is better not to make matters worse. Better simply to begin the task of quietly rebuilding and order will return. As you will see if you stay with us a little longer. I recommend you to do that, Mrs De Marly.'

Kate made her weary way to the ferry. Would Sam have accepted Leger's reasoning? Would Shyam?

And then she read in the evening paper that some unnamed suspect had been charged with Shyam's murder. Jesus! Stone had been right, she thought. What had he died for, she asked herself, if no one were to continue his work? His vision of

351

peace, of multi-racial harmony? Kate knew she must begin again, find the strength, taking with her all that she had discovered from him. Lesa represented a tiny patch of that.

She bent her thin body over the side of the boat and watched the plankton shine phosphorescent amongst the churning waves.

She felt stripped bare of everything, solitary now, nothing left to her since the day she had first crossed by water to Lesa, but she felt reconciled to herself. Finally. When had she last known such inner accord? As a child with her father? Those early childhood days. From the loss of him she had drifted into the comfort and security of Philippe, dear Philippe, cradling herself in a prison that she had not recognised. A prison of her own making. But now she was alone and the boundaries were her own. This was the beginning.

That evening Kate telephoned Philippe. 'It's over,' she said. 'I'm not coming back. I love you,' she told him, she had shed all anger, all resentment towards him, 'but it's just not what I want any more, our life.'

'I don't understand what's happened to you. What do you want? You can't stay there forever.'

'Perhaps I can.'

Later, lit by the glow from the hurricane lamp, she and Stone sat together on the wide verandah, drinking beer.

He lifted his hand towards her face and touched her pale cheek with the tips of his sturdy fingers. Such an alien touch after Shyam's, she pined.

'Why don't you stay here?' he said. 'Help me rebuild the place. We could run it together, like me and Sam did. I've been thinking, mebbe we could rent out a bit of land, or sell off a small patch to pay for a new sugar crop?'

Kate bent her head in silence, reflecting. Her liberation had been dearly won.

'What are our lives for,' Shyam had said to her, 'without liberation? We seek spiritual, economic and physical freedom. I dream of a humane society.'

'I could use your help, you know, and I'd be glad o' your company,' Stone persisted affectionately.

Yes, all right, she replied softly. For a while.

For Shyam and Sam, she thought. And for me.

A few days later Kate walked in the heat to the village where Sam had been buried. She laid flowers at his chapel grave, stayed a while with him, he was an old friend now, then walked on down the hill, drawn towards the disused mill. She had not visited that stretch of beach since before Ami's death.

The cyclone had caused considerable damage to the surrounding vegetation. The mill was no longer so protected. Curled wisps of barbed wire ripped from the main fencing lay about the beach, and the remains of damaged banana trees lay curling in the heat. The fruit had browned and rotted and was food now only for the ants and scavengers. In her carefully chosen sneakers and jeans she beat a path to its faded entrance. The door was bolted and barred. There was no way in. Further around, on the beach side of the building, she found a window set high. The glass was smashed and jagged. She scrambled up the side wall, using trunks of broken trees as wobbly steps, and peered inside. It was a dark cavernous building loaded with chunks of rusted machinery. It reeked of the cloying smell of burnt sugar. Sounds of rats scurrying to and fro terrified her away.

Later, in the cool of twilight, she returned with Stone. They opened up the building. Inside, in wooden boxes, stacked taller than a man's height and almost the length of coffins, they found guns. Kate's eyes burnt brightly as she spoke into the enclosed darkness.

'Leger will listen now,' she said. 'Won't he?'

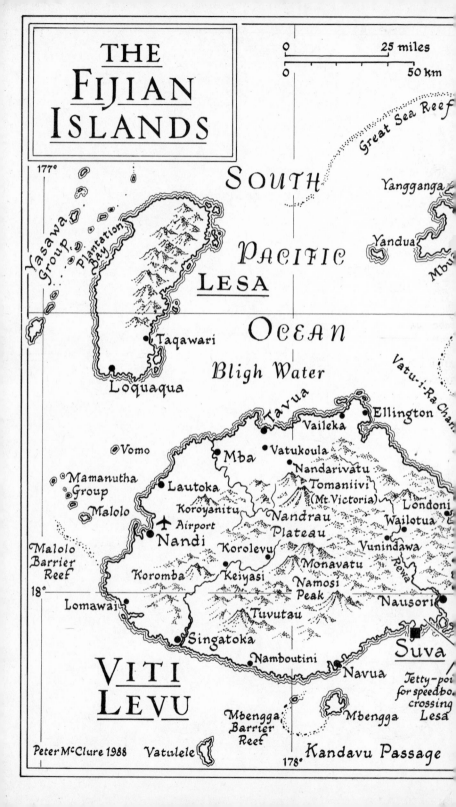

THE FIJIAN ISLANDS

0   25 miles

0   50 km

177°

SOUTH

PACIFIC

LESA

OCEAN

Great Sea Reef

Yangganga

Yandua

Mbua

Yasawa Group

Plantation Bay

Taqawari

Loquaqua

Bligh Water

Tavua

Vatu-i-Ra Chan.

Vaileka

Ellington

Vomo

Mba

Vatukoula

Nandarivatu

Tomaniivi
(Mt. Victoria)

Londoni

Mamanutha Group

Lautoka

Koroyanitu

Nandrau
Plateau

Wailotua

Malolo

Airport

Nandi

Korolevu

Vunindawa

Malolo
Barrier
Reef

Koromba

Keiyasi

Monavatu

Namosi
Peak

Rewa

18°

Lomawai

Tuvutau

Nausori

Singatoka

Namboutini

Suva

VITI
LEVU

Navua

Jetty-poi
for speedbo.
crossing
Lesa

Peter McClure 1988

Vatulele

Mbengga
Barrier
Reef

Mbengga

178°

Kandavu Passage